Annie O'Neil spent most of
leg draped over the family ro
in her hand. Novels, baking, a
teenage angst poetry ate up m
Annie splits her time between ....g ... husband
into helping her with their cows, baking, reading, barrel
racing (not really!) and spending some very happy hours
at her computer, writing.

Born and raised on the Wirral Peninsula in England,
Charlotte Hawkes is mum to two intrepid boys who
love her to play building block games with them, and
object loudly to the amount of time she spends on the
computer. When she isn't writing—or building with
blocks—she is company director for a small Anglo/
French construction firm. Charlotte loves to hear
from readers, and you can contact her at her website:
charlotte-hawkes.com.

Discover more at millsandboon.co.uk.

HAWAIIAN MEDIC TO RESCUE HIS HEART

ANNIE O'NEIL

TEMPTED BY HER CONVENIENT HUSBAND

CHARLOTTE HAWKES

MILLS & BOON

Published in Great Britain 2021
by Mills & Boon, an imprint of HarperCollins*Publishers* Ltd,
1 London Bridge Street, London, SE1 9GF

www.harpercollins.co.uk

HarperCollins*Publishers*
1st Floor, Watermarque Building,
Ringsend Road, Dublin 4, Ireland

Hawaiian Medic to Rescue His Heart © 2021 by Annie O'Neil

Tempted by Her Convenient Husband © 2021 by Charlotte Hawkes

ISBN: 978-0-263-29774-4

08/21

HAWAIIAN MEDIC TO RESCUE HIS HEART

ANNIE O'NEIL

MILLS & BOON

To my Hawaiian Hero

CHAPTER ONE

"HAILANA'S IS THE BEST—now zip it!"

Lulu ran her fingers along her mouth, then made the *shaka* sign with her hand, the more peaceful gesture finally managing to silence her colleagues, who were coming near to blows over who knew the best "secret" place to buy garlic shrimp farther up the coast.

Ono grinds—the Hawaiian version of choice fast food outlets—were often the main topic of discussion, when the crew members weren't retelling stories of recent rescues or actually rescuing someone. Which, to be fair, was most of the time. But the tourist season was coming to an end and there was an extra splash of "sitting-around time," during which conversation usually revolved around food.

Lulu had five big brothers—each and every one of them born and bred right here on Oahu—so if anyone knew where the best garlic shrimp were, she did. Besides, she was acting crew chief, and there was an all-island alert sounding on the emergency scanner. Perfect shrimp on a cloud of beautifully steamed rice with an unctuous lashing of teriyaki sauce would have to wait.

She pointed to the dispatch radio on the counter. "Listen."

The voice on the radio crackled though again. "Family of four out on Mokoli'i."

The jocular banter fell to an abrupt halt as they listened to the rest of the report. Mom and dad… Two little boys… Thought they'd walk out to Mokoliʻi, a tiny little island just under five hundred meters off the coast. The islet featured a couple of sea caves, two small idyllic beaches and, more to the point, no human population. People loved going out there for a taste of "desert island life." It was perfect… unless you didn't know when the tide came in.

This family had headed out toward the end of low tide, with a warning from the local lifeguards to come straight back. Because once the tide came in, walking back wasn't an option. The hotel they'd been staying in on the North Shore had been expecting them back for a dinner reservation an hour earlier, and there'd been no sign of them.

As a lifelong surfer, Lulu didn't need to be told there was no way they would be getting back without a boat. She knew the tidal schedule as well as she knew the menu at her local burger shack. And she ate out a lot. With the sun beginning its descent, and the tide only set to draw in higher, there was no time to waste.

Lulu swept the zipper round the first aid backpack she'd been restocking and shouldered it. "Casey, can you grab four life vests? Two adult, two children."

"Who wants to bet that they're *haoles*?" said Stewart, their helicopter pilot and sometimes speedboat captain, as he pulled on his Oahu Search and Rescue high-vis vest.

"What? You mean like you, mainlander?" ribbed Casey, her hair and make-up immaculate as ever as she shouldered her own first aid backpack, then howled in an imitation of how the Hawaiian word for foreigners was pronounced.

Casey howled a lot around Stew. The platinum-blonde medic and rescue staffer had been hired the same week as Lulu, and though they couldn't look more different—a tall, willowy funster against Lulu's petite surfer-girl vibe—

their core values were identical and they'd become instant friends.

Stewart threw up his hands and groaned. "Oh, c'mon, y'all! I've lived on the island forty years already! Surely that makes me a local."

"Not if you're still saying y'all," the rest of the team chorused as one.

Stew shook his head and grumbled something about islanders being stuck in their ways. Born in Texas, he'd used to try to shoot down their ribbing by insisting that Hawaii was his spiritual home. He'd moved here as soon as he'd been old enough to earn the airfare. Now, at sixty-three, he'd lived on the island long enough to learn the lingo, sport a teak-colored tan, and call all visitors to the islands foreigners—but not long enough to be considered a local.

Deep down, he knew the truth. You weren't Hawaiian unless you *were* Hawaiian. And his heart pumped Texas blood.

"Heads up." Lulu threw Stew the keys to the speedboat.

It was a small counterbalance for the regular ribbing he received. All the *You'll never be one of us* jibes had to be evened out by equal measures of appreciation. A crucial lesson being the youngest of six had taught her. It was all well and good to know where there was room for improvement—something her brothers regularly reminded her of—but it was equally important to be reminded that you were appreciated.

It was something she was still trying to teach them. She knew they loved her. Even if sometimes she had to dig incredibly deep beneath their insane overprotectiveness to see their love and respect—especially when it came across as claustrophobic and they seemed intent on never, *ever* letting her have a love life. But…whatever. If a prospective beau didn't want her enough to stand up to her brothers' *Don't you dare hurt my little sister* talks, she wasn't interested.

Not that a boyfriend was on her to-do list. Proving to their new boss—whoever he was—that she was top of her game was. And, more to the point, that she should've been given his job.

When their last crew chief—a cranky, sexist, would-rather-be-in-a-hammock-than-out-on-a-job boss—had retired a few weeks back, and Lulu had been made acting crew chief, she'd seen it as her personal mission to make every member of the crew feel appreciated. Worthy.

They were a small, motley, mismatched crew, and in the three years since she'd joined the team hundreds of lives had been saved because of them. Today was her last day as acting chief, and she wanted to make sure they all knew how much she appreciated their support of her leadership. Even if she might not have dotted every *i* or crossed every *t*.

Stew caught the keys and gave her a grateful nod. "Thanks, peanut."

"That's boss lady peanut to you, mister." She grinned, arcing her arm in a gesture for the others to follow her to the dock.

"Ticktock, time's running out on that." Casey grimaced, jogging up alongside Lulu. "How're you doing with that? Preparing for the new boss?"

Lulu pulled a face. Not particularly well. She'd had all sorts of plans about having everything in such amazing shape that he would immediately see she should have been given the job and fly back to wherever he'd come from. But…time. There was never enough of it. Especially when her choices were rescuing people or paperwork. Eating or paperwork. And surfing or paperwork.

She wanted the job, but in her more honest, private moments she had her doubts. The predominantly desk-based work that defined the senior position wasn't really her thing. Now, if the job came with a PA, whose sole responsibility was filling in the endless forms so she herself could go out on all the rescues…

She pursed her lips. Even the bump in pay these past few weeks hadn't inspired her to get the piles of paperwork done. Which did beg the question: Did she really want it? Or was she happy as she was?

Having just one job instead of the two she was currently juggling would be nice. Although her job as a paramedic did go hand in hand with her search and rescue job. With the complementary training each job had, she knew she always had a bit of an edge when it came to making critical life-and-death decisions, and choosing overtime over a social life meant her savings account was getting incredibly close to the magic number she needed to put down a deposit on the dream house she had practically moved into already.

Turtle Hideaway.

The small property she'd been coveting for almost two years now was a traditional Hawaiian beach house, tucked into a small, miraculously private cove. Living there would mean access to some gentle surf, some lazy morning swims with sea turtles, an insanely beautiful view of the sunrise and, like the cherry on top of a perfect ice cream sundae, it was on the opposite side of the island from her big brothers.

All except for Laird, of course, who was on the Big Island studying his precious volcanoes.

Her parents had totally messed up, naming him after a surfer. She smiled at that thought. But her smile faded away before it had a chance to gain purchase.

Her parents hadn't lived long enough to know that he'd become a respected volcanologist. They hadn't lived long enough to know what any of them had become.

The radio squawked again, pulling her back into the moment.

"C'mon everyone. Wheels up and motor in the water!"

She tried and failed to stuff her trademark braid under

her Oahu Search and Rescue cap. Hair down to your butt
tended to have a mind of its own. Sure, she could cut it,
but…she wasn't the *complete* tomboy her brothers accused
her of being.

Giving up, she flicked it back into its usual position,
down the line of her spine, and announced, "Let's go get
these goofballs."

"You coming?" Stewart feigned surprise.

Lulu hesitated, knowing her remit was to stay back and
man the radios at HQ. But it was her last day. Surely one
itty-bitty rescue wouldn't hurt?

Casey glanced at her phone, then made an *uh-oh* noise.
"What?"

"The dispatch has also gone to the OST."

Lulu's full lips thinned. Their "rivals"—the Ocean
Safety Team. Headed by none other than her brother
Makoa—aka the Mak Attack. The one man on the island
who knew each callout he took meant taking his little sister out of the ocean. It was a favorite pastime of his. Which
was precisely why they needed to get a move on.

"We're closest," she said, picking up her pace.

It wasn't strictly a lie. They were almost equidistant,
with an edge of maybe a kilometer or so. But her brother's
crew had bigger boats, with larger engines, and a huge team
waiting dockside for just this type of rescue. It shouldn't
be a competition, but thanks to her brothers' nonstop cam-
paign to get her to commit to a desk job, so nothing ever
happened to her like—

She stopped the memory short. Hanging on to the darkest day of their lives would never bring their parents back.

Fifteen minutes and one hair-raising boat ride later, Lulu
and her team pulled up to the tiny island where the family were backed up against a rock precipice, madly waving
their arms except for the father, who was holding one of
the little boys in his. They all looked terrified.

Any thoughts of shooting up a victorious flare gun to show her brother they'd "won" the race disappeared. This family needed help.

Lulu pulled off her regulation top so that she was only wearing her favorite long-sleeved short wetsuit and an ankle-height pair of ocean boots. The sea urchins round here were notorious.

Without waiting for the boat to fully come to a halt, she jumped into the waist-height water, backpack on, and waded to shore, pushed on by the rising tide while the rest of her crew secured the boat in the shallows.

"Please! Help our boy!" The tearstained mother cried, pointing to the dark-haired little boy cradled in his father's arms. "Jamie stepped on something spiky and we couldn't get it out. He refused to head back to the island before the tide came in and…and—"

The distraught woman released a sob of relief, then began to pour out an incredibly detailed story of how the day had begun and how they had ended up here, while Lulu focused her attention where it needed to be. On the boy.

One quick examination revealed that, yes, he'd stepped on a spiny sea urchin. The long spines could really sting, and it looked as though Jamie had stepped on not just one, but several of the spiky sea creatures—and with both of his feet. The odd puncture wound was generally easily rectified with a pair of tweezers, after a good old foot soak, but one glance at the boy's pallor and a quick tally of the black and blue puncture wounds told Lulu he would very likely need a course of antibiotics.

"How long have you been out here?"

The husband and wife exchanged a look. "Three hours? Maybe four?"

The husband shook his head and said he'd left his watch back at the hotel, wanting to really enjoy the last day of vacation with his family without worrying about the time. "I don't get much time with the kids when we're back home, see? So I told them—Jamie? Robbie? We're going to have a one hundred percent family day."

"Well, you got that, all right," Lulu said, her full lips narrowing into a wince. "And with a bit more drama than you anticipated."

Lulu got the father to lay Jamie down on the ever-decreasing beach while she examined his feet. "Are they stinging?" she asked him.

He nodded, tears beading in his eyes. Despite wanting to read the riot act to the family, for not checking the tide tables, her heart did go out to them. They'd been doing what families were meant to do—sticking with one another.

"Tell me, Jamie, how are your muscles feeling? Strong or weak?" She struck a muscle pose, then let herself wilt in a comedic flop. As she'd hoped, the little boy smiled and tried to make a muscle pose. Okay. So he was a bit weak. But he'd been scared for a few hours and those stings hurt without any sort of topical antibiotic or hydrocortisone cream.

She held her hand close to his feet, not touching the arch, where the concentration of spines was the heaviest. They were swollen and, yes, there was some heat radiating from them. At least no one had tried to pull the spines out by hand. They'd need a good soak in warm water and—her mother's home remedy—a healthy splash of vinegar.

The reminder of her mother gave her heart another short, sharp twist. She forced herself to reform the pain into pride.

Her mother would have loved knowing Lulu was using her remedies. Loved it that her daughter hadn't shied away from the career she'd always wanted, despite both of her parents' lives being cut so short in a similar one.

Logging the thought and shelving it, Lulu pulled out a temperature gun and held it to Jamie's forehead. "Hands up!" she commanded playfully.

Once again, the little boy did try to play along as she

took his temperature. It was up by a degree. Nothing serious, but something to keep an eye on. It was also a reason not to apply hydrocortisone cream straight away. That course of antibiotics was looking more and more likely.

"Is he going to have to go to the hospital?" asked the boy's father. "Our flights are first thing tomorrow morning, and if he needs extensive treatment I'm going to have to talk to the airlines. I heard you're meant to, you know..." the father lowered his voice "...urinate on the injury."

Lulu wrinkled her nose. "Luckily, that's a myth."

"Of course." He gave a nervous laugh. "I knew that. I was just confirming it for my wife."

His wife threw him a chastening look.

"Hey, chief!" Casey called from the side of the boat, where she was standing at the ready. "Need a stretcher?"

Lulu eyed the water depth, ever-increasing. Her very tall brother could have carried the boy. With one hand. All of her brothers could. It was like being related to five Jason Momoas or The Rocks. Tattoos... Muscles to spare... And more than enough attitude to circle the entire island group.

They constantly teased Lulu for her diminutive stature, insisting she'd been adopted because of her much smaller frame—which had, early on, earned her the nickname Mini-Menehune. She didn't know how many times she'd bellowed at them to take it back, telling them that, at five foot two, she was volumes taller than the island's mythical dwarves. Besides, she didn't have magical powers. If she did they'd know all about it.

These days when they Mini-Menehune'd her she just rolled her eyes. She'd made her stature work for her the same way they'd made theirs work for them. No one was better in an earthquake or collapse rescues than she was.

Boo-yah!

"A stretcher would be great," she said, and Casey began climbing over the edge of the boat with one.

They both knew the family's safety was more important than pride. They quickly transferred Jamie, then Robbie, and then the parents. Another quick boat ride and they were back at the OSR dock. A man they didn't recognize was waiting on the dock with a wheelchair.

The closer they got, the more Lulu's spine pulled up to attention. He was looking out at them with an unsmiling face. That wasn't what had her attention, though.

He was drop-dead gorgeous.

Frowning possibly made him even sexier. He was tall. Not as tall as her brothers, but he definitely would clock in at six foot something. Athletic… The lean variety as opposed to her brothers' bodybuilder aesthetic. Amazing blue eyes that could easily put a girl in a trance. Cheekbones begging for some fingertips to run the length of them. Chestnut-colored hair… Not sun-kissed… So a *haole*. A *haole* wearing an OSR jacket.

A wash of horror swept through her.

The grumpy hottie was the new boss.

She knew he was coming. Had known it for weeks. They all had. But…kind of like the mythical dwarves…she'd never entirely, actually believed he would come.

She forced on a smile and waved. *"Aloha!"*

Ew! That had been high-pitched. She didn't dare look at the rest of the crew, because she could feel them staring at her with *What kind of weird voice was that?* in their eyes.

He did that chin-lift thing guys did when they chose actions over words and didn't answer—which was rude. His eyes narrowed as if inspecting her for flaws.

A weird urge to rattle them all off for him seized her. She wasn't in regulation uniform. They shouldn't have taken this call. They should've left someone back at base. They should've locked the office. She should've done the towering pile of paperwork sitting in the in tray.

There were also the more personal flaws. Her hair was

probably mental. She chose gut reactions against by-the-book reactions. She hated peas. Probably could've eaten more vegetables in general. And there was always room for improvement in her flossing routine.

Bah!

Woulda...shoulda...coulda...

They'd saved this family from drowning. That was what mattered.

So she kept her smile bright, and waited for a response to her cheery island greeting other than a frown.

His bright sapphire-blue eyes scanned her, then flashed with an unchecked hit of warning when their eyes met. She fought the tiniest of trembles and turned it into a careless shrug. Their dueling *I see you* stares changed into something else. Something every bit as heated but...different. Like butterflies in her stomach. That kind of different.

Which was entirely unprofessional and made any *I'm right, you're wrong* posturing completely evaporate along with her high-pitched *aloha*.

She couldn't have the hots for him. No way.

Not for a *haole*. Not for someone who was this frowny and bereft of manners. And definitely not for a boss who had yet to say hello.

Hmmph.

From the thinning of his irritatingly sensual mouth, it was looking like *someone* needed a little lesson on island greetings.

She jumped onto the dock the second they pulled up and gave him a jaunty salute. Maybe he was ex-military, like their last chief.

He didn't salute back.

Okay. Whatever. She still wasn't going to let his whole stoic *I can play statues better than you can* thing unnerve her. Unlike the last boss man, this one was going to know that Lulu Kahale was a force to be reckoned with.

"Aloha," she said again, lifting her hand into the *shaka* sign. "Lulu Kahale. Acting crew chief at your service."

"Zach Murphy," he said, without returning the *shaka*. "You're grounded. I'll take over from here."

CHAPTER TWO

ZACH MIGHT AS well have pressed an "erupt" button on the
island's volcanoes for all the tension there was in the air.
Or maybe it was the tropical heat he was pretty sure he'd
never get used to. Either way, he was uncomfortable.

Hell.

He'd wanted to make an impression when he arrived
here at the station. A bad one, however, had not been the
goal. And this one was about as bad as it got.

Before he'd even met her, Lulu Kahale had managed to
crawl right under his skin. Which took some doing. Now
that he had met her, he knew his instincts had been spot-on.

Beautiful. Proud. Brimming with unchecked energy. She
was a force of nature. More hurricane than rainbow at this
exact moment. Although even that barely disguised sneer
of hers didn't detract from her striking aesthetic. It might
even be illuminating it.

Pitch-black hair he bet mimicked an oil slick when it
was fanned out on a pillow. Liquid eyes that looked like
molten gold. Lips so full and soft that a dangerous image
of what they'd look like bruised from kisses temporarily
blinded him.

He rubbed his thumbs in his eyes, refocused his brain
and forced himself to pour the energy she was pulling from
him back into the task at hand.

Even so, as he took the boy from one of the crew's arms and placed him in the wheelchair, Zach was giving himself invisible punches in the face.

His parents had warned him. *Hawaiians do things differently. There's another way of getting things done out here.* And, more pressingly, *Don't expect things to run by the same book they did back in New York.*

They'd got that right.

Rescue crews were extraordinary people. They willingly dove headfirst into scenarios most humans were genetically programmed to flee. Dangerous ones. Fires. Floods. Cliff edges. The whole damn ocean. They didn't deserve coddling, but they certainly deserved respect.

That ethos had been the key to managing the fire rescue medical teams he'd helmed back in New York. Gratitude combined with one crystal-clear edict: no bending the rules. *Ever.*

Which was precisely why the team behind Oahu Search and Rescue had brought him on board. According to the management, this team needed "a bit more starch in their collars."

They weren't part of Hawaii's famous Ocean Safety Team. This crew was more…off radar. They went a step beyond. Took the rescues the OST weren't trained for. Belayed into the steepest ravines to find hikers who'd lost their way. Dove out of helicopters into a stormy ocean to find surfers sucked out to sea by the powerful currents. And countless other scenarios. In short, they risked life and limb to save other people's.

His new bosses, based back on the mainland, had drilled a second message into him when granting his three-month mandatory probation. One that had been ringing in his head from the moment he'd accepted the job. Funding for Oahu Search and Rescue would only continue if everything was shipshape. From what he'd seen so far, it most assuredly wasn't.

He needed this job. He needed it as much as he needed the heart that beat in his chest. The heart that beat in his son's. They were both battered and bruised and they were relying on this new start more than he could put into words. So, yeah…

When he'd arrived at the office and found no one there, the door wide open and an overflowing tray of weeks-old paperwork, then eagle-eyed the crew returning, half in regulation gear, half very definitely not, he'd seen red. They weren't just compromising his professional future with this slapdash approach. They were compromising everyone's health and safety. And that was unacceptable.

If this had officially been his first day, he'd have been halfway through reading this woman the riot act. This… Lulu.

For the first time ever he felt as if his perfectly appropriate anger was hobbled.

Shouting at Lulu would feel like shouting at a happy-go-lucky puppy. Between his gut and the vibes she was arrowing straight at his jugular, he knew shouting would only turn things from bad to worse.

One eyebrow lifted in an imperious arc, she shifted from one hip to the other, droplets of water glistening on the high-cut arch of her wetsuit where her hip met her thigh. Caramel-colored thighs that should very definitely be hidden behind regulation board shorts or a knee-length wetsuit. Not this…this body-hugging short wetsuit that swept up and along her curves to her heart-shaped face.

Those flame-licked amber eyes were unblinking as she maintained her gaze on him, pulled some lip balm from who knew where and swept it along first her upper lip, then her lower, as if preparing for battle.

He felt as if they were speaking to him. Her lips. Begging him to kiss the disdain away. Turn it into something sweeter.

Or maybe the heat had officially sent him tropical.

He threw some imaginary cold water on his head.

He'd thought he was immune to "drop-dead gorgeous" after things with his wife had gone so spectacularly wrong, but no. This woman's beauty was something else altogether. Natural. Spirited. Every bit as heated as the lava threatening to make a show over on the Big Island.

As his eyes swept the length of her, hot licks of desire tugged at parts of him he'd rather not be dealing with right now. He saw her giving him the same once-over, with an expression that shifted from angry to impossible to read. One enemy sizing up the other? Or two people getting off on the wrong foot, then realizing seconds too late there was one hell of a mutual attraction?

He made a big mental X over the latter option and concentrated on the task at hand. Getting things back on track for a positive working relationship.

To keep the unwanted carnal sensations from making any visual impression, Zach pulled himself up to his full height and crossed his arms over his chest, hoping to draw Lulu's attention back to his face.

"So. What exactly does my being grounded entail?"

Lulu was staring him straight in the eye, clearly unintimidated by him physically or professionally.

"Are you sending me to my room? No dates for a month? No candy bars till Christmas?"

One of the crew behind her tried and failed to turn a snigger into a cough. This was Lulu's crowd, and he had five seconds to find a way not to be permanently branded The Bad Guy.

Zach shifted on his feet, transfixed by Lulu's amber-colored eyes that were flaring with coppery hits of indignation. He'd definitely made the wrong call. She wasn't belligerent—she was proud. She wasn't reckless—she was permanently poised for action. She wasn't trying to one-up him—she was trying to hang on to her hard-won rung on the ladder.

Not hard enough, though. He was the new chief, and as such there had to be some lines drawn in the sand.

"The patient's your priority for now," he said.

It was as much of an olive branch as he could give without throwing up his hands and conceding defeat.

"Oh? So you *do* want me to do my job, then?"

Lulu didn't bother double checking. She made a signal to her team that they should carry on what they were doing—which was, in fairness, their job. A blonde woman and two other men, all kitted out in regulation neon orange OSR shirts and board shorts, helped the rest of the family off the boat, while Lulu took command of the boy in the wheelchair.

One of the crew offered him a quick, apologetic, "Pretty sure she needs an extra set of hands…" in explanation as they hurried after Lulu, who was strutting down the dock as if she were a pop star who'd just swept the Grammys.

Whether her intent was to show off her curves or not was hard to tell, but suffice it to say she had it and she was flaunting it.

He couldn't help it. He grinned. Lulu was gutsy. He was going to have to match her point for point, then win some extra ones if he wanted to win the team's respect.

"Eh, bruh?" The man who had been piloting the speedboat clapped him on the shoulder. "I'm guessing you're the new boss man?"

Zach nodded.

He introduced himself as Stewart, rattled off a quick ream of credentials, then lowered his voice as he tilted his head toward Lulu, now disappearing into the clinic.

"She's all right—so cut her some slack, yeah? She's spent a lifetime proving to her five big brothers that she's just as tough as they are, so she tends to come on a bit strong at first."

Zach whistled. Five big brothers, eh?

There had been plenty of second-and-third-generation firemen at his station like that. Trying to prove they were just as good or better than those who had come before them. Hell… *He* was a bit like that.

Nothing like following in the wake of a father who had all but been the poster boy for the 9/11 rescue effort. Everyone on the fire crews had gone above and beyond, but his dad's rescue efforts had captured the press's attention. For a while. The fact that he'd had to take early retirement because of the battering his body had taken hadn't warranted so much as a column inch. No one had cared about pulmonary fibrosis in a fireman outside of his prime. They'd cared even less when he'd moved to Hawaii to try to give his lungs a break.

Anyway… He shook his head and focused on the problem at hand.

"Rules are the same for everyone," Zach said, almost by rote.

Stewart rocked back on his heels and made a noise that, once again, had Zach giving himself an invisible pop on the kisser. He was definitely walking an out-of-the-frying-pan-into-the-fire path today.

"Yeah, bruh… I see where you're going. But…" Stewart cleared his throat and gave his chin a scrub, obviously trying to put his words in an order he thought would penetrate Zach's thick skull. "The thing is…Lulu's got health and safety ingrained in her bones, you know? She's lived and breathed this stuff her entire life, but never been given proper recognition for it. The last boss…he tended to 'put Baby in the corner,' if you know what I mean."

Zach shook his head. No. He did not.

"You know…" Stewart opened his hands as if it was obvious. *"Dirty Dancing?"*

Another vision of those water droplets skidding along Lulu's bare thighs blinded Zach for a second. "Nope," he said.

"Not a film reference kind of guy?"

"I prefer facts to fiction," Zach said, knowing that the direction this conversation was headed wasn't endearing him to Stewart, who would inevitably report back to the rest of the crew. He put up a hand in an attempt to rescue the situation. "Look. I'm still a bit jet-lagged, and I probably shouldn't have rocked up barking orders in the middle of a rescue. I suspect we're all going to have to take a bit of time to get used to one another."

"Don't worry, man." Stewart gave him a congenial clap on the shoulder that made it very clear the man's age had done little to diminish his strength. "We all have false starts. The thing about Hawaii is…" He looked out to the sea, then up to the sun, then back to Zach. "We all come here seeking instant perfection, but the thing about paradise…"

He opened his eyes wide, actively inviting Zach to ask him to unveil the mysteries of Polynesia.

"What is the thing about paradise?" Zach asked, finally realizing that Stewart wasn't going to share his island wisdom until he was asked.

"You have to earn it." Stewart said tapping the side of his nose. *"Ho'oponopono."*

"Come again?"

Stewart repeated the word, then explained. "It's the Hawaiian practice of reconciliation and forgiveness. A way to free yourself from negative thoughts and feelings. Building a gateway to happiness and fulfilment of your dreams."

Zach looked at Stewart. Really looked at him. Beneath

the tan and the laid-back stance he saw a man who'd fought and failed and fought again, until he'd truly won that aura of inner calm and—dare he say it?—control of his own destiny.

Another thing to take note of. Just because a person was relaxed and smiley didn't necessarily mean they flaunted the rules. They respected them. They just had their own way of paying said respect.

Son of a gun...

He couldn't believe that he, Zach "Read the Regs" Murphy, was even thinking this. But maybe every now and again seeing the rules from another angle was the better option.

After all, the divorce lawyers had recommended he and his son stay in New York, but in the end he'd gone with his gut. Harry's special needs could as easily be catered for in Hawaii as they had been in New York, but if he was going to continue working he needed help. The kind you only got from family.

His ex, Christina, had always prioritized her work over the two of them. It had been one of the first fault lines in their marriage. Her modeling career had meant she was rarely in New York, so in order to be close to family— *proper* family—he'd sought out a nine-to-five job that tapped into his skill base, moved to Hawaii, and bought a house not far from his parents' condo.

He'd seen his parents transformed by island life, and was hoping that whatever was in the water out here would do the same for him and his son. The simple truth was that his parents had moved to Hawaii because they'd been hurting. Just like he was now. So, yeah. Like it or not, Zach needed some of this *ho'oponopono*. Big-time.

Stewart made the hand gesture Lulu had and said, "We good, boss?"

"Absolutely." Zach nodded, with a *Thanks for the insight* smile.

He watched him walk down the dock and disappear into the clinic, where a roar of laughter seemed to add an extra hit of color to the scene. Bright red plantation style building... White sand... Blue sky... Greener than green mountains soaring up in the background...

He decided to stay where he was. Absorb some of the atmosphere. After all, this was going to be where he worked and, to be fair, there were several highly trained emergency medical professionals in there with the boy and his family, who knew more about stepping on sea urchins than he did.

Not much call for sea urchin spine extraction in the heart of Manhattan.

About twenty minutes passed. Then the family left, the father carrying his little boy in his arms, white bandages round his feet, and the blonde woman—Casey, if he remembered correctly—walking with them to their car with a small sheaf of papers.

He gave a begrudging smile. Okay. They weren't so "off regulation" that they didn't give their patients the paperwork they'd need for their insurance and the doctors back home.

Before they got in the car, Casey put a fresh lei round the little boy's neck and called out a hearty *"Aloha!"* as they pulled away.

Zach leaned back on the rock he'd taken up residence on and let the sun hit him full on the face. It was a warm day, but not the kind of "city hot" Manhattan sometimes sweltered under. The air was a mix of sweet and salty. The breeze felt like silk. Even the birds seemed to ratchet their songs up a notch out here in the tropics.

"He *what*?"

Zach sat up. Definitely not a songbird's cry.

He looked round at the parking lot. The beach. The rescue HQ and—ah…there she was. Five feet and two inches of electricity and venom, heading straight toward him without so much as a trace of a smile on her face.

Lulu was wearing a pair of hip-hugging jeans and a long-sleeved T-shirt with the name of a security company on the front of it. The neck was ripped out so that it slipped off one of her shoulders as she stormed his way. She was also dragging an ominous black thunder cloud in her wake.

Zach felt the sand shift beneath his feet as he quite literally dug his heels in for whatever confrontation was about to come.

"Zach Murphy?" Lulu asked, her voice with a low, ominous tone.

"Yes?"

"I have a bone to pick with you."

He shrugged some fortitude into his bloodstream. It was better that they resolve whatever it was now rather than let things simmer.

"Fair enough." He closed the space between them, keeping his voice on the lighter side of neutral. "What's on your mind?"

"You bought my house."

CHAPTER THREE

ZACH GAVE LULU a double take—which, insanely, made her even angrier. There were the tiniest fractals of vulnerability piercing through the defensive stance he'd shifted into, and she didn't like thinking she'd put them there. She was angry. Sure. But she wasn't a bully.

Now she had to be angry with herself *and* him! *Jerk*. He really knew how to make a bad day worse.

His three-month probation was going to be exhausting if every day was like today. Particularly now that he'd bought a house. *Her* house. It meant he had no plans to fail the probation. No back-up plan in place back on the mainland. He was putting down roots. This was a man who planned to stay.

Zach Murphy scrubbed a hand through his regulation haircut, making it adorably messy. *Idiot*. He looked over his shoulders toward the sea, as if expecting a support team of combat mermaids to appear, and when that didn't happen he returned his gaze to her, the bright blueness of it knocking a lungful of air out of her for the second time today.

"I—sure. I bought a house. It was for sale. I have the paperwork and the mortgage to prove it."

He looked confused rather than confrontational—which, if she were in a reasonable mood, she knew was a pretty generous response. But in true Lulu style she had to finish what she'd started, and this little chat they were having wasn't about making nicey-nicey with the man who had not only bought her dream house but had also taken the job that would have enabled her to buy the house in question.

The fact that she didn't really want said job wasn't important now…

"The thing is," Lulu intoned, feeling the steam almost literally coming out of her ears, "Turtle Hideaway was *mine*." She poked herself in the chest with a bit more gusto than she probably should have.

Zach shook his head again, even more confused. "So…if you didn't want to sell it, why'd you put it on the market?"

"No!" Lulu threw up her hands, cross with herself for letting the conversation get so muddled. "I wanted to *buy* it and you beat me to it!"

"The Realtor didn't say anything about anyone else having put in an offer…"

Lulu barely stopped a low growl from roaring up and out of her throat. "I was *going* to put in an offer, but I needed a few more months to increase my deposit."

She bit down on the inside of her cheek. *Crud.* She hadn't meant to admit that.

Zach Murphy was an intelligent man. And talented. And married to all the rule books that had ever been written about anything ever.

Not that she'd ever admit it, but—*yes*. She'd totally looked him up on the internet just now, while Casey had picked sea urchin spines out of that poor little boy's feet. He had qualifications she couldn't imagine garnering. Emergency medicine clearly stoked his arterial fires.

His father had been a fire station medic during 9/11, in charge of multiple rescue crews and lauded as a hero by the press. His grandfather before him had actually *started* a fire station in a poor area of town where no one else would work. And Zach, in keeping with the family tradition, had led a junior firefighter youth group from the age of fourteen and had been the first to acquire all his first aid badges.

He'd risen through the New York City Fire Department ranks on his own merit rather than hanging on to the coattails of his forebears, and at last check had overseen half the medical crews operating out of over two hundred fire stations dotted across Manhattan. There was no chance she could outrank this superstud of emergency medicine. And yet again she'd given him the upper hand by admitting that he had not one, but two things she wanted.

She gritted her teeth. Something was going to have to give. Either she was going to have to find some way to work with this Mr. Goody-Rescue-Boots, or act on her years-old threat to pack up her surfboard and find a new shore.

As those thoughts rattled uncomfortably from her head down to her heart, Zach's demeanor shifted from defensive to composed, with the clear arrival of a light bulb moment. His stupid eyes were ridiculously expressive. A perfect window into his deep and incredibly detail-oriented thought-process.

This was not the lifeless, gimlet-like lizard gaze of his predecessor. No, Zach's eyes were more like a kaleidoscope. Dark sapphire-blue when he was angry—which he had been when they'd first met—and shot through with shards of flint when he had made up his mind about something. They were bright, like the sea beyond the reef, when he reached a place of understanding. As he had now.

The well-defined lines of his facial features relaxed into a strangely comforting expression. One that spoke of having hit a thousand rocky shores but, fueled by willpower alone, having found a way to pull himself out of the fray.

Every. Single. Time.

For heaven's sake. Even his emotional scar tissue was better than hers.

"It's a big house for one person," she muttered, hoping

the comment would serve as a concession that, yes, she got that it was his—but, no, she wasn't quite ready to buy him a housewarming present.

"I didn't buy it solely for myself," he said.

His tone was not exactly apologetic, but she could sense that he was sorry she was hurt. Which, of course, flicked off another plate from her armor. People who had compassion were impossible to be furious with.

She narrowed her eyes and tried to scan him for glimpses of insincerity, hoping he'd learned that pacifying technique in a management class.

Nope. It was organic. Real. He actually genuinely did look as though it bothered him that he'd upset her.

She absently traced some lines into the sand between them, realizing too late that she'd drawn a heart. She swiped it away with her foot before he could notice, then met his gaze. "Well, I hope you and your wife enjoy it."

His eyes darkened to near black, then cleared. "It's just me and my son," he said, his voice unnaturally bright. Or… no… It was affection. Protectiveness. The same way her brothers would say, *Oh. You've met Lulu, have you? She's my kid sister.* Two parts love to one part *If you do a single thing to hurt her…*

There was definitely a story there.

Something in her softened. She should probably cut the guy some slack. After all, he hadn't exactly been sent a memo warning him that he'd taken both her job *and* her house.

"Hey," he said, after a quick glance at his watch. "I've got to get back to the house. My parents are looking after my boy and I said I'd be back by now. We haven't unpacked anything yet… I don't know if it would rub salt in the wound, or serve as what it's intended to be—a peace offering—but maybe you could show us somewhere good to eat? My shout. It might give us a chance to…" His lashes brushed his cheeks as he lowered his eyes to choose his words. He looked back up at her. "I think we need a do-over in the first-impressions department."

A rush of excitement and half a dozen options flew to mind and, rather surprisingly, she felt a warm, happy smile replace the tense scowl she'd been wearing. Wednesday was two-for-one burger night at the Moo Oink Quack Shack.

"Burgers suit?" she asked, quickly adding, "They cater to all types. There's tuna, turkey, beef, pork and taro if you're veggie."

She gave his lean yet muscular physique a quick scan, trying to determine if someone that solid could be made of mushrooms and spinach. Her eldest brother was a vegan and he could pull a car down the road if necessary, so anything was possible really.

"Sounds good. I know Harry, my boy, will definitely be on board for a turkey burger."

"A carnivore, is he?" Lulu grinned and patted her tummy. "A man after my own heart. I like a boy who knows what he wants from life."

Something shadowed Zach's features, then slipped away before she could define it. He pointed toward a bright red convertible Jeep parked under a stand of palms shading the staff parking lot. He had, she could see, parked in the chief's spot.

"Can I give you a ride?"

"I've got my own, thanks. Shall I lead the way, seeing as you're a newbie on the island?"

"That'd be a big help. I'm still working on getting my bearings here."

Zach folded into a courtly bow. When he rose and met her eyes, she saw what she hadn't seen before. A kind man. A worthy man. Someone who was starting over after having been brought to his knees by an unexpected blow. As blindsided by life's cruelty as she'd been when her parents had died.

She turned away before he could see her eyes fog with the tears she'd sworn she'd never spill, semi-audibly muttering something about getting her backpack and keys.

Urgh. Now she had compassion for him as well.

Zach Murphy made hating him very, very difficult.

Shouldering her pack, emotions back in check, she tried to wipe the muddied shoreline of her mind clean, just as the tide swept the beach clean twice a day. It was a meditation thing her navy SEAL brother Kili did. He said if the beach could start over twice a day so could he.

Sure, he'd been talking about making it through boot camp with a broken arm at the time… But Lulu was sure the theory could be applied to rotten first impressions.

She totally got the "fresh start" thing. She saw it a lot on the island. *Haoles* arriving from the mainland, hoping to change their lives for the better. To leave whatever it was that had turned their lives dark behind them.

Heaven knew she'd threatened her brothers with a move to the mainland where no one knew her—or them—enough times. It was always threat enough to get them to back down. For a bit, anyway. There was a part of her that lived in fear of the day when one of them would call her bluff. A day she hoped would never come. She loved it here. Loved her family. She missed her parents—her mom, in particular—in the same way she'd miss her own blood pumping through her veins, but…she had her memories.

She decided there and then not to make Zach's probation harder than it already would be. Then again, she thought as she pulled on her helmet and revved up her motorcycle, she wouldn't make it entirely easy…

"What are you? Hawaii's answer to Steve McQueen?"

Zach was laughing as he spoke, getting out of his Jeep,

and he took Lulu's helmet from her after she'd tugged it off over her thick-as-molasses hair, but she could see a question in his eyes.

She couldn't help it. She bristled. Riding her bike was her happy time. Well... Surfing was her happy time. But when she wasn't in the water, riding her motorcycle was her happy time. Speed and a connection with all she held dear.

The thick, tropical air. The breeze off the ocean. The sharp scent of the coffee plantations they'd swept past (possibly at a mile or two above the speed limit). The warm, mouthwatering aroma of frying garlic about to be united with some gorgeous shrimp. The green jungle tang of unfettered growth as they'd passed Oahu's famed North Shore on the way to this quiet little slice of heaven she'd prayed she might one day call her own.

So, *Yeah, pal.* It was a big fat yes—because she'd driven to Turtle Hideaway at precisely the right speed. *Her* speed.

She already had five big brothers commenting on everything from the length of her hair to the shortness of her skirts. She didn't need to add a micromanaging boss to the mix. Even if he was as hot as blue blazes.

"That's Stephanie McQueen to you," she said with a grunt as she kicked the stand into place, trying to take as much of the bike's weight as she could as it fell into place.

Zach snorted good-naturedly, then sobered. "I thought fifty miles per hour was the maximum speed across the whole island?"

"You want to be a policeman now, as well? Solve crimes? The Five-O are always recruiting."

She winced at her tone. The comment had come out more snarky than jokey. "Okay. You got me." She held her hands wide, as if about to ask a universal question not even the wisest of souls could answer. "Who doesn't want to show off for the new boss?"

Zach's expression shifted to something inscrutably neutral, as if he were privately assessing her but saving his feedback for her staff assessment—which, annoyingly, he'd be giving her in a few weeks' time.

She might as well have told him she wanted to lick his sweaty chest then feed him grapes before they made mad, ferocious love under a moonlit sky.

Oh, man. Did she?

Kind of.

Maybe not the sweaty chest thing…but all the rest of it…

She rolled her eyes behind her lids, wondering if she should dig a hole now or wait for the earth to open up and swallow her whole.

If any of the Hawaiian gods were real, or helpful, or both, it would crack open any moment now.

She reminded herself of one of her grandmother's countless island proverbs. *Energy flows where attention goes.* If she kept drawing everything Zach said to a dark or sexy space, the way they related to one another would inevitably be combative. Or sexy. Or both. And that was no way to work with someone. Not with the job they did. Pure synchronicity was essential. They had to trust one another with their lives, and as such there wasn't any room for negativity or out-of-control hormones.

You can't stop the waves, but you can learn how to surf.

Her father's favorite saying.

Pffft.

She already knew how to surf.

She reached out to take her helmet back from Zach, scraping round for a new line of thought. His problems would be better to focus on than hers. What was it that had chased a man so inherently in control of things so very far away from home?

"Daddy!"

A young boy—six years old, maybe seven?—came running down the packed red earth path that led to her—to

Zach's new house. The boy's gait was a bit off. He was up on tiptoe and his arms windmilled as if he was constantly on the verge of tripping over his own feet. She did a lightning-fast scan of the boy as both she and Zach quickened their pace to meet him. His movements were definitely clumsy, and his hands weren't moving in sync with the rest of him.

"You're home!" the boy cried, virtually crashing into his father's solid wall of a chest for a big old bear hug. Just the type her brothers gave her when they knew she'd had a tough day.

Something about the way Zach hugged his son tight, bent down to kiss his wavy head of identical chestnut hair, pulled back to examine his face, then pulled him close again, brought a lump to Lulu's throat. There was real, genuine love there.

Sexy, smart *and* a good dad.

"Look!" Harry grinned up at his father and pointed at his mouth. His two front teeth were missing.

"Hey! I guess that means we're due a visit from the Tooth Fairy tonight." Zach's smile faltered. "Unless…you didn't have a fall, did you, big guy?"

Harry shook his head, his smile still very much from ear to ear. "No. They came out when I was eating watermelon. Grandma's got them in a jar."

"Ah, well, then. I'll be sure to give the Tooth Fairy a call once you've gone to bed tonight."

Zach held his hand up for a high five, which his son returned, but instead of just slapping the hand he held on to his father and started to do a little dance, jigging back and forth to the beat of a drummer neither Zach nor Lulu could hear.

Lulu couldn't help it. She giggled. This was one happy kid.

When Zach turned back to Lulu she saw that fatherly love had displaced everything else that had passed between them. His son was very clearly his here and now. His sun, his moon, his stars. His…yes…his Turtle Hideaway. And, though it was going to be tough to let that particular dream go, she knew right in the very center of her heart that the house had gone to someone who would love it and care for it as much as she did.

"Lulu?" Zach smiled down at his son, then back at her. "I'd like you to meet my boy. This is Harry."

Lulu squatted down so that she was at eye level with him and extended her hand. "How do you do, Harry?"

"I'm good, thank you." He grinned a huge happy, gap-toothed grin. "Especially now that Daddy's back." He gave Lulu a bit of a jerky handshake then beamed up at his father.

Cerebral palsy. That was it. She would lay money on it. Not that it felt good coming to that conclusion. Life wouldn't be easy for Harry.

Once a month she worked with a charity that brought all sorts of disabled children out onto the waves, either on surfboards or canoes—or, in the case of some children with extremely severe disabilities, an extrahuge inner tube. She loved experiencing the rush of surfing along with a child who would never be able to experience it on their own.

Her heart cracked open another notch for Zach Murphy.

No wonder he was a rule-book guy.

"Come!" Harry grabbed Lulu by the hand and began to pull her down the path toward the house. "I want to show you my room!"

CHAPTER FOUR

ZACH ERASED THE concerns he'd had about Lulu not treating his son like she might any other little boy. A lot of people were knocked off their stride when they realized Harry had cerebral palsy. His wife, for example.

He shoved the thought back where it belonged. In the past. They'd made their peace. Their decisions. Their separate moves toward a happier future. Even so…he couldn't bear it when people didn't see the same things he saw when he looked at his little boy. A loving, bright kid, kiboshed by a critical absence of oxygen during the birthing process. Sure, he could've sued. But a wad of cash wasn't going to change his boy's life. Good parenting was. Shame his wife hadn't seen things the same way…

Zach followed Lulu and Harry along the path lined with well-established banana trees and rounded a small stand of palms to see the house. His smile broadened when he saw Harry enthusiastically pulling Lulu up the handful of steps onto the wraparound wooden porch that had been pretty much all he'd needed to see of the house before asking the Realtor to take down the for-sale sign.

Their view back in Manhattan had been of a brick wall. Now it was the Pacific Ocean. The fact this place hadn't been sold the second it went on the market was a miracle. So it was a bit of a fixer-upper? He wasn't afraid of a hammer and a nail. What he couldn't do, there were likely trades-men around to help with.

Harry stumbled on the steps as he clambered to get to the top, which wasn't unusual. Zach's instinct was always to lurch forward and help, but he'd been trying to let his son learn from his own mistakes. One of the toughest lessons for a parent to grasp,

Harry stumbled again, slapping his hand down on the step and only just avoiding a few splinters in his knee. Instead of going into a hypercautionary mode, as many people did, Lulu laughed along with his son and, as if she were merely starting a new game, looped her arm through his for a spontaneous three-legged race to his bedroom—which, Zach realized, was her way of keeping Harry upright while providing him with a bit of dignity.

There was a clamor of voices in the living room as they entered. His parents. Rather than leap in and micromanage, as he might very well be accused of doing, he thought he'd try to give Lulu the space and respect to be the adult woman she was. His way of addressing the getting-to-know-you do-over.

He heard introductions. *Alohas.* His mother explaining that her real name was Francesca, but she preferred Frankie, and that Lulu was welcome to call her husband, Martin, Marty—everyone did. All of this was followed up by Lulu offering an explanation that her name was Polynesian for Pearl, but she found that far too girlie, and then, after Harry said something that made them all laugh, explaining the game they were playing. By the sounds of the thumping, the three-legged race was back on again.

Zach smiled.

Ten points to Lulu for dodging his mother's twenty questions. Another ten points for not calling out the special-needs kid for being a klutz. He'd always tried to keep his son's focus on what he *could* do, rather than what he couldn't. It looked as though Lulu was cut from the same cloth.

He knew it shouldn't be a huge surprise, seeing as anyone was capable of being kind. It was just... He guessed the last few years and his disaster of a marriage had been a life lesson in learning that love didn't always come from the most obvious candidates.

Not that he had the whole perfect-parenting thing down to a tee—possibly, never would. He used to caution people. Warn them. Mention what to look for when interacting with Harry, what to try to ignore. He used to do it to his wife.

It had taken his marriage falling apart and a telling off from his son after a particularly overprotective school sports day for him to realize that all his cushioning made people treat Harry differently—whereas if they'd met his son without all the preamble, they would have been every bit as disarmed by the sheer amount of joy his gorgeous, sunny-dispositioned boy possessed.

He parked himself on the porch, eyes trained on the sun as it began its descent. In New York, the summer sun hung in the sky deep into the evening hours. Here it looked like it was lights-out around six thirty—give or take half an hour—no matter what time of year it was.

Equatorial life was going to take some getting used to. And he wasn't just talking about the sun.

His mother appeared and sat herself down next to him with a light pat on the knee.

"She seems nice... Lulu. Pretty, too."

He nodded but avoided eye contact. Ever since the divorce had become final a year back she'd been intent on getting him back into the dating game. No amount of *I'm not going there again, Mother* had put her off.

She was a feisty second-generation Italian woman who'd married a feisty second-generation Irishman. The pair of them regularly set off fireworks by rubbing together in both the right and the wrong ways. But most of all their relationship was big on love. They might never agree on the perfect wattage for a reading lamp light bulb, but they'd never let Zach down.

However, he could do without their help in the matchmaking department. He'd learned the hard way that a physical attraction to someone did not a long-lasting relationship make. So, no matter how…erm…*pronounced* a reaction his body had to Lulu, he was going to have to ignore it.

"How'd your first appearance at work go?" his mother asked, in a tone suggesting that she'd seen his thoughts running through his eyes like a ticker tape.

He gave a self-effacing grunt. "Not great."

His mother looked back over her shoulder to where they could hear Lulu making dinosaur noises with Harry. No prizes for guessing that Harry was showing her his new Lego collection. His ex had bought him a fire-breathing dinosaur kit as prep for life on Hawaii, only to discover that only the dinosaur *film* had been set here… There had never been actual dinosaurs.

"Facts schmachts," she'd said.

And therein lay one of their many differences. Zach liked his feet solidly grounded in reality, while Christina was a dreamer through and through. He'd thought it would work. Being a ying-yang couple. His parents couldn't be more different from each other, but they were always able to see things from the other's perspective, claiming their differences had made them stronger as a couple.

But that hadn't been the case with Christina. Their differences had been like tectonic plates destined to crack apart—the gap growing ever wider as the stresses and strains of life took their toll. Eventually, he'd had to face facts. They had a disabled son who would need help for the rest of his life and Christina didn't want to do it.

His mother tapped him on the knee and pointed out

toward the bay, where a turtle was crawling up onto the beach. "There's Christopher."

"Christopher? How do you know? Are they tagged, or something?"

"No," she laughed. "It's what Harry's been calling all the turtles making an appearance."

A sting of guilt lanced his conscience. Back in New York, Harry's best friend was Christopher. His mother was a caregiver and she always took Harry in after school, or whenever Zach couldn't change his shifts to match his son's schedule.

It was one of the reasons he'd taken this nine-to-five job. Reliability. Sure, there would be the odd out-of-hours call, but the main point was, as he was the only one Harry had to rely on now, he wouldn't be risking his life at work the way he'd used to.

He made a mental note to take some pictures and send them back home. He stopped. Corrected himself. Back to New York. Their life was here now. With a bit of organization Harry and Christopher could have regular video calls. With a bit of ingenuity they could even have one from the beach, so they could show the real Christopher his new namesakes.

"I'm guessing you're going for the minimalist look?" Lulu appeared, laughing as she plonked herself down on the step next to Zach's mom, her elbows on her knees, leaning forward to catch his eye. "Or will you be building all of your furniture out of Lego?"

Zach gave her the thumbs up. "Got it in one."

She laughed. Their eyes cinched a bit tighter than they probably should have for a man and woman who'd hit it off so badly.

Zach broke the eye contact first and, because he was himself, explained, "I thought we'd go local on our purchases instead of shipping things in. We sold all of our furniture out East and…" He trailed off before he told the real truth.

He'd sold everything because he didn't want any reminders of his married life—apart, of course, from his son. Harry had been allowed to pack his favorite toys and books of course, but the bed Zach and Christina had once slept in…? *Uh-uh.* The kitchen table he'd knelt alongside to ask her to be his wife…? *Sold.* The gray sofa, side chairs and throw pillows she'd insisted upon buying, because gray was the new black? *No, thank you.* Blue skies, azure oceans and lush green mountains were his new color scheme and he liked it that way. He only prayed his boy did, too.

"Cool." Lulu genuinely sounded impressed. "If you want me to point you in the direction of some awesome local craftsmen, I'm more than happy to help."

"Well, now, that's a lovely offer—isn't it, Zachary?" Zach's mom said, her voice heavy with meaning. The kind that meant she'd happily offer to babysit if they wanted a joint shopping trip to involve some "adult time."

"Thanks." Zach pressed himself up to stand. "That'd be great. But right now…" He patted his belly. "I'm getting hungry, and Lulu here has been bragging on a local burger shack."

"Sure have." Lulu bounced up. "Are you and Mr. Murphy coming as well?"

"Frankie and Marty, dear," Zach's mom insisted, before throwing Zach an *I think this one's worth a few dates* look.

He only just managed to contain his eye roll as he called his son to come on out to the porch. And his dad. They might as well all go.

Half an hour later they were all glowing in the remains of the day's sunlight, their newly arrived meal covering the bulk of a huge round picnic table parked at the high end of the beach, but chained to a nearby coconut palm "just in case."

"So?" Lulu asked after a few minutes of contented munching. "What do you think?"

"Amazing," Zach said through a mouthful of barbecued pork and pineapple burger. "Never had anything like it."

Lulu beamed proudly—as if she had been the one to slow roast it in the barbecue and griddle the pineapple herself. Local pride, he guessed. The same way a native New Yorker would swear on his life that he knew the best local pizzeria or, in his dad's case, the best Irish pub.

"I can't believe we've lived here all these years and never eaten here," Zach's father said, wiping a bit of mayonnaise off his cheek. "This hamburger is out of this world!"

Frankie agreed about her own burger and then, her eyes darting between Lulu and Zach, added, "It's fantastic to see Marty eat so much. When we eat out, we normally go to the officers' club." She gave her husband a tender look, then said, "I haven't seen him devour anything they serve like this."

Lulu's brow furrowed. "The Naval Officers' Club?"

"Oh, no. Retired Fire and Rescue Officers'."

Zach's father jumped in. "What she's trying to say is we go to the same place too often. Don't explore enough." He coughed and then, turning away from the table, coughed some more.

Lulu didn't miss the creases of concern on Frankie and Zach's faces as Marty recovered, then turned back, his thin face wearing a *Nothing to see here* expression.

"Sorry 'bout that." He pointed at his throat. "A bit of a tickle. Anyhow, you were saying about exploring more...?"

Frankie gave her husband a pat on the arm. "We've lived on the island long enough to let go of our safety net. Perhaps Lulu will show us some more places like this now that we're all here."

Zach's eyebrows shot up to his hairline. Interesting... This would normally be the point where his mother hammered a poor, innocent woman with a thousand questions. Who were her parents? Where had she grown up? What were her hopes, her dreams? Was there anything they should know about her past? Her future?

Not this time. His mother was clearly taking a different tack. Deference. Trying to prove *they* were the ones worth considering. It was something he'd thought he might see when hell froze over, but certainly not before.

It had never occurred to him that their confidence might've been knocked by the move out here for his father's health.

Then again, it had also never occurred to him that some of his friends would stop returning his calls when his ex had filed for divorce.

Had his dad's fire station buddies done the same? Kept their distance once his dad's health prognosis had forced him into early retirement? It would've been a heck of a kick in the teeth after all the years of service and friendship his father had given.

He considered another possibility: that his parents had made the move in the way a wounded animal took itself far away from the pack to try its best to recover.

Neither option sat well.

He took a fry and swept it through some ketchup, dropping it at the memory of how shocked he'd been when his parents had met them at the airport. His dad had lost a lot of weight in the few months since he'd seen them last, and that cough of his was gaining traction. He felt ashamed that he'd been so involved in his own life that he hadn't noticed just how much his father's health had degenerated.

Now that he'd found a job, made the move, bought a house and was in a place where he could start settling Harry in, he finally had the brain space to see the bigger picture. He wasn't the only one who needed help. His parents needed him here every bit as much as he needed them.

They were all hurting. All trying to heal. And any ray of sunshine that came their way was worth its weight in gold.

His gaze instantly shifted to Lulu.

Even if it came in a five-foot-two-inch package of fire and electricity?

Before the thought could gain purchase, Harry lifted up his burger and oinked like a pig, mooed like a cow, then launched into his best chicken impression as they all began to laugh.

"I'll take that as a thumbs-up." Lulu laughed, giving him that hand signal Zach had seen several times now.

"What *is* that?" he asked.

"What? This?" Lulu curled her hand into a loose fist except for her thumb and pinky finger and waved it back and forth. "It's the *shaka* sign."

"What does it mean?"

"Hang loose. *Aloha*. That's cool."

"All at once?"

"It symbolizes a shared respect."

She gave a light shrug before Zach could attach too much meaning to the comment.

"It's basically whatever you want it to mean. So long as its friendly," she added, with a small but perceptible upward tilt of her chin.

Lulu's eyes met his head-on. They were flame colored. It was easy enough to see that it was the sun making her eyes appear as if they had a life of their own, but Zach knew the fire that burned in them flared bright and hot with a note of warning. The *shaka* sign was the first thing she'd done when she'd met him, and what had he done in return? He'd barked an instruction. Then he'd made it worse. Belittled her in front of her crew and the people they'd just rescued.

It had been a careless thing for a new chief to do and, more to the point, unkind and lacking in respect. The fact she'd agreed to come over to the house he'd unwittingly bought from under her *and* had been kind to his son and parents meant one thing and one thing only.

He owed her an apology.

He lifted up his hand and tucked his fingers into the sign. "Is this right?" He shook his hand back and forth, his eyes not leaving hers.

"Bit stiff," she said, trying and failing to keep a straight face. "You'll get there."

"You think so?"

She shrugged, then said in a sonorous voice, "Watch, and you will learn how to do it."

Zach frowned. "That's exactly what I did."

Lulu rocked back on her bench seat and laughed. "No, bruh. That's something my grandmother says. She's got, like, a thousand 'true Hawaiian' sayings. Most of them are probably made up…but sometimes there's a lot of sense in them."

"Oh, yeah? Like…" He opened his hands for her to continue then took another bite of his burger.

Lulu eyed him for a minute, as if deciding exactly which of her grandmother's sayings best suited the man and the moment.

"'You are a chief *because* of your people.'"

The words hit him where they'd been aimed. Right in the solar plexus.

"Good advice," his dad said, when Zach failed to reply. He gave the picnic table a thump with one hand and lifted his burger with the other and then, before he took a bite, stopped himself and nodded at Lulu and at Zach. "You're lucky to have this one on your team, son. You two make a good match."

They were a match, all right. Whether or not they were a good one only time would tell.

And with that the sun dropped behind the horizon, preparing itself to reappear on the other side of the island tomorrow morning, when they would begin again. And this time Zach knew he'd be pouring his all into trying to get it right.

CHAPTER FIVE

With the alert radio turned up to high volume, Lulu went outside to see if the inevitable storm clouds had gathered to break the day's intense humidity. Though she'd grown up with it, even she was feeling the closeness of this final day in August.

Today she was on dispatch duty, while the rest of the team performed what Zach referred to as "team building." It was the type of team building she was pretty sure in any other parlance was called cleaning.

Yesterday they'd team built the helicopter until it glinted in the sun. Today's focus was nautical. The speedboat and the RIB needed a scrub-down. The equipment needed checking over. Ropes and harnesses needed to be examined and repaired if necessary. It was the same kind of stuff she imagined they did at the firehouses and EMT headquarters back in New York—not because it was nice when things were shiny and clean, but because lives depended on it.

Her ear still tuned in to the radio, she wandered under a small clutch of palms, staying tucked mostly out of sight from the rest of the crew, who were farther down the stretch of grass just above the beach where they kept the boats. Laughing, talking, throwing jokes and good-natured insults back and forth, they were clearly having a good time.

It was a nice change from when Clive had run the crew.

He'd been... Well, she was sure he'd been nice enough back in the day, but she was also pretty sure that when he'd been assigned crew chief of their specialist search and rescue team he'd very clearly mistaken the modern world for the 1950s.

Being treated like little more than a coatrack when her specialty was emergency rescue and medicine had been quite a blow. And she had to admit Casey hadn't fared much better. But Casey was a whole lot better at doing the water-off-a-duck's-back thing. She might look like a beauty queen, but she was shot through with a core of steel.

Lulu gave her shoulders a shake, willing herself to literally and figuratively shake it off. Clive was gone now. Fishing, probably. Or napping. And, after a few heaven-sent weeks of proving to the guys that she had what it took to run the crew, she was "back in her place."

She silently chided herself for instantly going to the glass-half-empty scenario.

She stared down at her hands, forcing a bit more honesty to surface.

Zach wasn't as bad as she'd initially thought. Quite the opposite, in fact.

Divorced, his mother had whispered when she'd been over at their house the other day. *Knocked him sideways*, she'd managed, before Zach had come in to find them, no doubt trying to stem the passing of sensitive information.

It had added another layer to what little she knew about him. A level of complexity she hadn't gleaned from his opening *Me Boss, You Employee* maneuver.

No, Zach Murphy was definitely more than what you saw at first glance.

He liked things shipshape, but he didn't delegate. He joined in. Expected as much from himself as he did from the others. And, despite the whole *You're grounded* thing, he didn't seem at all focused on keeping her away from the big-boy jobs like Clive had. He already had them on a roster that was as egalitarian as it came. Alphabetical.

It could be tactical. In their small crew it didn't take long to see who came after Lulu Kahale.

That's right. Mr. Zachary Murphy.

Another huge burst of laughter came from the guys. Lulu looked across, felt her breath hitching at the base of her throat as her eyes landed on her new boss just as he was pulling his top off.

Oh, my.

It looked like a torso-of-the-week photo shoot.

Her tooth snagged on her lower lip as Zach grabbed the hose, tipped back his head and ran the cool water over himself. Her eyes were jealously glued to the stream of splashing liquid as it poured down his toned body.

Yum.

The politically correct part of her brain that was in a fury anytime she was treated differently because she was a woman knew she shouldn't be treating Zach's team-building exercise as a chance to appreciate his physical attributes, but... *Mmm...* Her hormones were overriding all normal brain functions.

It had been quite a while since she'd had a date, let alone a boyfriend, and Zach Murphy was exceedingly good-looking. Strong, but not bodybuilder bulky. His hair had gone from lightly wavy to extrawavy, thanks to the humidity. It was longer than a buzz cut, but not so long you'd mistake him for a transient surfer dude.

Which made her wonder... Did he surf? Was that a thing out East? His fluidity of movement suggested he'd be strong in the water if they needed an extra rescue swimmer. He'd not gone on any of their rescues yet, claiming he wanted to get a grip on the paperwork, discover the lay of the land before he went out with them. Instead, he'd put Lulu in charge.

Publicly, she'd said the decision was an obvious nod to

the fact she'd been helming the team since his predecessor had officially retired to his hammock. Privately, she felt ridiculously proud that he had even an ounce of trust in her after their first very false start.

He could have easily made an example of her. Suspended her back on Day Zero. He'd been right. She hadn't been in regulation gear. She'd left the office open. The medicine cabinet and gear were obviously locked up...but sometimes thieves didn't care about things like that. And, of course, there were the piles of undone paperwork that he was wordlessly plowing through, knowing damn straight she should've done it.

So, yeah... Right now, she really wanted to put her best foot forward.

It was a rare chance to be judged for her merits alone, rather than being mollycoddled and then ignored because of the "talking-to" her brothers had given Clive.

Something told her that even if her brothers did get to Zach, he'd hear them out, because he was fair that way, but he wouldn't be swayed by them.

One of the guys cracked a joke, winning a rare but heartfelt guffaw from Zach. He wasn't the most carefree of men...but his smiles could knock your socks off. If you were into that sort of thing.

In fact... Lulu scraped her teeth across her lip. If it weren't for the fact his two front teeth were crooked, he'd almost be too good-looking. Which was one of the many things on her no-go list when it came to considering potential dates. That tiny "flaw," such as it was, made him mortal. Which meant he was accessible to other mere mortals...like herself.

Hmm... Perhaps she should recommend one of the island's better orthodontists.

"Here's your shaved ice, girlfriend." Casey appeared by her side and handed her a palm leaf bowl filled with her favorite flavor—coconut and mango. She'd been out filling up the crew jeep's gas tank and obviously felt blasted by the weather as well. "What are we looking at?"

Lulu feigned an indifference she definitely didn't feel. "Just watching the boys doing some of the clean-up work for a change."

Casey snorted appreciatively. She leaned on the canoe Lulu had propped herself against, watched for a few moments, then shouted out, "Keep up the good work, boys!"

They laughed, waved and offered invitations to join in.

"Lunch break," Lulu parried, raising her shaved ice.

A volley of good-natured insults flew their way, melting in the heat before they landed. Lulu and Casey continued watching the guys at work the way they might watch a documentary on dolphins. Completely rapt.

"He's not as bad as we thought he was going to be, is he?" Casey nudged Lulu's foot with her flip-flop.

"Who?" Lulu asked, knowing exactly who Casey was talking about.

Casey tipped her head down and looked at her over her sunglasses. "Don't be stupid."

"I'm not!" Lulu protested hotly. Too hotly, judging from Casey's cackled response.

"You haven't looked at anyone like that in the history of me knowing you," she teased.

"That's not true! There was—" Lulu sought her memory for just one of her short-term boyfriends who had made goosebumps ripple up her arms in the middle of a summer's day and came up blank. Rather than admitting as much she offered Zach a backhanded compliment. "He definitely knows how to keep the bosses back on the mainland happy. Does the paperwork as if his life depended on it."

Casey shrugged. "Maybe it does."

Lulu kicked off her flip-flops and dug her toes into the sand. Casey might've nailed it.

As much as she'd wanted to find flaws in him after that first awful impression…she was struggling. When he'd invited her to his house—*her* house—she'd been prepared to play the happy islander right up until they were settled at the burger shack and then she was going to read him the riot act. Let him know how things really worked in Hawaii.

And then she'd met Harry. Funny, kind, a brilliant dinosaur impersonator and quite clearly the keeper of the solitary key to Zach Murphy's heart.

His parents were great, too. They probably had spare keys… Warm-hearted. Friendly. Eager to learn more about Hawaii. His dad had a worrying cough, but she hadn't felt it was appropriate to ask about it.

There'd been no mention of Harry's mother, and despite some rather epic earwigging over the past week she'd been unable to figure out why Zach's marriage had failed. One thing she was sure about: he wasn't much of a talker. Definitely an actions-speak-louder-than-words kind of guy. And, from what he'd done over the past week, also respectful, conscientious, hardworking. He was—as she'd admitted to herself late last night, when she might have been accidentally-on-purpose thinking about him—about a million times better than her initial impression.

He turned, saw her watching him, and winked.

A million and one times?

She caught herself smiling in response. He returned the smile. A dimple appeared on his left cheek. It was cute. It ranked up there with that seemingly untamable cowlick at the back of his head. And, of course, those bright blue eyes of his.

Then she felt something cold land on her collarbone.

Ah. Her shaved ice.

He hadn't been winking at her—he'd been signaling to her that she was about to become a victim of her own

ogling. Which, of course, hadn't been *ogling*. It had been...
critical observation.

She frowned and turned away, trying to shake off the
feelings as she swiped at the shaved ice. This wasn't like
her. Not even close. She wasn't a flirter. And definitely not
someone who dated. Well... She *dated*, but things never
really moved beyond that. Either her brothers freaked the
guys out by casually mentioning how much they could
bench-press, or she nipped it in the bud before anything
too close to feelings got involved.

It didn't take a psychiatrist to tell her that her idea of
true love had been well and truly screwed up the day her
father had grabbed his surfboard and paddled out to sea in
the middle of storm to find their mother. His actions had
declared one thing and one thing only: you should only
marry someone you would risk your life for.

Not so great if you were their little kid, standing on the
beach, holding your big brother's hand, wondering when
Mommy and Daddy were going to come back, but hey...
Whoever had named the Pacific Ocean for its peaceful nature had been having one hell of a laugh.

When she turned around Zach's back was to her and his
fingers were hitched on his lean hips as one of the guys
started pointing out something about the motor.

It was one of her favorite Zach poses—Zach with his
fingers hitched on his hips. There was also the thinking
pose, of which there were variations. Thinking with a head
scrub. Thinking with a chin rub. Thinking while looking
out to the ocean. Then there was Zach at her—*his*—desk.
With a pencil tucked behind his ear. With a pen tracing
along that deliciously full mouth of his. With his mouth
parted as if he were just on the brink of—

Absolutely nothing.

She took a big bite of shaved ice, instantly giving herself a full-on case of brain freeze. Just as well. She would

not and could not let herself crush on the new chief from the mainland. Swooning over him was too close to actual feelings, and feelings always got you in trouble. Just when she properly fell for him he would leave. Or she would get fired for inappropriate behavior. Or worse. As if there was anything "worse" than being fired.

A broken heart?

Pffft. She'd consigned her heart to the walk-in freezer of lost opportunities long, long ago.

As she sucked a few crystals of flavored ice off her knuckle their eyes met again. Something flared hot and bright between them, blurring out the rest of the world.

A flash image of a pair of his 'n' hers surfboards propped against the outdoor shower wall at Turtle Hideaway blinded her as the look intensified.

She rubbed her eyes to make it go away.

Insane fantasies like living with Zach were just that... fantasies. Mainlanders moved here convinced they wanted island life. But in the end all they actually needed was a monthlong vacation.

A surge of something that felt an awful lot like disappointment swept through her.

"Did you just sigh?" Casey asked.

"Ha!" She scoffed. "No."

Had she?

"OMG!" Casey cackled. "You totally did."

Lulu glared at her.

"You have the hots for him, don't you?" Casey asked, laughing as Lulu's cheeks pinked up.

"I totally do not."

Casey began laughing even harder. "You so completely do!" But as quickly as her laugh had begun, she went dead sober. "Don't you date him. You know you've got a trail of broken hearts in your wake and he's a good boss. We need to keep him here—and not just because he's a tasty bit of eye candy."

Lulu made a gagging noise. "As you very well know, I have rules. I don't date mainlanders. I don't date *haoles*. Nor do I date colleagues. Especially not a *haole* mainlander boss who buys my dream house. Just because he's sexy as a cake topper, it doesn't mean I'm going to rip his pants off, tear his heart out of his chest and dine on it for supper."

"Good to know," came a voice from behind her.

A very male and impossible to interpret voice that could only belong to Zach Murphy.

Awesome.

She turned around, doing her best to make her expression appear casually indifferent rather than completely mortified.

"I have high standards," she answered, as loftily as she could. That and she was scared to death of ever finding out what it was actually like to love someone.

"Hmm…" He hooked his fingers onto his hips. "Just as a matter of curiosity, is it a general Hawaiian thing not to date newcomers from the mainland, or something that's specific to you?"

His eyes didn't leave hers even though Casey was standing right there.

"Depends who's asking," she shot back.

"Asking what?" Stewart asked, joining them under the shady palms.

"Lulu here is giving Zach the rundown on her list of rules in order for her to date someone," Casey said.

"Oh, is she, now?" Stewart leaned against a palm, placing one food against it as a ballast. "I don't think I've ever known our Lulu not to stomp all over some poor unsuspecting suitor's heart." He crossed his arms over his chest and grinned. "This I would very much like to hear."

"Hear what?" another one of the other guys from the crew asked.

"Lulu's dating rules," Stewart said, pulling open a cool box and tossing cold bottles of water to everyone.

Lulu felt streaks of red working their way up from her chest to her collarbones then her neck, virtually strangling her as they burned their way across her cheeks. How completely mortifying.

"Are they your rules or your brothers' rules?" asked Kenji, aka Ken the Fin.

"I make up my own rules," Lulu retorted, unwillingly drawn into a conversational vortex she very much did not want to be in.

Everyone but Zach laughed.

Stewart took a swig of water and nodded at Zach. "Have you met the Kahales?"

He shook his head.

They all laughed again, shaking their heads and murmuring variants on, "Oh, this I gotta see!" And, "I hope someone's got a camera when that happens!" Or, "When's the Oahu tug-of-war again?"

"Will you guys shut up?" Lulu snapped. And then, to Zach, "Not you."

They laughed even harder.

Lulu saw red. "Oh, my God, you guys! Can it! If he was the last person on earth I wouldn't go out with Zach Murphy—all right?"

Too late, Lulu realized she'd screamed her little announcement aloud, and not in her head like a smart person would've done.

The team barely bothered hiding their snorts and guffaws behind their fists. Casey pretended to look slightly apologetic, but didn't really. And Zach looked bemused rather than hurt, which was even more irritating than the guys laughing.

Didn't he think she was worth dating? She knew she wasn't exactly bachelorette of the year, but it wasn't like she was grotesque. There'd been something between them just a few minutes ago. Enough to make him wink at her, anyway.

"Right. That's settled, then," Casey said, with a hand-wiping gesture that indicated the matter was closed to discussion. "We can all get back to work now, secure in the knowledge that Lulu and Zach will never, ever go on a date."

And just like that it was the only thing Lulu wanted to do.

Zach kept his gaze neutral, but he was wishing like hell he'd opted for the phone call version of this meeting with his boss instead of a video conference.

"You *what*, now?" he asked, instead of swearing.

"We'd like you and Lulu Kahale to represent the company at the Intra-Island Search and Rescue Games. Work out any problem points the two of you might have in advance."

"In advance of what?" he asked, instead of tearing the actual hair out of his head.

"The nationals," his boss said, as if it were obvious. "Of course there are also the International Search and Rescue Games to aim for, but we thought we'd start local."

What the actual—

"Sorry. I'm not following. You want me to play games with Lulu?"

He grimaced. That had come out all kinds of wrong.

His boss gave an easy laugh. The kind of laugh a man who delegated on a regular basis gave when asking someone to move a pyramid from one side of the desert to the other by the end of the week.

"It's a thing between the Coast Guard and the police force rescue squads. We thought we'd enter you all this year, to get some more visibility for the squad. See if we can attract some more investors. Long story short—you two have to win. No pressure."

If he could've volunteered to move a pyramid instead he would've done it, but Zach forced himself to smile and nod as his boss explained that the games would be held on the Big Island, where he and Lulu would stay in a hotel. Together. The games would take place over a long weekend in two weeks' time and would require the pair of them to work together "like a newly serviced sports car."

Zach only just managed to bite back a comment about how sports cars had a reputation for breaking down. Instead he smiled and nodded. He had never considered himself a yes-man, but two more months to go on his probation meant he wasn't in a position to say no.

He could, however, offer alternative suggestions. "Wouldn't someone who's been on the team a bit longer be better?"

"Nah," his boss replied, without bothering to think about it. "We've already done some research on the optics and the two of you make a good fit."

An image of Lulu that only belonged in the privacy of his bedroom cracked Zach's brain in half.

He shifted in his chair, trying to stem the images, while his boss rattled off a few ideas, then said he'd put it all in an email and zap it over so he and Lulu could hold a "blue sky meeting" about it.

"What? You want us to come up with ideas?"

"No. We want you to train together. Day and night. Let the rest of the crew put you through your paces. In two weeks' time you two must be on the same page—the *Oahu Search and Rescue are the winners* page. We want you to make one hell of an impression, if you get my meaning."

Zach did. They had to win. If they didn't, that probation threat hung in the air like a guillotine.

Thanking his boss for the "opportunity to promote the

team" and, of course, health and safety in Hawaii, he ended the call and dropped his forehead into his hands with a groan.

How on earth was he going to achieve synchronicity with Lulu when they currently repelled one another?

He'd thought he'd fixed things between them on that first day, but about a week in there had been that weird conversation with the crew talking about her brothers and dating. Zach's one big takeaway was that Lulu Kahale was not on the market for a boyfriend. And if she was she definitely wouldn't be knocking on his door.

A knock sounded and the office door opened.

Lulu.

He sucked in a sharp breath.

She bristled.

He tensed.

Their eyes met and sparks of flinty heat sprayed everywhere they shouldn't have.

"You got a minute, boss?"

She'd taken to calling him "boss"—which for some reason felt like an insult coming from her. A challenge.

"Absolutely. Come on in."

His desk was shoved up against the wall of the small office. The only other chair was right next to his. He held out his hand, gesturing for her to take a seat, just as she reached out to grab the back of it. Their fingers brushed. He felt as if he'd just stuck his hand in a candle flame. As tempting as it was dangerous.

She took the chair and pulled it a couple of feet away from him before she sat down, dropping her staff backpack between them.

Subtle.

Neither of them said anything for a minute, as if each of them was braced for round twenty-seven, or whatever it was, of the weird hate-tinged game of *I respect you but only as far as I can throw you* they'd been engaged in for the past few weeks.

"How'd the hiker from this morning get on at the hospital?" he finally asked.

Lulu tilted her chin up. She'd been the one to belay down from the helicopter to get the twentysomething hiker onto a stretcher. "Good. A bit shaken up. Fractured wrist and a few scrapes and cuts."

"Did you manage to figure out how he'd ended up on that outcrop?"

She shrugged casually, as if novice hikers were always falling off the sides of mountains and needing rescuing. "Bird-watching through binoculars. Wasn't looking where he was going." She sniggered. "He was more annoyed that he hadn't been able to figure out what type of bird it was than anything else. Oahu Elepaio."

"What's that?"

"The bird."

"Oh! You saw it?"

"Nah. Heard it."

He nodded, impressed. Athletic, competitive, beautiful—and able to identify birdsong. What other hidden talents lay beneath Lulu's implacable surface?

He silently made the question rhetorical. He didn't want to know.

They sat and stared at one another for a moment, the conversation drying up as it often did on the rare occasions they were alone.

"So!" He clapped his hands together too loudly, not quite ready to tell her about his call with the boss. "What can I help you with?"

"Nothing," she said, her eyes darting round the office that had once been hers.

He hadn't changed it much. Not at all, really—except for making it a bit tidier. Maybe that was what this was. A power play. A dethroned lioness prowling round the new leader of the pride.

The word struck a chord. She was a lot of things, but above them all she was a proud woman. This wasn't some false bravura or macho grandstanding. It was pride. And he liked that about her.

He liked a lot of things about her.

That long, thick braid that swung between her shoulder blades. That nook between her jaw and her neck. The way her tooth dug into her lip when she was biting back something she clearly wanted to say. But they were colleagues. *End of.*

After the ticking of the clock grew too loud to tolerate, he tried again. "So…did you come in here to point that out, or is this your way of saying you'll get the paperwork from this morning to me later?"

A wash of guilt and then delight rippled across her features. A look of triumph took purchase as she pulled her backpack off the floor and presented him with a clipboard thick with completed forms.

"Here you are."

He flicked through the papers. "Looks like it's all here."

"Should be. I went over it twice."

He looked up and met her eyes in time to catch a hint of vulnerability. A desire to please. And it felt personal.

This time he was the one to push his chair back.

"Is Harry around this weekend?" Lulu asked.

"Yes," Zach answered cautiously. "Why?"

"I wanted to take him out surfing."

Before Zach could explain the number of reasons why that was an insane idea, she continued.

"I thought since he likes the turtles so much he could see what it feels like—you know, to fly on water. Not that turtles fly."

She rolled her eyes at herself. Small streaks of red were

beginning to color her cheeks, as if she were silently willing herself to stop talking. But she didn't.

"I work for this charity. Well...not work. My brother and I volunteer there sometimes. We take special-needs kids out when we know the surf is going to be mellow. We've got special supports for kids with big physical hurdles, but I think Harry'd be good going out with me...so long as we slather him in sunblock. That kid is pale!"

Zach stared at her, then said, "He's not great at swimming."

"He doesn't have to be. We've got wetsuits, float vests, buoyancy aids. Everything he'll need." Her eyes flicked to his, the liquid amber irises a deep burnished gold. "He'll be safe with me."

Zach didn't know why, but he believed her. Which was huge. He'd never felt Harry would be safe when his ex-wife took him out. Especially when their outings were "visitations." Which was insane, because she was his mother, but...

A twist of acid stung his throat. Harry's cerebral palsy had closed something off in her—something he'd thought all mothers felt for their children, no matter what. An unbreakable, protective love.

"You can come, too." Lulu said, her eyes leaving his when he said nothing. "I mean, you have to, really, because I'll be taking other kids out, too. But..." She held her hands out in a *The choice is yours* gesture.

The invitation hung between them, and just as he saw her begin to adjust her posture, ready to take it back, he said, "Sounds great. We'd love to."

Her face broke into a broad grin. "Really? Awesome. Because I've already signed him up and your parents think it's a great idea."

"My parents?"

"Yeah, I—" Her expression turned hesitant. "I dropped

by their condo the other day and talked to them about it. Floated the idea."

"You went to my parents' condo and talked to them about taking my son surfing?"

Lulu nodded slowly, tensing her body as if waiting for him to blow up. "Yes. Was that a bad thing to do? I was bringing them the addresses for some food trucks I thought they'd like."

Zach gave his head a double-handed scrub, then laughed. Properly laughed. He'd thought she hated him. People who hated someone didn't drop by their parents' house with top tips for taco trucks and offers to take their disabled son surfing.

Maybe he'd been looking at it all wrong. Lulu was a strong, proud, hard-working woman. She'd wanted his job. She'd wanted his house. He'd unwittingly swanned in and taken both. So she was regrouping. Figuring out how to let go of her plans for the future and move on.

"What? Why is that funny?"

"No. Lulu. Please... Sorry, I just—" Zach held his hand out, gesturing for her to take her seat again, which she did. Reluctantly. "Your offer is an amazing one. Generous. Kind. Yes, please. I'm sure Harry would love it. And I—" A knot of emotion suddenly rose and jammed in his throat as he pictured the scene. The beach, the sea, his boy on a surfboard... "I'd love for Harry to have that experience."

There were a thousand other things he'd love to see Harry enjoy, but this would be a damn good start.

Lulu rose, her smile more cautious this time, but still a smile. "That's great. So...I'll pick you both up at six on Saturday."

"On the motorcycle?"

She snorted. "I think you'll find the Highway Code doesn't allow three people on the back of a motorcycle."

He tapped the side of his nose. "Good to know."

He enjoyed her smile. Not smug from being right, but satisfied to have proved she knew the rules as well as he did.

"I have a Jeep," she said.

He nodded. It suited her. As much as the bike did. "So, that's six a.m., then?"

She rolled her eyes good-naturedly. "We're not going night surfing, boss."

"Zach," he corrected. If he was going to trust her to take his son out into the ocean, he wanted to be on a first-name basis with her.

She scrunched her nose for a second and didn't repeat his name. Just nodded. She backed up to the door frame, as if turning her back on him would make her too vulnerable. And as she left, with that soft smile of hers and an over-the-shoulder wave, he suddenly saw the invitation for what it truly was. An olive branch.

She'd gone before he remembered the Intra-Island Search and Rescue Games.

He should run after her and explain it all, but the moment they'd just shared had felt like a fresh start. A chance for a genuine friendship.

Something deep in his gut told him friendship with Lulu was hard-earned and precious. And he didn't want to do a single thing to compromise it.

CHAPTER SIX

LULU'S HEART WAS hammering in her chest. She couldn't believe she was doing this. Bringing Zach and Harry to the Superstars Surf Club. Her *brother* was going to be there. She didn't want Makoa to see her with Zach. He knew her tells. Her blushes. Her hair flicks. The way she covered all of it up with an extra splash of *I don't care what anyone thinks of me*.

But what was even bigger was the fact that Zach had agreed to come. The tension between them might have relaxed a bit, but she knew he still thought of her as a wild card. Someone to keep an extra eye on.

And now Zach was going to trust her with his son?

He's not Zach, she silently corrected herself. *He's your boss.*

Calling him Zach felt like entering a completely different, touchy-feely universe. Ultrapersonal. The kind of personal that would give oxygen to the feelings that had all but consumed her since Casey had forced her to scream about not wanting to date him.

It was like she'd been cursed. Zach Murphy was in her brain nearly every second of every minute of every single shift they worked together. And pretty much all of the other minutes of the day since he'd walked out onto that pier and she'd tumbled headlong into those blue eyes of his. It was as if they'd swallowed her whole then spat her back out. She was someone she didn't recognize. Stupidly hungry to impress, strangely coquettish and ruled by a tummy filled with overactive butterflies that didn't seem to know when enough was enough.

These were teenage-girl-crush feelings. And now she was inviting him on one of her favorite days of the month to one of her favorite places on earth, where her brother would see her blushing like an idiot every time Zach Murphy laid eyes on her.

She pulled into the drive, not resenting the familiarity of the approach to the house as much as she had that first time she'd yanked her motorcycle onto the private little lane that led to Turtle Hideaway.

Knowing Harry was down here, tucked behind the palms and loving the little beach cove almost as much as she did, was an unexpected salve. Knowing the same about Zach was... Well, he hadn't yet announced any plans to knock the house down and replace it with some sort of chrome and steel number, like a lot of other mainlanders did to the traditional beach houses. That was something.

To her surprise they were already outside and waiting for her—rolled-up towels under their arms, board shorts on, smiles on their faces. What she could see of them, anyway. Both Zach and Harry were wearing snorkels and masks.

She'd barely brought her open-topped Jeep to a halt before Harry was doing his high-speed tiptoe running toward her. Her instinct was to get him to put the brakes on before he slammed into the side of the Jeep, but she'd hung around enough special-needs kids to know cushioning all the blows was worse than a few cuts and bruises.

Zach jogged behind him, tugging off his mask. Their eyes connected with a glint of mutual understanding that unleashed a warm glow of satisfaction in her chest.

Mahalo, he mouthed. *Thank you.*

He might as well have said *I want you* from the response it elicited. Her entire body was having a hot, tingly, glitter party. She'd never felt her clothes touch her body the way they were touching her now. Her T-shirt was brushing against her breasts, her cut-off jeans were brushing the tops of her thighs. Even her flip-flops brushed against the bottoms of her feet as if she were receiving her very first erotic foot rub.

"Load up—we're late," she said, instead of *I think I love you*—which, of course, would have been insanity. She didn't love Zach Murphy. She was crushing on him. Hard. But that was a hundred percent superficial and could be quashed with some concentrated mind over matter. He was her boss. And just because her entire body felt more alive than it had in years, that did not equate with a deep lifelong love. Certainly not the kind her parents had experienced.

"The moment I saw her...I knew."

And they'd wed two weeks later.

Lulu and Zach had known each other for five weeks and could barely be in the same room together, let alone on the same island, so it was pretty clear the two of them had nothing on her parents' love. Nor was this cloud cuckoo land.

She revved the engine and reversed out of the drive, doing her damnedest to ignore the fact that Zach had sat in the back seat. Right smack-dab in the center of her rear-view mirror.

Twenty minutes later they were down at the beach.

Harry and Zach climbed out of the Jeep and followed Lulu up a small bluff, from where they could see the crowd on the beach.

Zach stopped in his tracks. "Wow."

Lulu beamed. She always felt that weird kind of teary happy on Superstars Surf Club day, and today was no different.

"I didn't expect there to be so many people," Zach said, his voice a bit scratchier, a bit deeper than normal.

"It's pretty amazing, isn't it?"

Below them on the beach was a crowd of about sixty or seventy people, about a third of them children, the rest of them family members and, of course, volunteers in their bright orange T-shirts.

"And do all these kids—"

"They've all got obstacles to surmount," Lulu finished for him. "All sorts. Blindness, Down syndrome, autism, epilepsy, paralysis… But once they're out in the water with our volunteers—"

"None of it matters?" Zach finished for her.

"Exactly."

"Mini!"

Lulu cringed as Harry virtually leaped into his father's arms at the sound of her brother's huge foghorn of a voice.

"Mini-Menehune!"

She lasered her best evil eyes directly at her brother's chest. *Don't call me a magical dwarf!* And then caught herself adding, *Especially in front of Zach!*

"Hey! Mini! No *shaka* for the Mak-man?"

"Who's that?" Zach asked. "Friend of yours?"

"Brother," she growled.

She'd been hoping for a bit more time before Makoa spotted her, but that was the thing about her brothers. Always there when she both did and didn't need them. Her father's last words to Makoa had been *Look after your sister* and all five of them had taken the instruction to heart.

She popped on her brightest smile, hoping like hell that Mak would, for once, play it cool. "Hey, bruh! How's it hanging?"

"Great."

Her brother jogged up to them. Every insanely solid, muscled inch of his six foot five frame. He looked like a warrior with tattoos just about everywhere except his face. And that was only because their mother had made each of her sons promise that they'd never look battle-ready when she'd worked so hard to teach them the power of peace.

Makoa threw her a look. One that said, *You're being nice. What gives?*

She shrugged and nodded at Zach, as a reminder that they weren't alone.

Makoa rolled his shoulders back and turned to Zach. *"Aloha."*

Lulu was so used to men squaring themselves off against her brothers—each as big as the other—that she was more than quietly impressed when Zach stayed as he was, one arm casually slung over his son's shoulders, stance relaxed.

"Aloha," he said.

Her brother gave him the chin-lift and a *shaka* sign, then looked down at Harry. "Who's this little surfer man?"

Zach looked to his son. "Want to introduce yourself?"

Harry was staring up at Makoa as if he was Poseidon himself. In complete awe. Lulu was tempted to tell him that Mak's favorite dress-up outfit had been an old hula skirt and a coconut bra their mother had given them to play with as kids, but thought it best to let the moment play itself out. Her brother might drive her crazy, but he was a sucker for little kids, having three of them himself.

Mak knelt down, one knee on the sand, one tattooed forearm on his bent knee. He held out his hand. "I am Makoa. My friends call me Mak. You can call me Mak."

Harry beamed up at his father, then back at Mak. "I'm Harry. My friends call me…um…Harry."

"I like it." Her brother gave the boy's dark hair a scrub, then narrowed his gaze, as if inspecting him properly. He leaned forward conspiratorially and said, "You know, there was a King Harald. A Viking. A strong warrior of the sea. I bet you're like him. Show me your muscles!"

Mak struck a pose and then Harry did.

They all laughed. Lulu's brothers might be the most overprotective bears on the island, but moments like this reminded her that their hearts were made of solid gold. They also reminded her of how much she missed their big family gatherings. They were just so…complicated.

Did she show up with a plus one who would be put through her brothers' proverbial "boyfriend mangle"? Or did she show up single and endure the endless parade of men her brothers thought she should date?

She threw a surreptitious glance at Zach, who was still standing tall, relaxed and completely unintimidated by her big brother. Something tingled inside her. The unfamiliar heated spray of possibility.

Mak made a big show of being impressed by Harry's tiny little boy muscles, then challenged him to grab on to his flexed arm and be lifted up in the air. He swung him back and forth, much to Harry's delight and his father's concern.

Lulu knew that Zach had erased the crease in his brow before his eyes met hers, but she saw something there that she hadn't seen before. A core-deep need to protect his son at all costs, which sometimes involved stepping back and letting mishaps happen and at other times meant throwing himself in front of a speeding bus. It was a role that took precedence over everything.

Which made her wonder… What on earth had happened between him and his wife? Who could fail to be attracted to a man who honored his role as a parent so strongly? How on earth could you not want to do everything in your power to keep a kid this great safe and happy?

Whatever it was, there was definitely something dark and twisty keeping a stranglehold on Zach's free-and-easy side. It was a part of him she'd caught microglimpses of but had yet to properly unravel.

"So!" Mak pushed himself up to stand, his dark eyes still

on Harry. "You looking forward to surfing with a champion today?"

Zach looked to Lulu. "Are you a champion surfer?"

Mak laughed. "I meant me."

"What?" Lulu bristled. Really? Just because he had one more measly medal than she did, he was pulling rank? "*I'm* taking Harry out. You take your own kids out."

She felt Zach's eyes zap to her as both he and Mak absorbed the protectiveness in her voice.

She knew Mak would use it against her. Tease her pretty much until the world ended. But Zach...?

She didn't know.

She barely knew his little boy, but they'd hit it off and she'd genuinely been looking forward to his first, inevitable laugh of delight when the wave and the board connected. When he recognized the harmony that came from working with the ocean's strength rather than against it. Watching a child who had the cards stacked against him realizing he could be just like everyone else... There was no better feeling than that.

"Chill, little sister." Mak patted her head as if she were a sweet-natured but not very bright dog. "I meant champion of the games."

Lulu felt her forehead crinkle underneath her brother's hand, which was still absently patting her head. "What games?"

"The Intra-Island Search and Rescue Games," he said, in a way that also said, *Are there any other games worth talking about?* He gave her head a final scrub, then reached out to shake hands with Zach. "I presume you're the new boss-man? I'm Makoa Kahale."

"Good to meet you." Zach shook her brother's hand, then threw Lulu a quick look she couldn't read.

"What's going on? Those games are between the Coast Guard and your Ocean Safety lot, right?"

"Yes…" Mak drew the word out, then continued as if she were a simpleton. "And this year your little-bitty operation is in on the games."

"What?" Lulu looked at Zach and instantly saw that this was something he had known about and had actively chosen not to tell her. "Who's on the team?" she demanded.

"You are," Zach said, his blue eyes cinching with hers.

He looked nervous. Wary, even. As if he was waiting for a reproach for not having told her the instant he'd known. She didn't care. This was the best news since…since news had been invented.

"Are you kidding me? I'm on the team?"

She whooped and threw her arms around Zach, pressing her face against his chest before her brain caught up with her body and she pulled away.

He smelled good. Ocean, little boy…and maybe pineapple? He *felt* good, too. Strong, but lean. Not with that big monster-truck-style chest her brothers all had. And she wasn't positive, because her own heart had been hammering so hard, but she was pretty sure she'd felt his heart pounding through his T-shirt.

Panic? Or the same fizzy frisson she'd felt?

Whatever…

She started happy-dancing in front of her brother. "I'm gonna kick your booty!" She wiggled and shifted her dance toward Zach. "Who's going to be my teammate? Casey?"

"Me."

Her body stopped mid-dance. "You?"

"Yeah." He shifted his weight. "We're the team."

About a thousand feelings she couldn't identify fought for supremacy. Panic. Horror. Skittishness. But one overriding feeling canceled out all the negatives one by one.

Excitement.

She'd not seen him in proper rescue mode yet, but she had a feeling Zach Murphy was one of those quiet men who rose like a giant when challenged. And she was the one who was going to get to see his hidden talents revealed in all their glory. And then, of course, figure out how to smush all of her sexy feelings into competitive energy, so she could show her brothers she could stand on her own two feet once and for all.

"That's cool," she said, with an air of indifference she definitely didn't feel. She pointed two of her fingers at her own eyes then zapped them at her brother. "You're going *down*, bruh."

Mak laughed and slapped Zach on the back. "Good luck with that."

Zach didn't lurch forward under the weight of the thwack—instead he held his ground. "I'm willing to bet a barbecue dinner we'll win."

Lulu's eyes snapped from Zach to her brother and back again. He was? *Wow.*

She crossed her arms in front of her and gave her brother a *Now who's nervous?* nod.

Mak stuck out his hand, still laughing. "I am more than happy to take that bet. I like my chicken spicy and my burgers pink."

Zach shook his hand and Mak wandered down to the beach, still laughing and shaking his head.

"Wow," Lulu said finally. "That was brave."

Stupid, stupid, stupid, thought Zach. What had he been thinking? Challenging a man mountain who knew the islands as if they were part of his DNA to a search and rescue duel?

No prizes for guessing the answer to that one.

He'd wanted to impress Lulu.

The way she'd looked at him… The way she'd felt as she'd thrown her arms around him when she'd found out she was on the team… It had been like being hugged by an energy bomb. A surprisingly cuddly energy bomb. A surprisingly sexy energy bomb.

He hadn't missed the way her breasts had pressed against his chest. How perfectly her head had tucked beneath his chin. Her cheeks had pinked when, for a nanosecond, she'd looked up at him, and there had been nothing but sheer joy in her eyes.

So, despite every silent vow he'd made not to cross into the land of romance ever again, he'd found himself crossing it. Like a lovestruck knight intent on jousting for his lady's honor. Only this time the lady in question would be wearing a high-vis vest, a safety harness and belaying down the side of a cliff. She didn't need her honor saved. She needed it championed. And something he'd never before tapped into made him want to be the man who did just that.

A whistle sounded down at the beach.

"We'd better get down there." Lulu held out her hand for Harry, still taking little skippy hops of excitement, broken up by the odd victory swing of her shoulders and hips. "We're gonna beat my big brother!" she sang as she guided them down to where a dark-haired woman was beckoning everyone to gather in front of a row of wetsuits and surfboards.

"That's Chantal," Lulu whispered. "She teaches surfing, but her day job is lifeguard."

Something about the way she said the word *lifeguard* resonated with Zach. It was the same way he said *fireman* or *EMT*. Respect and humility mixed in with the complicated mess of emotions that went with really knowing the job—knowing the people who sometimes lost their lives because of it.

He wondered…

He scrubbed his head as too many memories of shouldering coffins leaped to the fore. He'd lost more colleagues than he cared to mention. He'd not seen what his father had, but he'd definitely offered his condolences more than anyone should have to.

He clocked up another silent notch for Lulu. She had no doubt lost people, too. She wasn't the type to get preachy, or parade around her life experiences to get respect. She wanted to gain it the old-fashioned way. By earning it.

When the safety talk had finished, and they'd zipped Harry up into a light wetsuit, Lulu looked at Zach but held her hand out to Harry. "This is where I take over. Is that cool?"

"Absolutely."

It was. But it didn't mean he wasn't nervous.

Twenty minutes later he had absorbed the fact that his concerns had been for nothing. Everything that had set him on edge about Lulu that first day they'd met—her air of recklessness, her need to win rather than be right, a daredevilry that left health and safety in the wind—had proved to be groundless worries.

Her work ethic should have resolved his concerns over the past few weeks, because in fairness it was flawless, but whatever it was that was sparking between them had kept him on edge.

He hadn't wanted to put a name to it, but now, seeing her coax his son into standing up on a surfboard on an actual wave, he knew what it was he'd been trying to deny. Attraction. It was a raw, untethered, grab-your-guts-and-won't-let-you-go type of attraction. And it scared the hell out of him.

It was completely different from what he'd shared with his ex. This felt bigger, somehow. More powerful. Impossible to walk away from. Like she was made of nickel and he was made of iron. Repelling and attracting one another in equal measure.

It wasn't even purely carnal. Not just about her slick of black hair trained into a thick plait down the center of her spine. Or her amber eyes, flashing with hints of copper whenever their eyes met. Or the curve of her hips as they swept into her thighs. Well…they all helped. But it was the smile on his son's face that he'd thank her for forever. His carefree laugh. The ease with which she showed him what was possible rather than, like his ex had, what wasn't.

The memories stung like venom. The pain was deep and long-lasting. But today, here on the beach, watching Lulu and his son swimming and surfing and, yes, occasionally falling into the sea, he felt a peace he hadn't felt in actual years.

He closed his eyes and let himself enjoy the sensation of trusting someone other than his parents with his son's happiness. It gave him access to a hundred other things he hadn't given himself time or permission for. Feeling the heat of the sun on his skin. Acknowledging the rhythmic cadence of the ocean. The soft whir of wind among the palm fronds.

He'd spent so much time thinking about what he didn't have these past few years. This was the first time in a long time that he'd sat back and felt grateful for what he had.

A gorgeous boy.

Loving parents.

A cool, slightly ramshackle house on the beach.

A job.

A beautiful colleague who drove him to the edge of reason…

He blinked his eyes open when he felt water dripping on him. "Hey!"

Lulu stood above him, her pitch-black hair haloed by the sun behind her. Her expression was unreadable.

His son threw himself into his lap, charged with energy and pride, asking over and over again if he had seen him up on the surfboard.

"I did, Harry. You were amazing."

The comment was meant for his son, but somehow Zach's eyes connected with Lulu when he said it. Her smile wavered for a second. She looked out at the ocean, then back at him, her fingers toying with the central zip of her short wetsuit. It took every ounce of strength Zach possessed to keep his eyes on hers and not dip them down to that sweet spot where her breasts arced away from her breastbone.

"*You* wouldn't want to go for a ride, would you?" Lulu asked.

Not what he'd been expecting. "What? With you?"

"No, with my brother," she said, with a roll of her eyes. "Yeah, with me."

He hesitated.

"Forget it." She turned away, as if to go.

"No, I—wait." He stepped toward her and caught her hand in his, scrabbling to form an actual sentence that was made up of real-life words, and short-circuiting because of the electricity buzzing between them, between their hands.

"Honestly…" She shook her head. "It was a stupid idea. It's hard for two adults to be on the same board together, anyway. There's…" Her eyes flicked to his, then dropped to his chest, his hips, his legs, and moved back up again. "There's a lot of contact."

"Dad, look!"

Lulu and Zach followed Harry's finger, which was pointing out to the ocean. There, in the center of the sea of surfers, was Lulu's brother, holding Chantal up with one hand as she arced into a variety of circus-style poses while he effortlessly surfed the pair of them onto the shore, before setting her down as if she were made of fairy dust.

Lulu looked back at Zach and deadpanned, "I'm not sure I have the upper body strength to achieve quite that level of finesse if we were to do the same."

Their eyes locked. The wattage between them ramped

up to something that hadn't been invented yet. And there it was again. That magnetic hunger to find out exactly what she felt like. To see how the soft, honeyed surface of her skin would respond to the rough whorls on his fingertips. To his lips.

Standing this close to her, he felt their differences keenly. He was all steel and cement and honking horns, while she was golden sand, soft breezes and rivulets of water shifting along a deep green palm frond. And yet something told him that right at the very center of her heart, of her mind— where it *mattered*—they were made from the same mold. With strong moral compasses. A built-in, unshakable conviction to serve their communities. A belief that everyone should be treated fairly and with kindness, no matter what package they came in.

"Dad?" Harry grabbed his hand and gave him a pleading look. "Can we do this again, please? Tomorrow?"

"Oh…" He faltered. "I think Lulu said it was only once a month…"

"I'll take you out, squirt," Lulu said over him. "If your dad's cool with it, we could practice at Turtle Hideaway."

"That'd be great."

Zach thanked her, trying to give Harry's head a scrub but missing, because his son was too busy jumping up and down. Lulu joined him for his happy dance—which was just as well, because he was finding it hard not to betray the sucker punch of emotion the offer had elicited in him.

She wouldn't know about the number of times Harry had asked his mother to go to the zoo, the park, the playground, only to receive a cringe and a paltry excuse as to why they couldn't go.

Christina's response to having a disabled son had been gutting. It was as if she'd expected her child to be an accessory to her almost unnatural beauty. But when two years of tests had revealed that their son definitely had cerebral palsy, a coldness had fallen in her—like a sheet of ice between her world and theirs.

It had been impossible to believe that she would reject both her son and then, as part of the fallout, him. But the lure of her career, world travel and being surrounded by nothing but beauty had trumped the vows they'd taken, the life they'd promised to share together, the son they'd sworn to protect. So when they'd separated three years ago and then divorced he had dragged about a hundred chains around his heart and locked it up tight. That sort of risk was never worth taking again.

"I do have one condition," Lulu said, aiming her comment at Zach.

"Name it," he said.

"You and me." She pointed at him, then at herself. "We train. Hard. And then we kick ass at the games." She winced an apology at Harry. "Sorry, bud. I wasn't meant to say ass."

Harry giggled.

Zach waved the apology away. Harry had heard worse. Much worse. Funny how he'd never realized how cruel children and parents could be until he'd started taking Harry to school. He'd caught the tag end of taunts and teasing from the kids, the sidelong glances from the parents and the distance they tried to keep between their children and his, as if Harry's condition was infectious.

Lulu pulled Harry in for a hug. "So? What do you think? Surfing lessons for this little dude in exchange for a bit of hardcore training?"

"Sounds reasonable. But why do you want to win the games so much? We're small fry compared to the teams we're going up against."

From her change of expression and the instant rush of cool air sweeping between them Zach knew he'd done a massive *open mouth, insert foot*.

"Oh? Is that what you think?" Lulu was tapping her

bare foot on the sand the way an interrogator might slap a leather baton in their hand. With barely controlled rage. "That we're small fry? That there's no point in trying?"

"No!" he protested. And honestly he didn't. "I don't. It's just that it's our first year in the games, and we've been chosen for optics more than ability—"

"Hold up!" she cut in, holding her hand out to stop him, as if she needed a moment to digest what he'd just said. She turned to Harry and pointed him a bit farther down the beach, to a couple of enormous cool boxes being manned by volunteers. "Hey, bud. Why don't you go grab some bottles of water, yeah? I think your father here is getting a bit of heatstroke." When he'd gone, she turned back to Zach and with barely concealed disgust said, "How did you even get hired if that's how little you think of us?"

"No! I misspoke. I don't think poorly of you or the team. I'm sure we have as much of a chance of winning as any of the others."

He caught a glimpse of Makoa, picking up two little kids, one under each arm, as if they were beach towels. *Oh, God. They didn't stand a chance.*

Lulu, catching the scene, spat back, "You said we were chosen for optics. So…what? We tick all the right boxes? Ethnic woman? Big, sexy, strong fireman? Is this a photo-op or a competition?"

He goldfished for a minute, stuck on the part where she'd called him a "sexy, strong fireman."

She dug her weight into her heels. "You know, when you came along I thought you were a jerk. A highly qualified, talented jerk. Turns out only one of the three was right."

He had to fix this. Fast. "I *am* highly qualified."

Despite her obvious ire, she sniggered. "But not very optimistic."

He sucked in a sharp breath and held up his hands.

"You've got me there. And *that's* why I think they put us together."

"Why? Because I'm a dreamer and you're an optics-only guy?"

"No. Because you see options where I don't. And…" He batted round in his frazzled brain for something smart to say. "And I can lift more stuff."

She sniggered again. "*Pfft.* You think you're strong?"

The atmosphere between them shifted, crackling with a whole new breed of tension. The kind that made him want to close the distance between them. So he did.

"Oh, I *know* I'm strong." He was close to her. Close enough that she had to tip that feisty little chin of hers up to meet his gaze.

"How strong?" she asked, in a voice that demanded proof.

"This strong."

Before he could think better of it, he reached out, picked her up, threw her over his shoulder and ran to the sea, gratified to hear her screams of protest turning into laughter. A lot of laughter.

He ran into the surf, deeper and deeper, until a wave slammed against his thighs and the two of them fell into the ocean, her body sliding down his chest, his arms wrapping round her waist to keep her above water, her hands lacing round his neck. When the wave retreated he was still holding her. The water dappled her skin like dewdrops. Their faces weren't even a handful of inches apart, and their bodies were pressed together as if their lives depended upon it…

"Is that all you two got?"

Mak appeared, towering above them, hands extended to pull them both up, the tropical water sloshing round his immovable body as if he were made of granite. He fixed

Zach with an intense and highly effective warning glance to get his hands off his little sister. *Immediately.*

Once he'd pulled them up, Mak gave Zach a proper thwack on the back as he chuckled. "You're going to have to prepare yourselves for an epic defeat."

Zach stood back, feigning a devil-may-care attitude he definitely didn't feel. *Hands off Lulu.* That was the unspoken part of that warning.

Message received. Loud and clear.

He glanced at Lulu. Her eyes were lowered to half-mast, her arms were crossed, and she was clearly mortified by her brother's thinly veiled threat.

When she looked up and met his gaze he caught a glimpse of something in her expression that sent a shot of warmth straight through to his heart.

Hope.

He stuck out his hand and did his best not to crumble when Makoa crushed it in his own enormous, meaty paw.

"Game on," he said, then forced himself to lower his voice an octave. "Game on."

CHAPTER SEVEN

Lulu handed Zach a carabiner. "Did you know your name means Sea Warrior?"

He snorted and took the metal loop, pushing the rope against the spring-loaded clasp before twisting it into a snug knot. "What? Have you been stalking me on the internet?"

It was a joke, but from Lulu's guilty expression, he saw that was precisely what she'd been doing.

"No," she snapped, handing him another. "I was looking up nicknames for Harry, and as I was at it I thought I'd look up some good nicknames for us. You know… For the competition."

"Sea Warrior, eh?"

She nodded, tempering the quick flare of defensiveness that had clouded her expression.

Zach grinned. "You tell me I'm a sea warrior just before I'm about to throw myself off the side of a mountain?"

They looked at the sheer drop they were just about to rappel down.

Lulu smirked. "I would've thought the King of Health and Safety wouldn't dream of describing his unparalleled rappelling efforts as 'throwing himself off the side of a mountain.'"

"Good point," he conceded with a smile—one he'd grown used to wearing whenever he was with Lulu.

Ever since he'd had virtually every bone in his hand pulverized into sand by her brother, he'd felt as if he and Lulu were joined in a silent truce. One in which they were united in their mission to show both the Hawaiian Coast Guard and the Ocean Safety Team that their little "ramshackle crew of misfits" were the best in the business.

It didn't mean they were a hundred percent simpatico. There were still a few knots and kinks to smooth out in their teamwork—wanting to rip her clothes off being top of the list.

He wasn't a vain man, but he couldn't help thinking she felt the same way. But something told him that if they broke the seal on whatever it was that was simmering between them there would be no turning back—and Lulu Kahale was not a woman he wanted to disappoint.

Despite his best efforts, his feelings for her were growing, no matter how "chalk and cheese" they appeared on paper.

He ran his life by the rule book.

She swore blind that it was critical to know when to go rogue.

He dialed back the risk in his life.

She liked nothing more than to push the limits.

And yet…the more he got to know her, the more he felt they had more in common than initially met the eye.

She'd not spelled it out, but it was clear her parents hadn't been with her for some time, and she'd pretty much been raised by five very protective older brothers. Anyone who fell in love with Lulu would have to have Superman-like resolve. He didn't know if he had that amount of love to give. And laying down a book of rules as thick as the complete works of Shakespeare, most of which would be about Harry, would send most women running for the hills.

Lulu likes a challenge…

And, of course, there was the undeniable fact that in the

love stakes Harry was utterly smitten. His son introduced Lulu to everyone as his best friend, and he counted down the days, hours and minutes until their surf lessons, which were pretty much every day after school now.

School. Snack. Surf lesson. A bit of larking around with the sea turtles.

Then Harry would go in to shower and help Zach's mom make dinner, while he and Lulu had an hour's training session on the beach.

Pushing enormous tires up and over in the wet sand. Climbing palm trees. Tying knots. Untying knots. Swimming out to the reef as fast as they could. Alternating turns in dragging one another back to the shore.

Pretending like hell that being close to her didn't turn him on more than he'd ever been turned on in his life…

So, yeah. Being at the top of this rappelling rope felt a lot like his life had felt these past couple of weeks. Like riding a yo-yo that went in only one direction.

He eased himself off the edge, both hands on the rope as he leaned back and found the sweet spot where the ropes and harnesses took his weight. His phone rang. They both looked at it, wedged into his top breast pocket.

"Want me to get that?" she asked.

He could get it. Rejigger his position so that he was holding the ropes with one hand. But the naughty devil he hadn't realized was perched on his shoulder had other ideas.

"Could you?"

She knelt down and pinched it between her fingers. The heat of her hand seared through the fabric of his shirt as she withdrew the phone. Their eyes met. Was she taking her time with this? Enjoying their proximity as much as he was? Or was she sharing the torture of indecision? Did they look at what this was humming between them or didn't they?

His phone rang again and she pushed herself back and up, her mixed scent of vanilla and frangipani surrounding him in a little cloud of Lulu that retreated as quickly as she did.

"Murphy's phone," she said, using her self-appointed "grown-up" voice. She listened for a second, then her eyes snapped to his, her body growing taut as if poised on a starting line.

"What?" he asked, already pulling himself back up and over the edge.

She hung up the call and handed the phone to him. "Hiker hasn't been seen in three days. Julia Thompson. Her husband called it in. He was searching for her himself, but lost his bearings. Some smoke was spotted farther up along this trail. Casey's waiting with Stewart. They're going to head over in the chopper if you and I find her."

"*When* you and I find her," Zach corrected, moving back from the ravine edge.

She smiled at him and made an approving noise. "I see some of my positivity is rubbing off on you."

"And some of my cautiousness is wearing off on *you*," he said, his brow furrowing as he realized it might actually be true.

He wasn't so sure he liked that. There was something unfettered and untamed about her that he never wanted to see trapped in a vise of strict regulations.

"Nah…" Lulu swiped at the air between them. "Don't you worry 'bout that, Mr. Rules and Regs. I'm sure there'll always be some fault you see in me to improve upon."

"I doubt that," he said, before he could stop himself.

Her eyes locked with his. Something charged and intimate exploded in the space between them.

"We'd better get going," she whispered, before the moment could fully take hold.

The two of them swiftly moved into a synchronized rhythm he hadn't realized they shared. Pulling in the ropes. Coiling them. Putting everything back in its exact place in the run bags. It spoke of the hours of training they'd put in together, but also nodded at something deeper. Something innate. A shared understanding that came with a heightened awareness of each other.

Zach was going to have to find a way to check it. He hadn't moved here to fall in love. He'd moved here to give his son a solid foundation upon which to build his life. He would force himself to remember the emotional scars his marriage had left.

"You okay?"

Lulu was looking up at him as he shouldered his pack.

"Yeah, why?"

"You look... I don't know... You don't look like you're in a good place to go out on a rescue hike."

"I'm good," he assured her. "C'mon. Let's go."

Lulu set off at her usual brisk pace. Five enormous brothers setting the pace throughout her childhood had pretty much meant running before she could walk. Which some people—like Zach, for instance—might say was her main problem. Racing headlong into situations before she'd drawn up the diagram. Calculated all the risks.

How could she explain to them that there was something in her, something innate, that she felt kept her safe? Privately, she thought it was her mother. A guardian angel watching out for her only daughter. But on a practical level she'd grown up with parents who had set the tone for a life of pushing limits. They'd been lifeguards. They'd known the ocean as well as themselves. Well... Almost as well.

They would never know if their mother had realized how bad the surf was when she'd grabbed her board and gone out looking for a tourist who'd decided surfing was a good idea well after the warning flags had been raised. What they did know was that their father had definitely known how bad it was and he'd gone out, anyway.

He'd always said life wouldn't be worth living if it didn't have their mother in it. Turned out he'd meant it literally.

Their deaths had irrevocably changed them. Her brothers all had jobs that pushed the limits—navy SEAL, volcanologist, bodyguard, stuntman, and, of course, Mak—her rival over at Ocean Safety. Even so, they all liked the firm set of rules and regulations that came with their jobs. But Lulu… She liked the fact that her crew went that one step beyond. Pushed harder. Further.

Zach had definitely bristled when he'd first met her, but now… Up until about thirty seconds ago she would've put money on the fact that he *liked* that about her.

But something had happened between them back there, and whatever it was had made the atmosphere between them awkward. First-day awkward. Awkward like back when they hadn't liked each other very much.

A desperate longing to revert to the strangely flirty, competitive, excited-to-see-each-other vibe that had been humming between them gripped her. She microscopically analyzed the exchange.

She'd said something about him finding fault with her…

He'd said he didn't think he could…

That comment had pulled them both up short, instigating another one of those magic moments they'd been sharing with increasing frequency. Those moments when their eyes connected and the rest of the world seemed to fade away, when their bodies—hers, anyway—buzzed with an energy that felt anything but earthbound.

Then they'd kind of leaned toward each other.

No. That wasn't right. It had been as if they were being *pulled* toward one another by an invisible force, proactively begging them to kiss. She might have even closed her eyes.

And then it had ended.

He'd got up, they'd sorted the gear, and from the look on

his face something had happened in that head of his that had turned their magic moment into a dark one.

She couldn't think what it could be apart from the almost-kiss.

Equal rushes of shame and anger twisted in her gut. Was she that horrendous an option?

A vulnerability she rarely let herself acknowledge exploded inside her. Zach was a class-A example of the type of man she had promised herself she would never, ever fall for. An uptight, regulations-mad mainlander. And yet none of it seemed to matter. This wasn't just a crush anymore. She genuinely liked him. Respected him. She also liked his kid.

If he had no plans on returning her feelings, she was going to have to find a way to rein hers in quick smart.

And then another thought occurred.

Makoa.

Her brother had quite the track record in meddling in her ever-diminishing private life. Maybe he'd got to Zach. Warned him off.

Another twist of white-hot frustration wrenched her stomach into a hot, tangled mess.

Her brothers didn't understand boundaries. They had no problem pulling unsuspecting suitors to one side for a "quiet word" that sent them running for the hills—or, as was more often the case, the airport. Hence the no-mainlanders rule.

But Zach didn't seem like someone who would be intimidated by her brother. He'd worked for the New York City Fire Department, for heaven's sake. She'd seen the calendars. Muscular hunks were a dime a dozen over there.

So what was it, then?

They hiked in silence.

An unbearable one.

Unable to take it anymore, she reeled on him. His body

slammed into hers, the impact forcing out the question running over and over in her mind.

"What?" she demanded. "What's wrong with me?"

They had grabbed on to one another for balance. Her fingers were pressing into the musculature of his lower back. Or were they? *Oh, no.* That wasn't his back. She'd just grabbed his butt.

His arms were wrapped around her entire body, as if he were protecting her from an avalanche. It was an instinctive move. One that had to mean he felt *something* for her. Didn't it?

She chanced a look up into his face.

Her question hung in what little space was left between them.

"Nothing," he whispered.

Again, that taut, hypnotic energy wrapped around the pair of them like a thick, opulent, tingle-inducing ribbon. Their breaths came deep and charged. His eyes darkened to a rich sapphire blue and shone with a brightness she'd not seen in them before. Before a single, helpful thought could find its way into Lulu's brain, he was lowering his mouth to hers. His touch was soft at first. Tentative. But when he felt she was returning his kisses they grew more heated. Hungry.

Her mouth was exploring his. His lips were teasing and taunting, then rewarding her for her curiosity. Her desire. She wasn't in charge of her body anymore. It had a mind of its own. As their kisses intensified she was vaguely aware that she was arching her chest into his, raising up on her tiptoes the better to pull his lower lip slowly, achingly against her teeth.

Her hips fitted perfectly between his. There was no doubt that his body had lost control as much as hers had. Her limbs twitched with the desire to regroup, find new handholds. To climb him like a tree, wrap her legs round his hips and press her mouth to his as if their kisses would save the world.

And then she heard the helicopter.

Her brain was instantly yanked back to reality.

What the actual hell? She was making out with her boss when they were supposed to be rescuing someone.

This was why "office" romances were verboten. This was also why there was always that added layer of frisson whenever she was with him. It was a relationship that had death knells tolling around it before it had even begun.

She stumbled back a few steps, instantly feeling cold in every part of her body that had been touched by his. "We should get on," she managed, through short, sharp exhalations.

"Yeah."

Zach's voice was rough. Not angry rough. Heated rough. As if they'd just been caught in a tornado, whisked up high enough to catch a glimpse of whatever it was on the other side of the rainbow, then unceremoniously dropped straight back down to earth again.

Pounding his fists into his own head wasn't an option. Nor was ripping up his contract. Nor was yanking his heart out of his chest and flinging it off the edge of the cliff.

Finding this hiker and getting her to safety was. Quickly followed by opening up his laptop, applying for a new job and booking a one-way flight to…

Where?

He couldn't move every time something happened that wasn't part of the plan.

Couldn't break up with it.

Couldn't divorce it.

Couldn't sugarcoat it with the godsend that Grandma and Grandpa would be there to take up the slack where Mommy had once been.

The pragmatics of his "well-laid plan" seemed insignificant now.

From the moment he'd met her, Zach had known right down to his very cell structure that falling for Lulu Kahale was out of the question. And yet he'd been the one to instigate it. The one who'd crossed the line he'd thought he'd drawn in the sand.

What on God's green earth had he been thinking?

Nothing. Obviously. He'd let his more primitive instincts take over when he should've pushed them off the side of this ravine they were now edging along.

He picked up the pace, curling his hands into fists, pumping them ahead of him as if trying to build up enough speed to take off and fly. Unspent energy, trying to find something useful to do with itself.

It was a real kick in the teeth to have been put in his place by the job. The one thing he prioritized after his son. Those were the two things that had kept him upright while he'd come to terms with the fact that his wife didn't want to parent their disabled child.

He let a stream of silent curse words loose in his brain to try to get his body to forget how good Lulu had felt in his arms. Pressed up against him. Matching the energy of his kisses as if she'd been waiting a lifetime for just that moment.

"Hey." Lulu stopped and pointed a hundred meters ahead toward the ravine.

He saw it in an instant. Smoke.

They began to jog, Lulu pulling out her phone and calling the station to give Stewart the coordinates.

A weak-voiced "Help…" bounced up the ravine walls.

Swiftly they pulled out their rappelling gear. Zach looked at Lulu. One of them had to stay up top to signal to the helicopter—the other would go down and perform as much first aid as possible.

"You go," she said.

"You sure?" Even after only a few weeks, he knew she would've happily jumped into the harness and onto the end of the rope line every single time.

"I'm sure."

The subtext of the decision was coming through loud and clear. *You're the boss. We shouldn't have kissed. Now, go.*

He swiftly lowered himself down the edge of the ravine into the jungle canopy. The hiker was only a few meters away from the spot where he touched down.

He gave a shout to Lulu that this was the spot, unclipped his harness and ran over to her. "I'm Zach. I'm guessing you're Julia?"

She was in obvious pain. Her ankle, just visible above her hiking boot, was a myriad of purples and blues.

She nodded. "Good guess. Did…" her voice faltered "…did my husband tell you I was missing?"

Zach nodded.

Her features tightened as if she was going to cry. She pointed at her right foot. "I didn't take my boot off because I thought if anything was sticking out I didn't want to see it." She winced as she readjusted her feet on the ground.

"That was smart. Compound fractures need to be kept as stabilized as possible, but I think you'd know if you had a break that bad." He knelt down beside her and gave her a quick scan. A few cuts and bruises. Dirt streaks on her face, arms and legs. Quite a few mosquito bites. "They'll take a proper look at that ankle in the hospital, but it looks like a long hot bath in some Epsom salts would be the best medicine for the rest of you."

"No!" She protested with a feeble laugh. "No hot baths. No hot anything. I'm desperate to be in a room with air-con. If you could put me in a room with a snowman I'd be over the moon."

Zach smiled, pleased she still had enough spirit to make lame jokes.

He unhooked his first aid kit from his shoulders and tugged out a bottle of water. "Here. You must be thirsty. Slow, steady sips. Don't gulp it."

She gave another tired, weak laugh. "That's the one thing I have managed to do. Drink lots of water." She nodded at a nearby stream. "I wasn't sure if it would be safe, but after a few hours in the heat I didn't really care."

He nodded, quickly taking note of her tiny day pack and the small fire she'd managed to build. She'd be hungry, too. He pulled an energy bar out of his backpack and, again, cautioned her to eat it slowly.

It had been three days since she'd disappeared. He was about to ask why it had taken her so long to build the fire when he pulled himself up short, wondering what Lulu would've done if she was in his shoes.

Focus on the positive, fix what you can, then find the facts.

"Good thing you brought matches," he said.

Her smile faltered. "Lighter, actually. It's the reason why I'm in this mess."

He arced an eyebrow.

"I suppose it's also the reason you found me." She made a small sobbing noise and a solitary tear trickled down her cheek before she covered her face with her hands and explained, "Even when he's angry with me he's always there, looking after me."

"Who?"

Zach looked up at a sharp noise and saw that Lulu had fired the flare gun for Stewart.

"Not long now," he said, pointing at the sky, where the helicopter could be heard approaching. He tugged a couple of instant ice packs out of his first aid kit to strap on to her ankle.

Absorbed in the story she had to tell, Julia began to speak as if her life depended upon it. "My husband and I were on a hike. We had a fight about his smoking. He got so angry he pulled out his cigarettes and his lighter, saying I made him so stressed he had to smoke. So I grabbed them and threw them into the ravine. But the lighter was his dad's, you see. Engraved and everything. I've never seen him so angry."

The words continued in a torrent.

"He stormed off. I stayed where I was for a while, certain he'd come back, but after an hour or so I figured he'd gone back to the hotel. So I thought, *I know! I'll find the lighter and take it to him, and we'll make up, and this won't be the worst vacation of our lives after all!* I love him so much… I just hate his smoking. But after one night in the jungle on my own I realized making a stand about something that really is his choice isn't worth living without him, you know? I just couldn't imagine a life without—"

Emotion strangled the rest of her sentence into nonexistence.

"Hey." Zach gave her hand a squeeze. "We've got you now. *And* you found the lighter. It helped us find you. That's got to be a sign that things will be all right, doesn't it?"

She nodded. "I hope so."

Zach gave her hand another squeeze, then excused himself to go and help as the helicopter approached, hovered overhead, then lowered the static stretcher, which Lulu jumped on from the hiking path above.

When their eyes connected he saw questions in them. Doubts. Seeds of insecurity he knew he'd sown because of his lug-headed response to having kissed her.

They loaded Julia onto the stretcher, and after Zach volunteered to hike out with the gear, Lulu silently agreed to ride in the chopper with her.

Come to think of it, she'd barely said a word since she'd

joined them. He didn't like seeing her this way. And he liked it less that her silence was his fault.

"I'll see you at the hospital, yeah?" he said before they began their ascent.

She gave him a sharp look. "I don't know. Will you?"

The question remained unanswered as Lulu gave the signal to pull them up.

Zach nodded at Julia, his mind still whirring on the fight she'd had with her husband over something that on the surface seemed small, but really was enormous. She wanted him to live a happy, healthy life. With her.

Zach wanted to live a happy, healthy life, too. A safe, secure, predictable life. It seemed the wisest option.

His eyes followed Lulu as she was pulled up and beyond the jungle canopy, and he thought of how she put herself in the face of danger every single day but came out unscathed.

He'd never allowed room for the possibility that he could love someone again. Least of all someone who did search and rescue. It wasn't just him he was looking after. It was his son.

An image flashed through his mind's eye of Harry and Lulu on the surfboard. Harry's slight, little-boy body being held upright on the board as he and Lulu caught a wave. His son's smile bigger than he'd ever seen it before at his achievement.

Would seeing that smile on a regular basis be worth risking his heart?

He zipped up his run bag, shouldered it, and began to hike. He didn't know. He didn't know anything anymore except that he and Lulu were going to be spending three entire days together on the Big Island, competing in those blasted games. The proximity would make or break them. Give them answers to the questions he was too damn scared to ask.

He looked up at the sky and caught a glimpse of the retreating helicopter.

One foot in front of the other, he told himself. That was how he'd climbed out of the dark hole he'd fallen into during the breakdown of his marriage, and eventually he'd made it to the top. He hadn't expected to find himself at the bottom all over again for the completely opposite reason. He'd thought falling for someone was supposed to feel good.

He caught himself up short. Was he falling for her?

He shook his head. Nope. He already had. Now he'd hit the crossroads where he had to figure out whether or not to do anything about it.

CHAPTER EIGHT

"WATER AND SUNBLOCK," Lulu said sternly to the little girl.

She pouted.

Her mother gave an exasperated sigh. "I've been telling her the only way to stop the freckles is to wear sunblock!"

Lulu gave the mother a quick scan, noted her immaculate make-up, nails and generally stylish aesthetic. Her little girl had almost succumbed to heatstroke and was only a couple of shades of red away from a dangerous sunburn.

She decided common sense and threats of skin cancer weren't going to work, so she tried another tack. "Are you cool with face painting?"

The mother shrugged, a bit confused, so Lulu asked the little girl what her favorite animal was.

"A cat!" she said, a big smile replacing the pout.

"Cool. Cats…"

Lulu grinned, then grabbed a couple of different tubes of colored sunblock. She was more of a dolphin person herself…but to each their own. She could work with a cat. Which kind of rhymed with Zach. Which instantly made a wash of guilt pour into her as she remembered the multiple texts she'd ignored from him after she'd taken herself off shift, claiming she was due vacation time, and then promptly signed up for some shifts with the ambulance crew and about a million training hours at the gym.

All time they could've spent training for the games.

Together.

Like a proper team.

Today's ambulance posting was at Waikiki Beach—the most popular expanse of surf and sand on the island.

She drew for a bit—a few whiskers, a splotch of a nose and, of course, some large freckles to cover the real ones—then leaned back and grinned. "Wanna see?"

The little girl clapped her hands. "Yes, please!"

Lulu dug her phone out of her pocket, took a picture, then showed the girl—who cooed at herself in the way only little girls could. With undiluted delight.

The mother gave Lulu a grateful smile of thanks, then the two of them padded off, hand in hand, the little girl skipping a bit now that she was rehydrated, and gabbling away about how much she loved it here.

Watching the two of them scraped against something in Lulu's heart she rarely let herself acknowledge. She'd never really wanted to have a baby. It was a tie that bound you to another human being in a way that freaked her right out. To two humans, actually. The father. The child itself.

How her parents had apportioned their hearts out to six children *and* each other boggled her mind.

The thought caught her up sharp.

The portions hadn't been equal.

The bonds of marital love were what had compelled her father to jump on his surfboard to go and find her mother, even though he had known two lives might be lost that day. From Lulu's perspective, it was indelible proof that loving someone meant making choices.

Who was worth living for and who was worth dying for?

It was a lose-lose tug of war she'd never been able to figure out when it came to her personal life, and most likely the thing that had always compelled her to keep her relationships short and sweet. Which did beg the question: Why have them at all?

Because deep down you know you want it, knucklehead. You know you want to love that hard. That big. That generously.

She forced herself to dial back the deep thoughts and remember what had pulled her down this rabbit hole in the first place.

Babies. That was it. Babies…

A little shudder swept through her, then stalled…

Primary school kids…teens…her ever-increasing gaggle of nieces and nephews… She couldn't get enough of them. Instead of decreasing the amount of love she had, each new arrival, whenever one appeared, opened up a fresh expanse of love she hadn't realized she could tap into. And it wasn't just her nieces and nephews. It was the kids down at the Superstars Surf Club. Harry…

The tug of longing turned into a tight, achy knot. Avoiding Zach hadn't meant neglecting Harry. She'd continued to teach him to surf. He shouldn't be penalized just because his dad had a fiercely grabbable ass and desperately kissable lips.

She closed her eyes as the knot in her stomach turned molten and started swirling around inside her. She could even smell him. That citrusy man scent that… Wait a minute…

She blinked her eyes open. If stomachs could plummet and flutter all at the same time, that was what hers was doing.

"Hey," Zach said, giving her a hip-height wave.

Hips she had fit into as if they were Lego pieces, born to nestle together, snug and perfect.

She swallowed and tried to look as if her insides weren't throwing themselves a party. "Hey, yourself."

Nice one, Lulu. Way to show him you aren't re-enacting your teenage how-to-snag-a-guy skills.

Zach cleared his throat, his body language shifting from wary to defensive. "Forgive me for being a bit slow on the uptake, but is this whole taking a vacation to work another job your way of saying you don't want to represent the OST at the games?"

Her entire body leaped to attention. "No. Absolutely not."

He didn't move, but she was pretty sure his eyes had turned a warmer shade of blue. "Okay. Well, in that case, you *are* aware we have to leave for the Big Island tonight, right?"

"Yes," she scoffed.

Duh. She knew the start date of the games like she knew the Fourth of July. It was one of those dates branded into her annual calendar. Which day, which island, which resort…

All of a sudden her brain was flooded with images of the resort where they'd be staying…the cocktails she'd have to resist drinking to stay out of the bed where Zach would be sleeping. And Zach must be having a similar sort of mental slideshow, because the already humid air had turned about as thick and sultry as it could without actually plunging the two of them into one of Hawaii's sudden downpours.

"How's Harry?" she asked.

"Good." Zach nodded. "Still loving his surf lessons, so… Thanks for keeping your word about that."

A protest caught in her throat, but she caught it just in time. She'd told Zach she'd train with him and she hadn't, so she deserved that jibe. Harry, though… She wasn't about to let her mixed-up feelings about his dad get in the way of their relationship. He was just a kid. He didn't deserve to be caught in the crossfire of whatever it was that was happening between them.

"Well…" Zach shifted a pile of sand from one foot to

the other. "Shame we've missed out on a week's worth of training."

His tone was impossible to read. Which, of course, made her insanely crazy. She wanted to strangle him and kiss him all at the same time. Scream at him. *How on earth do you think we're ever going to win the games if all I'm thinking about is what you feel like naked?*

And then, to her horror, she realized she'd just said all that in her out-loud voice.

"Hey, bruh." Lulu's colleague for the day, Jason, came round the corner, holding a couple of popsicles. He looked from Zach to Lulu and said, "Shift's over." He handed her one of the frozen treats, then gauged the energy surging between the pair of them. "I would've got another if I'd known you had company."

Lulu took her popsicle, made the introductions and then, to give herself something to do other than go back to her sexy, angry staring contest with Zach, began to eat it.

When she realized Zach was watching her with something a lot more like lust than disdain, she felt herself coil like a boa constrictor, seeing his desire.

"We're going to the Intra-Island Search and Rescue Games tonight," she said to Jason, and then, to Zach, "What time is the flight?"

"Seven. I can pick you up if you like," he said, his eyes not leaving her mouth as she tried and failed to stop her tongue from swirling round the top of her popsicle as if it were—

The ambulance radio squawked out a report.

"If you two lovebirds will excuse me?" Jason said.

Neither of them acknowledged the comment. They weren't lovebirds. They were lust monsters. One of them in a grotty end-of-shift uniform, one in a disturbingly sexy pair of completely ordinary cargo shorts and an old NYFD T-shirt.

How on earth did he *do* that? Make off-the-rack ath-leisure wear look as if it demanded attention? Demanded fingers on buttons, on zips, tugging, pulling, getting that waistband off those perfect hips and tugged down until—

"Lulu!" Jason banged on the side of the ambulance. "Someone was playing Tarzan up the road and needs an ambulance. Want some overtime?"

She could barely remember her own name right now, let alone divine if she wanted overtime or not. "Yes…"

"Wanna do a ride along?" Jason asked Zach. "See how the real rescue crews work?"

Lulu whirled on Jason. "Zach worked for Fire and Res-cue in New York," she said, far more defensively than she probably should have.

Jason smiled and put out his fist to Zach. "Respect, dude. Things run at a different pace out there. Wanna come along and see how we roll?"

"Sure."

"You two strap yourselves in the back," he said, with a wink to Lulu. "Give you a chance for some alone time."

They did as they were told, each of them buckling into a bench seat with nothing but a stretcher between them. It might have been the entire expanse of the Pacific Ocean or a toothpick. He felt both near and far away. Impossible to have and just as impossible not to.

After what felt like an eternity, but was actually about thirty seconds, Zach broke the silence. "We don't have to do this, you know."

"It's a bit late now!" She held out her hands, pointing out the obvious, then lurched forward as Jason took a sharp turn. Her hands landed on Zach's chest. He wrapped his fingers round her wrists and leaned in, holding her there, close. Too close.

"The games," he said.

She tugged her hands free. "Oh, no. No, no, no, you don't. We are definitely doing those."

Zach flinched, as if scorched by the fire in her pronouncement. "Why? Why're they so important to you?"

"Because it'll prove to my brothers I don't need to be protected. If I don't win these games and prove I have what it takes, they'll never leave me alone!"

There. She'd said it. She needed to prove her strength to her brothers once and for all. Now that Zach had taken her job, her house and her common sense, the games were all she had left.

He studied her in silence, his eyes searching hers in the same way he inspected a patient. Looking for the pain. For the real source of the injury beyond the superficial.

How could she explain what she was going through and not sound insane? How could she tell him that falling in love the way her parents had…the way she was doing with Zach this very second…was the most terrifying thing in the world? Love like theirs meant crossing the line. Paddling out into an ocean you knew could devour you whole.

It was why she pushed so hard. Accepted rescues that might mean possibly never coming back. She wanted to see just how far she could go and still retain control. Only when she'd pushed those limits far enough so that her brothers had to acknowledge her strength, her resilience, could she finally start to allow those other things she wanted in life some oxygen.

"Is that what you really want?" Zach finally asked. "To be left alone?"

It was a loaded question and they both knew it.

If she said yes, she knew he'd come to the games, behave impeccably, give them his all. But he wouldn't have that extra fire, the charged glow he always had when they pulled off some feat or another together.

If she said no…

Her heart strained at the thought of stopping this—whatever it was—before it even had a chance to begin.

"No."

"Well, then," Zach sat back, his eyes sparking with a determined resolve she'd not seen in them before. "What do you propose we do?"

Zach folded the cocktail napkin into ever-reducing squares, then watched it unfold when he released it. It was a metaphor, he told himself, for earlier this afternoon.

When Lulu hadn't answered his question in the ambulance he'd stayed quiet. He'd offered an extra pair of hands when "Tarzan" had needed his ribs wrapped but refused because it would "totes mess up" his tan line. He'd changed his mind when Zach had started asking Lulu about the dangers of punctured lungs.

He liked how they worked together. How they could each read a patient, pick an angle and go with it after a small shared acknowledgment. Her amber eyes would glow with the love of a challenge, with the rush of adrenaline that came from every rescue, every patient—no matter if it was a lack of sunblock on a toddler or a surfer with a bloodied nose and a concussion after his board had smashed against his face.

He liked her.

Plain and simple.

Probably more.

Definitely more.

But that was a drawbridge he wasn't yet prepared to cross. Not until she figured out what she wanted. He hadn't planned on falling in love, let alone finding himself neck-deep in unrequited love, but something deep in his gut told him this wasn't unrequited. More…undecided. And not because of him.

But he had his son to think about. To prioritize. Forever

and always. And if that meant backing away from a girl who made his heart pound against his rib cage every time he saw her so be it.

"Here you go!" Lulu appeared in front of him holding two cocktail glasses shaped like pineapples, one in front of each breast.

He looked away. They were here for the games. Not for him to ogle her breasts.

"Hope you like rum," Lulu said, putting the drink in front of him and taking a rather large gulp of her own. "It's pretty much all a mai tai is made out of."

He took a sip and choked. "Wow!" He drank deeply from his water glass. "You weren't kidding."

Lulu raised one of her eyebrows at him and, her eyes still connected to his, took a long, thirst-quenching drink of her own mai tai. No flinching. No wriggling as the alcohol hit her nervous system. Nothing apart from a tiny quirk at the corner of her mouth as if she'd just given him a test and he'd failed.

Maybe hers was a virgin cocktail.

Zach was about to ask what else was in the drink when a towering figure of a man thundered across the open-air bar.

"It's Mini-Menehune!"

"Oh, Lordy…" Lulu took another large gulp of her drink, shot a quick, "Prepare yourself," to Zach, then jumped up and did a double *shaka*. "Hey, bruh. Howzit?"

She threw a quick glance back at Zach. One that said, *Stand up. Don't let him tower over you.*

He stayed where he was. He'd met plenty of men like Makoa. Physically intimidating, made of machismo, but when push came to shove, if you found the right trigger, made of molten caramel inside. He had a pretty good idea that Lulu was his trigger…so he'd stay where he was.

Makoa, as anticipated, saw that Zach hadn't stood up

and, sensing his sister's nerves, crossed to him and put out his hand. "Hey, bruh. Good to see you again."

Tick!

Zach took the hand and shook it. "Nice to see you."

"Ready for the games tonight?"

Zach shook his head, confused. "I thought they didn't start until tomorrow?"

"No, bruh." Makoa unleashed one of his belly-jiggling laughs. "The *proper* games start tomorrow...the *team building* games start tonight."

"Team building?" Lulu's eyebrows arrowed toward her nose.

Makoa swiped an enormous paw in the air. "Aw, you know... It's all of that touchy-feely *If I trust you, we can do anything* sort of stuff."

"Oh, right. I see." Lulu took another, immensely large gulp of her drink and then, with a casual air Zach knew she wasn't owning, asked, "Are there prizes?"

Makoa patted her head, changing his voice so he sounded like a kindergarten teacher. "Yes, my darling little sister. There will be prizes." Then he leaned back and roared with laughter. "Probably the only ones *you'll* be winning this weekend."

Zach bristled on Lulu's behalf. Sibling rivalry was one thing, but he was pretty sure Makoa didn't understand how much these games meant to Lulu. Which killed him. She was smart, beautiful, fun, adventurous, talented and a thousand other things he shouldn't be thinking about if he wanted his feelings to stay anywhere near neutral. The last thing Lulu Kahale needed was a medal hanging round her neck to prove she was worth caring for.

As if sensing his understanding, she shot a glance at him, her amber eyes bright with ambition and a sliver of vulnerability. She rarely gave away her trust. And she was trusting him.

"Wanna join in?" she asked.

"Of course," Zach said, as if not joining had never occurred to him.

He pushed his drink away, then wove his fingers together and stretched them as if preparing for a workout. He silently thanked whatever Hawaiian gods were out there for the excuse not to get tipsy enough to try to kiss Lulu again. He didn't know if that ship had sailed, but he certainly wasn't going to try anything this weekend.

He pushed up and out of his chair and began to jog in place. "I'm ready when you are."

Makoa snorted. "Looks like my little sis is dropping you in it, my man."

"We're up for anything," Zach said, putting out his arm and pulling Lulu to his side, trying his best to ignore the physical satisfaction that came from feeling her nestle in close beneath his arm as she slipped one of her arms round his waist. "Aren't we, Lulu?"

He looked down at her, his entire body getting a full-force injection of pride when he saw her beaming back up at him.

"Totally," she said to him. Then, to her brother, "Bring it on."

An hour later Zach was deeply regretting the whole all-for-one-one-for-all bravura that had propelled him and Lulu up onto a stage with Makoa and his teammate—the last four standing—where they would complete the final trust exercise of the night.

Makoa's colleague—a petite woman, Kiko—was the human form of a firecracker. Fast, charged, and prone to go off when you least expected it. And Makoa was, of course, a mountain of muscle. Immovable if need be and surprisingly nimble when called to action. He'd be tough to beat tomorrow. He'd be tough to beat tonight.

Everyone had thought the very first trust exercise—the one where one partner had to fall into the arms of the other while wearing a blindfold—would finish Kiko because, of course, Makoa was the one chosen to fall into her arms. But she'd performed a circus-like stop-drop-and-roll maneuver that had broken his fall. Not strictly a pillow-soft landing, but…

Here they all were. In the finals.

The crowd, juiced up on mai tais, was whooping and cheering. Makoa and Kiko were obvious favorites because they were known commodities, whereas Zach, a mainlander *haole* and Lulu, the kid sister he was quickly realizing everyone had been forewarned to treat with kid gloves, were not.

As the evening had progressed, he'd gained a genuine understanding of what it must've been like for Lulu growing up in the shadows of her big brothers. He, after all, had only met one. And there were four more of them out there. As such, he'd put his all into the evening, easily allowing himself to unbuckle his tendency not to trust. This was for Lulu.

With each passing challenge the energy exchange between the pair of them had grown more and more fine-tuned. To the point where they'd even managed to gain some of their own cheerleaders—rescue crews who clearly liked seeing the underdog challenge the reigning champions, as Makoa's team had been for the last ten years.

"Quiet, you lot!" The emcee for the evening—a man with a steel-gray crew cut, who would also be leading events over the weekend—held out his hands to quiet down the whistles and the whooping. "The final event of the night is…" he paused for dramatic effect "…the handcuff challenge!"

The audience erupted with explosive laughter, hoots and hollers.

Zach threw Lulu a look. What the hell was the hand-cuff challenge?

She shrugged. This was her first time, too. She was as much in the dark as he was.

The emcee explained. The pair of them would be hand-cuffed together with "team-building cuffs"—whatever they were. It *was* possible to break free, they were told, but only by using the highest level of teamwork and taking onboard hints and suggestions from the audience, who would be split in two. One half for Makoa and Kiko. One half for Zach and Lulu. They'd have five minutes.

It had taken a Herculean effort for Zach not to notice that the few swigs of mai tai Lulu had taken as Dutch courage had made her a bit more…erm…*pliable* in the physicality department. She'd been the one to fall into his arms during the trust exercise. But, rather than doing it the old-fashioned way, she'd somehow twisted and whirled herself in the air so that she'd landed in his arms like a damsel in distress.

Well… A damsel who had then leaped out of his arms and paraded round the stage shouting, "That's how we roll!"

Now they were turned back to back, their wrists bound with some sort of rubbery rope. It wasn't very flexible, and allowed very little room for maneuver. The audience was shouting all sorts of options. Dislocate a shoulder. A thumb. Shred what little dignity they had and give up now.

All options Zach felt it wise to table.

Lulu turned her head away from the crowd, her hair brushing against his cheek as he turned to her. She whispered up to him, "Follow my lead, okay? I've got this."

He gave a quick affirmative noise, hoping she knew what she was talking about. Spending the rest of the evening tied to Lulu, who was already wriggling against his butt like a supercharged sexy Easter bunny, was going to be his biggest challenge yet. The last thing he needed was to get a hard-on in front of Hawaii's finest.

Mind over matter, he told himself on a loop. *Mind over matter.*

"Crouch down," Lulu said. "I'm going to have to climb over you."

"What?"

"Or maybe slip under you," she said, already lowering herself down so that he had no choice but to follow. "Not sure yet."

He felt her body press hard against his, then pull away. With a quick grunt and a tug on his hands, he felt Lulu do something like a somersault in the limited space between them. Their bound wrists were pressing into her chest... his back was still toward her. If he had the flexibility he thought he could slide her under his legs along with his bound hands.

He stretched his arms out and brushed what he was pretty sure was her breast—much to the merriment of the audience. The next thing he knew, Lulu was up on tip-toe, walking over his head. The audience was going insane with cheers and laughter—until he ducked down and pulled back, sliding her legs along his chest until she lost her balance, landed in a straddle on his lap, with their tied hands high above them.

He felt every single centimeter of her body as if they were both completely naked. Her body heat met and married with his. Her breath fell in short, hot, puffs upon his mouth, just as he was sure his breath was landing on hers. Their eyes met and clashed. Both of them were frozen in one of those moments that communicated one solitary thing: desire.

She felt so good. Legs tucked round his hips... Her hips cinching with his... Breasts pushing into his chest, the taut tips of her nipples making it clear that she wanted him as much as he wanted her...

More than he ever had before, he wanted to throw away

his dumbass rule book that made women off-limits. He wanted to forget about the *Will they? Won't they?* energy that had been running through him like adrenaline these past few weeks and open up his heart and his body to it all. He wanted to forget about the search and rescue games and spend the next three days in his room—or hers…it didn't matter. He wanted them to pour themselves into one another as if they were each molds that would make the other whole. He wanted to show her every level of pleasure he knew how to bring to a woman and explore all the others he had yet to learn.

Something about the way all the blood was rushing below his waistline told him that Lulu Kahale could wring him dry if she set her mind to it.

Somehow—miraculously—they both became aware of a countdown. Makoa and Kiko were still in deep discussion, their position unchanged. The audience was shouting a charged, "Five! Four! Three!"

"You okay with a bit of wrist burn?" Lulu asked, her lips brushing against his as she spoke.

It was the most erotic request for guaranteed pain that he'd ever received. "Yes."

She blinked, as if absorbing the deeper meaning of his assent—*I trust you*—then abruptly twisted her hands and yanked them free of the binding.

She leaped up in the air, hands held high, and danced around her brother and Kiko—who, seconds later, did a quick up-and-over arm-twist, as if they were performing a 1950s Lindy Hop, then faced one another, folded their hands together and slipped off the bands. Effectively achieving the required result without wanting to immediately have sex with one another.

The crowd went wild.

Zach rose and gave a red-faced bow, pleased for Lulu that they'd won, but hoping he could find the nearest exit—

and fast. He didn't need congratulatory slaps on the back, or the celebratory mai tais already being called for at the Tiki Bar, or even the supersize T-shirt he and Lulu were meant to wear together, to prove they were the reigning champs of the team-building challenges. No. He needed a cold shower.

CHAPTER NINE

"YOU DISAPPEARED FAST last night."

Lulu tried to make her tone and expression as neutral as possible. Zach was sitting at a table for one. If that didn't scream *Back the hell off*, she didn't know what did.

She nodded at his table when he took a sip of coffee instead of answering. "May I join you?"

"Please," he said, his tone much clearer than hers had been. It said, *Sure. You can sit down. But don't expect loads of chitchat.*

A shiver swept down her spine—and not because it was cold. This was the Zach Murphy she'd met on day one. The one who'd grounded her. The one who did everything by the book.

He was also the one she had thought was about as sizzling hot as a man could get, but was as much of an option for her on the dating front as a lemur.

Right then and there she realized she'd let all those barriers she'd kept up slide away. They'd kissed. She'd told him she thought about him naked. She'd climbed all over him as if he was her personal climbing wall and straddled him in front of the entire search and rescue corps.

And now it looked like he had made a decision. *Not today, buttercup. Not ever.*

Okay, then… If he wanted to be Mr. Rule Book again,

she would focus on the fact that they were meant to be winning these games for the Oahu Search and Rescue crew today. She was a big enough girl that she could set aside the mountain of hurt that had weighted her chest when she'd seen him sneak out of the bar last night without so much as wishing her sweet dreams.

"You okay?" She pulled up a chair, plonked down her plate and took a bite of scalding-hot scrambled eggs, too proud to let him know they were burning the roof of her mouth. It helped relocate the pain in her heart, so… useful, really.

"Never better," he said.

"Liar," she countered.

He looked across and met her eyes.

His irises were the same color as the sea about a mile away from shore during a storm. Dark blue, fathomless and a bit overwhelming.

She swallowed. Had she messed up everything last night by commandeering that final game instead of genuinely acting like a team member? *Screw it.* Teams needed leaders, and she'd led them to victory last night. She had even slept in that stupid T-shirt they'd awarded them, feeling the ache of loneliness at all the space in it that would've been filled by Zach if only she was normal and actually knew how to date someone.

They ate in silence for a few minutes, until she couldn't stand it anymore. They had the games to focus on, and if there was anything in the air between them that needed to be cleared they had about twenty-seven minutes to clear it before the first whistle blew.

"What's really going on?" she asked.

He shook his head. "Not important. Let's just focus on the games."

She bridled. "We *can't* focus on the games if you're

going to be wandering around with a cloud over your head the entire time."

"I'm not—" He stopped himself and held up his hands, took a breath and regrouped. He looked her straight in the eye and, in the same guilty way he might've told her he had forgotten to fill out the Health and Safety forms for the weekend, said, "I wanted to have sex with you last night."

Lulu did a double take. She had, too. But she certainly wasn't going to confess as much to him. Unless… Would it make it easier if they both knew they wanted the same thing?

"Me, too."

He looked at her. Really looked at her. "We've been dancing round this like…like dancers," he finished lamely, tipping his head into his hands. He gave that gorgeous chestnut hair a scrub, then looked back up at her. "I can't think about anything else. It's driving me nuts."

"Me, too!" A smile bloomed on her face and her heart felt about a thousand times lighter. "I mean, this is totally not like me. I don't normally kiss the boss on training hikes."

Zach's lips twitched. "But you do mention thinking about them naked?"

"No." She swatted at the air between them and put on her *How very dare you?* face. "That's for special people," she said primly.

"Special people who also happen to be your boss and as a result are in a very difficult position?"

She tipped her head into her palm and made herself consider things from his angle. New job. New state. New life. Trying to set things up for his boy. Still on a probationary contract. A horny-as-hell colleague who kept pouncing on him.

No. It wasn't an ideal scenario.

Hardly believing she was proposing the idea, she tapped

his plate with her fork to get his attention. "I could quit," she said.

"No." He instantly dismissed the idea. "No, you couldn't. I doubt you could even breathe without doing this job."

"Good point... But I like being a paramedic. I could do that full-time."

He laughed. "This isn't some weird team-building exercise, is it? Figuring out how we rearrange our lives so we can have sex?"

"No," she said, suddenly feeling the gravity of what they were really talking about.

Did they trust one another enough to be that close? Knowing there was a risk that it might all fall apart one day or...worse...that she might fall so head over heels in love that one day she'd have absolutely no control over the limits of how far she'd go to keep him safe?

She pressed her lips together, then released them. "I guess it's about deciding whether or not we want to change enough to break our own rules."

He sat back, threw his cloth napkin on top of his empty plate and considered her. "I know what some of your rules are and I seem to tick a lot of your don't-ever-go-there boxes."

"True."

"So..." He held his hands open. "If you haven't broken them for anyone else, why would you change them for me?"

Because she was pretty damn sure she was falling in love with him.

Instead, she said, "I'm beginning to wonder if all the rules and regulations I've imposed on my emotional life are holding me back professionally."

What a cop-out of an answer.

Unsurprisingly, he frowned. "What do you mean?"

She screwed her face up tight, then plumbed a level of honesty she rarely accessed. "I thought I wanted your job.

Really, really wanted it. Not just so I could earn enough to buy my house. *Your* house," she swiftly corrected, making it clear it wasn't a dig, "And not just for the kudos. Or for proving to my brothers that I'm every bit as good as they are. Which, obviously, I am."

She gave a self-deprecating snort and then, seeing Zach's change of expression, made herself dial back the defensiveness.

Zach nodded for her to continue.

"The higher-ups even interviewed me for it, but they saw what I didn't."

"Which was…?"

"I would hate doing your job."

They laughed, and unnecessarily Zach asked, "Why?"

"It requires something I don't have." When he didn't say anything she filled him in. "*i* dotting…*t* crossing… I don't do those things."

Zach feigned being affronted, then the part of him that was unbelievably good at his job caught up with him and he conceded, "Your skills do lie outside the office."

No offense taken, she pushed on, feeling this conversation was one they shouldn't let go of. "Exactly. So I have to find a way to be content, knowing I'm not perfect."

His soft smile shifted into a frown. "No one's perfect."

He wasn't giving her an ego-boost. He was making a confession.

"There's a lot you don't talk about, isn't there?" she said carefully. "Some vein of hurt you don't ever want to tap into again?"

In that instant she saw that she'd hit on the truth. He had been hurt. Badly. Straight down to the marrow. And he never ever wanted to feel that type of pain again.

One of her grandmother's old Hawaiian sayings popped into her head. "Love is like a cleansing dew."

She had no idea if there was a future for her and Zach,

but what she did know was that she cared enough for him and his son to throw herself in front of the proverbial bus for them. Which was both terrifying and exhilarating.

She put her hands on her pounding heart and said, "You can talk to me. What happens on the Big Island stays on the Big Island."

He huffed out a laugh. "I thought that was Vegas?"

She made a dismissive noise. "A girl can keep secrets wherever she pleases."

He shook his head and laughed, but then, to her surprise, he began to talk.

He talked about his ex-wife. How they'd met at a fire at a warehouse where some film crew had been doing a fashion shoot. She and a couple of the other models had been trapped. It had been scary. He'd had to carry her out over his shoulder and down a ladder to safety.

"Just like in the movies…" Lulu whispered, not exactly jealous of his ex, but wondering how on earth she could have ever walked away from someone who made her feel as safe as Zach could.

The relationship had grown from there. Zach and a couple of his colleagues had been asked to appear in a photo shoot. She'd asked him out. Actively pursued him from the sounds of things. So at least she had some brain cells.

Zach huffed out a laugh and brandished a ring-free hand. "But, as you can see, it didn't work out like in the movies. Not the kind with happy endings, anyway."

"What happened?" she asked.

"Harry happened," he said plainly.

Zach felt the shock of his blunt pronouncement as profoundly as Lulu seemed to. Her jaw literally dropped open and the hairs on her arms shot to attention.

Normally this would be the moment when the Lulu he'd

come to know would hammer him with a thousand questions. She liked to know the details about everything.

It was something he hadn't originally noticed about her. His first impression had been that she was foolhardy. Reckless. But in actual fact, she calculated risk and response with lightning-fast accuracy.

He could see in her eyes that she felt the weight of what he was doing. Entrusting her with access to the darkest moments in his life.

A surge of empowerment replaced any anxiety he'd felt about laying himself bare to this woman. He wanted her to know the whole story. Know the whole man. If they were really going to explore this energy surging between them they both needed to know the truth. And the truth was he was a wounded warrior doing his damnedest to build a new life for his son.

So he continued to talk.

He told her that this was only the second time he'd put into words the real reason behind the failure of his marriage. That the first time had been when he and Christina had had that all-night, final, harrowing fight over who got to divorce who and why.

"If we hadn't had Harry, would we be having this conversation?"

In the end, he'd wished he hadn't asked. He'd already known the answer. Hearing it had felt like being filled with boiling oil. It had incinerated everything he'd believed to be true about love.

Even though they'd both known what had happened to Harry had been down to a mistake at the hospital—a cruel, critical loss of oxygen—she'd blamed Zach for Harry's disability. It was his job. His exposure to "unnatural elements." It had already crippled his father, she'd mocked. How long would it be before it did the same to him?

It was the same job that had brought them together, that

had saved her life, and countless others during his career with the NYFD.

In that moment he'd seen their marriage for what it had always been. A photo opportunity. A photo opportunity that couldn't be sustained if their son was in the picture. And that simply hadn't been an option.

Lulu, despite the warm caramel color of her skin and the heat of the early-morning sun, had turned ashen.

But, as if the story was a raging torrent long held back against the weakening walls of a dam that had finally burst, he kept on talking.

He'd never hated anyone or anything before. But he'd hated Christina at that moment. His entire world had turned black and white. There were two camps. Those who loved Harry and those who didn't. Which meant there were a lot of people in the wrong camp.

It had brought out a darkness in him that had both terrified him and fueled his rage. How could anyone reject their child? Let alone a gorgeous little boy who, through no fault of his own, faced more of life's hurdles than most?

He'd forced himself to imagine carrying that rage around with him for the rest of his life. Acknowledged how all-consuming it would be. How it would color absolutely everything. And as the words she was hurling at him had blurred into a high-pitched whisper-scream he'd had an epiphany.

Though every word she spat at him was laced with venom, she was whispering so as not to wake Harry. There *was* something in that seemingly arctic heart of hers. A tendril of affection for her son. He saw her anger for what it really was. Fear.

It had been a turning point for the pair of them.

Fear brought out the worst in some people, the best in others, and his wife had proactively walked across a line he knew he could never cross.

Lulu shook her head, as if absorbing it all was physically weighing her down. "What did you do?"

He'd taken a lot of long walks with Harry asleep in the stroller. Talked with his friends down at the station house. His parents. Harry's doctors. Strangers… It felt like he'd walked every inch of Manhattan and talked to every soul he'd met, trying to figure out what the hell to do.

"Hanging on to the rage wasn't an option. There was no way I could raise my son with my blood running cold every time I thought of Harry's mother. So…" His eyes caught on Lulu's mouth as her teeth pressed down on her lower lip, its deep red turning white from the pressure. He looked away and continued. "After some pretty deep soul-searching we opted to call a truce, cite irreconcilable differences as the reason for a divorce, and go our separate ways. Try to hang on to what good memories remained."

Lulu harrumphed in a way that suggested she would've found it every bit as tough as he had to find any good memories among the ashes of their short-lived marriage.

"Irreconcilable differences was a pretty apt way to describe it in the end. My ex didn't want to find out if she had the strength that parenting a disabled son would require, and I couldn't imagine not digging as deep as I could to do exactly that."

"But…" Lulu's voice cracked as she swiped at tears glossing her eyes. "Harry's great! I love that kid. I'd hang out with him every day of the week if I could."

Her voice was filled with fire, compassion and a need to defend a little boy who wasn't able to do it for himself. As if the little boy who had been rejected was her own.

Their eyes met and clashed, cinching in a shared disbelief that anyone could treat Harry in that way.

She'd never spoken so freely. So passionately. But now that she had he saw that it was true. She was always popping by for a quick surf lesson. Suggesting places to take

Harry for burgers, shaved ice and who knew what else. Volunteering to cover for his parents if errands called.

Neither of them had put a name to what she'd become to them, their little tribe of two.

There was only one word for it.

Family.

But she had to know that his son was his priority. "Harry… Harry's the best thing that's ever happened to me," he said.

"And…" Lulu paused, visibly nervous about how to phrase her next question. "Does his mother see him at all? She must find it hard… You being so far away from New York."

The truth pressed against his chest and demanded oxygen. "She doesn't want to be a mom to a disabled kid. We've only been away for a few weeks, but from the day the divorce was finalized she's taken every overseas job offer going. Harry's not seen her for over a year."

Lulu looked as if this cruel slight to Harry had reached out and slapped her. "Gosh."

"Yeah," he agreed. "Gosh…" He traced his finger around a watermark on the table, then confessed, "It's probably been harder for me to wrap my head around than for Harry."

"How so?"

"She's never really been a hands-on mom. We had my parents' help at the beginning, of course. And specialists so we could understand just how much Harry's condition affected him. She would take him out on runs and things… you know, in his stroller. But as soon as she started working again, meeting up with her friends, I realized she only spent time with him when she absolutely had to."

Lulu whispered a heartfelt curse.

Zach nodded. "I know. I feel the same. But hanging on to that anger doesn't do Harry any good." He looked down at his hands, then back up into her eyes. "It's why seeing the friendship between the two of you develop has been so amazing."

He saw Lulu's gaze sharpen. They hadn't even defined whatever it was that was happening between the two of them, let alone what Lulu's relationship with his son was, but he knew she needed to know. "You're important to him. He talks about you all the time."

"He's a great kid."

Her voice was scratchy, and if he wasn't mistaken her eyes glossed over once again before she swept a palm across her face.

A whistle sounded and the emcee from last night's team-building games appeared at the edge of the dining room.

"Wheels up, everyone! Games commence in T minus ten!"

Lulu gave herself a wriggle, as if trying to clear herself of everything they'd just talked about, and when she looked at him there was something stronger, fiercer than in the looks they'd shared before.

"We're going to win these," she said, with a level of determination an army would've struggled to crush. "We're going to win these for Harry."

"Two more minutes!" Lulu insisted, one hand on top of the other, her body exhausted from the rhythmic compressions she'd been giving the "patient" they'd finally located far off the hiking trail.

It was well beyond the nine minutes of CPR most humans can receive without enduring severe and irreversible brain damage. Probably double that. Standard practice was to call time of death at twenty minutes, but there were some remarkable cases of thirty, forty and even fifty minutes of CPR preventing that crucial separation between life and death.

"Let me have a go." Zach held his hands over hers, ready to take over.

"No," Lulu growled, even while silently welcoming the heat of his hands above hers.

She wasn't cold—she was exhausted. But she couldn't stop. Not now. It was her fault it had taken them so long to find the CPR mannequin, cleverly kitted out with a device that allowed it to simulate having a heart attack. If she was successful a green light would ping on over its heart. If not the red light, already on, would turn black.

"Lulu..." Zach was using his *Be reasonable* voice. "If you exhaust yourself doing this, how are you going to have enough energy for the rope challenge?"

It was a good question.

Manhandling ropes in real life was tough.

Manhandling them in front of her giant of a brother after she'd drained all her strength on this exercise would be plain old humiliating. Especially when she'd have to throw them from one side of a ravine to another to "save" her partner.

Then she thought of Harry. Of how many hurdles he'd confronted during the course of his life. And another surge of strength replenished her waning stores.

Zach sat back on his heels, grim-faced, and watched her. He could've read her the riot act. Reminded her that this wasn't what the games were about. But something told her he knew why she was persisting. This mannequin represented a life. A real life they might very possibly have lost.

Two minutes later, the light on the mannequin's chest turned black.

The color seemed to fill her own chest with a cold, hollowed-out feeling that only equated with one thing: failure.

"Do you really think he's dead?" she asked, still giving syncopated compressions to the dummy's chest.

She was grateful for the rain, because she didn't want

Zach to know she had begun to cry. She was furious with herself for having insisted they follow a line of broken palm fronds that any idiot could've seen were because of a fallen tree, not the trail of clues they were meant to have followed.

"I do," Zach said, pulling out a pocketknife. He stood up and started sawing a thick piece of bamboo.

"What are you doing?" she asked.

"Making a stretcher," he said, as if it was the most logical thing in the world.

Her respect for him doubled. They were going to carry back the "body." Offer it to its family along with the respect they deserved by giving them a chance to say goodbye to their loved one.

Despite the black light, she continued compressions as he worked, until eventually a small sob of despair escaped her throat and she fell back onto her heels, arms as limp as noodles, her energy stores utterly zapped.

"Hey!" Zach was by her side in an instant, pulling her into his arms, holding her so close she could feel his heart pounding against her palm. "You did everything you could."

"No!" she cried. "It wasn't enough."

She'd been wrong. This was her fault. Little Miss Mini-Menehune had insisted her knowledge of reading the jungle was better than Mr. Urban Jungle's.

Too tired to fight, she let Zach pull her closer, weeping into his saturated top. The rain was pummeling them as if its sole purpose was to remind them that they were mortals up against the might of Mother Nature and that sometimes—exactly like with her parents—all the search and rescue skills in the world would never be enough.

"Hey," he soothed. "It's only a game."

"It's not!" She pulled away from the warm comfort of his arms and began compressions again, ignoring the pain, ignoring the ridiculousness of it all. "It's so much more than that!"

"Tell me?"

Something about the openness with which he asked the question uncorked years of pent-up sorrow and frustration. Perhaps it was because Zach had pulled the Band-Aids off his own wounds this morning. Perhaps it was being on the Big Island, where her parents had first met. Perhaps it was falling in love with someone when she'd least expected it—two someones, father and son—and feeling as though she had absolutely no control over it.

And then, of course, there was the here and now. Not saving the life she'd been charged to save—the culmination of her biggest fears.

Her answers poured out of her in a torrent as she persisted with the compressions.

It was about her parents. About losing them so young. About spending a lifetime trying to prove to herself that if she'd been old enough she could've saved them. Could have swum harder, longer, stronger than anyone else, even though she knew it was both stupid and impossible, because sometimes "stupid and impossible" worked.

It was about her brothers. Trying to crawl out from underneath the endless safety precautions they'd put in place to look after her. Precautions she found suffocating rather than comforting. Stifling instead of enabling.

It was about having to fight and claw for every inch of progress she'd made in her career. And realizing, once she'd got there, that being at the top would never bring her parents back.

"Were their deaths preventable?" Zach asked, when she finally paused to take a breath.

"Yes!" Lulu wailed, unable to hold back the one thing she'd never been able to say out loud. "They could've stayed on the shore with *me*!" Her tears ran in hot, angry streaks down her cheeks and she didn't even care. "They could've chosen me and my brothers, but they didn't."

"What happened?"

In short, choky bursts she began, "My mom was working that day. As a lifeguard."

Zach nodded, readjusting his stance in a way that said he'd listen for as long as she needed him to.

"My dad had brought me down to the beach with a couple of my brothers to pick her up. An alarm went off— a surfer had gone out too far and was caught in the build-up of a storm. My—" The words snagged in her throat until she forced them out. "My mom went out to get him, even though they told her it wasn't safe. When she didn't come back, my dad told my brothers to look after me…he was going to get my mom. Neither of them ever came back."

The story sat between them as if it were an actual living thing. In a way, it was. Her parents' deaths lived in her every waking moment. Even in her dreams. The dreams where she got on her surfboard, beat the ocean at its own powerful game of chance and returned, triumphant, with both of her parents—only then she woke up in the darkness, still alone, still the choice her parents hadn't made.

It struck her that perhaps her own past was why she had taken to Harry so much. She hadn't been rejected by her parents in the way Harry's mother had walked away from him, but she certainly hadn't been their first choice. Her respect for Zach and his decision to take a job that was more desk-based than life-and-death-based went up about a thousand notches. He'd chosen his son over his job. Forever and always.

Zach was the first to break the silence. "You do know you're not to blame, right? That you're worth loving?"

She looked at him as if he was mad. "They chose death with each other over a safe life with us."

Zach shook his head as if he disagreed, but instead of

saying as much he asked, "Why did you choose the same lifestyle? The same risks?"

"Isn't it obvious? I wasn't enough for them, so how on earth am I ever going to be enough for anyone else? I need to prove I can survive anything! Rescue whoever needs help, no matter what. I know it sounds insane, and that it'll never bring them back or change how people think about me, but I feel like I can't stop until I know *in here* that enough is enough."

She pressed her hand to her heart, feeling as raw and as vulnerable as she ever had. What she was about to say could get her fired…

"I'm not there yet—I'm simply not there."

Zach didn't shake his head. Didn't laugh or mock. Instead, he got up and handed her his pocketknife. "I guess you'd better let me take over the compressions for a while. You finish the stretcher."

She did as he instructed, grateful for the activity. She'd exposed so many pent-up fears she was feeling overwhelmed by a sense of openness she hadn't felt before. Of possibility. There was a huge space inside her chest that she could choose to fill with hope or despair.

She looked at Zach, drenched to the bone, diligently giving compressions to a mannequin they both knew was "dead." He wasn't being insulting or derisive. Nor was he furious that they weren't going to win the games when he knew his boss had all but demanded a red-letter day.

He had held her. Comforted her. Refused to judge her. Even when she had literally led them down the wrong path and arrived too late to "save" their patient.

Her brothers would've berated her for not listening to them if, like Zach, they had suggested an alternative route and been shot down. But, rather than humiliate her, Zach's response to her mistake intimated that he knew the job wasn't black and white. It was about choices. Most of them good. Some of them bad.

And she was going to have to find a way to live with the bad ones—because while she'd never yet lost a patient in real life, it would happen. She could let it plunge her into a depression or she could take the ego-blow and learn the lesson. And in this case, the lesson was *Don't let your ego overpower your ability to work as a team.*

She'd grown too confident after this morning. The first contest had been a relatively easy rescue from a capsized boat about a kilometer offshore. While the other teams had wasted time flinging ropes and buoys and, courtesy of a choppy ocean, failing, she'd grabbed a buoy and dived into the sea, bringing the tie line directly to the capsized boat.

Much to her brother's annoyance, she and Zach had been able to shoot their flare two whole minutes before his team had.

But she'd made the decision to dive in on her own.

It should be a bitter pill to swallow. Realizing how selfish she'd been. How myopic. Instead, Zach was giving her the space to learn that she could trust him. And with that came acceptance.

"Zach?"

He looked up, his shoulders steadily moving down and up, down and up, the fluid movements unrelenting even though they both knew it was pointless.

"I think we should call time of death."

"You sure?"

There wasn't a trace of scorn in his voice. He had her back. She felt the moment deeply, as if he had just offered her a part of himself in the same way she believed he'd offered himself to his son. Without reservation. With an abundance of love.

They called the time of death. Logged it into their phones. Loaded the "body" onto the stretcher.

She squatted down and stared at the mannequin. "It's hard not to feel like a failure."

Zach's eyes shot to hers. "You are a lot of things, Lulu Kahale, but a failure is not one of them."

She wanted to believe him. She really did. And the fact that the words came from him meant the world to her. But it was as if he could sense that his words weren't quite penetrating deep enough.

He beckoned her to him. "C'mere, you."

She gratefully crossed to him, letting herself be fully absorbed into his comforting embrace. As he held her a soft glow of optimism warmed the open space in her chest. Trusting someone didn't have to be a place of fear. It could be a place of resilience. Possibility...

If she let it.

She looked up at him, wanting to put words to the gratitude she felt, but she couldn't.

He cupped her cheeks in his hands and dipped his mouth to hers. It was the softest kiss she'd ever known, instantly turning her insides liquid. Each kiss that followed felt potent with meaning, with strength. And with that strength she felt her resolve return. They had exposed their raw wounds to one another. Their biggest vulnerabilities. Their greatest fears. It added a new layer to their obvious attraction to one another. A depth to the supercharged lust that had been fueling their interactions.

Somehow they managed to pull apart from one another. "Should we get back to the base?" she asked.

From the heat in his eyes, she might as well have asked, *Your room or mine?*

They made quick work of hoisting up the stretcher, then followed the path they'd broken through the undergrowth. They made it back to the hiking trail with the mannequin strapped beneath a heat blanket, and just as the sun broke through the clouds they reached the finish line.

Her brother was there. Of course. And a handful of other teams.

"Hey, Mini!" her brother shouted, throwing her a bottle of water. "We were about to send out the search parties."

"Ha-ha," she deadpanned.

He looked at her. Really looked at her. He dropped the attitude. "You okay?"

For the first time she felt as if he was going to listen to her answer and take it at face value. "Yeah," she said, throwing a smile at Zach. "I'm good."

Mak glanced at the body on the stretcher, then asked, "How long did you guys attempt resuscitation?"

"Over an hour."

He made a whooping noise and whistled. "Mini? You are a legend."

She and Zach threw one another questioning glances. "Why? We didn't resuscitate him."

"Maybe not, but you've always believed in trying your hardest. Respect." He held up a fist for her to bump. He looked over his shoulder at the pack of competitors, each throwing back deep slugs of water or kneading sore muscles. "None of us did over twenty minutes."

She and Zach shared another smile, this one shot through with a fresh, energizing sense of achievement—and then, because it was Zach, the look intensified into something far more intimate.

Mak didn't miss the exchange.

She braced herself, prepared for him to thwack one of his tree trunk arms over Zach's shoulders and take him on a little walk and talk to explain how things worked in the Kahale family.

Instead, he gave her a light punch on the arm and said, "I'm guessing you two probably need a long hot shower before the luau?"

Lulu practically choked on her surprise. Was her brother telling her he *approved*?

Mak gave a double *shaka* sign and congratulated them on a job well done, then left the pair of them standing there, temporarily speechless.

The only thing remaining between them now was a question she was too nervous to ask.

Do you want me?

Zach broke the silence first.

"I'm guessing this isn't the best way to show up to a luau." He looked down at his filthy outdoor gear, caked in red, iron-rich island mud.

Lulu instantly pictured herself peeling that top off him and scrubbing him clean. Heat darted into areas of her body she hadn't realized could light up with lust.

Shakily, she said, "The luau's not for a couple of hours."

"Maybe you could help me pick out the best shirt to wear?"

Lulu's eyes shot to Zach's. "I—I could do that. If you trust me."

Zach's eyes dropped to her mouth as she spoke. It felt tactile, his gaze…

She swallowed and reflexively licked her lips.

"I trust *you*."

Those three words… He knew how much they meant to her.

She became aware of her breasts growing heavy— not under the weight of the wet, muddy top, but under the weight of his eyes, which were noticing—yup—her nipples standing to attention.

"I should probably change, too," she managed.

"Mmm… And I'd better call Harry. A quick check-in."

"Yeah." She felt herself brighten. "Harry would be proud of you."

"Of us," Zach corrected.

And just like that they became an "us." She'd never been an "us" before. Sure, she'd dated. Had boyfriends. But none she'd ever really admitted to. It was like trying on a dress she'd never thought she'd look good in and realizing it made her look absolutely beautiful.

Us.

The word was catapulted to the top of her list of Most Wonderful Words in the World.

Us.

It even tasted good.

Zach shifted his weight, his eyes pinging to the hotel and back. He was making a decision. A big one. A single dad with a disabled kid wasn't going to let just anyone into his heart space, let alone his bed.

She held her breath.

His eyes met hers, decision made. "Apparently there's a really good club sandwich on the room service menu. I know the luau's coming up, but I'm a bit hungry now. We could call Harry… Go over tomorrow's schedule… Line our stomachs a bit before we try another one of those mai tais."

We.

Us.

"Good idea," Lulu said. Or maybe she didn't.

They were so busy staring at one another, trying to figure out what this new world order was, she didn't really have a clue what was happening.

Maybe they'd stand here all day, staring at one another like lovestruck idiots.

Maybe her brother would find them at midnight and clonk their heads together and point out the obvious. They needed to get a room.

Maybe they'd be struck by lightning.

Eventually—mercifully—one or both of them started walking. The outdoors became the indoors. One corridor led to another, and then the elevator, and then another corridor, and then, without so much as a word passing between them, they found themselves outside Zach's hotel room.

He tugged the key out of his back pocket. "You good with this?"

She nodded. She was. And there wouldn't be any need for the room service menu. She had everything she needed right in front of her.

CHAPTER TEN

THE SECOND THE door clicked shut Zach felt every chain he'd wrapped around his heart unlock and drop to the ground. He felt free in a way he hadn't in years.

At last. The fight was over. Resisting his attraction to Lulu hadn't made him stronger, wiser, or better able to defend his son. It had hobbled him. And Harry. And Lulu. And holding either of them back was the last thing he wanted to do.

He looked at her as if seeing her entirely anew.

Smart, funny, feisty, fiery, sexy Lulu. The ying to his yang. The fire to his ice. All of the opposites combining into something better, not worse.

Today his attraction to her had deepened into something he'd thought he'd never feel again. Love. Or at least the beginnings of it. He trusted her. With his heart and his son's. It was a powerful realization.

She looked up at him, those amber eyes of hers glinting through the inky darkness of her lashes. There was an openness in her expression he hadn't seen before. It wasn't vulnerability. It was consent. Belief. And unfettered desire.

"Should we call Harry?"

"Definitely."

He put his phone on speaker, and when Harry answered they described the day to him, their eyes glued to one another as they spoke, peeling off their boots and shoes. When the call ended they were still staring at one another, their breath coming short and fast as if they'd just run up a mountain. And in a way, they had. Both of them had opened up, baring their most vulnerable selves to the other, and had emerged from their admissions not only unscathed, but cared for. Deeply so.

His erection came so hard and fast he heard the leather on his belt strain in protest. He'd never wanted anyone more than he wanted Lulu, and from the dark gold glimmer of her eyes she felt the same way.

"You're shivering," he said.

"It's cold," she said.

It wasn't. She was shaking with adrenaline. So was he.

"Before we do anything…" He stopped and cleared his throat. "Um… Do we need to define what this is?"

"It's us," she said. "Trying to figure out what this is."

He nodded. Yeah. That was good. But… "Not much of a courtship…us hating each other at first sight."

"It wasn't hate," she countered. "It was…frustration."

He quirked his head to the side and nodded. That was right, too. "We're very different."

"That's not always a bad thing."

"What if it becomes a bad thing?"

"What if it doesn't?"

He smiled.

She smiled back.

So it was settled. They were going to see what this was. No matter the outcome.

"Shower?" she asked, her eyes doing a quick scan of their muddy and rain-drenched clothes.

He took her hand in his and, without bothering to take her clothes off, led them straight under the rainforest shower heads in the huge wet room.

He'd been upgraded by the hotel, but hadn't thought a

thing of it until now. The wet room was otherworldly, bringing the outdoors inside. It had two walls of bamboo, and the water was dewing on the surface, creating a tiny waterfall on the beautifully tiled shower bench. The other two "walls" were retractable glass doors that led onto a small, private rooftop garden, filled with lush tropical plants.

He threw them open, relishing everything he'd barely noticed the night before. With Lulu by his side the setting was pretty damn sexy. Then again, he would've happily made love to her just about anywhere right now. They could've been in a double wide trailer or a palm leaf shack for all he cared. But adding the element of luxury to this long-awaited moment was a very nice cherry on top of a long-awaited sundae.

He tipped her chin up and dipped his mouth to hers, then kissed her hard, enjoying the way her lips felt like that first incredible sensation of biting into a soft-serve ice cream cone. Yielding, but rewarding. Mouthwatering in a way that only made him want more.

Though they had both literally dragged themselves through the jungle, she somehow managed to taste of vanilla, mint and coconut. He didn't think he'd ever tire of the taste of her. And this was just the tip of the iceberg. Kissing. Standing in a shower with nothing more than a couple of flimsy T-shirts between them.

An insatiable hunger built inside him. It was beyond anything he'd felt before.

He'd thought what he and his ex had shared ranked up there, but he'd not had a clue.

His body's response to Lulu was in another league.

Holding her in his arms, tasting her, touching her…her back, her waist, her hips…he felt as if he was being consumed whole by an unquenchable thirst.

Knowing that he could trust her, that she cared for him and his son—loved his son, even, and possibly loved him—

meant more than he could ever put words to. He and Harry came as a unit, and until this moment he'd never realized how braced he'd been, ready to be found wanting because of it.

To Lulu, it seemed it was an asset. Having a boy so filled with love. Joy. Just like she was.

His kisses deepened. He wanted her. All of her. Taste. Touch. Sound. Pleasure. Pain. *All of it.*

"Wow..." she whispered against his lips as he turned on the matching shower heads.

"It's no Turtle Hideaway, but..."

"It'll do."

Lulu play-growled, grabbing fistfuls of his T-shirt and tugging him closer to her. Their lips met again, and his body felt saturated by an all-consuming temperature explosion. Lava meeting lava. Impact succumbing to immersion. It was impossible to know where he began and she ended. He didn't want to know. All he wanted was Lulu. Everything that made him who he was—common sense, lists, rules—was being swept into the drain along with the water pouring round the pair of them, energizing them as if it were a life-affirming ambrosia.

He felt her hands unceremoniously ruck up his T-shirt, her fingers pressing against his skin, tracing the lines of his stomach muscles, inching their way ever upwards, as if trying to commit the terrain of his torso to memory. Until, impatiently, she pushed his T-shirt up and over his head, her mouth leaving his only to find purchase on his nipples. Her tongue gave each one hot wet swirls of approbation, and her groans of pleasure at the sensation of skin on skin vibrated through to his chest. His heart. He'd never imagined being on fire would feel this good.

He slipped his fingers under her top and slowly...achingly slowly...pulled it up, enjoying feeling her body quiver in response to his touch.

"Take it off," she begged. "I want to feel you against me."

She was doing that, all right. Her hips were pressed into that sweet space that seemed to have been molded just for her, where his erection was taking on a life of its own… pulsing, demanding attention. If she so much as touched it with the tip of one of her fingers…

He grabbed her wrist as she began tugging at the clasp on his belt. "No."

"Yes."

Her chest arched into his, her hips nestling in closer, daring him to deny her access to all that strained at the fabric of his trousers. *Hell.* Every single pore in his body was aching to burst out of his clothes, rip hers off and take her right here and now on the tiled floor, but…

"Not yet."

"I want you naked. Now." Her voice was throaty. Hungry.

"When I say so."

Something flickered in her eyes. On and off. On and off. She was rewiring her response to him. Twenty-four hours ago Lulu would've let him have hell for being so absolute.

Half-naked, ravenous, horny, today's Lulu kind of liked it…handing the reins of control over to him. Her fingertips pressed into him as if she was trying to divine which direction to go. Push or pull. Take or be taken.

He saw the lights flick on again—full beam. She went up on tiptoe, leaning into him but not against him. "All right, then, Mr. Boss Man," she whispered into his ear, nipping his lobe as she paused for breath. "Have it your way."

He took the reins she'd just handed him and held on tight.

Her hunger for him made prolonging the moments of discovery all the more pleasurable. Finding the beauty mark just to the left of her belly button… The tiny tattoo of a starfish hidden between her ring and index fingers… The small scar etched into the divot between her hip and her rib cage…

"Coral…" she breathed against his neck as he traced his finger along the bump.

He didn't know how he did it, but he took his time.

Eventually, when she threatened to rip her own clothes off, and his too while she was at it, he pulled her T-shirt up and over her head. Her hair fell free of the messy top-knot she'd stacked it in, a slick of ebony cascading down her back.

He ran his hands over and through it as if it was one of the seven wonders of the world. "Let me wash it."

She looked up at him, surprised. "No one's asked to do that before."

"Well, I'm asking now."

"Why?"

There was the smallest hint of fragility in her voice. Defensiveness.

"I'd like to do it. Consider it my gift to you before I ravage you."

She pulled him to her again, and he felt the small triangles of her lace bra rub against his chest, the tight nubs of her nipples straining against the fabric.

"I want you," she whispered.

He wanted her, too. But he was enjoying this. Not just touching and holding her. It was the trust she was giving him. The openness. He wanted her to enjoy the luxury of caring and being cared for.

Lulu had locked the door of her emotional cupboard long ago. Way back when her parents had died, actively refusing help from anyone from that point forward.

He took the shampoo bottle off the small teak shelf, but she steered his hand back and he put it down.

"Why don't you want me to wash your hair?" he asked.

She hesitated, then said, "Because I won't be able to see your face."

He got it. They were both on new terrain.

He put her hand on his belt buckle. "Go on. Take it off."

He was handing back the reins. Letting her know this could go at whatever pace she wanted, stop or start whenever she blew the whistle—because this was something they had to do together, or they weren't going to do it at all.

Her fingers trembled for a moment. She looked up at him and then, decision made, took that belt buckle and whipped it out of its belt loops so fast he heard the clatter of the buckle on the tiled floor before he felt the exquisite release of his erection from his trousers.

He stepped out of the pile of saturated cotton and used his foot to flick it away. Lulu was right. Even a solitary thread of fabric between them was too much.

"Oh, my goodness me," she said, in a voice double-dipped with approval.

Her tongue swept across her lips. An intense pulse of longing throbbed deep inside him.

"May I return the pleasure?" he asked, his fingers hitching onto the waistline of her hiking trousers.

"Please…" she managed, her eyes still glued to his arousal.

He dropped to his hands and knees, hushing her protests that his moving wasn't fair because his body was too far away now as he undid the waist tie of her trousers and tugged them down in a oner. He threw them on top of his.

"Now," he said, sitting back on his heels and sliding his hands along her legs up to the perfect curve of her butt. "Now it's fair."

As he rose she pushed him back, so that he was forced to sit down on the bench. The energy between them flashed and morphed into yet another form. Neither of them was in charge now. It was as if they'd handed this moment over to the more primitive parts of their hearts—their souls—leaving their bodies to respond organically to each other.

He pulled her to him so that she was straddling him, his arousal taut and pressing against her belly. He undid the front clasp of her bra, felt his breath catching in his throat at her sheer beauty. A completely naked Lulu…right here on his lap. She was so perfect he could hardly breathe.

If he were to have conjured up his own Aphrodite to step out of a seashell and into his arms it would have been Lulu. He lightly stroked each of her breasts, cupping them, tracing them, and when her nails clawed into his back, her hips ground into his, he pulled one of her nipples into his mouth as he rubbed the pad of his thumb against the other nipple, enjoying her whimper of response.

"We need protection," she eventually managed. "Now."

He thanked just about every god there was that his friends back at the firehouse in New York had stuffed his toiletries bag with condoms on his last day. At the time he'd been certain they'd never be used. Now he wondered if there would be enough. He and Lulu were here on the Big Island for two more days, and from the way his body responded to hers they'd be needing that do-not-disturb sign for quite some time.

They turned off the shower and threw towels at one another, not caring if they were fully dried or not. He charged her with putting the sign on the door while he unearthed a fistful of condoms. When she got to the bed, a big huge fluffy towel wrapped round that gorgeous, curvy body of hers, he held them up.

She arced an eyebrow. "Hmm…" she said, her smile turning decidedly wicked. "Seems like we've got a busy night ahead of ourselves."

Lulu had engaged in foreplay before. But never like this.

Being with Zach Murphy was like taking a master class

in the senses. Learning one by one which of the pleasure zones did what and why. To the point where she almost felt guilty.

Almost.

Every second they'd spent together in the shower had shifted her low-grade hum of desire into a pounding, pulsing, energized ache. She wanted to throw herself into his arms. Impale herself on him. Tempt him. Torture him. Torture herself.

He tugged her to him, teasing away the tuck of the towel between her breasts as if he had all the time in the world. Every brush of his fingertips on her skin made her feel something new. Shimmery. Hedonistic. Carnal.

And above all completely safe.

She didn't have an ounce of fear that Zach Murphy would ever hurt her. Emotionally or physically. He had been so open with her about his past, so generous when she'd dumped a thousand pounds of pent-up misery on him earlier today, she was literally in awe of the generosity of his lovemaking.

He let the towel slip down along her body, the thick cotton skidding along her curves as if it had been specially designed to add another level of eroticism to the moment. She felt sexy and strong in a way she never really had before. Proud to stand in front of him without a stitch of clothing on, letting him drink her in as if he'd just crawled across a desert and she was a tall, cool glass of water he wanted to savor and gulp down.

Normally she would've been diving under the covers at this point, demanding the lights be turned off and all eyes shut as "the games" began.

But this was no game.

This was real life.

Someone like Zach—a man who'd loved and lost and been bruised like hell in the process—wouldn't be looking for a fling. He was an all-or-nothing kind of guy and this, right here and now, was his way of saying he was in.

He'd made it very clear she had a choice in the matter, too.

All.

Or nothing.

How could she not choose all? She was in love with him. Felt safe with him. Felt secure in a way she'd never felt with another man. She adored his son. Couldn't imagine a world without either of them.

She felt as if she'd lived a lifetime in these past eight hours, never mind the previous few weeks. She'd treated him like the enemy, had behaved like an idiot, then fallen in love with his son, with him, told him her secrets, fallen apart, pulled herself back together again and still he was here. Wanting her. Hungry for her.

It struck her that she'd been so busy holding that steel trap around her heart with one hand and a spear in the other, ensuring whoever she was with knew that she called the shots—*all* of them—she'd never fully opened herself up to the possibility that a relationship didn't have to be like that. Combative. Competitive.

It could be *this*. A shared energy that only made her want to be a better person. Everything about Zach filled her with peace. Well, sexy lust, too, but there wasn't anything about him that was in competition with her. He exuded an energy that made it very clear he didn't need to show her how male he was. How powerful. Zach Murphy wasn't proving anything to anyone. The only thing he was doing was making it very clear that he wanted her. And that made him the most alpha male she had ever met in her life.

He could have her with or without a pretty bow on top. In fact, it was time he learned how great it felt to have the spotlight thrown on him.

She pushed him onto the bed. Her hand barely met with

resistance as she put it on his sternum and guided him back to the huge nest of pillows before climbing on top of his lap and straddling him. She felt protected and wild. Drunk on hormones and yet more sane than she'd ever felt before. She felt honest and true. But most of all she felt as if a passion bomb had exploded in her. She was hot and wet and physically aching to feel him inside her.

After eliciting a few short, sharp breaths from him while she unfurled the condom on his beautiful erection, she lifted herself up a bit, using his shoulders as ballast, and then slowly, achingly slowly, she began to lower herself onto him.

Once she felt him fully inside her she began to rock her hips, amazed that she had been able to take all of him into her. His movements began to match hers. Soon they were moving with a synchronicity she wouldn't have believed possible. Action overwhelmed her ability to think straight. She tried to memorize every movement, savor each touch, each kiss, but the surges of pleasure completely washed away her ability to form a coherent thought.

They clutched at one another. Gave featherlight kisses. Tickled. Ravaged. Gasped. Groaned. Everything the senses allowed, she felt. And when, after she didn't know how many minutes or hours, they reached a mutual climax, they clung to one another as if their lives depended upon it. Shuddering and shaking in each other's arms as if they'd been taken apart and rebuilt again.

And in a way she had. She had never been more honest in her life than she had just been with Zach. She'd given herself to him completely. If she could unzip him and crawl inside him, give him everything he needed—extra heartbeats, more energy, more stamina, iron, magnesium, whatever it was he needed—she'd give it to him.

She slid off his big man chest onto the mattress. He rolled on his side and curved himself around her. His warm, muscled belly against her back… His thigh hair tickly against her bare legs… His breath on her neck, softer and sweeter than a breeze off the ocean… They dozed and nestled, all thoughts of attending the luau as far away as the moon.

When she woke, his arms were wrapped around her as easily as if he'd been doing it for years and the room was dark. She could smell him on her skin and herself on his. It made her hungry for more. She snuggled against him and, feeling his arousal against her bottom, was instantly ravenous for more.

Something told her it was going to be a long night—but the kind of long night she would happily stay up for.

CHAPTER ELEVEN

ZACH PULLED LULU'S wetsuit off the outdoor shower towel rail and hung it behind the curtain, out of sight. He smiled as yet another round of raucous laughter sounded from the beach, where Lulu and Harry were building sand castles.

She was a proper engineer when it came to bucket and spade architecture, drilling into Harry how critical it was to build the moat first, so that when the tide inevitably came in to try to sweep away their craftsmanship it stood a bit more of a chance against the inevitable.

The thought snagged and jarred as he caught himself pulling her bikini off the outdoor line and stuffing it into the laundry basket he had on his hip. It was almost exclusively filled with Lulu's belongings.

Zach was hosting a staff barbecue at his place this afternoon, which meant tidying up was inevitable. But why was he only picking up Lulu's things, with a plan to stow the basket out of sight under the bed?

Okay, sure… It had been three weeks since they'd returned from the games, and they'd stuck to their agreement to keep their relationship private. Zach was still on probation, and they were both pretty sure that the—*ahem*—new level of relations between the pair of them would be frowned upon, but…

What exactly were they doing, here? Were they keeping

their relationship private for professional reasons, or was it because both of them had concerns? Big ones.

From the outside, it looked a picture-perfect blossoming romance.

They spent a lot of time together. Pretty much all their time outside of work. And most of it here at Turtle Hideaway. No holding hands and gazing into one another's eyes over a candlelit table in the center of Honolulu for the two of them.

Was this secluded cove their moat against the rest of the world? A place to soak up as much of this loved-up feeling as they could before the inevitable occurred and the bubble popped?

He could almost see it playing out before him. The moment when their ying and yang views of the world were no longer the perfect combination but diametric opposites.

He hadn't missed the fact that they were still clashing at work, with Lulu pushing for the team to respond faster, harder, not taking the time to weigh up health and safety, until Zach stepped in and demanded it. He'd written off her behavior as a bit of a show for the rest of the team. But did it run deeper than that? Perhaps Lulu simply couldn't break free of that built-in need to press her full weight against any sort of restraint...

He shook his head. He didn't know. He just didn't know. And he had a little boy's heart to look after.

A collective cry of dismay came up from the beach, along with a wash of waves.

He heard Lulu's, "High five, li'l buddy," and, "Good work."

Ten minutes ago that would've been enough to assure him he was right to trust her with his son's heart. But now, as if letting one single solitary doubt through a razor-thin gap in their little love bubble, the floodgates opened.

He looked at the basket again. Keeping his job was important. Keeping Lulu felt just as important. But was respecting him and what he'd been through as important to her?

Harry and Lulu appeared from the beach. Her arm was wrapped around his shoulder and the two of them were oohing and ahhing over a shell one of them had found.

Guiltily, Zach stowed the laundry basket in the outdoor shower stall, out of sight. His son was his priority. So, for now their relationship was going to have to stay under wraps.

"Nice to have a break from the rains, isn't it?" Casey asked.

"Mmm…"

Lulu was half listening to Casey and half enjoying the sight of Zach manning the barbecue. He was wearing an apron. Board shorts, a T-shirt and some flip-flops completed his ensemble. Now that his tan had deepened and his body language had shifted from East Coast uptight to Hawaii's much more relaxed Island Time, he almost looked as if he was going to live here forever.

As if sensing her gaze on him, he turned and looked at her. A little zap of excitement spiked her pulse as their eyes met. And then a sliver of concern. Ever since she and Harry had come back from the beach this morning he'd been a bit off.

Maybe this whole inviting the team to his house thing wasn't really his jam. Or, more worryingly, maybe she wasn't.

"Want your burger medium rare or medium?" he called.

"Medium, please," Lulu yelled across the small group.

He gave her the guy chin-tilt thing, then turned back to the grill.

Hmm… Something was up with him. Definitely.

"Someone's happy with her New York beefcake." Casey

elbowed her in the ribs, her eyes flicking between her and Zach.

Lulu feigned a shocked expression. "The boss man, you mean? *Pfffft*."

Casey snorted, then turned her voice singsong. "Lulu's got a boyfriend."

"Shut up!"

Casey grinned, but then her expression sobered. "I'm totally happy for you two, but remember…he actually *is* the boss. And he's got a kid. And…baggage."

Lulu bristled. "We've all got baggage."

"I know. Cool your jets. I'm just saying…letting down a guy like that and a kid like that when you get tired of playing house… It'll be tough."

Every nerve ending in Lulu's body shot to high alert. Had Casey tapped into Zach's weird energy? Or had he…? No. He wouldn't have confided in Casey. Would he?

"I'm not playing house," she replied hotly.

Casey cackled and gave her the side-eye. "How long have you wanted to live in this house?"

Lulu's nose hitched up. Years. And Casey knew that. The question was clearly rhetorical. She didn't answer.

"And how about this new thing of volunteering at the Superstars Surf Club?"

"I've been doing that for ages."

Casey's eyebrows shot up. "Regularly?"

Okay. Maybe not regularly. But enough to have the place mean something to her. A lot, actually. And definitely enough for Casey's line of conversation to throw her hackles up.

"I hope you're not suggesting I orchestrated this whole thing." She was a lot of things, but conniving was not one of them.

"No, not at all," Casey said. "Seriously. Not at all. It's just…you seem to be moving pretty fast."

"I told you. We're not a couple."

"Then why is there a laundry basket in the outdoor shower full of your stuff?"

Zach had hidden her things away? Her tone turned icy. "Harry and I do a lot of swimming here."

"In your pajamas?"

Lulu stood up, properly angry now. What was this? The Spanish Inquisition?

Casey made a soothing gesture. "I'm just saying—this is the most serious I've ever seen you about someone and I'm trying to figure out when to prepare myself for the fallout."

What the hell…?

"What are you suggesting, Casey? That I set this whole thing up so I could dump him? Make bunny stew?"

"No, not at all." Casey gave an easy laugh. "Chill. Seriously. I'm not saying you did any of this on purpose, it's just…"

"It's just what?" Lulu demanded.

Casey lowered her voice and put her entire focus on Lulu. "He's got a lot of things you've wanted for a long time, but maybe it'd be smart to prepare him for the fallout when…you know…you decide to move on."

Shards of understanding lanced straight through her heart as she suddenly saw what Casey saw.

Her house.

Her job.

A beautiful little boy who loved learning how to surf.

A ready-made family tailored just for her.

Walking away from perfection would be insanity.

She wouldn't do that to Zach and Harry.

Would she?

"I'm thirsty," Casey announced, as if the topic was over. "Want a lemonade?"

Lulu nodded. Anything to get Casey away from her before she began stuffing everything she'd said back down her throat.

Casey's angle on the situation was off. Lulu wasn't living on fantasy island. Everything that was happening was real. *Very* real. Genuine. How dare she suggest Lulu would cut and run?

She pulled herself up short. Casey had known her a long time. They weren't the talk-on-the-phone-for-hours kind of friends, but they knew each other well. Casey knew her weak spots. Her tendencies. And Lulu's track record was almost exclusively devoted to diving in, surfacing, then walking away before so much as a bruise could appear on her heart.

She sat on top of the picnic table she and Casey had been leaning against and tried to squash all the questions Casey's interrogation had unleashed. She took deep breaths. Counted waves. Tried to let the happy-go-lucky energy of the small gathering surround her again.

Nope. No good.

She was properly agitated.

Ten minutes ago she wouldn't have believed feeling as happy and relaxed as she had was possible.

But the happiness obviously had fault lines. Casey had managed to crack the veneer of it with barely so much as a tap.

It was horrifying revelation when, just this morning, lying in Zach's arms, she'd thought being with him "stilled her," as her grandmother would say. Not when they were naked, obviously. But there was something about opening her heart up to him that made her feel stronger than she ever had. And giddier. She was falling head over heels in love with a strait-laced guy from New York City.

Maybe that was exactly the problem.

Opposites might attract, but how often did their relationships succeed? Maybe Zach was the one who was planning on doing the dumping, but had yet to figure out how to tactfully extract her from his and Harry's lives? Maybe she was just a rebound fling?

He wouldn't make her stop being friends with Harry, would he?

Now that the hounds of doubt were prowling round her brain, she thought maybe it was a good thing she'd not told him she loved him.

Or maybe it was old Lulu, justifying not committing again.

She sat there, shell-shocked, as if Casey's pronouncements and Zach's weird mood were physically chipping away at her confidence.

"Lulu!"

Her frown turned into a smile as Harry ran toward her, up on tiptoes, arms windmilling with excitement as they so often did, with the big starfish of sunblock she'd painted on his face when he'd complained a single stripe wasn't any fun.

"Look!" He held out a seashell as if it were a precious jewel.

She cooed over it and held it up, appreciating the gorgeous pearlescent colors.

He looked wistfully out at the sea, then back at her. "Are we going surfing tomorrow?"

She gave him a double thumbs-up and made a Herculean effort to attach a smile to it, because everything she'd thought she was sure of ten minutes ago was now being obliterated in a huge bubbling pot of insecurity stew.

"Absolutely," she made herself say. "Wild horses couldn't keep me away."

And they wouldn't.

It was one thing if Zach wanted to call their relationship quits, but there was no way she was letting Harry down the way his mother had. None.

"When do you think I'll be able to surf like you?" Harry asked.

Her heart twisted into a knot. She ruffled his hair and said, "It took me years, little man."

It wasn't a lie. But it wasn't the full truth. He'd never be as good as she was because of his disability. But why strip him of the joy of trying?

A huge, overwhelming urge to burst into tears consumed her. Over the past few weeks it had been watching interchanges like this pass between father and son that had made her fall even more in love with Zach than she already was.

His quiet, disciplined inner strength was one of the simplest and most beautiful joys to behold. He knew better than anyone that his son had limits, but he did his best to let him explore the outer reaches of those limits. It was a level of parenting bravery that there should be medals for. Heck—her brothers struggled with the fact that she did search and rescue to this day, despite her being at the top of her class in just about everything apart from size. She couldn't imagine what it was like for Zach. Especially knowing Harry's mother had lacked the strength to love her son as much as Zach did. Had rejected him even—rejected both of them. It genuinely did not compute.

She pulled Harry in for a hug, loving the openness with which he wrapped his arms round her waist, gave her a huge squeeze and then, with the same happy, wild energy, ran over to his father to do the same to him.

Her joy felt bittersweet when Zach gave a big "Oof…" as Harry careered into him, deftly shifting them both away from the grill with a gentle, "Easy there, H-man. Eyes on the prize."

She loved how Zach's body language changed when he was with his son. The way he handed him the tongs to take over hot dog–turning duties, his arm sliding over his son's slim shoulders. Protective, but not restrictive. She loved the way he called him "H-man" or "son" with the same level of pride an athlete might say they'd won a gold medal or a scientist a Nobel Prize. He thought his son was a wonder and his pride showed.

He was the gentlest, most patient, greatest dad she'd ever met. And that was saying something. Because, even though they annoyed the living daylights out of her, her brothers already had pole positions in that department. Seeing them with their little kids... It was something else.

Her smile faded a bit as her brothers crept into her consciousness. Would they be thinking the same things Casey was? That she lacked commitment and would leave Zach before he had a chance to leave her?

She shot a glare in Casey's direction, grateful that she'd been sidetracked by Stewart's retelling of a recent sea rescue the pair of them had pulled off.

What did she know?

Lulu had introduced Zach to both Makoa and her grandmother. Which was huge. No one she'd ever dated had met her grandmother. Sure, they'd accidentally run into her at a shaved ice stand, but she hadn't cut and run, or turned Zach and Harry around and walked the other way. She'd introduced them like the adult woman she was, only leaving out the part about how she was falling head over heels in love with the pair of them.

All of which meant...Casey might be right.

The table she was sitting on abruptly shifted, lurching her sideways, as if her brother had come and sat on the other side to send her off balance. She whirled round to tell him off, but no one was there.

Her eyes shot to Zach, who was catching some hot dogs that were falling off the grill while holding up Harry with his other hand.

All the conversations that had been light and cheery

turned into a swift volley of, "Did you feel that?" Followed up by, "Was that an earthquake?"

There were thousands of earthquakes a year in Hawaii, most of them low grade, but all worth paying attention to. This one hadn't felt big enough to trigger a tsunami, but it was always important to check.

All the locals began kicking into action. Getting Zach to put out the barbecue. Checking their phones for tsunami warnings. Discussing their designated safe spots at a higher elevation. Figuring out who had brought their first aid run kits in their cars.

For the first time ever, Lulu felt completely paralyzed. Normally she would've been the first to leap into action, helping the most obvious candidate who needed it, who in this case was Harry. If there were aftershocks, he'd need someone to help talk him through it all. She'd be organizing people into cars. Checking her own phone.

But she couldn't move.

Casey's words were pounding against her brain like dead weights.

Letting down a guy like that and a kid like that when you get tired of playing house... It'll be tough.

Lulu's phone began vibrating. Then she heard Zach's ring. And Casey's. Phones rang one after the other—until she realized what they'd felt was an aftershock. Something big had already happened.

She wouldn't have a chance to clear out her brain or to talk her worries out with Zach. They were all going to work. And whatever it was that awaited them was going to push them all to the limit.

Zach listened intently to the voice on the end of the phone. His eyes snapped to Lulu's as the information he was receiving sank in.

One of her brothers was missing in a landslide. Duke.

The stuntman. A movie company had been filming a chase scene on quad bikes for the blockbuster they were shooting. Duke and a stuntwoman had been riding up along some of the island's steepest ridges and the clifftop they'd been riding on had given way. It wasn't looking good.

Lulu was also on the phone, presumably hearing the same news. She was staring at him. Hard.

It was a strange look. One he couldn't read. He wanted to kick himself for being cool with her all afternoon. If he'd learned anything from his divorce, it was that keeping feelings bottled up inside was no use to anyone.

His instinct was to go to her. Pull her into his arms. Tell her he'd do everything in his power to make this bad situation right. But something about the way she was looking at him confirmed his fears rather than allayed them.

She'd just found out her brother was in trouble. It was very possible he wouldn't survive. And there was nothing that would send Lulu back to that dark place she'd only just crawled out of more than losing another family member.

She hung up her phone and gave him a *What gives?* gesture.

He pocketed his phone, his brain whirring with an extensive to-do list. Normally his body and his brain kicked into a familiar routine at moments like these. Sort out staff... equipment. Decide a course of action. He'd literally attended thousands of emergencies over his career. This one shouldn't be any different.

But his thoughts kept snagging on the one unfamiliar aspect of today's emergency.

It was personal.

He braced himself. She wasn't going to like the decision he had to make.

He would work this one.

She was getting benched.

As if she had read his mind and wanted to make sure

he knew she disagreed, she jogged over to him. "I'll head over to the site now."

"No." He shook his head. "You won't. Not on this one."

"You need me."

"I need you safe."

"I work safe."

Against his better judgment he huffed out a humorless, solitary, "Ha."

She went still. Too still. Her eyes were glued to him with a laser-sharp focus that seared right through to his heart. She knew why he'd made the call, but she didn't like it.

Not. One. Bit.

He was about to ask her to look after Harry, knowing she would definitely need something to do, but stopped himself short. Mixing personal and professional on a day like this was a very bad idea.

He gestured to indicate that he'd be with her in a minute, then asked his parents if they could look after Harry for a bit—preferably at their condo, which was inland and on a slightly higher elevation. A tsunami wasn't likely, but he'd hate to assure them that the beach house was safe. His dad agreed, as Zach had known he would, but his response was drowned out in a coughing fit.

Zach helped him regain his breath as yet another weight lodged in his chest. Relying on them for childcare was something he was going to have to reassess. He'd leaned on them big-time when his marriage had fallen apart, but he couldn't ignore the fact that his parents wouldn't be around forever.

His phone buzzed again. A pressing reminder that timing was critical.

"So." Lulu had her arms crossed over her chest. "Not even good enough to look after Harry anymore, am I?"

"Lulu—" There was a note of warning in his voice even he didn't like to hear. "This is for your safety."

"Is it?" she asked, and then, as she turned to walk away, she threw another question over her shoulder. "Or is it for yours?"

Unexpectedly, she wheeled on him, and a blaze of energy hit him straight in the solar plexus.

"You will not keep me from this rescue. That's my *brother* we're talking about."

"I know." He hated himself for resorting to his *Now, let's be reasonable* voice, but it was the first tool in his arsenal, so he grabbed it—because time was of the essence. The longer this played out, the less likely it was they'd find Duke. He held out his hands between them. "Lulu, you know that's not how this works. Just like surgeons, rescue crews don't go into delicate situations when it's personal."

"They're *all* personal," she bit out.

The words hit him like bullets. "Don't you think I know that?" he demanded. "Why the hell do you think I do this?"

"I don't know, Zach." She crossed her arms over her chest. "To lord it over other people? Show them how great you are? Be the big hero? It's what you do, isn't it? Show everyone that you're Mr. Perfect?"

Everything in him stilled. This wasn't how she really felt. Couldn't be. She'd been curled up in his arms this morning, all warm and cuddly, a smile on her sleeping face. When she'd woken and seen him there, his head beside hers on the pillow, her smile had doubled. She'd grinned, and whispered, "Wow. Dreams really do come true."

And now he was a self-aggrandizing hero?

He wanted to shout at her. Shake some common sense back into her. Remind her that this wasn't about her. Or her brother. Or trying to prove to the universe that she could've saved her parents if only her brothers hadn't held her back from the sea.

This was a bad thing that was happening. And it was his job to send in the best people to make it better.

"This is the right thing to do, Lulu, and you know it."

She dug her heels in. "Don't keep me off this job, Zach."

He did the same. She'd pissed him off and he felt emotion blaze up in him like flames. "You know I have to. It's how this works. How the job works."

"Well, then, why don't you take your job and shove it?" she spat back.

"What?"

"You heard me. I quit."

She shifted her weight to her other hip, her expression flickering between rage and something else. Shock at what had just come out of her mouth.

"Lulu, you love this job."

"Not if you hog-tie me and won't let me do it."

"What the hell…? Don't be like this. You know it's out of my hands."

"I know you're the boss and what you say goes. And right now I don't like what you're saying."

She was out of line, and she knew it, but what scared him was that she didn't seem to care. Her defiant expression shot him back to the first day they'd met, when his gut had told him one thing: *This girl's nothing but trouble.*

He was wishing like hell he'd listened to his gut.

He'd known there'd be hurdles in their way when they crossed the line from professional to personal. But now they were tripping him up on a level he hadn't seen coming. What if the same thing happened with Harry? What if she were to round on his boy the way she was now, fighting something she knew was the right decision?

And just like that the slim thread that had been holding his heart in place snapped. He leaned into her. Close. Real close. So no one would hear but her. "I trusted you," he said. "I trusted you more than I've ever trusted anyone since—"

He stopped himself. He wasn't going to give Lulu the satisfaction of hearing his voice crack. Screw that. If one by-the-book move was all it took to make her turn and run he and Harry didn't need her in their lives. Not now. Not ever. Lesson learned.

He pressed himself up to his full height, his voice more arctic than he'd ever heard it. "Have your resignation on my desk by the time I get back."

And then he turned and walked away.

CHAPTER TWELVE

LULU SWERVED ROUND the corner toward the EMT headquarters, narrowly missing a camper van as it trundled past in the other direction. Her heart jackhammered against her rib cage. That had been close. Too close.

An increasingly uncomfortable niggle wormed its way through to her conscience. Zach had been right to pull her off the job. She was too strung out, too frenetic, too *frightened* to work properly. But she couldn't stand by and do nothing.

She'd been too young to help when her mother had paddled out to sea, shortly followed by her father. Too inexperienced, ill-equipped, emotional. But they'd had to physically hold her down to keep her from throwing herself in and following them.

"Needle in a haystack," she'd heard one of the rescue guys say to another when the rescue boats had eventually returned, with no celebratory horn-honking to convey a success.

Needle in a haystack.

Today's rescue wasn't going to be that different. Mud was standing in for the ocean. With the same power to kill. To absorb a human—her brother—into the earth as if he hadn't existed at all.

She yanked her car into the EMT personnel parking lot,

swearing under her breath when, once again, her lack of focus caused her to nearly end up bumper to bumper with an oncoming vehicle.

She grabbed her uniform from the back seat of her Jeep and ran into the office. Chen, one of Duke's high school football buddies, was on duty. When he glanced up from the call he'd just finished, he looked about as grim as she felt.

Before she could utter a word, he put up his hands. "No."

"What do you mean, no?" she bridled. "I haven't even asked you anything yet."

"Lulu. You've got a freaking uniform on your shoulder and a *Send me into the deep end* expression on your face. Not going to happen. They've got rescue crews in place and they're doing everything they can."

"*'They'* don't have me."

He mimicked her air quotes. "And *'they'* are all highly qualified rescue staff."

"They're not me."

"And they shouldn't be. You know the rules."

She wanted to scream. Kick something. She closed her eyes, regrouped and forced her voice to remain steady when she opened them again. "I know when there's a big accident it's all hands on deck. No matter what's going on."

It hadn't just been Duke and the stuntwoman riding a quad bike who'd been involved in the accident. There'd been the film crew and their support teams, too. Not everyone would've taken the fall Duke had, but there were some twenty-odd people fighting for their lives in one way or another and she wanted to be there. Helping.

"Not today, Lulu." He stood up and crossed to her.

She took a step back, needing to keep the space between them. He wasn't threatening her. He was coming in for a hug. But she didn't want it. Didn't deserve it.

Zach had been right.

She wasn't any good to anyone right now, and he'd been

between an enormous rock and an immovable hard place. The best, the kindest thing she could have done was to have accepted what he'd said and let him do his job.

Even though it had been a good twenty minutes since she'd torn out of his driveway and down the coastal highway into Honolulu, she was still feeling Zach's presence as if he was right there in front of her. She could almost smell him in her nostrils. Barbecue smoke, pineapple and little boy. She could feel him in her space, leaning in close, his face taut with disbelief and unspilled anger, barely speaking above a whisper as he'd breathed out his admonishment. *I trusted you.*

She'd crossed the line. Gone way too far. Her age-old fears had roared up and superseded everything else. She'd crushed everything they'd been building into the ground as if it had never mattered at all. Which, of course, was the complete opposite of how she really felt.

She loved him. She loved Harry. The huge vacuum their absence would create in her heart was an acute reminder that the only people she had ever been able to treat this recklessly and still expect to be loved were her family.

But she'd just learned the hard way that you couldn't be reckless with a fragile heart like Zach's. It bordered on cruel.

If the shoe had been on the other foot she would've grounded Zach, too. Would've kept him away from her kid. She probably would've given him something to do…something to make him feel useful…but sometimes—like that day she'd stood on the shore, waiting and waiting for her parents to return—the only thing you could do was pray.

Her phone had been buzzing and pinging with messages from her brothers, but the truth was she'd been too frightened to look. Too terrified to hear the news if it was bad. Which—again—confirmed that Zach's decision was the right one. She wasn't in the right headspace to be dangling from a helicopter or clawing through a mudslide without compromising her own life and possibly the lives of others. Zach had been doing what he always did. Looking out for her.

She gave her shoulders a shake and then asked the EMT dispatcher, "Have you heard anything about him? About Duke?"

The fact he was on the island at all was rare. They'd made plans to meet up now he'd got back from a film set somewhere in Africa, but had yet to make good on it. She cursed herself for not having made it a priority.

He'd always been one of her favorite big brothers, but perhaps that was because he was the one she knew the least. He was ten years older and rarely on the island, because his work took him round the world doing stunt work for some of the world's most famous action stars. Her memories of him were mostly from when she'd been a little kid. She'd always thought of him as the fun one. The one who'd throw her on his back and run her round the backyard, neighing and whinnying like he was a horse, when she'd gone through her *I want a pony* phase. The fact he'd become a stuntman had been a surprise to no one. Tall, muscular and fearless, he was every action film director's dream come true.

She couldn't begin to imagine a world that didn't have all that energy in it.

She felt her face muscles twitch as reality hit. No matter who she went to, how many favors she tried to beg, she was going to hit wall after wall after wall. The only thing she could do was what the rest of her family was doing. Wait for news.

She found Makoa and Pekelo at her grandmother's house. The three of them were staring blankly at tall glasses of iced tea, ice cubes long melted. Her grandmother filled her in. Laird was on a flight over from Maui and Kili, the navy SEAL, was being kept updated by his admiral on the aircraft carrier he was posted on somewhere on the other side of the world.

"Where's your boyfriend?" Mak asked.

What little composure Lulu had left crumpled.

"Hey!" Her brother was up and by her side in an instant. "What'd he do to you? Want us to run him back to the mainland? He's still on probation, right?"

"No, it's nothing like that. It's me. I'm the one who messed up," Lulu said, tears finally surfacing and trickling down her cheeks.

"What'd you do?"

"I quit. I quit my job." She could barely believe she'd been such a stupid idiot.

"Why?" Pekelo asked.

"He grounded me."

Mak snorted in disbelief. "Lulu, you got problems."

"Yeah? Tell me about it, Mr. Perfect!" she snapped.

He rapped his knuckles on the table, commanding their attention. "It's how it works, Mini. You don't get to pick and choose which rules to follow. They exist to keep us alive, yeah? You think I want to be here when I know I'd be more helpful up there? I won those search and rescue games for a reason. I'm the best there is. And they've grounded me. If I didn't know in my heart that those rules are right I'd be up on that hillside trying to dig my brother out with my bare hands!"

Lulu nodded and buried her head in her hands, ashamed of having taken Zach's decision so personally. And, yes, of course she knew exactly what Mak was talking about. She'd be doing exactly the same if she was allowed. They all would. But instead they were having to find the same faith the general public placed in them when they set out to rescue their loved ones.

I trusted you.

The words played on a loop in her mind, over and over, grating against all the other decisions she should have made.

How on earth was she going to fix this?

When she looked up, Makoa was waiting for her, expectant. "What's really going on, Mini?"

It was a good question. One that had got so tangled up in the melee she hardly remembered where all her churned up feelings had begun. And then, clear as a bell, she remembered Casey, sitting on that picnic table, as casual as could be, wondering aloud when Lulu would leave Zach.

Her stomach turned as she realized just how beautifully Casey had put a name to her predictability. How it had proved true so quickly. It had taken...what? Two minutes? Three? A tiny earthquake had cracked her world in two. One decision that she knew Zach had struggled to take and she'd snapped like a twig. She'd taken everything she felt for him and his son and shoved it in his face as if they meant nothing to her.

"I messed up," she finally admitted.

Makoa pulled another chair up to the table they were all gathered round and had her sit down. She poured her heart out to them. Told them everything. How she'd not been sure about Zach at first, how they'd seemed to clash so much, but how, eventually, she'd seen how similar they both were. She told them how they'd been fighting off deeply embedded fears and overcoming them. Together. And then she'd gone and ruined it all when she'd wanted to fix something she never could.

No matter how many rescues she went on, her parents would never, ever come back. She saw that now. Saw the futility of her misplaced anger. The destructiveness it had wrought in her life. Never enabling her to establish deep, enduring friendships or relationships until...until she'd gone and done it with the single most wonderful man she'd ever met. Zach Murphy.

Her grandmother, who had sat silently throughout her emotional outpouring, took a long drink of her tea, then said, "'A humble person walks carefully so as not to hurt others.'"

"I think I already messed that part up, Gran," Lulu said miserably. "Got any other sayings that might help me out of this mess?"

Her grandmother's lips softened and twitched lightly into a smile. "Quite a few."

"Lay 'em on me. All of them."

Her grandmother gave them each a thoughtful inspection. When her eyes landed on Lulu she said, "'A child behaves like those who reared her.'"

Lulu and her brothers sat up at that. "What do you mean?" she asked.

"You're all headstrong! Tempestuous. Too quick to decide upon a solution to a problem."

Lulu huffed out a dark laugh. "Jeez, Gran. Kick a girl when she's down, why don't you?"

Makoa gave her a light fist bump, but because they all loved and respected their grandmother they fell silent as she cleared her throat to continue.

"There's another side to those traits all of you possess. Bravery. Strength. Wisdom. Especially you, Lulu. But it's up to you which traits you most want the world to see."

The comment landed where it had been meant to. In her heart.

She knew now, beyond a shadow of a doubt, that she loved Zach. She would eat a thousand humble pies—more, if it would fix what had happened between them. He had a son he cared for more than himself. He knew exactly what sacrifice was. What trust was. And she'd all but spat on the trust she knew he held sacred.

She wasn't sure he would ever forgive her for it. But she had to find out. And there was only one way to go about it.

Earn both his forgiveness and his trust.

"I've got to go." She gave her brothers each a hug, and her grandmother an extralong one. "Thanks, Gran. Wish me luck."

Her grandmother pulled back, her arms still around her, and smiled. "You don't need luck, child. You need to do what you've taken a lifetime to realize."

"Which is?"

"Look to the future. It is the only way to make peace with the past."

And in that instant Lulu suddenly understood how her grandmother was able to have such a Zen-like relationship with life. She'd been as hollowed out by grief as the rest of them when Lulu's parents had died. But she'd had six grandchildren to help raise, their futures to think about. Being consumed by the pain of loss would never have helped anything or anyone.

Lulu had fallen victim to exactly that. Pinning the urgency of each and every rescue to some sort of scorecard she'd made with the universe. If, one day, she got enough points, she'd get the top job at work and her dream house. Neither of which would mean anything without Zach and Harry by her side.

She gave her gran's cheek a kiss, then said, "I'll meet you all at the hospital in a bit."

Mak frowned at her. "What are you talking about?"

"Duke's going to need us there. Whether he's in surgery or just suffering from a bruised ego. And we'll be there for him."

Pek frowned, and started to say something, but she cut him off. "If Duke's not there…we'll be there for everyone else. Yeah? Like he'd want us to be."

Their frowns turned into soft smiles and nods of affirmation.

She held up her phone. "Keep in touch, yeah? I've got to put a few things right."

"Are you going to answer it this time?" asked Mak.

"Every time," she said, meaning it.

She wouldn't ignore her family, her friends—the people who loved her most—anymore. It was time to become the woman she'd always wanted to be. A good one.

CHAPTER THIRTEEN

THE LANDSLIDE WAS BAD. Real bad.

The only way the two of them would've stood a chance of surviving was to have been thrown beyond the crush of iron soil, rock and tree roots.

The helicopter was doing its best to navigate the ravine, where any survivors would be found.

"Lower," Zach instructed as he eagle-eyed the sun glinting off a bit of silver. He was sure he could see it now. The handlebar of a quad bike. "A couple more meters, Stew."

Stewart's voice crackled through his earpiece. "That's as far as I can get the chopper down, Zach. You're either going to have unclip and risk having to hike out, or we need to find somewhere else to put you down."

He thought of Lulu's face. The way it had drained of blood as she'd heard the news about her brother. The way tears had poured down her cheeks as she had performed CPR on the "dead" mannequin back when they'd been in the search and rescue games. She didn't give up. Not until she had to. And he was a long way from having to.

"I'll unclip."

"Is that wise?"

No. It wasn't. But there weren't an awful lot of rational thoughts going through his head right now. What he should've done was taken himself off the job, too, but right now he needed work like he needed oxygen. It was his go-to coping mechanism—slapping the blinkers on, closing off the rest of the world, so that his brain had a chance to absorb whatever the hell it was that had happened and do something positive. Something helpful.

Guilt pierced through his focus.

Exactly like Lulu.

If she wasn't helping, all her demons swarmed in. And he'd left her there on her own, with nothing but her fears and a demand for her resignation as companions.

As he unclipped the stretcher, and then himself, dropping to his knees for a body roll to take the impact of the fall, realization dawned. This was his pattern. If he screwed something up he had to go fix something else. Anything but the actual problem. When his dad had got sick after 9/11 he'd retrained as a medic. When his son had been born with a disability he'd started running marathons for the cerebral palsy charity instead of spending time where he should have. In his marriage.

Cause and effect. Cause and effect.

He'd fallen in love with Lulu. It had scared the hell out of him—not having control over her, not being able to predict her next move. Or, more to the point, keep her safe.

He'd cornered her into quitting. Forced her hand when he knew better than anyone that being handed a shovel and told to dig would've been a kinder, more loving thing to do.

But he'd seen red and walked away. Had wanted control of a situation he had no capacity or right to control.

Letting his wife go had been the safest option for his son.

Letting Lulu go…

Every pore in his body was telling him it had been the wrong decision. A cowardly way of making her take the fall for a situation that scared the hell out of him. Loving someone who knew her own mind. Her strengths. Her weaknesses. And his.

She'd read him like a book and when he'd shown her his true colors, his fears masked as machismo, she hadn't wanted any part of it. He didn't blame her.

He felt the ground shift beneath his feet as he tried to stand. There were tens of thousands of tons of earth here. Displaced soil and rock from the cliff… And one handlebar from a quad bike.

He shot off a flare gun, hoping the fire and rescue crew hiking in from the coast would see it through the jungle canopy, then dropped to his knees, pulled his collapsible spade from his backpack and began to dig.

A few minutes later the ground crew arrived. Perimeters were marked out. Trajectories calculated for how far Duke and the other quad rider—a stuntwoman called Jessica—would've been thrown. They dug and dug and dug as if their lives depended upon it. Theirs might not, but Duke's and Jessica's did.

A shout went up. They'd found Duke.

Zach was by his side in an instant. He'd unearthed more than his fair share of survivors from collapsed structures and the odd sinkhole. He knew one false move could make the difference between life and death.

With infinite care, they unearthed him, relief flooding through the group like the sun coming out from behind a storm cloud when they discovered he was alive. He'd obviously sustained some internal injuries—that was made apparent by his low, thready pulse—but the fact he'd been wearing a helmet had played a massive role in his survival. From the angle of one of his legs, there would be at least one compound fracture to tend to as well.

After carefully securing him to the stretcher, Zach put a neck brace on him, checked for any outward signs of bleeding or additional compound fractures that needed immediate attention, and then, fairly certain that the only thing holding him together was his cleverly designed costume—

a padded motorcycle suit sewn into a business suit—left him intact.

Zach radioed Stewart, asking him to try to get the cables down one last time before they made the decision to walk him out. The half hour or so it would take to carry him to the nearest road was time that might mean the difference between life and death. And there was no way Zach was going to tell Lulu they hadn't done everything humanly possible to ensure the outcome they all wanted.

It took Stewart a minute or two longer than it normally would have, but he did it. Zach clipped himself to the safety basket and rode up with Duke, telling him over and over how much his family was looking forward to seeing him again…how much they cared…how he should hang on because help was close at hand.

When they landed on the roof of the hospital, emergency medical staff were there to take over, but Zach ran in with them, anyway.

"You can't come in, man," said one of the doctors, his eyes on Zach's dirt-covered uniform. "Operating room has to stay sterile."

Zach backed off, the swinging doors of the OR practically hitting him in the face. He felt his phone vibrate. He grabbed it out of his safety vest. Twenty messages were sitting there. The phone buzzed again. Twenty-one. All of them from Lulu.

She was here. In the hospital. He wasn't to worry, but—

He jammed the phone in his pocket and took off for the emergency room entrance at a run, heart pounding, brain buzzing with too many possibilities—all of them dark—to let just one take purchase.

He scanned the busy waiting room. He saw Harry first, and then Lulu. They were playing a board game on a little table in the children's play area. Lulu was keeping Harry actively engaged while sending yet another text under the table out of Harry's eye line.

Zach didn't know what he felt. Relief. Gratitude. Fear. They weren't here for the fun of it.

"Duke's in surgery," he said.

"Your dad's had a heart attack," Lulu said at the same time.

"He's going to make it." They spoke simultaneously. Then again. "You go."

Nervous laughter filled the space between them until Zach gestured for her to speak.

"Your dad had a heart attack. He's alive. I got some aspirin into him straight away, which helped. He's getting a couple of stents put in, but other than that he should be good as new. Your mom's with him now."

Harry grabbed his dad in a waist-high hug and beamed up at him. "Lulu saved Grandpa!"

Zach shook his head, not understanding. "Were you in the ambulance?"

"No. I was over at your parents'."

He gave her a blank look.

She lowered her voice, giving Harry's head a little scrub. "I owed this little man an apology for running out on him. And your parents. And you." She winced and gave an apologetic smile. "I might've said a few things I didn't mean…"

"You had every right. I was thinking more like an overprotective boyfriend than a boss."

She opened her mouth and goldfished, a sheen of emotion glossing her eyes.

"Don't cry, Lulu!" Harry dug into his pocket and handed her a tissue.

She thanked him and looked across at Zach, as though she wanted to say something but couldn't.

Harry jumped in and explained how Lulu had come over and apologized to them all for leaving the barbecue.

"She said she was scared for her brother, and needed to see her family, but that made her realize she felt like *we* were family, too! She said she loved you, Daddy. That you made her a better person." He started singing a little song, the lyrics composed of three words. "Lulu loves Daddy… Lulu loves Daddy…"

Their eyes met, and the connection was so strong between them that Zach felt as if she had actually handed him her heart.

Lulu still loved him.

Harry tugged his hand, keen to finish his story. "And then Grandma and Grandpa were so happy they said we better have ice cream. So Grandpa went to the freezer, but he fell down, and Lulu pressed on his chest until the ambulance came, and now he's okay."

Again his eyes snapped to hers. "You did CPR on my dad?"

She nodded. "And you dug my brother out of a mountain."

And there it was. Love in a nutshell. You did whatever you had to do, whether or not you knew that your love was going to be returned.

A not entirely settled peace surrounded them. They both had questions. Lots of them.

They started with facts.

He filled her in on how they'd found Duke and the injuries he thought he had. "I suspect he'll need quite a bit of recovery time, and a lot of physio, but from the looks of this waiting room he's got a pretty amazing support team."

They both looked round and saw that the room had filled up. It was so full, friends were actually having to wait outside as well as in.

"Thank you," she said, her voice scratchy with emotion. "You went above and beyond. If you hadn't pushed things…" she took a wavery breath "…he might not have a recovery to fight through."

Zach shook his head. "I did what I had to."

"You did more than that," she replied, with a fierceness that warmed him straight through to his heart. "I have it on good authority that you stepped outside the rule book to find him."

"What? How?"

Lulu pointed over to another section of the waiting room— one that was filled to the gunnels with tall, muscular, dark-haired men in various uniforms. Her brothers and their in-laws, and their brothers, and everyone else she'd grown up with. There in the middle of them was Makoa, who gave her a little flick of the chin to say he saw what was going on.

A gathering like this a year ago—hell, a month ago— would've sent her running for the ocean, surfboard tucked under her arm, ready to paddle out as far and as fast as she could. Doubly so if they'd caught her baring her heart to someone right here in the middle of it all.

But she'd learned something today. Protectiveness didn't have to mean suffocation. It could mean support. Something to hold all the emotions she felt in balance, catching her as she negotiated the best course of action. Sometimes she'd be right. Sometimes she'd be wrong.

She'd been wrong to think Zach was trying to sideline her.

She'd been right to find his parents and Harry, even not knowing if Zach would speak with her again.

When Harry saw where Lulu was looking, he waved at Mak. Her brother grinned at the little boy, his hand instantly folding into the island greeting. Harry jumped up and down, thrilled to have someone so spectacular singling him out for a *shaka*.

Mak, clearly sensing that Lulu and Zach were having an important talk, beckoned the little boy over.

"You cool with that?" Lulu asked, hanging on to the hood of Harry's hoodie so that he wouldn't run off.

"Of course," Zach said. "I know he'll be safe."

It was his version of saying that he trusted her and her family, and it meant the world. He might as well have got down on bended knee and asked her to spend the rest of his life with her. Told her he loved her. But they weren't there just yet.

Lulu gave Mak a wave of thanks when she saw him pick the boy up and start introducing him to everyone as Harry the Beast, well aware that a six-year-old around a sea of supersize men would be a lot to handle.

Mahalo, she mouthed to her brother, and then to Zach she said, "I heard Duke was coming in from Casey. I was already here with your dad, so I let these guys know. They wanted to be here in case—you know—in case it hadn't gone according to plan..." She continued in a rush. "Everyone's gathered here now, and they will head out to help the crews who are looking for Jessica." Her eyes flicked to the waiting room clock. "Only a couple more hours until sunset."

She looked up at him. His blue eyes were filled with the love she'd been so frightened of receiving. The love she had to put through one more test.

"If it's cool with you, I'm going to help."

Zach pulled her to him and tipped his head to hers. "I shouldn't have stopped you before. It wasn't my place."

"No," she corrected. "You were right. I was out of my mind. I needed the proverbial slap in the face."

He flinched and pulled back at her choice of words.

She held up her hands. "I know you weren't doing what you did to hurt me. Quite the opposite."

He nodded. "I've got to go see my dad—but, Lulu, we need to talk. Properly."

"I know. We will. For as long as we need to. Days, if necessary. Which reminds me…" She dug in her pocket for a piece of paper. "I have to give you this."

He knew what it was without looking at it. "No. I won't accept it."

"You have to."

"No, I don't."

She gave a gentle laugh, her features softening with affection. "You made me realize something really important today."

"What? That you hated your boss?"

"No. That I really, genuinely, do not want that job anymore."

"What? You love it."

"I do…but I love giving back more."

He shook his head, clearly not understanding.

"I want to work for Superstars Surf Club. Full-time."

"I don't understand… I thought Chantal was the only paid staff member."

"She was," Lulu said. "Until she got an offer to set up another Superstars Surf Club in Australia."

Zach let out a low whistle. "That sounds like an offer that would be hard to say no to." His brow creased. "How did you fit all these things into an afternoon? Visiting your family, my family, saving my dad's life, writing a resignation letter and finding a new job?"

She gave him a sheepish smile. "I can do a lot when I put my mind to it."

His smile was soft and sincere, infused with the deep kindness she'd first spotted in him back when she'd thought he was someone who would make her life hell. Meeting him hadn't been hell, but she felt as though she'd been through a journey. One of those epic, life-changing ones that had taken her heart and mind and plunged her deep into the parts of her life she'd been actively ignoring.

Falling in love with Zach had meant confronting demons and, to her disbelief, she had come out whole. Better than whole. She was in love, and she couldn't wait to spend a lifetime of sharing this amazing feeling with Zach and Harry.

He ran a couple of fingers through her hair, tucking it back behind her ear. "I love you, Lulu Kahale. You're mad as a hatter, but you're good for me. You remind me that being a better person doesn't always mean sticking to the rule book."

"I love you, too. And Harry," she added, wanting him to know that she knew they came as a package deal. She went up on tiptoe and gave him a kiss. "Go see your dad. I'll meet you in a few hours, yeah?"

He returned the kiss, and the depth of connection they'd just shared was transferred between them like energy. She'd never do anything again to compromise what they had together. No matter what.

"*Mahalo*, Zach."

"Thank you? For what?"

"For being you. For taking a chance on me."

"There was no chance in this, my love," Zach said, cupping her cheeks with his hands. "This was destiny. And don't you forget it."

She wouldn't. She wouldn't ever forget. Not as long as she had a heart beating in her chest.

EPILOGUE

One year later

LULU HID BEHIND a palm tree, watching as everyone filtered down onto the beach, where there were huge plank benches spread in a massive circle. And her grandmother, her brothers—Duke walking without his cane for the first time in a year.

They were all so different from the people they'd been just one year ago.

Duke had ended up needing months of recovery in the hospital. His injuries had been far more profound than they'd originally thought. He'd spent those long months not only diligently following his strict rehab routine, but coming up with new safety guidelines for stuntmen and women.

Today he was pushing Jessica in her new wheelchair, sportier than the one she'd initially had after her injuries had made it clear she wouldn't walk again. But she swam. Every day with her rehab specialist in the pool, and twice a week with Lulu in the ocean, on a surfboard kitted out with special support harnesses.

Makoa was wearing a traditional outfit, of course. As were her grandmother and her brother Laird. Kili was wearing his Navy dress whites uniform and looking stupidly handsome, even if he was her brother. And Pekelo was wearing one of his trademark Hawaiian sunset shirts... the goof.

All of them were wearing leis. All of them except for Lulu, who was wearing a crown of flowers because today, of all of the days in her life, she truly felt like Hawaiian royalty.

Harry had insisted upon wearing a traditional Hawaiian shirt, covered in flowers and surfboards. Zach was wearing a gorgeous linen suit that, if possible, made him look even more gorgeous than he'd been that first day, when she'd seen him and thought, *Uh-oh, here we go... Fire and ice don't mix.*

But it turned out they did when they worked together. Lived together. Loved together.

When most of the guests had arrived, Mak pulled out the family's conch shell horn and sounded several long calls—the Hawaiian way of calling the gathering together and bringing everyone they'd asked to join them into the same mind space—into the beautiful reflective energy that was charged with the power of bringing Zach and Lulu together as husband and wife.

As the reverend began to chant the *Oli Aloha*, Lulu began her journey down the "aisle" to the center of the circle, where Zach stood. They'd agreed together that they wanted a circle. A shared space for friends and family to witness their public declaration of shared love. A reminder that once they were joined together they wouldn't just be two people—or, in their case, three—but an entire community made up of family and friends. It fitted perfectly with the *Oli Aloha*'s verses, which spoke of seeking a loved one, finding them and becoming one with each other and with all who loved them.

Throughout the ceremony—complete with the exchanging of leis and the Hawaiian ring blessing—Zach and Lulu beamed at one another. They'd been through it all with the reverend several times, but this time it was as if every cell in their bodies knew it was the one that counted.

Once they had exchanged their vows, and their hands had been bound together with a lei for a blessing that reminded them that it wasn't anything physical that bound them together, it was love, they were invited to kiss and seal the marriage.

Zach pulled her so close to him she actually felt her feet lift up and off the ground. The guests began to laugh.

"Why are they laughing?" Zach whispered against her lips. "Don't they do kissing the bride in Hawaii?"

"They do," she said, kissing him in between ever fewer words. "But normally the bride's flip-flops don't fall off when the groom kisses her."

"Just like Cinderella!" He grinned.

"Better than Cinderella," she said, as the reverend asked them to face one another for the final step of the ceremony.

"Why's that?" asked Zach, reluctantly returning her to the ground, weaving his fingers through hers.

"Because Prince Charming lives in a castle and we live somewhere far, far superior."

They grinned and looked up at Turtle Hideaway, which was absolutely covered in tropical flowers and looked more as if it should be a float in an Aloha Parade than the place where they were going to spend their honeymoon.

The reverend began to recite the *He Alo A He Alo*.

Lulu beamed at Zach as the short prayer invited them to share *aloha* in their marriage.

"For those of you who do not know," said the reverend, "*Alo* means person and *ha* means breath. Together Lulu and Zach will honor the breath of life they have each been given and the added strength that comes from the love they share."

"Do we get to kiss again?" Zach asked.

"By all means. It's your life to live. Together."

And that was the joy of giving herself to Zach, Lulu thought as she willingly tucked herself into her husband's warm embrace. Giving meant receiving. Until she'd learned to give herself completely to him, without any hope or expectation of anything in return, she hadn't known the true meaning of love. And now that she had it was better than she could ever have imagined.

* * * * *

TEMPTED BY HER CONVENIENT HUSBAND

CHARLOTTE HAWKES

MILLS & BOON

To Vic.
Happy Birthday to the newest little wolf
in your fearless pack! X

CHAPTER ONE

'How long has the kid been on the oxytocin drip, Oti?'

'Two hours,' Octavia Hendlington murmured softly. 'Six drops per minute.'

Not turning around as her colleague joined her, Oti continued to eye the young woman perched uncomfortably on the end of the bed and being cared for by her sister. The labour ward—or what passed for the labour ward in this end of the large hospital tent in her medical camp in South Sudan—was tiny.

But they had worked so many miracles in this place over the past four years, she could only hope tonight—her last night—would be a good one.

'Dilation?' Amelia queried.

'She's been at six centimetres for the past ten hours. Her name is Kahsha; she's eighteen, primigravida.'

'And the baby's head still shows no sign of descending?' Amelia frowned.

Oti's teeth worried at her lower lip, and she stopped herself abruptly. In a matter of days she would be back in the UK, and her father would not accept such unattractive, *unladylike* habits.

Five more days of being herself, and then she would be back to playing a role again.

Would her new husband be just as irritated by her as her

father had always been? Oti shoved the thought from her head and focused on her colleague.

'No sign of the baby descending at all,' she told Amelia.

She cast her gaze around the tent and tried to swallow down the thick lump of emotion that lodged itself so uncomfortably in her throat. If it hadn't been for the fact that it looked as if it was going to be a complicated labour, Oti might have been grateful for the distraction from her own thoughts tonight.

She had been volunteering with the medical charity HOP—Health Overseas Project—for four years, ever since her brother's accident, and this was the only place where she'd ever felt herself. Possibly the only time in her life—certainly in the last fifteen years.

Dr Oti.

It was simple and clean, and she thought that was perhaps what she loved the most. Out here, far away from the clamour of home, it was just about helping people and making a difference.

She had value.

Surely that was as uncomplicated as it got?

But soon that would all be over. And it didn't matter which mask she would be donning this time—Oti the socialite, the It-girl, or Lady Octavia Hendlington, daughter of the Earl of Sedeshire and soon-to-be Lady Octavia Woods—it would still suffocate her, just the same.

What would Amelia and the other volunteers think if they knew she was about to marry the much-lusted-after billionaire, Lukas Woods? Or *Sir* Lukas Woods—given the knighthood he had received in the previous year's New Year's Honours list. Not the youngest recipient, but certainly one of the youngest.

Busying herself with the oxytocin drip, as though occupying her hands could also occupy her wayward mind, Oti tried to pretend that her stomach hadn't just flip-flopped at the thought.

The man was one of the most eligible bachelors in the world right now—certainly one of the most eligible in the country—and in five days she would be marrying him. The thought was terrifying.

Lukas Woods wasn't merely good-looking...he was practically elemental. As though there was fire, earth, wind and water...and then there was *him*. And that beautifully muscled exterior was rivalled only by his inner core of pure steel. Ruthless business magnate, media personality and self-made billionaire. How many other kids had written an app at the age of fifteen, and made their first million by the age of eighteen?

She might have met him on only that one intimidating occasion five months earlier, but it had been enough to leave her with the impression that he might as well have been honed from the very magma of the planet itself.

How was she ever to endure a marriage to this man? This stranger? What if she couldn't even stand him?

Her body prickled in protest, and she ignored the tiny voice inside taunting her that she already knew the answer to that question.

Then again, the alternative had been a forced marriage to Louis Rockman, son of the Sixth Earl of Highmount, vicious, dictatorial and cruel. Even now, fifteen years on, she could still feel the grip of his fingers biting into her arms, his weight pinning her down...

'You're thinking a C-section?'

Amelia's voice dragged her mercifully back to the present.

'Yes. But now Kahsha wants to return to her own village to seek out help from a traditional healer.'

'Right.' Amelia nodded grimly. 'It's her choice, Oti.'

Oti dipped her head. They both knew that they couldn't

stop the young girl from seeking traditional help if that was what she chose to do. HOP had long drilled it into their volunteers that they were there to offer medical advice and options, but not dictate. Some of the women they encountered had little enough autonomy over their own lives as it was. They didn't need a group of foreigners swooping in and taking away their choices on how they wanted to give birth.

It was enough that the charity's volunteers showed respect for the decisions the Sudanese women made about their own deliveries and their own health.

'It just doesn't help when it isn't what's medically best for them.' Oti folded her arms over her chest, making her friend frown at her.

'You okay? I've never seen you quite this on edge.'

Oti had no idea how she managed to summon what she hoped was a bright smile.

'Of course. Just tired probably. It's been another twenty-hour shift.'

Her colleague looked unconvinced, and Oti knew why. Shifts were always long in a camp like this, but she'd never been this down. Perhaps a version of the truth would be better. She tried ramping the smile up a little more.

'I'm think I'm going to miss this place.'

'I'm so sorry.' Amelia grimaced, understanding washing over her expression. 'I forgot you were leaving tomorrow. But you'll be back in a few months, right? You always are. What is it now, forty months out of the past four years that you've been out here?'

'Something like that.' Oti forced a laugh, as though she was any normal person looking forward to spending some time back home again. Ironically, another role that she knew how to play.

She hadn't told anyone that this would be her last mission, any more than she'd told them that she was getting married. It would only invite too many questions that she wouldn't know how to answer.

Or perhaps it was more that saying it aloud would somehow make it too real.

'Go and get something to eat, and get your head down,' her colleague advised. 'You've got a five-hour drive just to the nearest airstrip.'

'Sure.' It felt more like an awkward jerk of her head than a nod, but at least Amelia didn't seem to notice anything amiss.

She felt foolish. But what choice did she have, either about telling her colleagues, or about agreeing to the marriage in the first instance?

You could have said no, a voice whispered in her head, but Oti shut it down quickly.

True, Lukas Woods had asked her if she was sure she knew what she was doing, but declining him had never been a real option. Not if she wanted to save her brother. Her father had made that abundantly clear.

Her father hadn't earned the title The Odious Earl for nothing, even if no one dared say it to his face. Not even her.

Especially not her.

Shaking her head free of the dark thoughts that threatened to overtake her, Oti watched the young mum-to-be struggle off the bed with the help of her sister and managed another smile at her colleague.

'I think I might accompany Kahsha just a short way out of camp. You never know, the walking might help the baby to descend and we won't need to try for a C-section after all.'

It was always possible. And, anyway, if this was to be her last trip out to Sub-Saharan Africa for a while—or ever—then she might as well absorb every last second of it.

Because all she saw for her future were even more fences to hem her in than she'd ever had to endure before.

* * *

As the organist played a virtuosic performance of Bizet's 'Farandole,' Lukas watched his bride being led up the aisle by her father. Though *led* might be too mild a word for it, given that the man could evidently barely restrain himself. The Odious Earl—a nickname that the man had earned for his pomposity, his gambling and his penchant for young girls barely older than his own daughter—was practically racing to deliver Lady Octavia to her fate.

Not that Lukas cared to look too closely, but he was sure that if he did he would actually be able to see pound signs imprinted in the Earl's eyes, the older man's podgy fingers virtually grasping for the hefty sum of money that would be his on conclusion of the ceremony.

Involuntarily, Lukas's gaze shifted to the taller than average, slightly willowy figure walking beside him with no fewer than seven bridesmaids in tow, although she eclipsed every one of them. An observation which he chose to ignore—along with the inconvenient and somewhat galling way that his body tightened in response.

This marriage wasn't about love, or even lust. It was about securing the controlling interest in Octavia's late brother's company, Sedeshire International, as the latest acquisition for Lukas's own company, LVW Industries. Preferably before the idiot Earl ran his late son's company into the ground, as he had been doing in the short time that he'd had his hands on it.

And if marrying the old Earl's socialite daughter was the price he had to pay for it—along with an eye-watering sum, of course—then Lukas considered it money well spent.

The business was actually a good investment, but the fact that he'd stolen it from right under the nose of Andrew Rockman, the Sixth Earl of Highmount, had been a delicious bonus.

How fitting that this was how Lukas would finally be

able to fulfil the vow he had made to himself as a twelve-year-old, the week his mother had been lowered into that black hole in the ground—that he would one day take his revenge on the Rockman family. In particular that he would take his revenge on Rockman, the man who had effectively driven her there, along with Lady Octavia's father, the man who had helped Rockman get away with his lies.

And, by marrying him, Lady Octavia would unwittingly help him to bring her repugnant father into line.

Yet as Lukas watched their approach closely, he was sure he saw her wobble. The faintest stumble before her father lowered his head to hers and murmured something that looked tender but which Lukas imagined was anything but. His bride-to-be seemed to stiffen her resolve even as a beatific smile graced her full mouth, and her eyes flickered up to meet Lukas's own.

And something slammed into him.

Just as it had five months ago, when he'd visited Sedeshire Hall to ensure that she knew and agreed to the marriage, only for Lady Octavia to walk—no, *stride*—into that conservatory at her family home, carrying herself like a queen rather than a mere *lady*. She'd made his entire body leap on sight, even as she'd declared confidently that, deal or not, she knew what she was doing and she was prepared to marry him.

As though the decision had been hers.

Desire had walloped him then, just as it did now. Hard. Like a punch to the gut when a fighter dropped his guard in a bout—which he *never* did. He'd wanted her right there and then. Like nothing he'd ever known before.

And then she'd fixed him with that inscrutable stare of hers—with eyes far too intelligent and fierce and assessing than the air-headed, social-climbing creature he'd been led to believe she was.

Making him wonder at the veracity of all those rumours.

Making him wonder if she really was such a vacuous socialite and making him want to piece together the fascinating puzzle that this woman suggested she was.

And that killer body that she seemed to have absolutely no idea that she possessed.

He'd known she was pretty enough. The photos of her exploits as an It-girl—clad in scraps of metallic dress or barely-there bikinis—revealed as much, though he'd believed that her personality would be as plasticky as so many socialites of his acquaintance. Perhaps that explained why he hadn't been prepared for the almost visceral reaction he'd had to her.

In that one moment, five months ago, he'd been taken over by a desire that he'd never experienced before in his life. He had never wanted a woman so badly, with such a *need* that he thought he might go mad if he didn't have her.

And yet at the same time, crazily, he'd wanted to protect her. From her father. And maybe from others. Perhaps that was the part of it which made the least sense.

He'd wanted to throw her over his shoulder and carry her out of that place, and if he'd had a damned horse then he'd believed he might have thrown her over that too. Rescuing her as if he was some medieval knight instead of a modern-day one, and she was his damsel in distress.

He, who had never been given to flights of fantasy in all his years.

It was the moment Lukas had realised that Lady Octavia Hendlington was the last woman on earth he should ever marry. Yet he'd done nothing to stop it, and now this vision was gliding gracefully up the aisle towards him, and she was no pretty-but-plastic girl. She appeared every inch a stunning woman with an indefinable quality that Lukas could neither put his finger on nor dismiss.

It unsettled him.

Not for the first time, he felt the tiptoeing steps of doubt creep into his brain, casting the faintest black shadow.

And, not for the first time, Lukas shut it out.

So she was attractive. It meant nothing that he noticed—he was, after all, a red-blooded male—but it didn't mean he couldn't control it, this jolt of heat that she seemed capable of igniting within him.

Attraction was fleeting; flames died. And, no matter how innocent his bride-to-be appeared on the outside, he could not afford to forget that Lady Octavia Hendlington was an autumn crocus—beautiful to look at and seemingly harmless, but in reality she was toxic right through. Just like her father.

Finally, she drew to an elegant halt beside him and he was suddenly struck once again by quite how vivid, how piercing her eyes were. A blue that almost seemed to reach inside him and strike that black thing which had long since resided where a heart would normally be.

He couldn't bring himself to look away. Worse, he didn't want to.

So as she stood before him, calmly allowing her bridesmaids to sort out the ridiculously long train of her wedding gown, Lukas fought to rein himself in, telling himself that the interlude was also a chance to get a grip on his own traitorous reactions.

'You made it then,' he remarked drily. For her ears only. As though engaging in banal conversation could somehow lessen her impact on him.

But, as she tilted her head up to him even further, that punch became a fist, tightening around his lower gut. He forced himself to ignore it.

'Did you think I wouldn't?' she asked.

'It crossed my mind. Especially since your father told me that you were at your *special* spa retreat, which I understand is your social circle's euphemism for *rehab*. Again.'

'I wasn't in rehab,' she bit out, and he couldn't have said why he thought she hadn't intended to speak.

For a moment it appeared that she was going to say something else, but then she blinked at him and closed her mouth. The air seemed to shift around them, leaving Lukas uncharacteristically unsettled. As though he'd somehow missed the mark.

But he hadn't. It had been well-documented in the media that the first time she'd attended some kind of rehab she'd been fifteen, about the time her out-of-control partying had really begun to hit the headlines. Although she'd been decidedly more discreet in the past decade or so, the rumours had persisted.

That was presumably why her father had insisted on Lukas marrying her as part of the deal for Sedeshire International.

Without warning, his bride-to-be turned her head elegantly to look around the cathedral.

'Verging on overkill, don't you think?'

He followed her eyes as she glanced around. Bedecked in flowers, with the bells pealing and the world-renowned organist still playing, it was acutely apparent that no expense had been spared. Ordered—though none of it paid for—by her father, of course.

Luxurious wreaths and wide velvet ribbons hung from the magnificent, towering stone columns, while generous bouquets of calla lilies and baby's breath decorated each and every pew filled with the four hundred or so guests.

'Precisely how I believe you instructed it,' Lukas replied drily.

Or perhaps, more likely, as had been instructed by some young twenty-something would-be party planner, and the Earl's latest badly kept secret.

If he hadn't known better, he might have thought his

bride-to-be actually winced. But if she did, she caught herself quickly.

'Of course. And the fitted lace gown, a six-foot-long train and thirty silk buttons complete with rouleau loops?' she bit out.

'It's from the most sought-after designer of the moment—just as I believe you requested.'

'Really? You believe I requested a wedding gown so tight that I had to pour myself into it and then be sewn in place?' She couldn't help herself; her discreet tone did nothing to disguise the barbed note to her words. 'It leaves nothing to the imagination.'

The organist was concluding now and the bishop was preparing to deliver his address, so Lukas had to move his head even closer to her ear to ensure they weren't heard.

Instantly he became aware that her scent—fresh and light, and not remotely cloying—was assailing his senses.

Making his body tighten all the more.

'If you'd wanted a say in the design of your wedding dress, and if you weren't in rehab, *Lady* Octavia…' he didn't know why he felt the need to emphasise her name just then—perhaps to keep his mind on the game? '…then perhaps you should have bothered to come back and deal with it, rather than spending the last few months partying and sunning yourself on one beach after the next.'

She glowered. 'Are you guessing now?'

'I don't need to. Your glowing tan rather gives it away,' he made himself say. 'But, either way, does it matter?'

There was the briefest of pauses, as though she wanted to say something—perhaps along the lines that it mattered to her. But instead she flashed a bright smile which he couldn't help feeling was a little too practised.

'Of course not.' Her smile had an edge that felt an awful lot like a blade. 'I've long held the title of Sedeshire's lost cause heiress, after all.'

'Then all the more reason to make it a show and quell any rumours that this is some hastily arranged marriage simply because you are pregnant with my—or any other man's—child.'

She bristled, though he suspected he was the only one close enough to spot it.

'Does that title concern you?' he couldn't help himself from asking.

'Lost cause heiress?' Her head snapped up. 'Of course not. I learned years ago not to care what anyone thought.'

He couldn't have said why, but he didn't entirely believe her.

'And, for what it's worth, the lace alone on your bridesmaids' gowns took months to sew,' Lukas added, 'so there will be no question that this wedding took care, and planning, and time. I hope you enjoyed those last months of heady indulgence. But I should warn you, your partying lifestyle is now at an end.'

'How very autocratic of you,' she bit out before she could stop herself. 'And between the intricate lace of my bridesmaids' dresses and the tightness of this one to show that there is no baby bump concealed beneath, I'm flattered that you paid such close attention.'

'As you should be.'

Before she could work out whether he was serious or still mocking, he flashed her a wolfish smile.

'Perhaps, though, having you as the mother of my heir could be a wise selection. Good stock, as they say.'

He knew he would score a hit even before he said the words. There had never been any mention of heirs before, even if he couldn't entirely explain what had made him even say it.

It seemed his bride-to-be got under his skin a little too much, but she didn't need to know that. Neither did she need to know that he was lying about heirs; he had never had any intention of ever perpetuating his cold, damaged bloodline.

Not with a father—biologically, if nothing else—like his.

Still, something in Lukas had uttered the words, and now he relished the way his soon-to-be-bride practically bubbled with indignation.

And something else he chose not to identify.

CHAPTER TWO

HE COULD NOT be serious?

Oti bristled as his eyes raked over her and pretended that he didn't leave a scorching trail of awareness right from the top of her head to the tips of her toes. And everything in between.

Especially everything in between.

'And should I present my head for inspection so that you can ensure there are no bulges or depressions which may indicate any dental issues?' she sniped, her voice just on the brink of being loud enough to be overheard, before she caught herself. 'Perhaps you'd care to examine my legs to ensure they're symmetrical and well balanced, and that there is no sensitivity or similar problem to the structure?'

'I'll presume that's how you inspect a horse or some such animal, shall I?' His low voice seemed to ripple the air in the space between them. 'How clichéd that someone with your upbringing should use that as a frame of reference.'

'And how banal that a self-made man from one of the worst estates in the country would look down on me for doing so,' she shot back acerbically, though she made sure the smile never slipped from her lips.

'Touché,' he acknowledged instead. 'It seems we each continue to prejudge the other.'

'Although, in my case, I believe my judgement is rather more accurate, is it not?'

Even as she said it, she couldn't stop herself from shivering at the way every single person was watching her. Prejudging her in exactly the way that Lukas was talking about.

Weighing her up. Measuring her. Damning her.

All of them wanting to know what she'd done to land the much-chased infamous playboy and marriage-phobic Lukas Woods.

He'd been right about the dress—as galling as that was— half of them probably thought she was already pregnant. Deliberately.

'Smile,' he instructed brusquely, offering a flash of straight white teeth that any onlooker might believe was a genuine smile.

And Oti obeyed, ignoring the way her heart was pounding in her chest—assuring her that her adrenaline was all fired up and ready to carry her at speed, straight back out and to the waiting car.

But she couldn't. Not just because of her father, whose grip on her arm had been so tight as he'd propelled her down the aisle that she could still feel the bruise forming under her skin even now. Not just because she couldn't bring herself to humiliate Lukas like that, when, despite everything, he had at least given her a chance—two chances—to back out of this marriage. But because she had no idea where that would leave Edward.

Edward—how could she leave him to their father? Her heart had practically broken the last time she'd visited and he'd begged her to help him end it all with dignity, only to threaten to ban her from visiting again when she'd refused.

'Octavia? What is it?'

She tried to speak but choked on the words, yet the bishop droned on, oblivious, mercifully too caught up in his own self-important role to notice.

'Did he hurt you?'

She blinked, taking a moment to realise that she was massaging the tender spot on her arm. She dropped her hand instantly. Lukas already looked furious, as though he was just looking for an excuse to call the wedding off.

She couldn't blame him; marrying Lukas, taking his money, was all a lie. But it would give her a chance to help save Edward's life, so how could she refuse?

'Of course he didn't hurt me,' she lied smoothly. But she couldn't help adding, 'After all, my father *is* an honourable man.'

She hadn't expected Lukas to get the reference, but he arched an eyebrow almost imperceptibly.

'Marc Antony?' his voice rumbled. 'His oration at Julius Caesar's funeral.'

It was a long-standing joke between her and Edward. She certainly hadn't expected Lukas Woods to get it. She blinked quickly.

'Yes.'

'Interesting,' he murmured, his eyes holding hers.

Rare, dark granite-grey with perhaps the faintest hint of a midnight blue flecked through them. And they rooted her to the mosaic floor.

'If you see yourself as some kind of Marc Antony, and your father as Brutus, then who might you cast in the role of Cassius, I wonder? Or even Caesar himself?'

Wordlessly, Oti stared at him.

If she'd hoped that her months away would diminish the effect he had on her—even during their one single meeting, five months ago in the conservatory of Sedeshire Hall—then Oti now realised she'd been wholly naïve.

'I keep looking at you and thinking you present yourself as quite the incapable, guileless young woman in this entire agreement. But you aren't, are you?'

She blinked. It was true that she wasn't herself around Lukas. She hadn't been even from that first moment.

For a woman who had always prided herself on her gentle nature and giving personality, she seemed to turn into this smart-mouthed sass machine whenever Lukas Woods was near. It would have been disconcerting if she hadn't decided it was a good defence mechanism. And she was only with him for Edward's sake. Not her own.

'Perhaps we should try needling each other a little less?' he suggested as the bishop began to wrap up his opening speech. 'Given that we're about to become husband and wife.'

Husband and wife.

Oti knew it had been meant as a light quip, but the words echoed through her head as a strange sensation poured through her. And this time it had nothing to do with the low, impossibly rich voice that coiled around her unexpectedly, seeming to permeate her very bones and making her feel...*odd.* Or the way his mouth was so close to her ear that his warming breath brought jolts of unwanted attraction straight down her centre. To her core.

Husband and wife, it echoed again.

And she tried to pretend that something didn't kick hard in her chest. Or lower, if she were to be shamefully honest.

What was she thinking, taking on a man like this... marrying him?

Even for her brother. But what choice had she had? She could finally see the light at the end of the proverbial tunnel, when the last four years had pitched them all into the blackness. How could she have done anything but run towards it and hope that it was the way out, and not another oncoming train?

It was odd, wasn't it? The way her life seemed to be cleaved into such clear segments. It was as if she'd been reeling from one thing to another—her attack, her mother's death, then Edward's accident—these past fifteen years. Reacting. Countering. Hopelessly out of control. But always playing catch-up.

She hadn't had time to breathe or think. Or even work out the person she was.

She'd thought she'd been getting closer to finding herself these last years with HOP. Working in South Sudan had been the first thing that had truly felt her own. It had helped to ground her. At least her last memory out there was of the walk with the young mum Kahsha, where the prolonged exercise had finally helped the baby to shift and descend.

Now there was a five-day-old baby back near their camp called Ayshani-Oti. Her heart actually felt as though it was going to swell its way out of her chest.

If only her father's Machiavellian wrangling hadn't once again caught up with her. He started fires wherever he went. Destroyed everything. He'd used Edward against her, and she'd had no choice but to fling herself once more into a burning building in the hope that she could put the fire out.

Only this time the fire was Lukas Woods. And she couldn't help fearing that he was going to be the one to finally burn her.

'If any person present knows of any lawful impediment to this marriage, speak now or for ever hold your peace.'

Oti tuned back in as the bishop was speaking, the silence descending in the cathedral seeming suddenly so loud in her ears. The vaulted ceilings echoed with the sound of a guest coughing. Someone sneezing. And all she could think was that she had a hundred objections to going through with the marriage.

Not least the fact that she no longer trusted herself or her motives. Not entirely.

And then she caught Lukas's grim expression and she couldn't have said what that sensation was that rolled through her; it was as though he was waiting for someone to object. But no one did.

Another cough.

Another shuffle of bottom against wooden pew.

And Lukas merely watched her. Challenging her. And taunting her. Baring his teeth in something that might appear to be a smile but made Oti think of wolves and sharpened fangs.

She needed to keep her head in the game, lest she end up being ripped to shreds. And she could pretend to be offended by the entire agreement all she liked—she certainly ought to be—but the truth was that she was floored by her insane attraction to Lukas.

She had been, right from the moment she'd walked into that room in Sedeshire Hall five months ago. He'd made every reservation she had about the ludicrous marriage disappear from her brain.

Or maybe it was more that her brain had ceased working altogether.

Despite all the pictures she'd ever seen of him in the papers—and there was a plethora of them, all displaying the man in all his honed magnificence—not one of them had even come close to conveying quite how *breathtaking* he was up close.

Quite how *heart-stopping*.

Six feet and four inches of pure, sizzling muscle that— she'd realised after a startling instant—had her hands actually itching to reach out and touch. To see if, beneath that exquisitely tailored suit that had clung so lovingly to his broad shoulders, he could possibly be as rock-solid as he looked. As though he was magnificent enough to rival even the most famous of the Greek statues. Myron's *Discobolus*, perhaps. Or Glykon's *Farnese Herakles*.

Oti had always considered herself relatively cultured, interested in such works of art on a purely intellectual level.

Up until that moment. But, standing there in that room, it had been as though her whole world had suddenly tipped up on end and shifted. She'd felt more and more pyretic the longer she'd been in Lukas's company and though she'd pretended it was just the circumstances of their meeting, she'd known it had all been a lie.

Now, there was no lying any more.

The bishop smiled benevolently at them and declared his delight at leading the marriage vows.

Oti's heart gave another lurch.

'And so it begins,' Lukas murmured as he shot her a smile that, to the congregation, would surely have looked like a smile between lovers.

But she knew better. She was close enough to see the expression in those hard grey eyes. And the smile wasn't reflected in them at all. Her heart began to hammer.

It hammered so loudly, in fact, that she could scarcely hear anything else for the rest of the service. Not the bishop's loquacious additions, nor Lukas as he recited his vows, and not even herself as she echoed them.

It was like being in a fog, somewhere in the middle of the hedge maze that used to dominate the west part of the gardens of the Sedeshire estate when her mother had been alive.

As though the entire ceremony was happening to someone else on the other side of the eight-foot evergreens. She could see them but she could barely even hear them.

She would have been happy to stay like that for ever.

Lost.

It was only as the bishop was declaring them husband and wife that Oti finally began to come back to herself.

'You may kiss the bride,' he concluded with a flourish that she felt was wholly unnecessary.

Later, when she was alone, she would quiz herself over why she'd had it in her head that Lukas *wouldn't* kiss her.

Why a part of her had felt so ruffled by the idea of him…
declining to do so. Later.

Not now.

Instead, Oti watched, almost transfixed, as he lifted one
hand and moved it to her cheek; then he slid it around the
back of her neck in a way that any onlooker might have
even considered to be romantic. She knew the truth, and
yet it almost fooled her.

Then he hauled her towards him, his eyes burning
through her, wild and untamed and stirring up sensations
inside that she was sure she'd never felt before. Then he
lowered his head and, as he claimed her mouth with his, her
entire body seemed to combust in flashes of white-hot heat.

And Oti's world as she knew it imploded.

He should never have kissed her, Lukas castigated himself
a short while later when he had finally ushered his too-
lovely new bride into the back seat of their wedding car,
barking out a low command to his driver before climbing
in after her.

He should never have married her either. But that was
hard to remember when he was still floored by their kiss.
And it didn't help that she was touching her fingers to her
lips, with that same dazed expression shining in her too-
blue eyes. He tried to pull his gaze away and look out of
the window, but it was impossible.

Slowly, she turned her head to look at him. Her throat
worked a few times.

'What…was that?'

'If I have to tell you—' his voice was sharp, and not at
all like himself '—then I can't have been doing it right.
And we both know that isn't the case.'

It spoke volumes that she didn't respond to that with one
of her witty put-downs. As if she was too punch-drunk to

manage it. Any other time, he might have taken that as a triumph.

But, right now, Lukas was still trying to rationalise what had happened back in the cathedral. He'd intended a kiss which would satisfy their critics without being inappropriate, but then he'd felt the soft fullness of her mouth open up under his, and everything...*everything* had fallen away.

The cathedral, the guests, even the damned plan itself.

In that split second there had been only him and her. And something that felt oddly like a truth between them.

Which meant that he really was in trouble.

Merely being tempted by the woman was one thing. But it was quite another to forget that anything else even existed. Worse, that he didn't care, because he could still taste her on his tongue. And he found himself savouring it.

Muttering a curse under his breath, he reached towards the limousine's minibar and selected a tumbler before pouring himself a few generous fingers of whisky.

Yeah, he'd realised the kiss had been a mistake even as her breath was heating his mouth back there in the cathedral. He'd tried telling himself that he'd had no choice, that the kiss was an integral part of the ceremony, that he was playing the part of the newly married husband.

But it hadn't felt like playing a part when his mouth had been sliding so perfectly over hers, as though he'd been waiting for this very moment ever since their first encounter. As though *she* was the reason he'd been feeling so edgy for the better part of the last five months, rather than the fact that the plan he had set in motion more than two decades earlier was finally drawing closer.

Close enough to smell.

The first step had been buying out Sedeshire International before the Rockman family could get hold of it, and now those papers were finally signed off and the ink was almost dry. Lukas didn't care that he'd paid over the odds to do so. It was only money and these days he had more of it than his dirt-poor childhood self could ever have even imagined.

The second step was, admittedly, a little harder to swallow, especially for a self-confirmed bachelor—marrying Lady Octavia on the dubious promise that her father would finally tell the truth and set the record straight about his mother.

Just as he had vowed to her as a twelve-year-old.

And it didn't matter that she was no longer around to see justice done, to see her tarnished reputation finally being restored. It would be enough that he had kept his promise to her.

He'd watched the expression of old Andrew Rockman in that front pew, practically incandescent with rage at the marriage.

Lukas had half expected Rockman to storm to the front when the bishop had asked if there were any objections—maybe he would have even welcomed it. The barbaric man would at least have had to finally show his true colours, and the charade would have been over.

But, of course, the opportunity had passed. Rockman had swallowed the rage that only Lukas himself had noticed, and the service had continued. And he'd felt as if he was on autopilot right up to the moment where the slick brush of his lips over Octavia's had made Lukas forget where he was. *Who* he was.

Heat had poured through him as his new bride had melted against him. Right into him. And oh, how there had been a part of him that had craved exactly that.

Lukas couldn't understand it.

Taking a long pull of the expensive drink, he let the heat pour though him and soothe him. But, strangely, he didn't really taste it.

He could only taste *her*. Roaring through his veins, thundering around his being. Flooding him. He could barely restrain himself from reaching over to haul her back to him and explore that delicious friction between them all over again.

His only consolation was that she wanted him just as badly. He knew women well enough to be able to read his new bride like an open book.

Tension emanated off her as she sat across the luxurious seats from him. He could see that she too fought to get herself back under control, the taut lines of her elegant neck at odds with the way she kept her hands neatly folded in her lap, too neat, too precise. As if she could read every last traitorous thought in his head and felt every one of them.

He needed to break the silence, but no words came.

'Drink?' he offered at last, more for something to say. 'Or perhaps that would undermine whatever programme you're following.'

'You mean like a twelve-step one?' She sniffed. 'No, thank you. Though, as I said, I wasn't in rehab. It's just that it's barely eleven thirty.'

Her attempt at a put-down might have amused him under any other circumstances. It certainly wouldn't have got to him. What was wrong with him?

'Says the woman who is well known for partying 24/7,' he countered instead. 'It's a bit late to start pretending to have standards, isn't it?'

'Evidently,' she shot back, though her tone was ridiculously polite. 'Since I just married you. Or perhaps I'm lying and it's the booze and drugs talking.'

He gave a snort of laughter despite himself. Her comebacks were like a fine blade slicing through the air, neither dull nor confused.

Without knowing what he was doing, Lukas stretched one long arm out across the seats. He took her chin in his fingers and—not unkindly—forced her to look at him.

'That's twice you've seemed offended when I've mentioned your past. But your pupils aren't dilated, and you don't sound compromised. You certainly don't smell like you're drunk. For that matter, you didn't seem under the influence when last we met either. One might actually suspect that the rumours about you weren't wholly true.'

Octavia froze. Her glorious sapphire eyes—which he hated himself for noticing, let alone being unable to draw his gaze away from—widened. Her breathing grew more rapid and shallow. He could see her pulse battering wildly in her neck, the beat seeming to echo throughout his entire body.

It shouldn't have been so hard to make his hand open up. To release her.

Belatedly, his new bride wrenched her head away as if she'd been just as frozen as he had been. If he wasn't careful he could end up blowing this whole scheme on a woman who seemed to be capable of doing the one thing that only one person had ever managed.

It seemed that his new bride was developing a knack for getting under his skin.

The sooner they got this wedding breakfast over with and he could get back to the relative peace of his home—and, more important, his office—the better.

CHAPTER THREE

Oᴛɪ ᴡᴀs ʀᴇʟɪᴇᴠᴇᴅ when their car finally drew up at the reception venue.

She'd spent the entire journey replaying their discussion in church as though they'd been two naughty school children in Sunday service, instead of bride and groom at their own wedding.

It was ludicrous.

Yet even now, thinking of doing…*intimate things* with this man only made her feel all the more edgy. Hotter. And heavier. Right *there*…between her legs.

What was wrong with her?

She couldn't imagine what he would say if he knew the truth. If Lukas found out that she was a virgin. It was embarrassing, certainly at her age. He wouldn't believe her, anyway. Not unless she explained why she'd barely done more than kiss a man in the past decade. Not unless she told him the whole story. And there was no chance she would do that.

She'd put that part of her life—that awful night—behind her a long time ago.

If her brother hadn't come along exactly when he had… well, she didn't like to think what might have—*would* have—happened. It sickened her enough that it had got as far as it had. But she'd been lucky. Edward had rescued her. Too many other women weren't so fortunate.

But Lukas Woods didn't need to know any of it.

Still, as he slid far too gracefully out of the car and then turned to help her follow, she almost batted his hand away, only spotting her bridesmaids—girls she barely knew any more, let alone friends—waiting for her. Every one of them was her father's choice. Mostly daughters of high-ranking nobility with whom he was trying to ingratiate himself. Perhaps one of them was the girl that he was currently sleeping with—though she was barely older than Oti, and possibly a little younger.

Odious didn't quite cover it. If it wasn't for Edward, she would have cut her father out of her life years ago.

Perhaps she would be able to visit her brother soon. Maybe even in the next few days. There was no honeymoon planned; to be fair, she felt as if she was going to be more of a mistress than a wife, since Lukas was already married to his work.

But, for now, she still had the wedding breakfast to get through. Shoving her thoughts to the back of her mind, Oti feigned another smile—her cheeks were beginning to ache—and allowed Lukas to take her hand and assist her out of the vintage vehicle and tried not to wince.

She might have known the infamously sharp-eyed Lukas wouldn't miss it.

'What is it?' He stopped instantly.

'It's nothing,' she lied, trying to turn her arm so that he couldn't see.

Taking her arm and stilling her movements, he noted the bruise that was already beginning to form.

'Was this your father?' he demanded. 'Before, in the cathedral? What was it that he said to you?'

'It's fine. Let's just go inside.'

Not a rebuttal, she noted. As if she wanted Lukas to know.

She eyed the marks, practically feeling her father's vice-like grip as it had tightened around her. His fingers biting painfully into her arm.

'Don't mess this up, girl,' he'd hissed. 'Or, so help you, you and that vegetable brother of yours will regret it.'

Anger had shot through her and she remembered jerking her head up and forcing herself to take one step then another, until finally she drew to an elegant halt at the top of the aisle, where her father finally released her.

If she was going to bolt, *that* had been her chance.

Instead, she'd looked at Lukas and all her fears, all her anger, had seemed to simply…dissolve. As though it was all going to be okay.

Which was why, right now, she just wanted to forget her father and return to whatever verbal jousting she and Lukas had discovered back in the cathedral. As absurd as it was, she'd found some degree of comfort in their barbed exchanges.

'I can't help but notice the inordinate number of devastated-looking Z-list actresses dressed as though they're in mourning,' she murmured as they strode into the magnificent venue.

His jaw locked, and she silently prayed that he wasn't going to continue interrogating her about her father.

'What can I say?' Relenting unexpectedly, Lukas apparently decided to play along. 'I'm quite the catch.'

'It might have been amusing to watch, had I been in the congregation watching that car crash of a wedding, instead of standing right there at the front—one of the main participants.'

'You didn't enjoy being the centre of attention, Octavia? You do surprise me.'

'And then there was Andrew, looking apoplectic.' She snorted indelicately, a fraction of a second before she realised Lukas had stiffened slightly beside her.

'Andrew?' He sounded as though he could barely bring himself to spit the word out.

Oti frowned. 'Andrew Rockman, Sixth Earl of Highmount?' she clarified. 'He and my father are as thick as thieves, which should tell you everything you need to know about the man.'

'I know who he is.' The clipped tone made her stomach flip.

'You're not friends?' She didn't know if she could stand that.

'We are most certainly not.'

She was pretty sure that the unrufflable Lukas Woods was seething beneath his too-flattering morning suit.

How curious.

'Good,' she offered. 'Because I don't think I could stand it if you were. He's such a bully, as are his sons. My family has known them for years. Did you know that he stormed into Sedeshire Hall, bawling at my father to call off this wedding?'

'I did not know that,' Lukas answered, and she got the impression he was fighting to keep his emotions in check.

She filed that away for later.

'What exactly did he tell your father?'

'I don't know.' She shrugged. 'I can't say that I was listening. Though he was raging about my father betraying him.'

And then she waited for her new husband to fill in the gaps for which she was sure he had the pieces.

She told herself that she shouldn't be surprised when he merely shrugged, made his excuses and disappeared. Leaving her to greet the rest of their unimpressed guests alone.

'You can marry as many daughters of earls as you like— it won't make you any less of an illegitimate bastard.'

Lukas eyed the enraged, spluttering Andrew Rockman,

Sixth Earl of Highmount, and forced down the bile that always threatened to drown him from the inside whenever he thought of him. The man who was—as much as Lukas would have cut out his own tongue before admitting it aloud—his biological father.

It took everything Lukas had to keep his voice even and light, as though those insulting words didn't resonate so deafeningly in his head. As though they didn't scrape inside him where he'd always felt so raw.

'I'm fairly certain that marrying as many daughters of earls as I like would make me a bigamist. But never fear, I only needed to marry the one in order for her father to give me a controlling share of Sedeshire International. The company you've been trying to get your grubby little paws on for years.'

He even offered a sardonic smile and was rewarded when the older man's eyes bulged with fury.

'You're an utter disgrace,' the Earl spat out.

'On the contrary, I'm a success. In business and now, it seems, in marriage. I may be an *illegitimate bastard*—' the words nearly lodged in Lukas's throat, but he made himself say them anyway '—yet to the world I'm the man who bagged an earl's daughter. And secured a company, all at once. Though I wonder what that says about my new father-in-law's loyalty to you? It's no secret that you've been desperate to get your greedy fingers on Sedeshire International, and yet he chose not to sell to you.'

'You're nothing!' the old Earl exploded viciously. 'A nobody.'

'Indeed, as your closest…' Lukas paused thoughtfully. 'Well, I wouldn't go so far as to call him a friend—I'm not certain that you understand the meaning of the term—so let's go with…ally. As your closest ally, I wonder what conclusions will be drawn from the fact that he agreed to marry

Lady Octavia off to me, rather than one of your sons. Or, should I clarify, one of your legitimate sons.'

'You're no son of mine.'

For most of his life Lukas had chosen to tell himself the same thing. It had suited him to pretend that he could not be connected to such a man—more than *suited him*. Denying the Earl's existence—even if only in his own head—had been as necessary to Lukas's well-being as learning to breathe. Now, though, seeing the old man's rage, Lukas felt compelled to fuel the fire.

'I couldn't agree more. Yet you can call me a *bastard*, just as you called my mother a whore, but it doesn't change the fact that we share the same blood.' The words almost curdled in his mouth, and Lukas made no attempt to disguise his contempt.

'Watch your tongue, boy,' the Earl snarled.

Lukas stood his ground. The old man might intimidate most people—even himself as a twelve-year-old boy carrying a message from his dying mother, only to be thrown, quite literally, from the Earl's home—but Lukas had long since learned how to stand up to bullies.

'One of your offspring is in prison for tax evasion, one can barely run his trust fund let alone a company, and the third has a reputation for plying young socialites with alcohol and drugs and then taking advantage.'

'Anyone who believes that will be made to pay,' the Earl hissed, as Lukas gave a bark of hollow laughter.

'Because you're a master at manipulating the truth, and getting people to lie for you? Just as my new wife's father lied for you when it came to the truth about my mother, and my parentage, all those years ago?' Lukas bunched his fists into his pockets as though that might control the grief and resentment that was rising inside his chest.

The older man sneered. 'Your new wife is as feeble and inadequate as your mother was. Another waste of a life.'

Lukas clenched his jaw so tight that he thought it might break. He had spent so many years resenting the fact that he'd had to look after his mother when, by rights, she should have been the one looking after him. Resenting her. Hating her, even. But he'd be damned if this oxygen thief standing in front of him needed to know that.

'You drove her to her grave,' Lukas managed. 'She told me how you tried to get her to terminate the pregnancy when you found out, then ensured she was left homeless and jobless when she refused.'

He might have known the Earl could sniff out any hint of weakness. The old man's eyes narrowed thoughtfully, then glinted.

'You think you know it all, don't you?' His smile was nothing short of brutal. 'But you don't know a thing, boy. You think she had morals, defying me to have you? You weren't her first baby. You're just the one that survived a failed attempt to get rid of you.'

'That's a lie.' The denial was out before Lukas could stop it. Before his brain could kick in and warn him that this was exactly the reaction the man standing in front of him had wanted. Even now, the old man's eyes gleamed with victory.

'Oh, no lie.' He grinned, a cold, cruel baring of teeth. 'Your mother didn't want you any more than I did. She tried to rid herself of you, like I told her to. She always did what I told her to do. She never loved you, because there wasn't room in that weak, pathetic heart of hers for anyone but me. But, then, you already knew that, didn't you, boy?'

Lukas had no idea how he managed to hold himself together, let alone stopped himself from dropping the sorry excuse for a man to the ground. But he'd long ago learned to control that frustrated, angry streak that seemed to run through him and he wasn't about to give in to it now.

'I know that whatever she did was because you pushed

her. You took advantage of a woman who loved you, so who was weaker and more pathetic? All you ever did was use her.'

The old man snorted in disdain. '*Love?* You talk of love, yet here I am, attending the wedding of my oldest friend's daughter and some upstart.' The Earl waved a gnarled hand at him. 'Not because you love her—you don't even know her—but because you wanted to steal their company from my grasp.'

'Octavia knew the deal from the start,' Lukas scorned. He had no intention of letting the old man know that the marriage part of the deal wasn't exactly concerned with the business side. 'I didn't make her believe I cared, only to then use her. Unlike the way you treated my mother, my new bride knew the circumstances of the agreement all along.'

But still it didn't stop those cold fingers of apprehension from slinking down his spine. The image of her walking down the aisle in her father's grip.

'You tell yourself that so that you can believe you're better than me. But you'll ruin her all the same. You don't have it in you not to do so. You're no better than a mangy dog from the gutter.'

'You're mellowing in your old age,' Lukas mocked. 'You managed far crueller put-downs when I was a kid. You, the bully who took such delight in mocking a twelve-year-old boy—telling me that I should stay in the gutter, where I belonged, that I would never amount to anything. I've no doubt you comfort yourself daily with the notion that landed gentry isn't true nobility.'

'And if I hadn't mocked you, would you have been so driven to get to where you are today? That dirty, worthless kid would never have had it in him to make it this far. Perhaps you should be thanking me for giving you the drive that you so sorely needed back then.'

The Earl stopped thoughtfully as some of the contempt faded from his expression. 'You're focused and ruthless, just like me. Perhaps the apple didn't fall too far from the tree after all.'

Loathing coursed through Lukas. 'I'm nothing like you,' he ground out, appalled.

He hated that that only seemed to make the Earl all the more exultant.

'You're more like me than you might think. And, as much as you might hate me, I have no doubt that one day it will be you standing where I am, and some bastard kid of yours standing where you are, staring at you with the same deep loathing.'

'I will never have kids,' Lukas refuted. 'No child deserves to have your tainted blood running through its veins.'

'You have fire, boy. Perhaps I shouldn't have been so quick to throw you out of my house all those years ago. Maybe you're worthy of the Rockman name and title after all.'

'I don't need your title.' Lukas gritted his teeth. 'I have my own. What's more, I worked for mine. You don't get to claim credit for it.'

The Earl curled his lip. 'You have a knighthood. As quaint as that is, it's no peerage. And I blocked you in that when I refused to acknowledge your mother.'

'Which is the only thing you recognise, isn't it?' Lukas disparaged. 'Have you ever considered that one day I might find a way to prove you lied all those years ago?'

Lukas couldn't be sure if it was the mere threat or if the Earl had begun to piece it together, but, either way, the old man looked as though he was about to lose his mind, right there in that anteroom…right up until he dropped to the ground like a sack of potatoes.

It was odd how there was no warning. No clutching of his chest. No calling out. One moment the Earl was standing in front of Lukas, and the next moment the man simply toppled to the ground as if his legs had suddenly gone from under him. For a moment Lukas could only look on, stunned. A part of him even suspected it was some new ploy by the old man. But there was just silence.

Not quite believing what was happening, Lukas dropped to his heels and reached out to check the Earl's pulse.

There wasn't one.

For a fraction of a second Lukas thought he might actually have considered just walking away. Just leaving this man who had caused him—and his mother, as weak as she had been—so much unnecessary pain. How many times over the years had he wished this man dead?

But then instinct cut in and, with a low curse, Lukas hurried to the door, flung it open and bellowed down the empty corridor for one of the hotel staff. Then, moving quickly back across the room, he dropped onto his knees and began chest compressions.

Oti was in the Grosvenor Wing, gritting her teeth as she greeted the guests alone, wondering if she'd already been ditched—with a cluster of sombre-looking female Z-list guests who would have loved that to have been the case— when she heard Lukas's shout, as faint as it was in the main hall.

She wondered what it said about how tuned-in she was to her fake husband, as she slid through the oblivious crowd and hurried along an endless plushly carpeted corridor. She only knew she was heading in the right direction because a couple of members of staff were ducking into a room a little ahead of her.

Silently lamenting the weight and encumbrance of her dress's long train, Oti surged after them.

'Lukas? Did you…? Oh, good grief.'

He glanced up and she wished she could read the expression that flickered in his eyes when he saw her. But then it was gone, and Lukas was all business.

'Call for an ambulance. He collapsed less than a minute ago—there was no indication.' Lukas didn't miss a compression. 'He isn't breathing, and he has no pulse.'

Oti didn't wait to hear any more. Pushing through the dithering hotel staff, she circled the patient—only then realising the man's identity—and knelt down on the other side to Lukas and carried out her own brief assessment.

'I'll do the rescue breathing if you want to continue with compressions.' She glanced up at the still staring staff, starting with a young man. 'Right, you go and call an ambulance *now* and tell them that we've begun CPR. *Go!* And you—does the hotel have a defibrillator?'

As the young man stumbled away, the girl blinked at her.

'I need you to stop panicking and think.' Oti kept her tone calm but firm. 'If you don't know, then I need you to go straight to your manager and ask. A defibrillator, understand? Also, ask if you keep shots of epinephrine. Got it? Now you need to hurry.'

She jerked her head shakily then turned and hurried out of the room. Oti could only hope that the girl could hold herself together long enough to get what they needed.

Briefly, she wondered what had been so urgent that Lukas and Andrew Rockman had been discussing it alone. Certainly without her father. But she could contemplate that later. Right now, she had to focus on working with Lukas to save the man's life. Even if a part of her suspected the world would be a better place without the likes of the Earl of Highmount. The current one, or the son who would inherit the title if Andrew were to die.

For the next five minutes she and Lukas worked together, soon establishing a surprisingly efficient rhythm until the girl returned with the defibrillator, and what looked like a manager.

'The ambulance is on its way, and I've sent someone to stand at the entrance to bring them straight here.'

'Great.' Oti nodded, her eyes not leaving the patient as she silently counted Lukas's compressions. 'Okay, turn the defib on.'

'I don't know how to use it.' The manager shook his head. 'We only got it last week and training isn't until next week.'

Bending her head, Oti was unable to answer as she began two short rescue breaths.

'It's okay—I know,' Lukas muttered. 'Just turn the machine on and follow the instructions on the read-out whilst I complete one more cycle of compressions, then you can hand the defib to me.'

Finishing the rescue breaths, Oti sat up as Lukas began compressions again. When the Earl's life was on the line, was it right for her to allow Lukas to take charge, just to preserve her own secret?

Watching Lukas working on the older man, Oti weighed up her options. Clearly, he knew what he was doing in terms of the pace and pressure of the chest compressions—and although it was a draining task he made it look deceptively easy—which was good to see, but using the defib could be a different story.

'…twenty-eight, twenty-nine, thirty.'

As Oti bent her head for another two rescue breaths, she was aware of the manager handing the defib to Lukas, who, having already unbuttoned the Earl's shirt, removed the sticky pads and began to place them down on the man's bare chest. A perfect position for the one beneath the right clavicle, but the other one was slightly off. There was nothing else for it.

'Wait.' She reached out to stay his hand, fighting off the jolt of awareness that shot through her at the contact.

And it had nothing to do with the defibrillator.

Valiantly trying to ignore it, Oti guided his hand a few centimetres lower and set it down.

'What do you think you're doing?' She was sure that it wasn't just her imagination that his voice sounded hoarser.

'Moving you to a more lateral position.' She shook her head, struggling to regroup. 'Even amongst medical professionals, the location of the apical pad can often be too medial.' She barely recognised her own voice. 'The result is reduced separation between the pads, causing the current to pass through non-cardiac tissue and potentially reducing the successfulness of the defibrillation.'

He eyed her intently for a brief moment and she thought he was going to say something more. Instead, he merely inclined his head.

'You sound like you know better than I do.'

She told herself that it was good that he wasn't so full of his own self-importance that he refused to listen to her, but she shouldn't feel so ridiculously flattered.

Attaching the pad to the Earl's chest, she turned her attention back to the machine as it analysed their patient's heartbeat.

'Stand clear.' She glanced at Lukas, but he'd already edged back a little from the man, his hands up to indicate he was no longer in contact. 'Shocking.'

As the machine delivered a shock, Oti waited long enough to check the read-out before setting it aside and continuing CPR.

Lukas matched her without a word, as if they were in perfect sync. As if he was someone she'd worked with for years. But she didn't allow herself to consider it any further.

For a couple more minutes they continued CPR, with Oti giving two breaths for every thirty compressions from Lukas. After five cycles she delivered a second shock to the Earl, and more compressions, but still to no effect.

'Any idea on the ambulance?' she demanded, turning

to the manager, who was on his walkie-talkie and looking rather ashen himself.

'It's coming down the lanes now…a minute or so out.'

'Yes.' She nodded, though her eyes didn't leave the patient as Lukas began.

So a good few minutes before they got to the patient. Another cycle and another shock by her and Lukas, and if that wasn't successful, at least they should be able to administer epinephrine before administering a fourth shock.

And one thought niggled at her. If the Earl should need an IV, given the shape that he was in, her recommendation would have to be an intraosseous infusion for a non-collapsible entry point, since intravenous wouldn't be feasible. And what if the crew weren't trained for IO? She could end up having to administer it herself. How many questions would that raise with her new husband?

'Another set?' Lukas said grimly, interrupting her thoughts, half a command, half a question.

Blinking, she took a moment to reassess.

'Yes.' Oti nodded at last. 'Another set.'

For the next few minutes they resumed their roles, the time passing all too fast before she administered another shock. Then, abruptly, the old Earl's heart kicked back in, just as the ambulance crew hurried into the room.

For the next few moments Oti was occupied with handing over in a timely manner, relieved that they accepted what she and Lukas had done as though there were quasi-trained guests, rather than her being a doctor.

And still Oti couldn't work out whether Lukas was happy that they'd been successful in saving the Earl's life—or not.

'What were you talking about in that room, anyway?' she attempted casually. She might have known Lukas wouldn't fall for it.

'Who says we were talking?'

'He didn't want me to marry you,' she commented instead, and she thought it said a lot that he didn't pretend not to know who she was talking about.

She tried to recall the argument between Andrew Rockman and her father that evening, wishing that she hadn't dismissed it at the time, but little that her father did interested her. She had even less interest in what the Rockman family did.

Now her brain was beginning to whirl, throwing up snippets of old information that she'd thought the two older men would long since have forgotten about.

'They were arguing about the past.' She bit her lip thoughtfully. 'A group of hotel chains and luxury boutiques that the Rockman family once owned, until they lost it all in a hostile takeover.'

It had been a successful chain but, instead of trading on the name, by all accounts it had been stripped down methodically and ruthlessly. Andrew Rockman had always claimed that it had been about more than business, that it had been personal. Some young upstart targeting him.

Now she couldn't stop herself from asking Lukas if he had been that upstart.

'What else do you remember?' Lukas demanded, which wasn't the answer Oti had been expecting, yet it was somehow more of an answer.

'Not a lot more.' She shrugged. 'I'm afraid I wasn't exactly paying attention. Ten years ago I *was* that party girl you accused me of still being.'

She eyed him defiantly, but he didn't offer a put-down this time. Not that it made her feel any less ashamed when she thought back to the way she'd spent her life schlepping from one luxury beach holiday to the next. From a party on some billionaire's yacht to a celebration in Monaco. Between the ages of fifteen and nineteen, she'd played the part of the airheaded socialite only too shamefully well. She could hardly blame Lukas for thinking she was still that girl. It had been nearly a decade and yet the rest of her so-called social circle had never let her forget it.

'And ten years ago I was that young upstart,' Lukas ground out unexpectedly. 'We both have a past, Octavia. The point now is to make this marriage—this business transaction—work for us. Are you prepared to do that?'

She was still reeling from her new husband's shock revelation, her brain still trying to piece it together. It was as though she was seeing tiny sections but missing the big picture.

'I am prepared,' she offered at length. 'So what now?'

'Now we get through the next few hours and then I'll drop you off back home. My home,' he clarified tightly.

'Drop me off?' Oti frowned. 'Where are you going?'

Her skin was starting to prickle at his unexpected change of tone as she frantically tried to work out what had just happened. He was no longer the teasing, amused Lukas of before. Now he was sharper, colder, more withdrawn. And it shouldn't have mattered to her.

But it did.

'I have conference calls to attend to,' he told her coolly. 'Work doesn't stop just because today is my wedding day.'

'Heaven forbid,' she remarked, but he didn't even crack a smile. 'And what about me? What should I do?'

Lukas looked almost disdainful. 'You should do… whatever it is that you do.'

And even as she told herself that she should be glad she'd just been presented with the perfect opportunity to visit Edward—the brother who she hated having to pretend had died in that accident—she was powerless to stop a sting of hurt from working its way under her skin.

CHAPTER FOUR

'LOOK, I'VE DONE my research.' Oti eyed her brother. 'I've used every contact I could as a doctor, to really make sure, and I truly believe you're a perfect candidate. Nerve transfer surgery has a high success rate for C5 to C6 spinal cord injuries.'

'But it won't make me walk again,' Edward threw back.

It sliced right through her to hear him so uncharacteristically angry and bitter. Not that she blamed him—how could she?—but the Edward she'd known and loved had always been ready with a light-hearted quip or a joke to lighten the moment.

She missed that Edward, more than she liked to admit.

She *needed* her brother back. For all that their father had ever put them through, they'd always had each other. For support, for counsel, or even for simple sibling teasing. But the accident hadn't just robbed Edward of his ability to walk or move; it had also robbed him of his sense of self.

And it had robbed her of her big brother.

Without him, she'd felt more alone these past four years than she could have imagined.

Before she could catch herself, Oti reached for her wedding rings, as though to twirl them on her finger the way she had done virtually all last night, unable to sleep. But she'd removed her rings before visiting Edward—he would have spotted them instantly and demanded to know about them, and she'd never been able to lie to her big brother.

But it was disconcerting how bare her hand felt without them. After less than twenty-four hours. Oti didn't care to examine what that said about her. She forced her focus back to Edward.

'No, it won't help you to walk again,' she agreed evenly. 'But this procedure could allow you to regain use of your arms. You might be able to lift a cup and feed yourself. You could be able to lift your arms above your head to dress yourself, or even turn on a light switch. Maybe you could even have enough strength to turn a door handle and push your own wheelchair. You could even make one of your godawful peanut butter sandwiches, which always glued my tongue to the roof of my mouth. You could be independent again, Edward. You wouldn't have to have carers on hand 24/7. Feeding you, cleaning you, even having to scratch your damned nose for you if it itches. I know how you hate it. But, this way, you could get some quality of life back.'

'*Could. Might. Maybe...*' He echoed the words hollowly. 'Do you hear yourself?'

It broke her heart, but she couldn't afford to let him see that. This was Edward, her incredible brother, who had been able to do anything. *Every*thing. He was tough and he wasn't a quitter. He never had been.

She just had to bring that back out of him now.

'Oh, I'm sorry, did you have some better plan?' she forced herself to say. 'My mistake. I see your life is just how you want it right now.'

'Funny,' he threw at her.

But she was sure she saw just a glint of something in his eyes. As though the old Edward was still in there—somewhere. It was more than she'd seen in four years. But, then, this was the first time she'd been able to give him something akin to hope in the past four years.

She made herself press on. 'Or you could just give up, of course. Prove Father right and be the quitter he keeps saying you are. Is that what you want, Edward? To let him win by giving up on yourself? On me? On your own life?'

For one long, horrible moment he stared at her and Oti felt the words of apology racing up through her, ready to spill out everywhere. And then, all of a sudden, he offered a twisted kind of smile.

It wasn't perfect, but it was better than nothing.

'Who the hell wants to let that repulsive old bully win anything?'

'Right.' She hesitated. It wasn't exactly the resounding agreement she'd hoped for. But neither was it the stonewalling for which she'd been preparing herself.

She waited as the silence enveloped them again. Should she say something more? Or wait for Edward to speak?

Oti clenched her fingers together in her lap and forced herself to be patient. If Edward was going to go for it, he would need to be the one to instigate it.

'Nerve transfers aren't new,' he pointed out, after what seemed like a lifetime. 'But they've never really been successful on spinal cord injuries.'

'You know about them?'

He snorted loudly. 'You think I haven't constantly looked for new procedures, sitting here in this damned chair all day, unable to even lift my own glass of water to drink?'

It was all Oti could do not to smile. Or cry. Possibly both. Instead, she focused on keeping her emotions in check and her voice even. Edward wouldn't thank her for a song and dance—though he might enjoy the irony of her pun—and, in any case, she didn't want to oversell it.

There were still no guarantees, after all.

She moved around the table, sitting down carefully and

trying not to look too eager. And all the while pushing to the back of her mind that all this hinged on their father honouring his agreement to her and paying for the surgery.

Looking at her brother's face, agreeing to marry Lukas in return seemed like a small price to pay.

She wasn't an idiot. Her father would have always found someone to marry her off to—and some way to have leverage over her to do so. She was lucky it was Lukas and not one of his boorish friends. Or one of their hard-partying sons.

And it wasn't as though she had someone of her own to love. Not that she wouldn't have liked that…but her social circle, and her job, made that rather difficult.

She ignored the sensation that rippled through her when she thought of Lukas. A fleeting chemical attraction. Nothing more.

'It's a combination of nerve transfer for dexterity, and tendon transfer for strength. Both of these are well-established procedures, just for other areas. For example, tendon transfer is well described in the area of hand surgeries.'

'I need upper arm strength.'

'Right,' Oti agreed. 'So they would remove a working nerve from a donor site in the shoulder, close to the damaged section of nerve preventing the signal from reaching the lower arm, and then use that working nerve to effectively bypass the damaged section. Then it is connected back to the spinal cord. But where, previously, they might have used one donor, here we would be talking about two, or even multiple.'

'And then I can move my arms again. As if by magic,' Edward ground out, getting angry again, his bitterness intertwined with frustration and sheer exhaustion.

She couldn't blame him; she could only imagine what

he was going through. He'd been like this for the better part of four years.

Oti weighed her options. She could go in gently, or she could see if the tough love option was still her best bet.

'Not by magic,' she told him firmly. 'The surgery is just the start of it. After that you have months of rehab and hard work.'

'Sounds appealing,' her brother gritted out.

'Or years of rehab, if you don't put in the effort.'

He didn't answer for a moment. But when he finally did speak, Oti wasn't prepared for it.

'So, what you're saying is that I'm going to need to put my back into it.'

She blinked at him.

'But I will,' he continued, deadpan. 'Because I know that you, my sweet baby sister, will have my back.'

'Hilarious,' she managed, still shocked.

It was a terrible pun, but she wasn't sure she cared. It had been so long since Edward had made a joke about anything—certainly not his disability—that she couldn't help feeling this was progress.

It was certainly better than calling himself a *head on a stick*.

She thought that particular self-description had broken her heart worst of all.

'Edward...'

'It's going to be just *spine*.'

And then, without warning, he laughed.

It was a slightly stiff, awkward laugh. But it was a laugh all the same. And Oti didn't know if it was hearing Edward make bad puns, or the emotion of her marriage to Lukas— or perhaps it was the fact that she knew she never could have dreamt of offering Edward this glimmer of hope had she failed to go through with the marriage to Lukas—but she lost it.

It rushed over her and she dropped her head in her hands and sobbed.

'Don't cry, Oats,' Edward growled.

He hadn't called her by that childhood nickname for years. Somehow, that only made her cry a little harder.

'Please, Oats,' her brother tried again after a moment. 'I feel useless—I can't give you a hug. I can't even take your hand.'

Sniffing hard, half crying and half laughing, she took his hand. What she wouldn't give to have her brother haul her into one of his old bearlike hugs and tell her everything would be okay.

But he couldn't.

And she needed to be the one to be strong for him. There was no one to be strong for her.

Lukas?

The question popped, unbidden, into her brain. Oti stuffed it back down hastily.

Lukas Woods couldn't be trusted with the truth.

No one could.

'Sorry.' Pulling herself together, Oti wiped her arm across her eyes. 'It's just been a long couple of days. But it's done now. So let's get back to the rehab after your operation.'

'The gruelling bit, you said.'

'True. But since when were you ever bothered by a little hard work, Edward?'

'I'm not.' He blew out a frustrated breath. 'But do you really think they'll take me on, Oats? The candidates they've chosen were all less than eighteen months post-spinal-cord accident. I'm nearly five years.'

'They're making strides with it all the time, Edward.' She focused on her brother. 'The experiences they had with the first few groups have informed their understanding of the procedures. Of nerve topography itself.'

'Which means…?'

'It means they studied how spasticity allows preserved muscle function and stops atrophy.'

'I have no idea what you're saying to me.' Edward frowned. 'You might as well be speaking Sudanese for all I know.'

'Nuer,' she corrected absently. 'Or Dinka.'

'Which raises another question,' Edward cut in. 'These trials are new, and I don't qualify for any current clinical trials, which means we'd have to pay for this surgery.'

Oti schooled herself not to panic. 'No, there's a new trial…'

'There isn't.' He stopped her again. 'How are you intending to pay for this, Oats? Because volunteering as a doctor in Sub-Saharan Africa might feed your soul, little sister, but it doesn't do much for your wallet. And I don't have anything since Father seized control of my company after the accident. If I hadn't had private insurance, I wouldn't even have this place.'

'Father will…'

'Spare me,' Edward snorted. 'He wouldn't throw a pound my way even if he had it. Which he doesn't, given that he's gambled away everything owned by the Sedeshire estate, bar the damned Hall itself.'

'He's…made some money.' Oti tried to sound convincing, but she'd never found it easy to lie to her big brother.

It was one of the reasons she worked in Africa—to avoid having to lie to his face. That, and the fact that he'd banned her from visiting for the first couple of years after the accident, and she hadn't been able to stand being just down the road from his hospital whilst he'd refused to even see her.

The fact that their father had been only too inexplicably happy to wash his hands of a tetraplegic son had only heightened her sense of injustice.

As though, somehow, the Earl felt that Edward's lack

of mobility might somehow reflect on his own image of apparent virility.

How many more ways could their father have left to disappoint either of his children?

'No, he hasn't,' Edward contradicted smoothly. 'If he had, he'd have gambled it away again faster than you could say *Quit whilst you're ahead.*'

He pinned her with a sharp stare, and it was all Oti could do not to squirm. She smoothed down her grey jersey trousers, picking off a sliver of some imaginary lint.

'What gives, Oats?'

A hundred different excuses darted around her head, though nothing that she thought her brother might believe. But then he spoke again, his voice cracking as he asked her not to bring him hope of an operation there was no chance they could afford.

'Of course not. I wouldn't…' The words tumbled out in her horror. 'Trust me. We can afford the operation.'

'How?'

Another skewering gaze. Her heart pounded in her chest. There was nothing else for it but to come clean.

'I got married.'

He didn't answer; he simply stared at her. And that was worse, somehow. Without knowing what she was doing, Oti reached inside her pocket and retrieved her wedding rings and slid them nervously back onto her finger.

It shouldn't have felt so…*comforting* to do so.

'You got married?' Edward managed at last, his expression little short of thunderous. 'For me?'

'No,' she lied, far more smoothly than she might have thought possible.

'For me,' he confirmed in sheer disgust. 'Not one of those lecherous old sops Father kept pushing you to marry, just so his own debts could be expunged?'

'No.'

'Not Louis Rockman?' Edward's face twisted. 'After what he tried to do to you as a kid?'

'No.' Oti couldn't suppress a shudder at the thought. 'He's a successful businessman. And he's...*nice*.'

And there was no reason at all for her to feel quite so guarded.

'But he's still paying Father off, isn't he?' Edward demanded harshly.

'Yes, but this time I made him promise to pay for this surgery.'

Her brother snorted. 'He'll never honour it. You know that.'

'He'll have to—it's written into the contract,' she lied.

'So you see,' she continued loftily, 'everyone wins. I can't be married off twice.'

Her father might try it, of course, but once Edward had undergone the surgery, the old Earl would have no more leverage over her.

'And at least this way it's someone with whom I can actually stand to be in the same room,' she continued when Edward still didn't reply.

It was supposed to be an explanation that would placate her brother but, even as she said the words, Oti realised there was a grain of truth in it.

A memory of Lukas in the cathedral, and that kiss, lit up her brain as heat flushed through her.

Okay, more than a grain, then.

'Who is it?' Edward demanded abruptly, his eyes raking over her face. 'Which of his cronies did he force you to marry, Oats?'

She fought to compose herself.

'Lukas Woods.'

He stared at her for such a long moment that she wasn't sure if he'd actually heard her. And then he spluttered with disbelief, *'Lukas Woods?'*

'He's…'

'You can't be serious, Oats?'

Well, at least he wasn't back to calling her Octavia, which meant he couldn't be *that* mad. Now that she considered it, he didn't look even half as cross as she might have expected.

'Have you ever met him?' She wasn't sure what made her ask the question, but she hadn't really expected it to be true.

'I have, actually. Yes. A couple of times, several years ago. Once at a business event, and once at the racetrack.'

'Lukas races cars, like you?' she asked, before catching herself. 'Like you used to do.'

'No, he was more into the mechanics side. He liked to build them, and just raced to see how they performed. He told me one of his first jobs was for a car mechanic when he was a kid, and in his spare time he used to go to the scrapyard and he used what he could find to build old engines. I guess when his company took off he kept it going as a hobby.'

But a serious hobby, by the sound of it. Just like Edward's racing used to be.

Her first thought was that she liked the fact that her brother kind of liked Lukas. Her second was that it shouldn't matter what her big brother thought.

'I thought he was a decent bloke. So why did Woods marry you? What did he get out of the deal?'

She didn't want to tell him, but at the same time she couldn't bring herself to lie to him.

'Father sold him a controlling interest in Sedeshire International.'

For a moment Edward dropped his head down and her heart suddenly lurched. His hair would once have fallen in his eyes when he did that, and he'd had this habit of thrusting his fingers into it to rake it back. It was a mannerism that she'd never really paid attention to before. But now he couldn't even lift his arm to do that. And his hair was so short that it didn't move a single millimetre when his head moved.

God, how she missed such a simple gesture.

'Well, if my company had to go, better it's in Woods's hands than in Father's.'

'Or Andrew Rockman's,' she told him quietly.

'Christ, is that who else was interested?'

She nodded slowly.

'Then yeah.' He sounded resigned. 'Definitely better with Lukas Woods. But you shouldn't have married him. He might be a decent bloke to another bloke, but he isn't who I would want my baby sister marrying. Why did you do it, Oats?'

'Because it was either him or Louis Rockman. Can we discuss that later?' She tried to smooth things over. 'I just want to focus on you right now.'

'Forget it, Oti.' Edward blew out a breath and her heart ached that he was thinking of her even as he must be seeing his own chance—however slim—at some degree of recovery slipping away.

She reached forward, catching herself as she was about to put her hand over his—he wouldn't even feel her—and moving it to his cheek instead.

'Too late, Edward.' Her voice was soft. 'I already married him. The deed is done. So unless you want a bully like Father to be the only one to win, then you might as well accept it.'

'No, Oti.'

'You have to.' Frustration, and an old sense of guilt, bubbled up inside her, leaving her helpless to control her outburst. 'You wouldn't be in this state if it hadn't been for me.'

He blew out a sharp breath. 'For pity's sake, you weren't driving. I was. You weren't even in the car with me.'

'But if you hadn't been racing to collect me...' She

splayed her hands. 'If I hadn't called you, panicking, because *he* was at that party...'

'Stop it, Oats. It wasn't your fault.'

'It *was* my fault.' Oti let her head drop, her throat tight and clogged. 'If I'd never called you...'

'So what happens if I have a lower motor neuron intact?' he asked abruptly.

'What?' She jerked her head up, confused.

'Tell me about the procedure,' Edward ground out.

He was making an effort again. Pulling himself together despite everything. And she needed to do the same.

Oti smiled a watery smile. This was precisely why it didn't matter what she'd had to promise to Lukas, or her father.

Edward was worth it.

'Then the peripheral nerve transfer procedure can work to reroute expendable donors to non-functional nerves.'

For the next hour or so they talked through options and procedures. And it felt promising that Edward was listening to her, and they weren't fighting any more.

All that was left to do now was to call her father and get the funds he'd agreed to give her. She would do it as soon as she left Edward.

Her father must have received the money by now. The deal had stipulated that it be transferred to him from Lukas the moment they walked out of that cathedral as husband and wife. And—the Roc Holdings takeover aside—Lukas had a reputation for being utterly scrupulous where business was concerned.

She hoped with every fibre of her being that her father would honour the deal. Because if Lukas was softening towards her at all—and maybe it was just fancifulness on her part to think that was the case—then he wasn't going to feel that way if she had to go to him to try to inveigle more money out of him.

It would make her seem, certainly in Lukas's eyes, as greedy and grasping as her father himself.

CHAPTER FIVE

'CARE TO TELL me where you've been?'

Oti jumped as she closed the door to her suite. Slowly, she turned to look at Lukas as he stood—he felt as though he'd been lurking—by the connecting doors.

The expression in her stunning blue eyes was like a hand reaching inside his chest and clutching that thing which passed for a heart. Then twisting.

'What is it, Octavia?'

He heard the words before it even registered that he'd been going to say them, and he didn't like it that her eyes widened, as if the concern in his tone surprised her. As though she didn't expect kindness from him.

He fought back a wave of what felt astonishingly like... remorse.

'I was just...' She shook her head, clearly rattled. 'I phoned my father.'

'Oh...?' he prompted when she fell abruptly silent.

She didn't answer. Lukas wasn't even certain that she'd heard him.

'Octavia?'

She jerked her head up, her gaze colliding with his again. And then...something changed. The air around her shifted. She shook her head back so that her glorious curtain of hair danced over her shoulders, and with almost controlled deliberation she sashayed into the bedroom and past where he stood, wholly unconcerned.

'To answer your original question, I've been out,' she replied casually.

A feral growl rumbled up through his body. 'I can see that,' he said. 'Out where?'

'Who are you? My father?'

She almost laughed as she dropped her bag on the chair, began to unwind the long scarf from around her neck and removed her earrings, whilst he watched transfixed and feeling downright murderous.

'No, Octavia.' He let the doors go with a sweep of his arms, then stalked into the room. 'I'm your husband. Or do you need a reminder about that?'

And then he felt shocked at how jealous he was. As though he didn't know whether he was more annoyed at her or disgusted with himself. Perhaps because he hadn't been able to chase images of her wearing nothing but some scraps of snow-white lace, that he'd ached to tear off with his teeth, for God's sake—out of his head.

He'd actually convinced himself that he'd succeeded. All day at work he'd pretended to himself that he'd pushed her from his head, only to return home this evening to find the place distinctly Octavia-free and his driver gone.

It had felt inexplicably empty.

And now she'd practically floated back in, with a glow that he recognised from the women he'd slept with in the past. Only…he hadn't slept with her, which meant only one thing.

And a kind of primal rage seethed through his veins, even as he told himself that he didn't care.

That he *shouldn't* care.

But ever since their damned kiss at the altar he'd felt as edgy as an adolescent. Unfocused in an important business meeting today, and unable to distract himself with even the more herculean of physical exercise.

'I know you're my husband,' she said calmly, snapping him back to reality. 'We were married less than twenty-four hours ago—I'm hardly likely to forget.'

'So where were you?' he growled, not even recognising himself.

What was it about her that had him turning himself inside out?

She lowered her hands to her lap so damned calmly that it scraped at him all the more. Then she cocked her head towards him.

'Why do you care?'

Lukas didn't answer. Words would have been impossible. He wasn't just angry; he was furious. Emotions that were unfamiliar, and certainly unappreciated, surged through him. He didn't even know what he was doing.

Fake marriage or not, out of respect he had decided not to indulge in extramarital affairs. He'd at least expected her to show the same courtesy.

They'd only just had the ceremony, and it was about the optics of the situation.

Yeah, right...the optics.

Thrusting aside the unwelcome voice, Lukas forced himself to move to a chair, throwing himself down with his usual insouciance and stretching his arms out behind his head. No need for his deceitful new bride to know just how pent-up he was.

But then he watched as her eyes followed the line of his chest, as though drawn there against her will. That tiny intake of breath. The flicker of her tongue over her lips. It appalled and thrilled him in equal measure.

That attraction between them was still there. That was something. He could use that to his advantage.

Is that all it is? a voice taunted inside his head.

Lukas chose to ignore it.

'Perhaps I failed to be clear before, but I am very protective of what is mine. And since, as you so conveniently pointed out a few moments ago, we only married yesterday.'

'Is that so?' She surprised him. 'I didn't think we would be playing by those rules.'

'Well, we are.'

'Both of us?' she demanded. 'Or just me?'

For a long moment Lukas stared at her. And slowly he began to realise what was going on, the truth of it making him want to jump up and punch the air in triumph.

Inexplicably.

'Is that what this is about?' He grinned. And she blinked at him as though she wasn't sure how or why the tables had turned. 'Tit for tat? You think I'll cat around, so you're getting your kicks in first?'

'I *think* you'll cat around?' she echoed scornfully, doing a half-decent job of pretending that she was aghast, in Lukas's opinion. 'I don't *think* it, Lukas. I *know* it. Look at your reputation.'

'And so you intend to do the same?' He wasn't sure how he managed to stay in his seat.

Especially when she shrugged so easily.

'Why not?'

'This will not continue now that we are married,' he told her. Serenely.

Taking it as a victory that she stiffened perceptibly.

'I beg your pardon?'

Another flash of a smile that felt too sharp on his own mouth. He didn't understand what he was doing, or why he felt so…*outside* himself. But it didn't seem to matter. The words were coming out, anyway.

'Whoever you met this afternoon, you will not meet him again. Do you understand?'

'I know your reputation,' she continued too evenly, as

she casually plucked a tiny piece of non-existent lint from those deliciously backside-hugging jersey trousers.

It was a habit of hers he'd noticed right from that first night, five months ago. Though he couldn't have said why he'd been so paying so much attention.

'The whole world knows it, of course.' She was still speaking, frowning at him. 'And it isn't what a new bride would like to hear.'

'Is that so?' Lukas demanded, that full mouth of hers… *doing things* to him.

He told himself it was the whisky still running through his veins from the limo drive home, though he suspected that was not actually the source of his perturbation. He'd probably sweated that out after the first couple of hours of beasting himself.

Across from him, Oti lifted her shoulders as elegantly as she possibly could.

'You like to live life to its fullest. You drink and gamble and carouse.'

'Carouse?'

Her eyes narrowed at him. 'Now you wish to take issue with my choice of words?'

Despite everything, amusement tugged at the corners of his mouth. 'Forgive me, *Lady* Octavia.'

She glowered at him, and he liked that rather more than he ought to.

'My point is,' she emphasised irritably, 'that you are infamous for having a string of lovers. So I would ask whether you intend for your endless string of affairs and flings to continue?'

It was puzzling how little the idea appealed to him suddenly.

'Does it matter?'

'It does when you're dictating who I may and may not

meet now that we are married. Sauce for the goose and all that.'

'There will be no sauce,' he ground out, barely able to focus. His head was being turned inside out. 'No taking my driver to meet other men. No affairs.'

'And you?' she pressed. 'Not that I care about the affairs per se, of course. More that I don't wish to be made to look a fool any more than it appears you do.'

She leaned back on the bed then, her arms extended behind her. Lukas suspected she had no idea how that put her breasts on display in that figure-hugging top. Less idea still of quite how her gentle unpretentiousness was affecting him.

He'd never much cared for *sweet* women before, preferring those who knew what they were getting themselves into with him. He desired women, sure, and he prided himself on being a thorough, generous lover. But he'd never been so preoccupied with fantasies about peeling their clothes off, slowly and delicately. Taking such time and care.

It was all that had consumed his thoughts ever since she'd hauled that insane wedding dress around his house last night.

Ever since he'd opened that door and seen her standing there in those scraps of lace like some kind of real-life erotic pin-up.

'Are you offering yourself as an alternative?' His voice was little more than a rasp as he deliberately avoided her question.

He barely recognised himself. Or the primal creature that howled inside him, making him take one step, and then another, getting all too close to where she sat. To the *bed* on which she sat.

And he found that he felt altogether too much like an untried, overeager adolescent.

'If you want me to yourself, *my lady*, then you need only say so.'

She laughed, a sensual sound that seemed to wind itself around his groin like a fist. A very soft but firm Octavia-style fist.

What the hell was wrong with him? He didn't even *want* to want her. She was everything he despised. From her life-style to her morals. And whilst that might be okay for a single night of mutual satisfaction with a woman he would never have to see again, it wasn't a good idea to complicate things in this clear-cut arrangement of theirs. Why blur the lines with a woman he would have to see day in, day out for the foreseeable future?

And still he kept advancing.

'I realise you may find this difficult to understand, given the sheer volume of women who follow you around just hoping you'll notice them for a night, but you are not at all my type, Lukas. I am not the slightest bit attracted to you.'

Victory smashed through him. It made him want to punch his hand into the air.

Because here, at last, he finally knew she was lying.

He knew women, and he knew how his new bride had looked at him. Yesterday, on their wedding day and the first time they had met. She might not like him much, and she might like his reputation even less, but she *was* attracted to him. She couldn't help herself any more than he could. It was apparent in every line of that lush body of hers.

'I know you want me,' he rumbled, revelling in this sensation that was moving through him. 'I can read it in the way you respond to me. Every time. You can't help yourself.'

'I don't do any such thing,' she argued, but her voice was faltering. Insubstantial.

A revelation.

'Would you care to put that to the test?' he asked gruffly, the ache stirring inside him all the more.

There was a beat of hesitation before she answered. 'What kind of test?'

A thousand thoughts raced through his head. Each one dirtier than the last. He reined them in quickly.

'A kiss,' he told her simply.

'A kiss?' Her eyes raked over him searchingly. It might as well have been her fingertips.

He shivered.

'Yes,' he confirmed. 'If you respond, you'll admit the attraction. If you don't respond… Well, that won't happen.'

'Such humility,' she needled. But her eyebrows knitted together, as if she was trying to see the catch. 'That's it?'

'That's it,' he confirmed, willing her to accept.

When was the last time he'd wanted anything so much?

Oti pursed her lips, her brow pulling tighter as she tried to decide whether she could deceive him.

He didn't know why he held his breath, willing her to bite. And then she lifted her head and jerked her chin to him defiantly.

'Sure, why not? One kiss to prove you wrong.'

It was almost comical, the way she sat up, folded her hands into their usual place on her lap and closed her eyes as she tilted her head to the side.

Before he could think better of it, Lukas scooped her up and lifted her off the bed.

'Wait—where are we going?'

Wordlessly, he carried her out of her bedroom and to the sitting area, before sinking onto one of the couches with Octavia sprawled in his lap.

She struggled to right herself. 'What are you doing?'

'Setting your mind at ease,' he lied. 'I figured you would prefer to do this…*test* kiss in here, rather than on a bed. I don't know if I can trust you not to get too carried away.'

No need to tell her that he barely trusted himself not to get too carried away.

'Right,' she muttered huskily, not even realising that he hadn't tried to deny it.

He rather liked that. Just as liked the heat of her backside against the solid length of his sex. Making it more of a gratifying ache than a painful one.

'Now what?' she quipped. But the tremor in her voice gave her away, betraying her desire, just as he'd hoped.

Encouraging her to loop her arms around his neck, Lukas dipped his head to her, inhaling that fresh scent he remembered from the cathedral. It smelled more of tropical hair shampoo than any heavy, cloying perfume—only making her seem that much more innocent.

'Now what?' Her voice seemed to flutter around her, and he couldn't hold himself back any longer.

Bending his head, he didn't wait, he didn't warn. He just took.

Everything in Oti jolted, like grabbing hold of one of the electrified fences that had once been set up around their camp in Sudan.

Only far, far more pleasant.

Lukas was just as charged, just as stirring. And there had to be something seriously amiss with her because she revelled in every second of it.

The delicious crush of his mouth on hers, and the glorious sweep of that clever tongue.

Her arms were already around his neck, but now she used them to pull him closer, pressing her body tighter up against his, the feel of his hard length beneath her doing nothing to ease that heavy throb between her legs. And there was no way she could silence those giveaway sounds that were coming from her throat, of longing and of greed.

But, for his part, Lukas didn't appear any more controlled. His low growl of approval when she'd rocked over him had slid through her like honey. Warming her and spreading inside her. She tried it again, and this time he wrenched his mouth away from her.

'Be very careful,' he began, his voice so hoarse with desire that it made her breasts ache. 'I suggest you don't waken what you aren't prepared to deal with.'

And despite the fact that she had no real idea what she was doing, having never slept with any man before, Oti dropped her head to graze her teeth gently against the column of his neck.

'I'm more than prepared to deal with anything I awaken.'

He didn't hesitate. Dropping his head to reclaim her mouth, kissing her as thoroughly as if he were branding her, Lukas moved his attention to her jaw. Soft, butterfly-like kisses that had her murmuring softly, followed by a trail leading down her elegant neck and to her collarbone.

Oti couldn't help it. She became pliable and soft in his arms, moulding herself to him, just like she had in the cathedral, except this time, without an audience, she allowed her hands to roam freely over that sculpted chest, intent on exploring every inch of his incredible body and learning every ridge and every dip.

But it was getting harder and harder to concentrate when Lukas was tracing whorls on her skin like that as he moved. Until, at last, he reached the deep V neckline of her top. His mouth, his tongue, traced their way over her skin, the top of her chest, and dipped beneath the fabric.

And all she could think was how much more she wanted. How badly she ached for him. She tried to tell him what she wanted—*needed*—but then, seeming to read her body like a glorious book, Lukas hooked his fingers under her top and lifted it over her head with an impressive economy of movement.

'You've practised that,' she tried to joke, something

prodding her that she ought to be more wary about his sheer skill and efficiency.

But as she watched him fingering the delicate electric blue lace of her bra, something approaching marvel clouding his features, it was hard to even breathe, let alone talk.

'Stunning,' he growled.

And then he dispensed with that too, leaving her naked from the waist up, and feeling more feminine and wanton than she thought she'd ever felt before.

His eyes were almost black with the same desire that echoed within her. In all the places that no one had ever touched. Then they locked with hers as he cupped one of her breasts in his palm and she could only look on, transfixed, as he tested it, gloried in it and tasted it.

She had no idea what the sound was that came out of her mouth. Something primitive. Her body seemed to arch involuntarily, as if offering herself up to him all the more.

He feasted on her for a lifetime, maybe two, before switching sides to repeat the entire process. As if he had all the time in the world. Nowhere else to ever be. Nothing else to ever do.

He treated her as if she were infinitely precious, and even though a voice in her head tried to remind her that it was all fake, she didn't care.

And then, with deliberate care and his eyes still holding hers, he rubbed one calloused thumb pad over her taut, tender nipple and a low sigh escaped her as her eyes drifted closed. She wasn't prepared for the wallop of sensation when his mouth suddenly closed over it, drawing it into his mouth, sucking it deeper and letting his teeth slide over it, then soothing it with his cool, wicked tongue.

It was entirely possible, and embarrassing, that she was going to come apart just at that, and Oti couldn't bring herself to care. It was too good.

Too right.

Never, in all her wildest dreams, had she thought this was how she and Lukas would end up.

The convenient reality of their situation splashed into her head like a douse of cold water.

Lukas lifted his head up instantly. 'What is it?'

She'd almost forgotten when she'd started this…or agreed to it? Oti couldn't quite remember how it had begun; Lukas had her so twisted inside out with pleasure.

But the fact was that she'd called her father as soon as she'd left Edward, asking for her share of the money he'd extorted from Lukas.

He'd laughed callously at her before hanging up. Reneging on his promise, just as she'd always feared he would.

Begging Lukas for the money for Edward's surgery was now her only chance. Getting caught up in his kisses and forgetting the endgame certainly wasn't part of her plan.

'I have to ask you…' She faltered.

It was crazy how much she wanted to swallow the words down, stuff them away and simply enjoy this one night with Lukas. To let him show her what she'd been saving herself for all these years.

But Edward and his needs were supposed to be the entire reason she had gone through with this charade. With everything that her brother had put up with these past few years, was she really selfish enough to put a few hours of carnal lust ahead of what might save Edward's life?

Struggling to a more upright position, acutely aware that she was naked from the waist up, Oti kept her arms around Lukas's neck, as if that could somehow afford her a little dignity.

What if she told him the truth? Maybe she could appeal to his sense of decency. He certainly had some—more than she'd initially given him credit for, and certainly more than her father had ever had.

But what if he used it as leverage against her, just as

her own father had done? Could she really trust a man she barely knew, just because he made her body come alive in a way that she hadn't known it was capable of doing?

'What is it, Octavia?' Lukas demanded, and his concern only added to her guilt.

'I need to ask you a favour,' she began, flicking out her tongue in a fruitless effort to moisten her suddenly dry lips.

Beneath her, Lukas had grown still, tense, his hooded eyes disguising his reaction from her. But she forced herself to carry on.

'Like you said, consummation wasn't part of the deal you made with my father.'

'The deal?' Lukas echoed, and she knew she didn't imagine the mounting fury in his tone.

Still, she pressed on. For Edward.

'Yes, the deal. You got my brother's company, my father got money and he got to wash his hands of me. But now it's my turn.'

'Your turn?'

There was no doubting his expression of disgust. Unlinking her hands from around him, he thrust her away and onto the couch, hardly able to get away from her any faster.

'I want to come out of this with something too.'

'Is that what this was all about?' he spat out. 'Money?'

'No,' she cried instinctively, before realising her mistake. 'Yes, but…for a good reason.'

Misery racked her.

'Save it, Octavia.' His voice was harsh, and it seemed to claw at her from the inside out. 'You really are your father's daughter now. Save the excuses, however. I don't want to hear them. How much?'

'Lukas…please…'

'How much?' he repeated, and she didn't dare argue again.

She named a sum that she knew would cover the cost

of the operation, not a penny more, and couldn't stop herself from lamenting the fact that if her father had shared the pot he'd extorted from Lukas she wouldn't have to be asking for this now.

'You will have your money…'

'Lukas, please know that…'

'The money will be there,' he bit out. 'You don't need to whore yourself out for it.'

And then, before she could say anything else—even if she'd had a clue what to say—he had stalked across the room and into his own suite, the unmistakable sound of the key turning in the lock making it clear that he was rejecting her.

She could hardly blame him. But it didn't stop her from throwing herself onto the huge marshmallow pillows of her bed and sobbing herself to sleep.

Yet what choice did she have?

The day could hardly have gone much worse. And it was all her own doing.

CHAPTER SIX

SINKING BACK INTO the creamy soft seats of the limousine, Oti fought the urge to close her eyes.

She hadn't slept a wink for the last couple of days, tossing and turning each night, her thoughts returning over and over to Lukas. And that kiss.

The way her whole body ignited each time she replayed it in her head. No one had ever come close to making her feel like Lukas did. Making her ache like he did.

After what had happened to her that ghastly night almost fifteen years ago, she'd begun to think that no one ever would.

In fact, she'd begun to conclude that there had to be something wrong with her. Why had she insisted on carrying it with her, letting it overshadow any hint of a relationship with any man since?

Ultimately, she'd been rescued. Other women went through far, far worse ordeals. So why had she carried it with her all these years? Why didn't she feel the same drive that other young women her age felt?

And then Lukas had stepped into her life and she'd felt something shift inside her, even from their first meeting. However much she'd tried to pretend otherwise, there had been something about Lukas that had simply lifted all those heavy, suffocating layers away.

She'd thought their kiss in the cathedral had been un-balancing enough, but the other night had just upended her world completely.

Oti couldn't stop replaying it. It was on a loop that she couldn't—didn't want to—break. And that made the man so much more dangerous to her. Just like she'd always thought he was.

God, how she'd wanted him to keep kissing her. To touch her, the way he'd deliciously threatened to do. That rich, dark voice of his had played with her senses, turning them in on themselves so that she could barely think straight.

So that all she'd been able to think of was Lukas, and the way he'd been tasting her. Teasing her. She'd felt so wanton—desired and desirable. More than that, he'd made her feel as if there was nothing lacking about her at all. As if she'd just been waiting for this—for *him*—all this time. It was surely one of Lukas's greatest skills, and she'd been helpless to resist him.

If he hadn't stopped, then Oti was in no doubt that she would have given herself up to him right there and then, on that sofa in her bedroom suite.

Giving her virginity to a man who barely liked her, let alone loved her.

She might ask herself what she'd been thinking, except the truth of it was that she hadn't been *thinking*. She hadn't been capable of thinking at all.

Edward was right. She'd been playing with fire the mo-ment she'd agreed to her father's preposterous plan to marry her off to a man like Lukas Woods. Whilst she might have told herself that she was sacrificing herself for a greater purpose—to get money for Edward's surgery—the truth was far less noble.

She had wanted Lukas from that very first meeting, in a terrifyingly exciting, utterly carnal way. Her body had recognised it, even if her mind had refused to accept it.

But it was getting harder and harder to lie to herself. Not least because the money was there—from Lukas—in her account, and still...that raw, urgent longing hadn't gone away.

It was all so confusing.

The fact that she hadn't even had to sleep with the man told her so much more about what kind of a person he was. And it didn't match the ruthlessness of his reputation.

She should have everything she wanted. And yet she didn't. Because what a part of her really seemed to want—physically if not emotionally, of course; she wasn't that crazy—was Lukas. And she couldn't shake that sense of regret and blame over what had happened between them the other night.

Nor the rawness that scraped somewhere unfathomable, deep inside her chest.

Perhaps talking to Edward again today would clear that up. Being able to finally assure him that the procedure was a possibility—that, as long as the tests proved him to be a viable candidate, money wouldn't be a stumbling block—should erase any lingering doubts about Lukas from her mind.

As well as any final remnants of guilt.

'Commandeering my driver again?'

For the third time in almost as many days, Oti found herself startled by her fake husband. She watched, horrified, as he slid into the back seat across from her. She tried—and failed—to stop her eyes from soaking up the sight of his long, mouth-wateringly muscular legs, which his tailored suit did nothing to diminish. Quite the contrary; they stretched out in front of him so very languidly, practically inviting her gaze to roam upward.

Oti blew out a breath of frustration. Even here, in the back seat of a car, he wore power like a bespoke suit. And, like everything else, it fitted him immaculately.

'What are you doing, Lukas?' she managed, her voice scratchier than she would have liked. But that couldn't be helped.

'Heading into the office. Some of us work for a living.'

She bit her lip to stop herself from answering. There was no need to tell him about her job—it didn't matter to her at all what he thought.

If only she could believe that.

'You aren't driving yourself? Only you have done the last few days.'

'You haven't used my driver the last few days,' he pointed out.

'So you're only here because I am?' She could hardly matter that much to him, surely?

'After last time, can you blame me?'

Shame and anger bled into each other and Oti opened her mouth to answer, only for the driver to alert them to an accident further up the road.

'The report says that traffic is gridlocked, sir,' George, the driver, continued. 'We could go the longer way around—the roads that way are quieter.'

'Do that,' Lukas confirmed as Oti's heart lurched.

A longer car ride, with the tension already palpable? Just what she didn't need.

The car turned and they drove in silence for a while and Oti forced herself to stare out of the window. Anything not to have to engage with him.

More because she feared confusion and—shamefully—lust would be written all over her features.

It was only as they pulled up at a set of red lights that Oti found her gaze pulled to the commotion going on in a car parked awkwardly in the kerb, though it took her a few moments to work out exactly what she was seeing.

'Stop the car!' she yelled, just as George began to pull away again.

It vaguely registered that it took Lukas repeating the instruction for the driver to obey.

'What's going on?' His voice was low, almost guarded.

'Unlock the doors, George. *Now*. I think the woman in that car is in labour, and she's on her own.'

The door clicked and she practically stumbled out as she hurried back to the other car, only realising that Lukas was right alongside her as she reached the passenger side.

'George is calling an ambulance,' he told her quickly. 'I don't think it's wise to interfere. Leave it to the professionals when they arrive.'

Oti didn't reply; she just picked up her pace. Tapping on the car window, she then stepped back to give the grunting woman space.

'I'm Oti, I'm a doctor. I'm here to help.'

With another grunt and a twisted expression, the woman managed to unlock the car door, and Oti hauled it open.

'My husband…' the woman managed between groans. 'He forgot his mobile in the panic to leave the house. He… he ran to the petrol station down the road with our son to… make the call.'

'Okay, so is this your second baby?' Oti asked. 'Can you tell me your name?'

'Debi… This is my…second. Yes… I was…in labour for ten hours with him… This one can't come…yet.'

'Yeah, it happens that way sometimes.' Oti offered a gentle laugh. 'Hours for the first, but the second is quick. Nothing to worry about. I can tell your contractions aren't far apart at all. Can we get you into the back seat so there's a little more room for me to examine you?'

She felt Lukas's hand at her elbow, drawing her away.

'You need to wait for the professionals,' he ground out in a low voice.

'I'm a doctor,' she reminded him irritably, beginning to wrench her arm away.

His grip tightened.

'You might have bought your degree,' he hissed, 'but that doesn't make you a practising doctor. You can't play superhero with this woman's baby.'

Oti had had enough. Never mind her own sense of privacy or keeping her secrets. This woman needed her, and she wasn't about to let Lukas stop her from doing the one thing she did best.

'For pity's sake, Lukas, I *am* a professional,' she hissed up at him. 'I haven't been on the beach, or whatever my father has claimed. I've been working in South Sudan for the past four years, looking after women and children, including delivering babies. On an average day, our small unit can help deliver sixty babies in a twenty-four-hour period. I know what I'm doing.'

Later, she would savour that stunned expression which passed over his face. The way he stopped looking at her with quite such a mixture of pity and disdain. The moment he began to see her in a different light.

Later.

But right now she had a job to do.

'Get the first aid kit from your limo—your driver will know where it is if you don't. I need gloves, and hand sanitizer if there is any.'

She occupied herself with helping Debi from the passenger seat to the back seat, settling the woman into position just as Lukas returned with the gloves and gel.

'Okay, Debi, it's going to be okay. I just need to check how dilated you are, and see if I can feel the baby's head.'

'The ambulance is on its way,' Lukas murmured just before Oti moved back to her patient. 'But that accident we were avoiding is blocking the road for everyone.'

'Understood.' She nodded, stepping away from him. 'Okay, Debi, let's see how you're doing.'

She dropped down to begin her check, but even in that

instant her suspicions were confirmed. Still, she took a moment to confirm all was okay before pasting a bright smile on her face as she stood up.

'Okay, so you're fully dilated, Debi, and I can see the baby's head. Your baby is clearly eager to meet you, so I don't think we're going to be able to wait until the ambulance arrives.'

'I can't deliver here,' Debi gasped. 'In the back seat of the car, in the middle of the road.'

'It happens more often than you might think,' Oti soothed, turning quickly to Lukas. 'Can you get me water, paper towels or something like it, and scissors?'

Then she glanced him up and down, her eyes alighting on his suit footwear.

'And give me your shoelaces.'

His curt nod before swinging around to obey her gave Oti a ridiculous kick of pleasure. As though something had *shifted* between them. In a good way. She thrust it aside, focusing on her patient instead and busying herself with keeping Debi calm, and breathing properly.

But the birth was happening fast.

Crouching down on the ground, she watched the baby as she heard her patient give a more guttural grunt. There was nothing else for it.

'Push,' Oti ordered. *'Push.'*

With a loud cry, the woman pushed, and the baby slithered straight out and into Oti's arms, and all she could do was pray that she didn't drop it.

'Scissors, water, paper towels, and the rug from the car.' Lukas's voice came from behind her as she swung around to face him. 'Oh.'

He stopped abruptly, gazing in horror at the baby in her arms. It might have been comical under any other circumstances. To see the all-powerful, always controlled Lukas Woods look so thrown.

'Lay the paper towels on the seat,' she instructed. 'Quickly.'

To his credit, he gathered himself instantly, laying them down so that Oti was able to clean and massage the baby until she heard that first beautiful cry.

'Shoelaces and scissors?' She turned to Lukas as he was just standing up from untying them.

Wordlessly, he handed her both and, conscious that his eyes were still on her, she busied herself with tying off the umbilical cord and then cutting it. Finally, wrapping the baby up warmly, Oti handed the precious bundle to an emotional but happy mother.

'Meet your daughter—ten fingers, ten toes and a healthy set of lungs.'

'My husband…?'

'I'll head up the road to look for him.' Lukas didn't hesitate. 'Let him know what's happened.'

And as he left Oti was almost grateful for the space. It was a chance to decompress. This time, she was in no doubt that Lukas would have questions but, far from dreading them as she might have a week ago, she thought she might actually welcome them.

It would be a chance to let Lukas see the real her and maybe erase some of the less than flattering opinion he had of her as some dumb socialite.

And even though she knew it should worry her that his opinion of her mattered so much, Oti couldn't seem to escape the notion.

She was still fighting her own thoughts when Lukas returned with the rather frantic-looking husband and the couple's relatively nonplussed son in tow. Keeping their distance, the two of them tried to give the family space as they all waited for the ambulance.

'You should have told me,' Lukas bit out eventually.

Oti paused in the process of shoving the bloodied paper

towels into the bin-liner, though she deliberately didn't look at him. She didn't need to ask what he was talking about.

'Would you have believed me?' she asked quietly.

'I'd have had it looked into.'

The saddest part, Oti thought, was that he actually thought she would find that reassuring.

'So you wouldn't have believed me,' she pointed out. 'You wouldn't have taken my word for it.'

He actually hesitated. The man renowned for never missing a beat. It felt like a small victory, even as she chastened herself for caring about that.

'Why would you let people paint you as some vacuous, party-hard It-girl who's permanently living it up on some extended tropical holiday? Or that you're in rehab yet again?'

She tilted her head up to him. 'What difference does it make?'

'What difference?' he echoed, appalled. 'Look at what you just did. That was…*incredible*.'

He shook his head as though he couldn't actually find the words and, even though Oti tried to pretend his words didn't affect her, there was no denying that ball of pride which swelled inside her, just hearing the admiration in his tone.

Lukas Woods thought she was *incredible*.

'What could you possibly gain by not telling anyone the truth?' he demanded angrily.

Oti didn't know how, but she managed a shrug.

'The truth gets distorted by what people want to see.'

'All the more reason to tell them.'

'They wouldn't have wanted to hear it,' she countered evenly.

'Then you make them.'

'Why? What does their opinion matter to me?' She even let a laugh escape her, a genuine one. Because her next observation, at least, was true. 'You certainly don't let yourself get affected by what other people think.'

'They don't think I'm a party girl.'

'But *I* know I'm not. And besides, they think you're a ruthless playboy. But you aren't really, are you?'

He didn't answer, but the glare that he shot at her might have skewered a lesser woman. Right now, though, she felt anything but *lesser.*

'You really don't care what people think, do you?' His eyes seemed to root her to the spot.

She couldn't move. She wasn't even sure she could breathe.

It was as though Lukas was seeing her for the first time. Or, if not that, then certainly through fresh eyes. And she found the whole experience almost exhilarating.

'You're not at all the girl I thought.'

'Well, then—' she wasn't entirely sure how she managed to sound so breezy '—it serves you right for not doing your homework on me properly, doesn't it? I can't imagine you're usually so lax when it comes to business. I can only take it as further proof that you aren't as cold-blooded as you like people to believe.'

'In fact,' he continued as if she hadn't spoken, 'you're not a *girl* at all, are you?'

And, before she could answer, he reached out and took a lock of her hair, rolling it between his thumb and forefinger for a moment, before tucking it behind her ear.

It was such a soft, unexpected, *intimate* gesture. And it wiped all thought from Oti's mind.

But then he simply took the rubbish bag from her, stalking to the public bin on the pavement and dropped their rubbish in the slot which would take it to the underground storage.

Then he paced back to her, before turning to sit on the bonnet of the limo, his legs stretched in their usual position, his arms folded across his chest, highlighting his chest and biceps. Not a close-cut hair out of place. The trousers and waistcoat of his bespoke suit as immaculate as usual on his sculpted frame.

And Oti watched his every movement as though beguiled. A billionaire who was accustomed to snapping his fingers and everyone leaping to attention, yet he hadn't been too proud to help her with the baby, and the clean-up afterwards. A man who wasn't afraid of getting his hands dirty—quite literally.

Despite all her caution, the more time she spent with Lukas, the more she found herself admiring him. Respecting him. And having that respect reflected back at her now when he looked at her was…exhilarating.

Yet it was also terrifying. Because, if she wasn't careful, she could end up confusing attraction and respect, could end up falling for the man. A man who didn't remotely feel the same way about her.

She eyed the horizon as a hundred—a thousand—thoughts crashed around her head. But there were so many of them and they were all so intertwined that she had no idea where to even begin unravelling the truth. And at the centre of it was that one single event that she didn't want to have to talk about to anyone.

Certainly not to Lukas.

'Then why did your father perpetuate those rumours?' Lukas demanded after a while.

'Because he doesn't know the truth.'

'You can't expect me to believe that, surely?'

'My father hasn't noticed me since I was *that* girl, all those years ago. He's a selfish and self-serving man, but I think you already know that.'

'I do indeed. So surely he would have preferred to use your success as a doctor to somehow turn it around to his own success as a father?'

'He would have, yes,' she agreed evenly. 'Which is why I never told him. I suppose I thought he'd work it out eventually. The fact that he never has speaks for itself, I think.'

'So he would rather paint you as an addict who wastes her life partying abroad, and ends up in rehab all too often?' Lukas's disdain was unmistakable, and Oti felt her mouth twist into a hollow smile.

'Ironically, that helps him.'

'I fail to see how.'

'That's because you aren't like my father.' Her gaze was drawn to Lukas despite herself, and her smile became a little less hollow and a little warmer. 'That's a compliment.'

'Indeed it is,' he answered grimly.

'You may be calculating and ruthless when it comes to work, but you aren't nearly as intrusive when it comes to more personal matters.' She smiled. 'You're a nicer person than you want the world to see. I just don't understand why.'

'And again—' Lukas arched an eyebrow at her, making her hands actually itch to reach out and smooth it '—this isn't about me.'

'Perhaps I'm hoping that if I open up to you then you might afford me the same courtesy.'

She didn't realise how true that was until she heard the words come out of her mouth.

'Don't bank on it,' he growled softly.

But it lacked any bite and Oti felt her smile warming her from the inside. She dipped her head to conceal it.

'Fair enough. Either way, my point is that it suited my father to let people think I was still that wild child. Whilst they were speculating about me, they weren't looking at him. Plus, there were rumours that he was having some financial trouble, and I became the perfect scapegoat.'

'He could tell them that you had blown through your inheritance on exotic holidays, wild parties and drugs,'

Lukas realised. 'That way, no one would think he was the one who'd lost it all gambling.'

'He could also claim that he'd spent hundreds of thousands sending me to rehab.'

'The man's a degenerate,' Lukas snarled. 'But you're a fool for letting him get away with painting you that way. Why wouldn't you say something?'

She could tell him about HOP, and how she'd always feared her father would piggyback onto the charity and try to use her involvement with it to somehow improve his image. And then she thought about Edward, and how his accident was the reason that she'd ended up fleeing to the charity in the first instance.

She couldn't tell Lukas about one without the other.

'It's complicated,' she hedged at last.

'And that's a cop-out.'

His look of disappointment cut through her, but the distant wail of an ambulance siren saved her from the need to answer. They each lapsed into silence, waiting for the sound to get closer, as Oti tried to pretend to herself that she didn't care that Lukas had been so easily stopped from asking her anything more.

And yet she waited and held her breath. But he still didn't speak. She needed to pull herself together.

'I'd better go and alert my new patient,' she commented, standing up straight. 'They look like they're all too preoccupied to have heard it.'

'Will you need to accompany them to the hospital?' Lukas asked.

'I don't think so.' She shook her head. 'There were no complications, so a handover to the paramedics should suffice.'

'Good. Then we'll head back home and talk properly.'

'No, I can't...' The words came out in a panicked rush. 'I have to go and see... I have to go.'

She could feel the change in Lukas instantly. Even if she hadn't been so close that she could feel him tense, she would have felt it in the way the air around them tightened. It thickened.

'That will not happen, Octavia. You're not going anywhere until we've talked.'

'I don't know what you think is going on here,' Oti cried desperately. 'But I have to go. I need to see Edward.'

'Edward?'

'My brother.' She watched Lukas's expression change from anger to disbelief to shock, all in the space of about a second, and it occurred to her that she was far too tuned in to the man if she could recognise all that so easily. 'The money I needed from you was for him. For an operation.'

'I thought your brother died,' he said slowly.

'He didn't.' Misery washed over her at the disgust beginning to settle over Lukas's features. 'That was another of my father's lies.'

And one that Edward had wanted her repeat, if only for his own dignity. But she wasn't about to tell Lukas that.

The sirens' wail was louder now, and Oti knew she had to go. But she felt rooted to the spot. Paralysed.

'Go and help your patient. I'll leave George to take you to Edward.'

'You're going?' She didn't know why she felt so surprised. Or so deflated.

'I have a meeting to get to.'

There really was no reason for her to feel disappointed. So why did she?

'Then take the car, Lukas.'

He pushed himself off the bonnet and began to move away.

'I'll walk.' His tone was inscrutable. 'I need to think, anyway, and the fresh air will do me good.'

He stepped around the car and reached inside to retrieve

his phone and jacket, slinging it over his shoulder as he walked away. Try as she might, she couldn't seem to drag her eyes from him.

'And what then?' she asked thickly.

Lukas turned to look at her, the expression in his eyes almost ominous.

'Then, Octavia, you are going to come home, and you are going to tell me everything.'

And it struck Oti as more than a little telling that the part her unguarded heart clung on to most tightly in that instruction was when he told her to *come home*.

CHAPTER SEVEN

OCTAVIA WAS IN his sleek living room, already waiting for him, when Lukas finally arrived home that evening.

She looked serene and composed, and utterly in control—just as she had done that morning helping the mother give birth to her child inside that car. As though this was the kind of thing she did every day.

He suspected, from all the research he had spent the day doing, including her charity work with Health Overseas Project, that it wasn't too far from the truth.

Octavia—or Oti, as she preferred to be called—wasn't at all the woman that he'd believed her to be.

Had he ever been so mistaken about someone?

The question had been running through his head for the past several hours, though he knew the answer of course. It was because that was all he'd been expecting her to be. It was all that he'd *wanted* her to be.

He'd known her reputation didn't fit from practically the first moment they'd met, when she'd sent all his senses into full alert. But he'd ignored it because it hadn't suited the narrative he'd wanted to write.

Then he'd realised it again in the cathedral, when she'd stood in front of him and he'd felt as if his skull was cracking with the effort of resisting her. And he'd certainly realised it on witnessing the way she'd taken charge during

Andrew Rockman's heart attack. But he'd ignored it on those occasions too, because he'd been so focused on stealing Sedeshire International out from under Rockman's nose. And he'd been using her to finally trounce that man, once and for all.

Now, though, it was time to face up to the fact that he should never have married her. Oti deserved better than to be a pawn in such a game, and he should have known that.

Lukas crossed the room to pour himself a drink from the cabinet—more for something to do than because he actually wanted one—and then took out a glass for her.

'I take it you do drink?' he asked brusquely. 'Given that you're clearly not in need of any twelve-step programme after all.'

He hadn't intended to sound quite so abrasive and, in any case, his anger was directed more at himself than at Oti. But he wasn't accustomed to missing things, certainly not in business. Oti might believe it showed he wasn't quite as ruthless as he liked to appear, and it was ridiculous how much Lukas wanted to be the man she thought he was. However, he suspected the truth was far less selfless.

The simple fact was that whilst business was always clear and easy for him, marrying Oti had been about furthering his revenge for his mother. He had nearly—finally—succeeded in the plan he'd formulated back when he'd been a twelve-year-old kid. A plan he'd tweaked slightly over the years, but which had essentially stayed the same.

A plan which he'd been impatient to execute because he'd wanted to move on with his life. Truth be told, he'd wanted it over with a decade ago. But he couldn't simply abandon it—he couldn't simply let his mother's death go without exacting some sort of punishment.

'I do drink, yes.' Oti's quiet voice dragged him mercifully back to the present. 'Though I prefer wine to brandy.'

'Red or white?'

'Red, if there's a choice,' she replied, unfailingly polite, which nearly killed him.

He opened the bespoke wine cabinet and selected a bottle, then set about opening it. In silence again, feigning a patience that he didn't feel, until at last he was crossing the room towards her and setting the glass of wine down on the expensive coffee table.

'Thank you,' she murmured, lifting the glass elegantly and taking a sip before setting it back down.

He wasn't sure why, but he wondered if she found it as tasteless as he currently found his favourite brandy.

Moving away, Lukas found himself at the huge picture window. The view had always made him feel as though the city—and what felt like the entire world—was at his feet, but now Lukas peered down the long, straight, wide roads as if seeing past the city's boundaries would somehow let him see the big picture that he'd been missing all this time.

'Ask me what you want to know, Lukas.' Her quiet voice flowed over him.

He didn't turn around.

'How about we start with why you went along with your father's sick story that your brother was dead?'

His choice of words was designed to twist into her, too barbed to go unnoticed. Yet it didn't escape him that he deliberately kept his back to her so that he didn't have to see the expression in her eyes. So it surprised him when her tone stayed even.

'I didn't go along with my father's sick story.'

He turned despite himself.

'It was Edward's request,' she continued smoothly. 'It just happened to have the same result as my father intended.'

'*Edward* asked you to say he was dead?' Lukas asked, wholly unprepared for the look of pain that crossed her delicate features before she seemed to steel herself.

And in that instant he hated that she had to wear such a mask around him.

'My brother told me on multiple occasions that he wanted to…die.'

Lukas didn't answer, not having a clue what to even begin to say.

'The crash was bad.'

'I saw the news reports at the time,' Lukas confirmed.

Not to mention the fact that he'd done an internet search that afternoon, unable to concentrate on his meeting. Or any of the work that demanded his attention, for that matter.

It had been late on Christmas Eve, and Edward had allegedly been driving on a narrow, unlit valley road in the driving rain when an oncoming driver had lost control and skidded around the bend on Edward's side of the road.

His vehicle had been rammed through the drystone wall and who knew how many times it had tumbled down the steep rocky slope before coming to a halt at the bottom, on its roof.

When had he crossed the room again? When had he lowered himself into the chair opposite her?

'His injuries were…*are* significant.'

'But he's alive,' Lukas clarified. 'Is he in a coma?'

'No, he isn't.'

He didn't particularly appreciate the feeling creeping through him at that moment.

'He has brain damage?'

'No, he's alert, and his mind is as sharp as it ever was.'

'I just bought the controlling shares of his company.' Lukas eyed her grimly. He'd never regretted a business deal in his life. Until now.

'Edward's well aware.' Her expression was rueful. 'But, as far as he's concerned, it's better in your hands than Rockman's.'

'If his mind is still sharp, then why not keep the company? I only met him a couple of times, but he always struck me as a good CEO.'

'He was. Most of the board agreed,' she told him in a voice that Lukas now recognised was too calm, too controlled. As if she had a tight lid on myriad emotions which bubbled within but couldn't afford to let a single one of them show. 'Sadly, a few didn't, and Edward agreed.'

She stopped abruptly. Lukas could have asked more, but he wanted her to tell him when she was ready. Clamping his jaw shut, he forced himself to wait.

'He's tetraplegic,' she announced after what felt like an age. 'He's stuck in a wheelchair, he can't move his arms or legs, he can't even grasp things, and as far as Edward is concerned it's no life at all.'

'Yet, asking you to pretend he was dead—' Lukas shook his head '—isn't that a bit extreme?'

'Not if he wanted to protect his privacy. His dignity.' She shook her head. 'He was an amateur racing car enthusiast, Lukas. The media were seriously attracted to him. Almost as much as you. Can you imagine if you were in an accident? The lengths they would go to get to you? In the first few days alone, after Edward's accident, we caught three reporters or photographers dressed up as hospital porters, or a nurse, just to get in and get a photo of him. One of them even succeeded.'

He remembered it in that instant, the image flashing into his mind, making him wonder how he'd forgotten it. He'd been hooked up to machines and surrounded by tubes and wires. If it were himself, he could see how it would unnerve the board at LVW Industries.

'So the photo of him in a coma, four years ago, wasn't released by the family, as was claimed?' Lukas realised with a jolt.

'No, it was not. Not even my father would admit to Edward's condition, even for money.'

This was what Oti had gone through? Having to deal

with a relentless press whilst trying to come to terms with the seriousness of her brother's accident. Especially after losing her mother six years earlier.

'We had him moved to a private, very discreet medical facility. Fortunately, as company founder, he had the highest level of medical cover. Plus, the board wanted to keep the extent of his injuries concealed until they knew more, so as not to frighten any shareholders. Which was fortunate, since I can't imagine my father had the means or the inclination to pay for Edward's treatment.'

Neither could Lukas, but he wisely stayed silent.

'At first, all I prayed for was that he would wake up. Then, when he couldn't feel anything, I prayed that it was just bruising. We kept hoping that once the swelling went down he would be okay, albeit with rehabilitation. By the time we realised the full extent of his injuries, Edward had decided that he didn't want anyone to know until he had come to terms with it himself, and the board agreed. It was decided that, as the press would be relentless in trying to get a photo of him as long as they knew he was alive, it was easier to pretend otherwise.'

'And your father?'

'He was only too happy to wash his hands of a son with a disability.' Finally, she couldn't keep the bitterness from her tone.

She looked so broken and defeated, so unlike the woman he'd imagined she was. And suddenly all Lukas wanted to do was go to her, scoop her into his arms and take all her pain away.

He had no idea where that came from.

Not least because he never allowed himself to feel anything. It made no sense.

'Is that why you started volunteering in South Sudan?'

'I wouldn't have, if Edward hadn't banned me from even

visiting him for the first two years.' She jerked her head up, her tone defensive.

'I wasn't attacking you.'

She eyed him warily, and he found he didn't much like that either.

'I had to get away. I needed to do something meaningful. And, although I'd managed to drop off the media's radar for years, without Edward to pursue any more, they turned their attention back to me.'

'I believe there were articles,' he mused, 'and photos of wild parties and reckless behaviour.'

'Old photos that hadn't been released before.' She looked embarrassed nonetheless. 'I suspect people released them for money. Maybe even my father. And I could have fought them, but what would have been the point? People only want the salacious story. The pictures were of me—no one really cared whether they were out of date or not. Besides, I earned my wild-child reputation by my own actions.'

There was such a bleak turn to her countenance that it scraped at something inside Lukas. He couldn't have said why he suspected there was far more to the story. Nor could he explain how he knew that now wasn't the time to press her on it. So instead he asked her something else.

'You said the money I gave you is for Edward?'

'There's an operation.' She scrunched up her face and he got the impression that she was trying to decide how best to explain it.

He, a man who usually had to explain the intricate workings of computer programming or robotic workings to others. It might have been amusing, under other circumstances.

'There's a new operation. A combined nerve and tendon transfer, which could help him. Possibly. There's no guarantee. It's in clinical trials.'

'So he's in a trial?'

'No, the nature of his injuries mean that he isn't eligible for the trials. But we can still pay privately. I just didn't have a way of guaranteeing the money and so I couldn't even get him to agree to have an assessment to see if he would be a good candidate.'

'And now you have my money.'

'I won't apologise, Lukas.' She glowered.

'I don't expect you to. I'm assuring you that, no matter what else happens, you have my money. *Your* money. Whatever your brother needs, come to me. It's just money, Oti.'

Shock then relief skittered over her lovely face. And then she smiled and her face lit up. It was like being dazzled by the light from the glory of the sun itself.

More than that, it seemed to warm his very soul. It seemed to make it feel whole again.

'I called them today and they'll see him at the end of the week.' She shifted in her chair and he realised it was with excitement.

And something else that he couldn't quite isolate. As much as he didn't want to dampen her mood, Lukas couldn't help asking more questions.

'Do you mean that?' She sounded almost breathless, and what did it say about him that he liked the impact he'd had on her?

'I do. So your father wouldn't pay for any of it?' he asked.

'He said he would. He promised he would pay for it with the obscene sum he extorted from you. But…' She trailed off.

'That's why you agreed to marry me,' Lukas realised. 'Your father promised to pay for Edward's operation if you married me.'

'Yes.'

'He reneged, though. That's why you asked me. As your husband, I'd be honour-bound to agree? It was a last resort, but you still thought I needed buttering up?'

He didn't need to spell it out for her; she was clearly embarrassed enough. She was also torn. He could read it in every line of her tense body. Still, he wasn't surprised when she tried to defend the repugnant man.

'I hoped he would honour it.'

'Your father is too greedy for honour, Oti,' Lukas murmured quietly. 'He wanted the money for himself, whilst you wanted the money to save your brother's life.'

'You make it sound entirely noble and selfless.' She frowned.

'Because it is.' Remorse stirred within him. 'You're the only one who hasn't been self-serving throughout this entire arrangement.'

'Am I?' Her gaze slammed into his without warning. 'So why *did* you marry me, Lukas? What's in it for you? I mean, I understand the part of the deal where you got Edward's company, and my father got his money, but why me?'

It was on the tip of his tongue to tell her that this conversation was about her, not him—just as he had back at the roadside that morning—but the words didn't come.

'I'm guessing my father thought our marriage might somehow keep you around to tap for more money when he blows through the first lot. But why agree, Lukas? You could have refused that part of the deal. He would still have taken your deal—it was almost double anything Rockman could offer.'

What was it about this one unique woman that had him twisting and turning, no longer sure of the difference between black and white, night and day? It was all a glorious confusion where Oti was concerned.

And, for the first time, he felt an inexplicable urge to talk to her as he'd never talked to anyone in his life.

Oti wasn't sure at what point she realised she was holding her breath, but suddenly she was aware of the feeling that her lungs were about to burst.

Lukas had been silent for so long that it seemed as though he was actually going to talk to her. She desperately wanted him to. What wouldn't she give to be the person Lukas Woods talked to? In a way she seriously doubted the notoriously closed-off man had ever talked to anyone.

But then, without warning, he shut down again.

'You should have told me what was going on, Oti. I asked you several times if you knew what you were doing.'

'I remember.' She drew in a long breath, trying not to let the disappointment flood through her. 'And in that sense, yes, I knew. But I couldn't tell you about Edward, I didn't know what you would do—if you would use it as further leverage against me.'

'You think I'm capable of that?'

He looked utterly appalled. But there was something adding to her disappointment now. Something more. Something like the beginnings of anger.

He wouldn't answer a single one of her questions, yet he was virtually flaying her with every one of his. And she was supposed to answer without complaint?

'Yes. No. I don't know.' She exhaled her confusion. 'I thought so…but the more I've got to know you…'

And yet if the emergency this morning hadn't happened, she couldn't be sure that she would have said anything.

'How did you even get to be a doctor without everyone knowing?' He caught her by surprise.

'It's a long story.'

This was verging into territory that she didn't want to go.

'We have all night,' he answered evenly, but there was an unmistakable steel to his tone.

'It isn't that interesting.'

'It is to me,' he refuted.

'As is your life to me.' She didn't know where it came from, but she heard the words spilling out. 'Yet you keep all your secrets whilst demanding all of mine.'

He scowled at her, but he didn't refute what she said. Oti took that as progress.

'Tell me something about you, Lukas. Something no one else knows.'

The room fell quiet. Almost deafeningly silent. And even though she knew he wouldn't answer her, she couldn't bring herself to break it. She didn't want to be the one to speak first.

'Something like what?' he gritted out, taking her by surprise.

It took her a moment to regroup, her heart knocking around her chest as her mind rapidly sifted through the hundreds of questions that had flitted across her brain at once.

'Tell me about your parents,' she asked abruptly.

'My parents are dead, but you know that. I think the world knows I wrote my first app aged fifteen in the bedroom of my foster home.'

'A two-metre by one-metre cupboard that barely passed as a bedroom,' she couldn't help herself from saying. 'Yes, I've read that, but…'

'The size of the room was irrelevant.' He cut her off unexpectedly. 'It was my room. All mine. And the family left me in peace. I got shunted between multiple foster homes and care homes in the four years between my mother dying and my reaching sixteen, and that foster home was the only one where I felt safe. Secure.'

'I never knew that.'

And, deep down, she'd never expected Lukas to share anything real with her.

'No, well, the media prefer the lonely orphan story.' His tone was impartial. As though he hadn't told her something so personal. 'And I let them use that line because it kept the press away from the foster family's door, which has made it safer for other foster kids in care.'

There was something about his choice of language that caught her attention.

'*Has made?*' she queried. 'As in, you're still in touch with them?'

That definitely wasn't widely known. Lukas narrowed his eyes at her, giving her the sense that he was weighing her up.

'I hear from them occasionally. And I call from time to time. They're in their eighties now.'

'I didn't know.' She shook her head.

'Why would you?'

The air grew heavy and expectant again, until Oti was sure she could hear the very hair growing on her head. He'd already told her such a lot—far more than anything she'd ever read on the internet or in magazines over the years—and yet she couldn't seem to let the conversation end. She was suddenly hungry to know more, to understand better, and the voraciousness of her appetite should have terrified her.

'But before the foster home?' she began. 'Before your mother died?'

He didn't answer and, after a moment, she felt compelled to fill the silence.

'I'd just turned nineteen when my mother died. It was her death that shook me out of acting the wild child and made me realise I wanted to do something more with my life. That was when I went back to school, sat my A-levels and got myself into med school.'

'Is that why you let your father keep pretending that you were the out-of-control social-climber?' he asked almost offhandedly. 'Because you felt guilty that you hadn't got yourself together *before* your mother's death?'

Oti pursed her lips and let her eyes slide from Lukas. She'd never thought of it that way, and she didn't like what she heard. At the same time, it irked her to find she couldn't deny it.

'Maybe that was your penance for never having let your mother see your success.'

'And maybe you're making assumptions based on what you think my relationship with her was like.' She bristled unexpectedly. 'Maybe my relationship with my mother was never particularly good, especially considering how she venerated my sorry excuse for a father her entire married life.'

Her words seemed to charge the air. She could almost see it crackling before her eyes.

'I presume you had a stellar relationship with your mother before she died,' she snapped before she could stop herself.

'Not really. I never knew my father. He ditched us before I was even born. But, like your mother, mine exalted him my entire life.' His expression was so impassive that it was impossible to tell what he was really thinking. And yet she desperately wanted to know.

'She'd been a chambermaid before I came along,' he continued. 'Possibly her favourite recrimination to me, from my earliest memory through to her death, was that he would have lifted her from that life…if only I had never come along.'

'Sorry—' she pulled a face, appalled at her own self-centred outburst '—I shouldn't have lost my temper.'

'Is that your idea of a temper?' he challenged, his voice still giving nothing away, although now he had one trademark eyebrow cocked. 'It's remarkably…restrained.'

'Don't worry,' she announced before she caught herself, desperate to lift the mood from whatever trench she'd just been digging. 'I'm sure you're unrestrained enough for the both of us.'

Where the heck had that come from?

The air around them shifted, closing in on her like summer skies before a thrilling storm.

'Careful, Octavia, that could be taken as something approaching an invitation.'

A wiser woman might have paid heed to the note in his voice. The warning sign that she should start treading carefully.

The problem was that she'd spent her whole life being careful. She couldn't put her finger on what it was about Lukas that was so different, but suddenly she didn't want to be that overly retiring version of herself any more.

'I do hope so.' She held his gaze. 'It's *Oti*. Calling me by my full name won't alleviate whatever this…this thing is between us.'

'That's enough…*Oti*.'

It seemed she'd scored a direct hit when she hadn't really even known what she was doing. Lukas's jaw clenched so tightly that she could see the muscle twitching.

'I did tell you, back on our wedding day, that you risked being all mouth and no trousers.'

Did she really just tease him on a sexual level? Her? Who had less experience than anyone she knew?

'I said *that's enough*.'

She wasn't even sure that he'd opened his mouth to speak. The words seemed to hiss out of him, the most deliciously dangerous warning.

'What a shame, Lukas…'

'If you can't silence yourself—' his voice throbbed in the space that separated them '—then trust me, Octavia, I will do it for you.'

He moved out of his seat so fast that she didn't have time to process what was happening. But, unaccountably, she found herself hauled to her unsteady feet and pressed up against his solid, hewn chest, her head as light-headed as if she were drunk.

Maybe she was. But not on the wine.

'I warned you,' he growled. And she recognised that tautness in his voice, as though he fought to rein himself in.

Suddenly, that was the last thing she wanted.

'You did warn me,' she agreed all too huskily. 'But I never was very good at following instructions.'

Then, before he could set her aside, just as he had done a few nights earlier, she surged against him and pressed her lips to his.

CHAPTER EIGHT

HE HADN'T INTENDED to kiss her.

He'd intended merely to…intimidate her. To stop her from talking. From telling him how he'd felt about her all those months ago. And how he'd come to choose her as his future bride.

He had sworn to himself, those few nights ago, that he would never touch her again after his alarming lack of control.

In fact, Lukas had rapidly come to the conclusion that staying away from this particular woman would be in both of their interests.

But still it took all his resolve to break the kiss and set her aside. More gently this time than he had the other night.

'You don't have to do this, Oti,' he rasped out, ignoring the fact that his body was clamouring for her. 'The money is yours. No strings.'

'And if I want to?' she managed breathlessly. Almost making him surrender right there, on the spot.

He growled, forcing himself to cross the room. To put that space he'd thought about between them.

'You don't want to.'

And then he left the living room and stalked down the hallway to his suite. Stepping through the doors, he stared at his empty bedroom and wondered what the hell was going on that he still lusted after this woman with such intensity.

He didn't hear the click of the door. He didn't even realise she had stepped through the connecting archway between their bedrooms until she said his name, and he turned around.

And his body went into overdrive.

His sweet bride, his shy Oti, was standing against the door wearing nothing but a lace lingerie set—in cherry-red this time—and a pair of *Do me* heels. And it was killing him not to simply obey.

'Go back in your room,' he managed hoarsely.

'I don't think so.' She laughed softly, and he wondered if she knew he heard the nervousness.

'Octavia. I'm not going to tell you again.'

She took another step forward. 'Thank goodness for that. Too much rejection could damage a woman's ego.'

He wasn't a green, inexperienced adolescent. He knew women—and their bodies—as well as he knew his own.

Better, perhaps.

He could read the short, shallow breaths which indicated her interest as easily as he could read the hard, pert nipples that virtually called out for him to touch. His eyes had alighted on those sleek, endless legs of hers. He hadn't been able to stop imagining them wrapped around his waist—or, better yet, draped over his shoulders—since the other night.

The memory of those scraps of electric blue lace that barely concealed her modesty still haunted his dreams. Waking and sleeping.

But he could also read the uncertainty in her eyes.

'This isn't what you want. I can read it in your expression.'

And still she advanced into his room, his space, and he knew what was coming. He thought he was ready. Prepared.

His hands prepared to snag her wrists, to hold her away, to *control* this spiralling situation.

'This is *exactly* what I want, Lukas. I'm just terrified you'll throw me out again.'

And he intended to resist her. He really did. But then she took a final step and he caught her scent—soft, fresh, vaguely floral, and that gentle musk that was all woman— and every thought tumbled from his head.

Need punched through him. So hard that he didn't know how he had stayed standing. He had never, *not once*, wanted a woman the way he'd wanted Oti. Still wanted her now. With an uncharacteristic recklessness. As if he'd never had anyone else before.

Dazed, all Lukas could see was images of Oti, stretching in front and behind him. And then she put that hot, sharp mouth of hers on his and something detonated inside him, blowing up any sane thought in the process.

Before he knew it, his hand curled around that elegant neck of hers and he hauled her all-too-willing body to his, revelling in the way she melded herself to him as if it was the most natural thing in the world.

He wanted to lift her into his arms, carry her across to his bed and spread her out on it. And then he wanted to feast on her as if she were his own private buffet.

Lukas had no idea how he managed not to do any of these things. Instead, he took his time. He let her mouth explore his in her own time, as if she was still in control the way she thought she was.

Then again, maybe she was. Or maybe neither of them were?

So he indulged himself. Kissing her over and over, deeper, harder, revelling in the slide of her tongue over his, triumphing in those greedy little sounds she made at the back of her throat.

And the only thought in his head was that he didn't want it to end.

More.

The word pounded through him with every thump of his heart. Like a drumbeat that thundered in his veins.

Every taste of her was like a drug, slipping through him and leaving him feeling more intoxicated than he thought he'd ever felt in all his years.

Slowly, almost lazily, Lukas allowed his free hand to travel her body. Starting with the long, sensuous line of her spine which he made his fingers walk down with excruciating deliberation, relishing the shivers which his teasing elicited from her.

She arched into him, pressing her breasts against him, abrading her nipples against his chest as though she couldn't stand not to be touched any longer. And he found he rather liked that image.

Lukas tore his mouth from hers, allowing his fingers, his mouth, his tongue to begin their wondrous journey of discovery. To trace their way down her jaw, down that sensitive column of her throat and to the hollow at the base.

He thought the needy groans she made might actually kill him. As if a storm was raging through him. Only the voice of reason telling him why this was a bad idea holding him back.

But he couldn't bring himself to care. Not with his bride pressing her body to his as though she couldn't get close enough, the carnal sounds she made racing along his sex as surely as if it were her very tongue.

And he stopped pretending he had any control left whatsoever where his new bride was concerned.

Oti was sure that he was going to drive her insane with need. Somewhere along the line, she seemed to have lost the control she'd thought she had. She wasn't sure that she cared.

Not when her aching, heavy breasts were pressed so deliciously into Lukas's rock of a chest, and every movement he made chafed them like some kind of exquisite torture. And somehow she couldn't remember why she'd ever thought it was a bad idea to consummate this marriage of theirs.

Or that she'd been trying to seduce him for any other reason but this driving, primal need that she had never even known that she possessed.

He seemed intent on glutting himself on every inch of her, learning her curves with his hands, then his mouth. He dropped down her body, worshipping every last swell and dip, cupping her backside in his hands as his mouth brushed over her stomach, and abdomen, and...*dear Lord*...lower.

And then she was being swept up, carried across the room and laid out on his bed whilst Lukas shouldered her legs apart, the darkest, hungriest, wildest expression in that grey stare of his. It made a fluttering chase through her whole body.

'I don't... I haven't...'

'I have,' he muttered darkly.

Then, his eyes not leaving hers for a moment as she watched, transfixed, he lowered his head and licked his way inside her.

Oti combusted. Like a thousand glorious sparks firing off all at once. Like the most spectacular fireworks. It was nothing she'd ever known before. How could it have been?

As Lukas used his mouth, his tongue, to trace her core and dip into her silken heat, all she could do was surrender to him. Moaning with each taunting stroke and bucking against him when she couldn't help herself any longer. And when he laughed, a low, deep sound that vibrated against her very sex, she thought she would shatter into a million tiny shards.

He teased her and toyed with her. Knowing exactly what she needed to carry her out on wave after wave of incredible sensation, whilst he built the storm inside her. Higher and higher. Her hips rocked and jolted, chained to the rhythm that he was setting. Performing the dance that he wanted her to perform.

She didn't care. Just so long as he never, *never* stopped.

And then she felt that final wave swelling beneath her. Lifting higher than she'd ever been before. Panic—banished until that moment—rushed back into her, racing through her body and threatening to overwhelm her.

'Lukas...' She barely recognised her own voice, as breathless and urgent as it sounded.

But, as though he knew exactly what she was feeling, he grazed one hand over her body, making her belly tremble as it skimmed the skin. Then, suddenly, he slid a finger inside her and did something magical with his mouth, and Oti was hurled straight back into the glory of those rolling waves.

This time was all the more devastating than before. With every sweep of his tongue she shook and she shook, spinning higher and higher and more out of control. And then Lukas did something magical, and those last flimsy threads holding Oti to reality were broken.

She was gone. Spiralling up into nothingness with a cry so primal that it surely couldn't have been her. It was as if she were fragmenting. Splintering into so many pieces that she doubted they could ever be put back together properly again. She doubted *she* could ever be put back together again.

She had no idea how long she soared, but when she finally, *finally* came back to herself, it was to find Lukas moving up the bed and gathering her in his arms as though she was something infinitely precious.

But that was fanciful. And foolish. Sex was sex, and... love was love. Only a fool would confuse the two.

So then you're a fool.

But she didn't have time to dwell. As he rolled onto his back, he carried her with him, settling her down on top of him, his solid, velvety length pressing against her wet heat. And she shivered again, though this time for a slightly different reason.

'Lukas…'

'Stunning,' he breathed, his hand reaching up to cup her breasts and making her bite her lip again.

Was it the incredible sensations or the intensity of his gaze that emptied her head of all rational thought? She didn't know; she could only hear her own breathing, shallow and panting slightly, as he reached between them and traced her swollen core again.

Then, suddenly, he was lined up and Oti found herself waiting, *needing*, desire overcoming anything else she might—or perhaps ought—to be feeling.

And finally, as his eyes locked with hers and she forgot how to breathe, she moved her hands to cover his as they cupped her hips and let him plunge inside her.

It hurts.

Oti stiffened as her fists shot out involuntarily and slammed hard against his unforgiving chest. The pain lanced though her, searingly hot and so very, very sharp that it chased every bit of air from her lungs so that she couldn't even breathe.

He was much too big, much too thick, much too *everything*…so deep inside her. Though, slowly, it dawned on her that he was no longer moving. That he too had gone still, holding her above him with an impressive self-control of which—she was vaguely aware—any other man would have been incapable.

She couldn't move, couldn't speak, couldn't even bring herself to meet Lukas's gaze, though there was no way to avert her face so that he couldn't look at her. Not that she needed to. She could tell by the way her skin burned that he was glowering at her.

That he was furious.

'Are you going to explain this?' he bit out at last, a dangerous edge to his tone despite the quiet, too-controlled pitch that he employed.

A sudden sob made its way up through her and it was all she could do to swallow it back. How had she been so foolish as to think she could deceive Lukas? That he wouldn't discover she was some untried, untested virgin?

His opinion of her had already been low. It seemed that she couldn't even seduce a man without showing her abject lack of experience. And now he wanted her to *explain* herself.

Oti shook her head, helpless against the sting of bitter tears as they welled behind her eyes.

'Ahh, don't cry, Oti.' His tone changed in an instant. It softened in a way she hadn't heard him speak before. 'Not because of a man like me. I'm no good. I'm not worth it.'

Oti's eyes flew to his before she realised what she was doing.

He sounded so...*different*, and she couldn't put her finger on what that emotion was which skittered across his impossibly handsome face, but she knew it was better than what had gone before. And he was still *there*, inside her. Filling her. Stretching her.

What was she to think?

'You should have told me, though,' he added with a slight frown.

'And you would have believed me, of course.'

She didn't know how she kept her tone light. Conversational. Not that it seemed to lessen the impact on Lukas. Another dark cloud crossed his features and Oti waited for him to deny it, but he didn't even attempt to do so. She wasn't sure if that made it better or worse.

'I don't blame you.' The words tumbled out before she'd realised she was going to speak. 'I played my part as the party girl at one time. Not to mention, my father put enough rumours out there about my lifestyle, my partying.'

'I should have asked.'

'Like I said, you wouldn't have listened, and I can understand why.'

'I'm listening now.'

'Now?' She snapped her head to him, praying he couldn't read all the embarrassment that was surely written all over her face. 'With you...*inside* me?'

'I can think of a better time,' he drawled. 'But that boat sailed when you walked into my bedroom looking like a damned siren.'

She shouldn't let his words heat her so easily. And still she felt the grin tug at her mouth.

'A siren?'

'A damned irresistible one,' he groaned. 'And now I find out you were saving yourself.'

'I wasn't saving myself...' She paused, acutely aware that he was still so deep inside her. It seemed like such an odd time to be holding such a conversation. 'I just...didn't find anyone I liked enough.'

Lukas groaned again. Emphatically.

'That's hardly the best thing to tell a guy who's just become your first. It tends to inflate the ego.'

'Really?' she murmured. 'Well, if it helps, I can tell you that you've been a disappointment.'

'A disappointment?' he growled, clearly taken aback.

'A terrible, terrible disappointment,' she teased. Because somehow, in spite of all her lack of experience, he'd made her feel powerful. And utterly desirable. 'It's supposed to be about shattering my earth and rocking my world, is it not? And yet I feel quite...unmoved.'

'Is that so?' Lukas remarked drily.

'It is.' She fought to keep a straight face. 'Because if...'

Lukas began to shift. Slowly drawing out of her, then back in, not so deep this time. Oti caught her breath and waited for the pain, but this time, though it felt odd, the searing sensation had gone, replaced instead by a dull ache. Then, gradually, as he began to move in a lazy rhythm inside her, that ache too began to dissipate.

Little by little, she began to move her hips to meet his, following an instinct that she didn't recognise. Testing him and learning him, even as he moved himself so carefully above her.

Her hands had long since released from their fists, and now she pressed her palms against the solid wall of Lukas's chest, allowing herself to feel the definitive beat of his heart and letting his heat seep into her. Revelling in the way that same heat spread through her, warming her. As if he could heal her...if only she might let him.

And, fanciful or not, Oti finally surrendered, giving in to everything as she'd told herself she must never do.

She forgot about the circumstances of their marriage and she simply relaxed into the moment. Into the incredibly glorious slide of their bodies, so intertwined that she couldn't have said where she ended and he began.

As though she were handcrafted to fit him.

There was nothing but her and Lukas, and that incredible fire he was building within her. Stoking it slowly but surely with every roll of his hips and every pull out and thrust in. Making everything in her world hotter and brighter with each passing moment. Its intensity terrified her and thrilled her in equal measure.

It felt like a lifetime before she came back to herself, floating on sensations she had never experienced before, she'd never even dreamed about, just as nerve endings she hadn't known existed still fired for an age afterwards.

But when she did come back to herself, it was to see

Lukas walking back into the bedroom, still gloriously naked, which at least gave her confidence that he wasn't making a bolt for it.

'So—' she licked her lips as she tentatively sat up '—where do we go from here?'

'From here?' he said slowly. Scooping her into his arms, he carried her through to where a hot bath was running, before lowering her in and then sliding in behind her. 'You start to talk to me.'

'What is it I should tell you?' Oti asked a few minutes later. After he'd taken a sponge and squeezed it over her exquisite body.

He was still trying to get his head around the discovery that she'd been a virgin. Still trying to work out how a woman so intelligent and beautiful could possibly have still been untouched.

'Shall we start with the obvious?' he muttered gently, unable to help himself from lifting a wet curl from her neck and dropping a kiss where it had lain.

His body was already—impossibly—beginning to tighten again with need. As though he hadn't just had her— his *wife*—less than ten minutes earlier.

'You want to know why I was still a virgin,' she said flatly.

'For a start.' He dropped another kiss, and her body relaxed just a fraction.

They didn't speak for a moment, the sound of gently splashing water filling the room instead. But then Oti drew in a breath, as though steadying herself, and she began.

'I told you that I picked myself up when I was nineteen, right after my mum died.'

He didn't answer. He didn't need to. He just kept slowly sponging her down.

'But I didn't tell you why I went off the rails in the first place.'

'Take your time,' he murmured when she paused again, this time clearly waiting for some kind of response.

She gave an almost imperceptible dip of her head.

'When I was fifteen I was attacked.'

'Attacked how? Sexually?' Lukas bit out, stilling for a moment, unprepared for the anger that stabbed through him at her unexpected admission. She stiffened again, and he instinctively resumed his ministrations.

'Sort of.' She sucked in a deep breath. 'It was on some holiday, on a beach one night. My family…and the Rockman family.'

Lukas didn't know how he controlled himself. How he didn't spit out the next question.

'One of the Earl's sons?'

'Yes,' she admitted almost soundlessly.

Whatever he'd felt before about the way the Earl—his biological father, for want of any other term—had treated his mother, it was nothing compared to the sheer violence he felt at the knowledge that one of his sons had attacked Oti.

'He raped you?' Lukas rasped out.

'He tried to.' She hunched her shoulders and Lukas had to clench the sides of the bath not to drag her around. Just to give her space.

'I was lucky… Edward came looking for me and he found us in time…before anything serious happened.'

'You were…okay?' Lukas demanded, immediately regretting his choice of words.

Of course she hadn't been *okay*.

'Edward went mad. I think he would have killed him if I hadn't pulled him away. But when he told our parents, and they told us not to upset the Rockmans by making a big deal of it, he really went crazy.'

'Your parents said what?'

Lukas didn't know how he stayed calm. It was only because he knew that him blowing up would be the last thing that Oti needed.

'That's when our family really started to come apart. I went crazy, turning into that girl we all know so well from the press. I drank, tried drugs and generally wasted my life. But the one thing I couldn't stand to do was be around boys, or men. And I haven't had a serious relationship since.

'Meanwhile, Edward couldn't stand to be around any of us. I think he blamed himself for not being there sooner to stop it getting even as far as it did.'

'I can understand that.' Lukas barely recognised his own voice. 'I can't believe that you could stand to be near your parents after that.'

'I couldn't.' She shook her head, but he noticed her shoulders were relaxing slightly and she was beginning to sit up straight again. 'I think it's why I turned so wild.'

'But you picked yourself up. You got to medical school. That's to be commended.'

'Only once my mother had died and I felt like living that lifestyle was only punishing myself. I was lucky that I'd got good grades through school, despite all my coasting. But once I got my head down I worked hard, and I became a doctor.'

And then her brother's accident had happened, and she'd ended up running away to Africa.

Lukas shook his head, his mind still grappling with everything that he'd discovered in the past twenty-four hours. 'I can only imagine what you've been going through these past years.'

He needed to stay focused and strong, for Oti. The wife he hadn't wanted, but now found he couldn't remember life without. The woman who hadn't even felt able to tell him that she had been a virgin.

He felt like a complete cad.

If he was any kind of decent man he would walk away now. They'd agreed from the start that there would be no physical side to their marriage, and he should have stuck to that. He should never have given in to his overwhelming desire for her; he should have been strong enough for both of them.

He owed her that much.

And then she spun around abruptly in the bath, and he definitely wasn't expecting the bright, almost dazzling expression on her face.

'I haven't been going through anything, Lukas,' she told him earnestly. 'Not any more. I've been focused on the positives and I've been living my best life being the doctor I always wanted to be in South Sudan.'

Lukas was still fighting to make sense of everything she was telling him. Revelation after revelation had fallen from her lips, building up a picture of a woman who was a million miles away from the creature he'd told himself, a matter of months ago, that she was.

She made him feel all at sea. And humbled.

'I'm so sorry.' He shook his head. 'If it hadn't been for this marriage you would still be out in Africa, doing the job you love so much. And this…*us* should never have happened. Go back—I won't stop you.'

He began to lift himself out of the bath, to give Oti her space, vowing to himself that he would never touch her again, when she grabbed his wrists and held him in place.

'Lukas—' she cut him off, not even trying to conceal the excitement in her tone '—you could come out with me. Even just for a month or two. See what I do… *Did.*'

'Oti…'

'You asked me if there was anything you could do,' she challenged. 'This is it. Come back to South Sudan with me.'

'Oti…'

But it appeared that now she had the proverbial bit between her teeth she wasn't about to let go.

'Please, Lukas. We'll call it our honeymoon.'

And it should concern him more that his head told him to let her go whilst his…chest pulled tight with the effort of stopping himself from agreeing.

CHAPTER NINE

LESS THAN A week later, after an eleven-hour flight from London to Juba, the capital, and then a fifty-minute flight to a small airstrip in the middle of nowhere—the closest serviceable one given the season—Lukas found himself with Oti in South Sudan.

The paperwork for him to join her had taken a bit more work, as he'd not been on the charity's books nor been through their lengthy application process. But it never failed to strike Lukas just how far limitless pockets of cash could get a person. Coupled with the fact that they'd clearly been prepared to move heaven and earth to get Oti back there.

It was crazy how the more he was around her the more he wanted her. Like an addiction, when the only addiction he'd ever had before had been to succeed and drag himself out of the council estate where he'd spent the formative years of his life.

They were four hours into their five-hour drive to the medical camp when they passed a woman on the road carrying a screaming, rigid baby, its arms locked in an uncomfortable outstretched position.

Lukas wasn't surprised when the driver stopped the car and Oti leapt out. He followed out of instinct, but it was odd, after a professional lifetime of being the person people automatically looked to in order to resolve any number of problems, to now be the person relegated to standing on the sidelines watching.

The only plus side was that it afforded him the opportunity to watch Oti in what was clearly her environment. She had a quiet authority about her that was eminently watchable. A grace and an efficiency, just like she'd demonstrated that day back home when she'd helped the woman deliver her baby at the roadside.

Oti clearly cared deeply about her patients, just as there was no doubt in Lukas's mind that she loved her job. And marriage to him had nearly robbed her of all of that, yet she'd been prepared to do so out of love for her brother.

She made him feel humbled. Which was why there was no way that he was going to spoil things for Oti by letting her see his discomfort at quite how redundant he already felt out here. All he could do was be here in case she needed him for now, and once he got to camp she'd assured him there would be plenty of non-medical jobs to occupy any volunteer.

He fervently hoped that was true. He hadn't had a full week away from work since he'd written his first app at fifteen; there was no way he could sit and twiddle his thumbs for the next couple of months.

Keeping his distance by the four-by-four, Lukas watched as Oti chatted to the mother, mostly using her own grasp of the language, with their driver and translator standing by for backup, though she didn't appear to need it.

It wasn't long before Oti headed back over to him, and he wasn't surprised that the relieved mother was in tow.

'This is Larhan and her baby. I suspect he's contracted neonatal tetanus, so the earlier we start treatment, the more chance he has of survival.'

'She was walking to the camp?' He didn't know why he felt so shocked. 'It's an hour's drive away. And even at our slow driving speed on these so-called roads, there is no way someone walking would get there before nightfall.'

'That's why we're taking her with us,' Oti confirmed. 'I'll sit in the back with them, but her baby is going to need space. Could you get the rucksacks out and keep them in the front with you? It'll be tight, but rather that than them falling against him. He's in enough pain as it is.'

'Are the limbs meant to be locked out like that?' He frowned. 'I mean, obviously they're not *meant* to be but…'

'I know what you mean.' She even offered him a smile. 'The muscle rigidity is caused by the toxin acting on the baby's central nervous system.'

'But he's…what…a few weeks old?' He had no idea about babies, but he looked small. 'How did he get tetanus?'

'Given that he's only five days old, I'd say it's likely he contracted it due to poor umbilical-cord-cutting practices when he was born. A dirty blade or, more often out here, the practice of drying out the cord by sealing it with cow dung. Sort of like a poultice. We see it a lot out here.'

'Isn't the cow sacred to some of the tribes out here?' he reflected carefully.

'Exactly, but right now this baby is suffering with spasms, and if we don't get him back quickly then he'll most likely die. In our camp, around three in every four babies that we see die of it, usually because they don't get to us in time, but also because we have limited resources out here.'

Shock ran through Lukas as he hauled the rucksacks onto his back and ran them around to the front of the vehicle. He wasn't sure what he'd expected when he'd agreed to travel out here with her, but it hadn't been this. It was quite a rude awakening.

'It gets worse, though,' Oti added quietly as she came around with the last bag. 'We call it the silent killer because we only get to see about five per cent of the babies who suffer from it. As far as we can estimate, many thousands more die at home, in terrible pain.'

'But even if we get him back to your camp in time, the probability is that he won't survive?'

She didn't answer. She didn't need to. Instead, he followed her around the back of the four-by-four to help her and the mother and baby into the back. Then he slammed the old creaking door as gently as he could and prepared to push the vehicle out of the boggy mud where it had sunk after being stationary for even that short period.

At least that way he felt useful.

And an hour later they were finally at the compound, a high brush fence surrounding baked clay brick huts and various tents, from nine-by-nines to larger marquee-style offerings.

He watched Oti leap down into a handful of other medical volunteers who looked to be coming out to greet them.

Their expressions of delight and welcome switched instantly to professional mode as Oti approached, their gaze dropping from her to the wailing baby in her arms.

'This is Shangok. He's five days old. We saw his mother, Larhan, about an hour down the road to the camp, so we brought them in. As far as I can gather, he was born a healthy two point eight kilograms, and for the first few days he fed, slept and cried as normal. Yesterday, however, he stopped feeding and began to turn stiff. He hasn't slept or stopped crying since.'

'MNT?' one of her colleagues posited.

Oti gave a curt bob of her head. 'I suspect so.'

'We'll take him inside and get treatment started if you want to get settled in?'

'No.' Oti shook her head. 'I'll do it. Give me one moment.'

'You're jumping straight back into work,' Lukas said as she hurried over to him.

She looked momentarily abashed. 'Do you mind?'

'Would it matter if I did?' He smiled despite himself. 'This is why we're here, is it not? You want to show me the role you love.'

The brilliance of her smile punched through him. In all the time he'd known her—and, admittedly, it wasn't that much—he'd never seen her smile like that. As if she was truly happy being back, despite the circumstances of their arrival. Her joy was truly intoxicating.

'I'm sorry.' She was already heading away from him. 'They'll want to get him into a quiet environment with little stimuli, so if I don't go now then I won't be able to go in afterwards.'

'Go.' He waved her away with his hand, even though he didn't have a clue what he was supposed to do next.

'Look for the big boss. She'll tell you where your *tukul* is, and then we'll compare house guests when we meet next. Mine has a hedgehog who likes to snuffle about in the middle of the night.'

Before he could answer, she had turned around and hurried off.

Everyone seemed to have a task, a purpose, hurrying around quickly. The sooner he was one of them the better.

It was a good couple of hours before Oti finally left the medical tent, making her way across the compound to the *tukul* where she'd been told Lukas was, still shocked that no one appeared to have recognised him yet. It felt like fate that he hadn't shaved since their wedding, because it was amazing what a couple of weeks' worth of facial hair and a baseball cap could do.

To her, it was still obvious that Lukas Woods was the man beneath, but to people who weren't expecting him to be out here in the first place it was enough to cast shadows over the sharper contours of his face, to soften his telltale square jaw and to conceal the giveaway cleft in his chin.

She doubted they would get away with it for too long, but she would be grateful for every day they were able to settle in without too much scrutiny. Hopefully enough time to help them find a groove.

She could still hardly believe that he had agreed to come out here with her. As though he actually cared about her, as though she mattered to him. And it didn't matter how much she told herself it was all deeply fanciful and ridiculous— every time Lukas watched her with those intense granite-grey eyes she felt as though he was seeing her for the first time all over again.

But right now she should check he was settling in before heading back to her own old hut for a bit of alone time. She could hardly wait.

Sure about that? a voice questioned silently in her head. Oti ignored it.

'Knock-knock,' she began as she reached the open door to one of the larger *tukuls*.

A grin pulled at her lips despite everything. No doubt he'd already realised how sweltering it was in those huts, until the temperature dropped later in the night.

'Are you settling in okay?'

The hut was usually reserved for the main project managers or surgeons. It was about twice the size of her *tukul*, complete with a king-size bed and a new-looking mosquito net. She was used to an old one that had been repaired at least a couple of times, using silver tape. Why wasn't she surprised the billionaire was being treated like royalty?

'I've been...*playing house*, it seems,' he replied drily, his head turning to look at her. 'Unpacking as best I can, given that all clothes have to be bagged to keep any unpleasant insects or arachnids from crawling into them.'

'It's a bit of an art form,' she agreed, laughing. Then she

spotted her own half-empty rucksack. 'Wait, why did you unpack my stuff? I have my own *tukul*—it's just over there.'

Turning to point between a few other huts, she noticed a decoration on the door that she hadn't left there. As though someone else was now occupying it.

'You *had* your own *tukul*,' Lukas corrected quietly.

Something flip-flopped inside her.

'Well, it doesn't matter.' She forced a smile. 'I'm sure my new one will be fine. Not as salubrious as yours, of course.'

'This is our *tukul*, Oti.'

She blinked at him, a cold sensation rushing over her body as she stood statuelike, followed by a rush of heat which she preferred not to dwell on.

'It can't be. It's too…' she bit back the word *intimate* '…big. And it's usually reserved for people more senior than me.'

'Your project chief said it was going spare and she thought, as a newly married couple, we would appreciate it. I wasn't about to lay out the details of our arrangement to her.'

'No, obviously not.' She bit her lower lip.

'I suspect you'll have a fair few questions to answer next time you see people, though. She was rather shocked you'd never mentioned me before.'

She could well imagine it. Everyone had been so focused on the baby, Shangok, that there hadn't been chance for anyone to ask her about her sudden change in marital status. But tonight, and tomorrow, Oti had no doubt there would be a veritable barrage of questions fired her way.

'But we can't share a hut, Lukas.' Her voice shook and there wasn't a darn thing she could do about it. Her eyes slid, almost against her will, to the king-size bed. 'We can't share…*that*.'

They hadn't been intimate again since that one night, almost a week ago. Not that she hadn't enjoyed it—*more* than enjoyed it—but after that bath, and her shocking revelation, Lukas had closed and bolted the door between their suites and practically moved out of their—*his*—home and into his city centre office, making it clear that he had no intention of a repeat performance.

She'd tried not to let it hurt her. Clearly he was the kind of man who liked the thrill of the chase more than he liked a sure thing—but hadn't she known that about him already?

And he hadn't been the one to instigate that night, had he?

Either that, or she'd been so appallingly bad in bed that he didn't want a repeat performance. Just because she'd found their night together so wholly electrifying didn't mean that Lukas had been equally enthused.

Oti felt a hot flush spread over her cheeks; how had she failed to recognise that at the time?

'I agree—it isn't ideal.'

'Ideal?' She tried for another laugh, but it sounded flat.

From the safety of the doorway, she once again eyed up the king-size mattress on the old pallet frame. There was also a battered old dresser desk, a rickety chair and a newly woven rug.

As *tukuls* went, it looked lovely. And that wouldn't do at all.

She and Lukas might have pretended to the objecting board members of his various companies that they were going on a delayed honeymoon, but that didn't actually mean it had to feel like one.

'We should have a hut each,' she muttered faintly, not daring to look at Lukas. 'I didn't plan this. You have to understand that.'

'Obviously you didn't plan it.' He had crossed the tiny space before she had a chance to move, his hands going to her shoulders. 'You don't believe that *I* manipulated this situation?'

'Of course not.' Her gaze seemed to be locked with his, and she couldn't have disconnected even if she'd wanted to. 'You made it abundantly clear, even back at the house, that you wouldn't be…inviting any further intimacy between us.'

'Right.' He nodded with evident relief, and she tried not to feel irrationally hurt. 'I'm glad that was clear.'

'But you didn't insist on separate accommodation?' She swallowed heavily.

Even though she tried, there was no suppressing the glimmer of hope that he just might admit it was because a part of him had wanted to share. And then he moved closer to her, so fast that she didn't have time to think. But her heart had time to beat faster.

'This isn't a conversation for other ears,' Lukas muttered tersely, his large hand circling her wrist gently as he tugged her inside.

'No.' He didn't hesitate once the door was closed. 'But only because I believe it would only raise suspicion. After all, we're supposed to be a newly married couple.'

Yanking herself out of his grasp, Oti tried to push back the sense of disappointment that raced through her. It was shamefully telling that she didn't open the door or try to leave. They were alone and, despite everything, her entire body was prickling with awareness.

She swallowed heavily. 'Yet we can't stay here and… share a bed.'

'There's no choice.' His voice held a sort of grimness that made her feel perversely insulted. She wondered what was wrong with her. 'We're married. We're sharing. It's done.'

Oti stared at the bed, then at the floor. She felt like some gauche teenager again, and hated herself for it.

'We're grown adults, not unschooled adolescents,' he pressed on, as if reading her thoughts. She hated the way he could do that. 'I'm sure we can sleep in the same bed without touching each other.'

A memory of their night together slid, unbidden, into her head. He had reached for her so many times that night, as though he could glut on her for ever and still never have enough. He'd made her feel so cherished, so incredible, and she'd never, *ever*, felt like that before.

She'd never thought she was capable of it, especially after the attack.

It was as if Lukas had made her come alive, and she'd suddenly realised what she'd been missing out on all those years. Yet now he was like a different man, keeping her at arm's length and making it clear he didn't remotely feel that same draw, that same desire, whilst she couldn't imagine ever wanting to be with anyone else.

He'd ruined her. And the worst of it was that if she could go back in time and choose to have one night with Lukas or a lifetime with anyone else, then she wouldn't hesitate to choose him. Every time.

'Of course we can,' she replied, wondering if her voice sounded as hollow to Lukas's ears as it did to hers. She hoped not.

'Besides, you'll be in that hospital eighteen hours a day, from what you've told me, grabbing a few hours' sleep when you can, sometimes working through the night. And I've already been given a list of tasks, so I have plenty to do. We won't even be in here at the same time for much of it.'

'And when we are, we'll be so tired that we'll be asleep before our heads even hit the pillow,' she added, wishing that she could believe that for even a minute.

She couldn't actually imagine anyone being able to sleep if they were sharing a bed with Lukas. She doubted anyone ever had.

Her body signalled its approval instantly.

'Are you okay?' He eyed her closely. 'You appear to be a little flushed.'

'It's a little hot in here, don't you think?' Beginning to babble, she headed for the door. 'Sometimes you marinate in your own sweat in these places. I've known people to pull their beds outside and sleep in the cool air.'

'That's an option,' he replied evenly. 'But for now, acting like we can actually stand to be around each other would be a start.'

She nodded stiffly, her mind searching for a topic but coming up short. He made it sound so easy. Then again, it probably was easy for him.

In the end, it was Lukas who spoke first. 'How is the baby, anyway?'

'Shangok?'

Did his voice sound hoarser than usual? No, it was no doubt just her imagination. At least this was a topic she could discuss with some ease.

'Shangok. Yes.'

She lifted her shoulders sadly. 'We won't know for a while. That is to say, we're more likely to know if he's getting worse than if he is responding. We put him on a drip, and we'll use as much of our limited resources as we can.'

'Is he still in pain?'

'Incredible pain.' She nodded. 'We inserted an IV line and administered medications to control the muscle spasms, otherwise he'd be unable to move his rigid body yet feel every single one of them.'

'It sounds horrendous.'

'You have no idea.' She sucked in a breath. 'The slightest thing can set a spasm off, from a soft noise to the lightest touch, even a whisper of wind gliding over their skin.'

'I take it that's why you mentioned putting him in an environment with little stimuli?'

'Yes.' No point in thinking about their home—*his*

home—now. 'The hut we have is darkened, with a more consistent temperature than elsewhere.'

'And it will be enough?'

He actually sounded as though he cared. But then, why wouldn't he? He wasn't some heartless monster. Except, perhaps, where her own traitorous heart was concerned. And that was hardly his fault, since he'd warned her from the start that she should know what she was signing up to.

She dragged her mind back to the little baby in the *tukul*. Would the measures be enough?

'I don't know,' she told him sadly. 'He really needs human tetanus immune globulin, but our stores are virtually depleted. There should have been a supply run a few weeks ago, but the rains meant that the runways were impassable. Last time I was here, we had three babies die within a thirty-hour period.'

'That many? I thought illnesses like tetanus were virtually eradicated.'

Oti tried to concentrate on the topic at hand and not the way that his sense of compassion somehow made him that much *more* than the man she was already beginning to fall for.

'That doesn't come close to the true extent of the problem, Lukas. It's estimated that out here, in the bush, around ninety per cent of births happen in the home, and a high percentage of those births will result in maternal and neonatal tetanus being contracted when the umbilical cord is cut. Most of the time, they never make it to us—maybe as little as five per cent of the time—and because of the way it moves through the body, the mother and/or the baby will be dead within days.'

'That's…staggering.' His brow pulled up tight, and there was an expression in his gaze which she didn't entirely recognise. 'Surely that can't be across the entire country?'

'It isn't.' She forced a half-smile. 'In the cities, where

there are hospitals, the incidence is much lower. The charities and the government have been working together for a long time, establishing vaccine roll-outs and educating people.'

'But out here in the middle of nowhere, not everyone has access to healthcare and so immunisation rates are lower?' he guessed.

'Plus, so many people are displaced.' She nodded, loving the way he took an interest because she did. As though it mattered to him because it mattered to her. 'They have enough trouble finding clean water, food and building new shelter for themselves. And they have their traditional healers—some of whom are actually very good at what they do, and some are completely ineffective. Either way, western-influenced health education is very much a low priority for them.'

'What about vaccine drives? Education drives?'

She was beginning to see what Lukas relished the most. A project. A goal. It gave him purpose.

Just like being out here had always made her feel as if she had value.

She couldn't help wondering if it was tied to the way his mother had worshipped his biological father, despite him abandoning her and Lukas. Just as her self-worth had been damaged the day her parents had refused to side with her over what had happened with the Rockman boy—she didn't even like to think of him by name.

They'd valued money and connections over her wellbeing. It had taken her years to get over that, and this place had helped.

As had Lukas, though that made no sense.

'Obviously we educate people.' She nodded softly, pushing the confused thoughts from her head. 'Multiple charities, not just HOP, have worked together with the government for years, on huge public awareness and vaccine drives. And we are making ground. But it's an ongoing issue. And money only goes so far, you know. We aren't all billionaires.'

She stopped, horrified, waiting for him to say something. He didn't speak.

'I wasn't asking for more money,' she choked out, hating how she'd let things get awkward between them.

'I know.'

'I didn't mean…'

'I know.' He silenced her. 'It's been a long few days. I suggest we get some sleep and regroup tomorrow.'

Sleep? How was she supposed to sleep whilst lying in a bed next to Lukas? Not least because all she wanted to do was be close to him, touch him, be touched by him. Just like the other night.

And he didn't want any of that.

'I think sleep is a good idea,' she lied as brightly as she could. 'I'll get changed in the shower block.'

'No, you stay here. I'll change over there. I want to check tomorrow's schedule with one of the guys I met this afternoon, anyway. You may well be asleep by the time I get back.'

'Great.' Another lie. 'Well, see you in the morning, Lukas. Goodnight.'

CHAPTER TEN

Despite fearing that she would never be able to sleep with Lukas next to her—his back to hers—Oti woke up the following morning having had one of the most peaceful nights she'd experienced in a while.

The early-morning sounds of camp floated around the *tukul*, but the sound she found her ears straining for was Lukas.

Nothing.

Rolling gingerly onto her back, she turned her head to his side of the bed, only to find that he'd gone. Her stomach lurched, though she told herself not to be so dramatic. Lukas was a notoriously early riser; just because he wasn't here didn't mean he was trying to avoid her.

Stretching out her hand, she checked his side of the bed, to find that it was cold. He'd clearly left some time ago.

To avoid her?

It was a question she couldn't possibly answer, and yet she felt she already knew.

Slipping out of the mosquito nets and throwing on fresh shorts and a T-shirt, Oti slipped into the ablution hut to shower. It was nothing like the glorious, hot power shower that she'd enjoyed back home—back at *Lukas's* home—but it felt familiar and somehow comforting. From the low-pressure, tepid trickle that rolled briefly over her body to dodging the bats above her head, it was everything she'd grown accustomed to over the past four years.

Still, as she dried off and returned to their hut, Oti found herself hoping that he would be back there. But he wasn't.

Eventually, she headed over to check on Shangok, relieved to discover that, whilst there wasn't yet any improvement, he hadn't significantly deteriorated. That, at least, was the best she could hope for at this stage.

By his bedside, the baby's mother could only watch on, her face impassive. And, not for the first time, Oti's chest pulled tight. Death was such a part of life out here, with mothers forced to watch so many sick, dying children that their attitudes were far more stoic than Oti wished they had to be, but that didn't mean they felt the loss any less acutely. Here, the mothers seemed to permanently hold and cradle their babies, which only made tetanus all the more cruel. And it never got easier, trying to explain why—with this particular infection—cradling their suffering babies made it worse, not better.

Offering the mother a small smile and a brief word, Oti made her way from the tetanus hut to the main medical tent and began to familiarise herself with the new cases that had come in during the couple of weeks since she'd left. She was so absorbed in her work that she didn't notice Amelia join her until she felt herself embraced in a huge hug.

'You dark horse.' Her friend laughed. 'You never said anything about getting married. Congratulations!'

Delight swept through Oti, though it was swiftly followed by a stab of guilt.

'I'm sorry I didn't say anything,' she began, returning the embrace. 'I just...'

'I get it—you didn't want to jinx it.'

'Something like that,' Oti lied, feeling another jab of shame, especially when Amelia linked her arm.

'What did they tell me his name is—Luke?'

'Lukas,' Oti clarified, waiting for her friend to connect the dots. But Amelia was already focusing on her patients. 'I'll introduce you later. Maybe at lunch, if there isn't a sudden influx.'

She didn't know why she'd said that. More for something to say than anything else, but her colleague looked up in surprise.

'There's a supply drop coming in at lunchtime. Your husband went with the loggies to collect it. They left a few hours ago. You didn't know?'

Lukas had already joined the logisticians on a supply run? And notably one that would keep them away from camp for a few days.

Oti plastered a smile on her face. 'Ah, well, I can introduce you when they get back. By the look of all these new cases, we won't be getting out of here for a couple of days, anyway.'

'I hear you.' Amelia offered a wry smile. 'Come on, let me introduce you to Jalka. She was admitted a few days ago after suffering from a miscarriage at fifteen weeks and after carrying out tests we discovered she's suffering from malaria.'

Oti nodded grimly. Out here malaria accounted for just under half the miscarriages and stillbirths that their medical camp saw.

'Haemoglobin levels?'

'Investigative screening showed a level of around half normal levels, at four point eight,' Amelia confirmed. 'We were lucky that her mother was a safe match and prepared to donate blood for her.'

'Great.' It was good to hear that she had a relative.

Superstition often prevented blood donations, and certainly not to a stranger. If the patient didn't have a relative who was a match and cleared by the lab technicians as a safe donor, it was often hard to find any blood to donate.

Consequently, Oti had known the volunteer doctors and nurses come off twenty-hour shifts, only to donate their own blood, in the hope that it might save a life.

'And this was a few days ago?' Oti confirmed.

'Yep, your task today is a relatively pleasant one to get you back into the swing of it.' Her colleague grinned. 'Carry out a final test on Jalka and, hopefully, discharge her with iron tablets. She should be free to return home.'

'Great.' Oti smiled. 'If only they were all that pleasant.'

'À gauche...à gauche,' Lukas relayed to the driver, Jean-Christophe, as he received instructions over the walkie-talkie from the vehicle that had gone ahead of them.

It had been several days of bumpy driving and the recent rains meant it was all only just passable. Even so, they had finally managed to reach the airstrip to collect the supplies and were finally on their way back to camp. To Oti.

He thrust the thought from his mind.

Had it not been for the skill of their drivers, Lukas was fairly certain they'd have been bogged down in mud more than just the once so far.

It had been unexpectedly satisfying leaping out with the rest of the team to push the four-by-four out of the mud and dirt. The physical exertion had somehow helped towards clearing his mind, just as he'd hoped getting out of the compound would do.

Getting away from Oti.

Spending the night next to her in bed, pretending to himself that he didn't ache to simply turn over and haul her back into his arms, had been torturous. If he'd thought it had been challenging those last few days back in the UK, keeping his distance from her by spending most of his time at the office, then being stuck in that compound with her for the next month or so was going to be agonising.

He'd needed to find something to do that would exhaust

him both mentally and physically. By the looks of things, working with the logisticians would be an ideal solution. From everything he'd been able to glean so far, there were two main areas of work in the HOP camps. The medical team who took care of all the patients and the logistics team who took care of everything else, from the erection of the tents and huts to the working of the generators, the digging of wells, going on supply runs—the list seemed never-ending.

Just the kind of work that Lukas felt he could really get his teeth into—getting back to the mechanical work he had always enjoyed, even from a kid back in that garage. Before LVW Industries had even been a dream.

And exactly the kind of thing that could help him keep his mind off his new wife.

Right?

'We should have to be stopping soon,' one of the other logisticians in the back, a softly spoken German lad, announced. 'It is time we are stoking the generator in the truck.'

'I'll alert the other vehicles,' Lukas confirmed, picking up the walkie-talkie again, grateful that they had given him something tangible to do rather than just being a useless addition to the team.

They'd claimed it wasn't a big deal, and that they were so shattered that handing over to someone else would free them up to grab a few extra hours' kip in the back seat. But it didn't matter to Lukas so long as he was a valuable member of the team.

He didn't give free rides in business, so he certainly didn't intend to accept them on this posting. And already, he thought, he was beginning to understand why Oti had spent the better part of the past four years so committed to the charity.

'José says there's a bit of a flat area on higher ground a

couple of kilometres down the road.' Lukas replaced the handset again. 'He thinks that would be the most logical place to stop. Less chance of any of the vehicles getting bogged down.'

'*D'accord.*' Jean-Christophe signalled his agreement. 'Okay. I stop there. But you are ready for interrogation from José, yes?'

'Sorry?' Lukas turned sharply to the laughing driver.

'You have of the luck, travelling with us. This is first mission in this camp for Alex and me, and we are not knowing Oti much well. But José is knowing her for years. He is nice guy, but he is not knowing about you, and I am thinking that he is not being happy.'

'Something to look forward to, then.' Lukas grinned.

'Yes, indeed.' Jean-Christophe laughed all the harder.

Lukas settled back, unconcerned. He wasn't bothered about José asking him questions, or anyone else for that matter. In truth, the closeness of the team was a good thing. Oti had likened it to a close family and now he could see what she'd meant. And that should make it easier for her when their marriage—their fake marriage—finally came to an end.

She would have this job, and this family, to come back to. A place where she felt safer, surrounded by people who cared about her. So why did the prospect fill him with something that felt less like relief…and more like jealousy?

'There. *Là-bas.*' Lukas indicated suddenly, rounding a bend to see one of the vehicles ahead of them heading up a dirt path on the side of a slight hill.

There had to be a turn-off somewhere; it didn't look as though this road headed that way. It didn't help to peer through the fly-splattered windscreen—water being too much of a luxury to waste too often, especially not on the passenger side—he stuck his head out of the window.

'About one hundred metres—there looks to be a turn-off.'

Really, it was more of a muddy patch, but it looked promising. Jean-Christophe clearly agreed since, as he reached the point Lukas had indicated, he turned the wheel carefully, inching the vehicle between the worst of the mud pit and the rocky outcrop on the other side.

The road—not that it could be called that—was so narrow that Lukas wondered how the truck driver had navigated it without the wheels sliding off the side. But by the time they arrived on the flatter top, the other two vehicles were already parked in a circle along with two more old charity cars he didn't recognise. A small group was gathered around the truck, looking concerned.

Jumping out, Lukas, Jean-Christophe and Alex all hurried over to join them. And as they stepped aside he caught sight of Oti in the middle of the group.

What the hell is she even doing here? he thought as his stomach lurched—but, tellingly, it was a good lurch, not a bad one.

Without a word, they edged slightly away from the group, just as the driver was telling them the generator to the truck had packed in, and Alex the loggie was stepping forward to take a closer look.

'I didn't plan this,' Oti began quietly. 'We just knew you guys were heading back this way, and there's a camp in this direction where we've been intending to run a measles vaccination drive for months. We just didn't have the supplies.'

'So you thought you'd save time and meet us en route.' Lukas kept his tone steady. 'It makes sense.'

What made less sense was quite how erratic his pulse was. He could feel it slamming around, especially at his neck.

'Exactly.' She looked relieved. 'So, we're…good?'

'Sure.'

He didn't feel *good*. He felt something a whole lot

more—almost dangerously so. He wanted to say something. Or, worse, *do* something. Like touch her. Taste her.

With deliberate nonchalance, he turned back to the group in time to hear Alex deliver his verdict.

'Looks like the filter, maybe?' he declared. 'But we'd need Clem to fix it.'

'Who's Clem?' Lukas asked as a rumble of concern made its way around the group.

'Clem is mechanic.' Jean-Christophe pulled a face. 'He is being back in camp.'

Another rumble ran around the group. The supplies they'd collected included anti-malaria drugs and tetanus vaccine, along with some other medical supplies which all needed to be kept in a carefully controlled cool environment. Only a working generator could keep the back of the truck cold enough.

'And Clem is only one can fix.' Alex pointed to the generator.

'Unless you can?' Oti ventured hesitantly, looking at him.

'You are mechanic?' Jean-Christophe frowned.

'I used to tinker a bit.'

'He used to build his own racing cars.' Oti stepped in, glancing at him. 'Sorry, but this is no time for false modesty. Edward told me he met you at the racetrack once or twice. And if we don't get this fixed, we could lose a significant amount of the supplies.'

As a murmur of agreement made its way around, Lukas acknowledged her point and peered at the machine. It didn't take him long to determine that Alex was right; it was the fuel filter that needed replacing.

'Do we have any spares?'

'Should have been on supply plane, but no.' Jean-Christophe bunched his shoulders. 'Was expected fifteen days ago. We cannot be keeping much supplies in camp, in case of being attacked of bandits.'

Yeah, Oti had explained to him that everything was kept to a minimum the further out the camps were from any main towns or cities. The more remote, the more they depended on regular supplies. The less they kept on site, the less of a target the hospital, the staff and the patients would be to any potential thieves.

In a roundabout way, Lukas supposed it made sense, though it didn't help in situations like this.

'There's nothing?' he checked. 'Not even an old generator?'

'Yes, old generator in car,' one of the other drivers jumped in suddenly. 'But is not work.'

'It doesn't matter if it works.' Lukas thought quickly. 'It's the fuel filter I need. It just might do.'

'I get, I get.' The driver hurried over to his vehicle as Lukas began working at the generator in the truck.

'Is not same type generator.' The driver frowned, bringing it over. 'Filter does not fit.'

'Let me see?' demanded Lukas, stretching out his hand. He investigated it closely. 'No, it isn't the same, but I reckon I could file the leads down and jimmy something up.'

'Who is this Jimmy?' Jean-Christophe frowned as the group began to crowd around Lukas. 'We backing up, yes? Giving the man space to work. Showing us that he is not being our little Oti's plus one after all.'

'Jean-Christophe…' Oti sounded agitated but a laugh sprung out of Lukas.

'Is that what they're calling me?'

He realised he hadn't heard himself quite that relaxed or happy in a long time. Ironic, given the situation. But it had been creeping up on him for the past month or so.

Ever since his marriage.

'Oti's plus one, *sí*,' confirmed José, clearly delighted he wasn't taking it personally.

'Right, well—' sliding the screwdriver inside and prising the filter out with a grunt, Lukas cast the grimy diesel-covered part a triumphant grin '—we'd better show everyone—including my beautiful new wife—that I'm more than that, don't you think, gentlemen?'

And he told himself that his chest didn't swell when Oti flushed that delicious shade of pink that he was beginning to get to know so well.

Not in the slightest.

'You know you're the hero of the week?'

Lukas glanced up as she approached. His face was already taking on a golden colour from the sun, making him all the more handsome, if that was even possible.

She valiantly tried to stop her heart from hammering in her chest.

'Is that so?' he drawled.

The hammering increased in intensity.

'Everyone is buzzing about you.' She made herself laugh, looking around the small group as they waved their newly acquired supply run beers in the air and turned up the volume a little more on the music. 'You can't go anywhere without being a success, can you?'

'I just rigged up a bit of filter repair.' He brushed it off in typical Lukas fashion. 'It was a bit hammy, but it did the job. The vehicles are with Clem, the mechanic, now for some proper repairs.'

'Don't underestimate your value,' she told him, suddenly serious. 'If you hadn't cooled that truck in time, we wouldn't have much in the way of usable medicines, and we sorely needed everything we got. The rains here really impacted our supplies this past month.'

'Speaking of which, you rushed off so quickly to do

that medical drive, once we got the truck generator working again, that I didn't get chance to ask how the baby is—
Shangok, right?'

'He developed sleep apnoea that second day and the
spasms increased, so we feared the worst.' She didn't tell
him that neither she nor Amelia had gone to bed that night,
or the next day. 'Then, just as we feared he was starting to
slip away, the drugs must have begun to kick in and everything stopped getting worse. And then, all of a sudden, he
began to improve. Just a little, but enough to give us hope.'

'And now, with these drugs?'

She nodded, hopeful but not wanting to be unrealistic.

'Now he really stands a chance of recovery. I hope he
does,' she couldn't help but emphasise.

She eyed him carefully before speaking again.

'Did you take the mission with the loggies to keep away
from me?'

She noted that he took a long pull of his beer before answering.

'I think staying away from each other, at least in an intimate setting, is for the best, wouldn't you agree?'

'Why?' She shook her head, careful to keep her voice
low.

'Because the last thing I should have done was sleep
with you that night.'

'Was it really that bad for you?' Oti blurted out suddenly,
even as she squeezed her eyes shut and wished she could
swallow the words back.

'What?'

'Forget it.' She shook her head violently. She was such
an idiot.

'Oti…'

'No, really.' She backed up, hitting a wooden pillar in
her haste. 'Forget I said anything.'

'You think it was bad for me?'

Fight or flight?

Back home, she might well have done the latter. But out here she always felt different. Bolder. Stronger. More herself.

Straightening her shoulders, Oti looked directly at him. 'Obviously it was, because you've been very fastidious about not being alone with me ever since that night.'

She could hear her heart beating in the long pause before he answered.

'I was giving you space.'

'Please,' she snorted, as if that could somehow conceal her hurt. Her shame. 'You don't need to sugar-coat it.'

'I'm not trying to sugar-coat anything,' he refuted. 'I'm trying to be sensitive. More sensitive than it seemed I was when I took you to my bed.'

She frowned. 'I seem to remember that I was the one who came to your bed.'

'Because you felt you had to.' Lukas looked disgusted, but she knew it wasn't aimed at her. 'You felt you had to have sex with me.'

'I assure you I didn't.'

Was that really what he'd thought?

'We had sex, I found out that you were a virgin, and then you told me that the most intimate you'd ever been before with anyone had been some scum who had attacked you.'

He was clearly fighting to keep his voice down, yet she knew none of his frustration was aimed at her. It was a liberating experience.

'I came to you that night because I wanted to. Because I *chose* to.'

'I'm not the man a woman like you should *choose* to give such a gift to, Oti. I don't think you fully appreciate that. This is an arrangement, not a proper marriage. The two shouldn't be confused, and sleeping together just seemed to be blurring those lines.'

'Are you saying you don't think you can trust us to share a bed without…blurring the lines?'

'I'm saying that I'm *sure* I don't trust us to.' His voice turned gravelly, and just like that her body started to melt again. And it had nothing to do with the heat.

A heavy silence settled around them, loaded with meaning and thick with desire. She opened her mouth to try to break it, but it felt as if it was impossible.

Perhaps he had a point. Every time she found herself close to him, sensations she didn't care to analyse tangled inside her, and it was getting harder and harder to push them back down. It didn't matter how ferociously she reminded herself, it seemed all too easy to forget that the agreement wasn't about *wanting* to be with the man; it was about *having* to do it.

'There's been a Hep E outbreak in the local village,' Lukas said, startling her, after a while. 'I was talking to Clay earlier and he has already been to investigate, and he found no detectable free residual chlorine in the supplies the villagers are keeping in their homes.'

'That's strange.' Oti frowned, not entirely sure why Lukas had changed the subject but trying to follow his lead, aware that Clay was their go-to water and sanitation guy. 'We always chlorinate our water before distribution. We have to. Hep E and acute watery diarrhoea can kill quickly out here. If the water isn't protected then that would likely provide a clear, active pathway for the waterborne diseases.'

'We're wondering whether contamination occurred at the tap stand, in the water container or elsewhere, and if recontamination can occur. We need some turbidimeters and photometers, as well as some chemical analysers, and then we'll head out and conduct a full investigation.'

'Great.' Oti cranked her smile up a notch, still not quite certain what was going on. 'It will be good to see the results. If there's something going wrong it's a chance to put it right and save lives.'

'I thought maybe you'd want to put together a medical team to go and vaccinate them, or treat them, or whatever Hep E needs. We could work together,' he suggested carefully. 'Albeit from different sides of the problem.'

It didn't matter how Oti tried to tell herself to rein it in, her heart started doing a little race of its own.

She didn't want to tell him that there was very little her team could do for waterborne diseases such as Hep E or acute watery diarrhoea. They could test to see if people were positive, but usually it was about preventative measures and good hygiene education.

But if Lukas wanted them to work together and maybe use that shared goal to forge a new connection and find their way back to where they'd been before, then maybe he was right.

It made sense to work alongside each other whilst forcing a little space between them on a personal level. It was logical.

The problem was...her mind and her body didn't seem to agree that *logic* was the right way to go.

CHAPTER ELEVEN

'WE'VE ISOLATED SEVERAL men and women who have tested positive for Hep E,' Oti told Lukas a few days later when he popped his head into her temporary medical tent. 'But one of them is pregnant, and another has a pregnant wife. I really need you to isolate the source before we leave, or the entire camp is going to come down with it.'

'Clay and I checked the water supplies HOP set up and they're all clean. Plus, we've done a random check on households in the camp and they've all been clean too.'

'There's definitely a source somewhere.' She frowned. 'I have too many patients suffering.'

'Which part of the camp do your patients live in?' Lukas asked. 'Maybe that will help narrow it down.'

'Yes, that might work.' Turning to her translator, Oti asked her to get the locations of their *tukuls*.

Although there was little she could do for the patients with waterborne illnesses, she'd taken the opportunity to run a children's measles drive out of the camp, and at least a thousand new displaced kids had turned up.

'Here's the list,' Oti said, thanking her colleague as she took the paper with a sketch of the area of camp and the homes. 'I'm coming with you.'

She grabbed a bagful of testing kits and instructed her staff to do the same.

As Lukas had predicted, they were clustered fairly closely together. On the downside, the tightly packed area coupled with the transmission method for the illnesses meant she was anticipating many more patients.

On the plus side, at least it meant it was likely it was something they had locally, and not a main pump or water source that had been contaminated.

'How much longer do you want to stay out here?' he asked. 'Or does your team need to get back to the main compound?'

'No, we'll be here for at least another couple of days. The number of kids who are here, and who we could vaccinate, makes it more than worthwhile. Are you and Clay heading back, then?'

She tried not to look too disappointed. It had actually proved a good idea, she and Lukas working together. Taking their various teams out of the main camp seemed to also be giving the two of them a fresh outlook, and the odd awkwardness that had settled over them ever since they'd slept together finally seemed as though it was dissipating.

'No. Even if the problem turns out to be a communal bucket which they're filling from some kind of surface water pool instead of the clean water source the charity has set up, we found one of the pumps in a deep water well on its last legs and we want to swap that out before we go back. Clay's due to be leaving in a few days so he wants to close off any jobs like this whilst he can.'

'Okay, that's good.' She fought to suppress her grin of delight. 'So we'll probably head back to camp all together the day after tomorrow.'

'Yeah, well, that's the night Clay's leaving party is scheduled, so he's pretty determined to be back by then.' Lukas laughed.

It was hopeless not to grin back at him. 'Ah, that means barbecue and beer. I can't let my team miss that or they'll never volunteer to come out with me on another away mission again.'

'Maybe we could have a drink together.'

Oti tucked her hands into her shorts pockets, just so that she didn't throw them around in delight. 'That would be nice.'

'Good.' He dipped his head as though that confirmed it. 'Then we'll have a drink at the party.'

'Okay,' she managed quietly, but he was already going, leaving her to watch his retreating rear for far longer than she knew was acceptable.

It had been a good mission, Lukas thought two days later, back at the medical camp, as he made his way across the compound to finally get a hot—hot-*ish*—shower.

Several days away and, despite the T-shirts and field washes they'd had, the work had been manual and gruelling, even without the heat to contend with. But it had been as satisfying as ever—the feeling that what he was doing was really making a difference out here.

Money was all well and good back home, but what he did here wasn't about money—it was about saving lives. Literally. And somehow it left him feeling more at peace with himself than he thought he'd ever felt.

Or maybe that was the effect Oti had on him. He couldn't deny that working alongside her had been harmonious and somehow...*right*.

But now what?

Sharing a tent with Oti the past couple of days had been taxing enough, and that was before they'd broken that invisible barrier between them. Tonight they would be back in their *tukul*—back to sharing a bed—and Lukas was forced to admit, as he crossed the compound again, he wanted her more than ever.

Perhaps he could commandeer one of the outside hammocks? It might avoid any further conflict with Oti, and he was tired enough to sleep on a clothesline, and the mosquitoes weren't a real problem during the heat of the day. It was only the evening and night when you seemed to get eaten alive.

But he'd face that problem when it arose.

Ducking into the *tukul*, he grabbed clean gear and his wash bag, then headed over to the shower block; one of the cubicles was already in use as he walked in. It didn't take him long to strip off and stand under the shower head, his foot on the manual lever that was connected to the solar-heated water collector above which would tip to rain warm water down on him.

It might not be the steaming hot power shower he had grown accustomed to, but somehow, out here, these jury-rigged systems seemed all the more blissful.

By the time he emerged from the shower, towelled off with fresh shorts on, he felt cleaner and fresher than he had in the last couple of days on the road. What was more, he felt ready to face anything, even another night in the same bed as Oti, with their backs to each other as he resisted that roaring need to turn her over and remind her just how good they had been together.

Gathering up his stuff, Lukas made to leave just as the other cubicle opened and Oti stepped out, a long, soft white shirtdress giving way to those incredible legs, her hair wrapped in a towel. Her blue eyes widened as she saw him standing there.

'I thought you were restocking the vehicle?' It was only half an accusation.

'And I understood you were going for something to eat first,' he countered lightly, not bothering to answer the question. 'But I see you're trying to avoid me.'

'I'm not.' She tried to deny it, but suddenly Lukas decided he was sick of the game.

There was altogether too much rawness and leftover heat between them every time they found themselves alone. And the more they tried to deny themselves, the more intense it seemed to become. Which was why he found himself advancing on his new wife, revelling in that too-aware look in her eyes as he backed her up to the baked clay brick wall of the block, one arm braced against the wall behind her head and the other by his side.

Deliberately not touching her. Deliberately angling his body just enough that she could push past him if she really wanted to.

Oti didn't even attempt to.

'You missed me, didn't you?' he demanded, his voice hoarser than he'd expected.

'No.' She flushed. That deep colour which disappeared beneath the falling neckline of her top, making his hands itch to follow it. To trace her soft skin.

'Do I need to remind you what happened last time you lied?' he asked softly.

'Do I need to remind *you*?' she echoed unexpectedly, making his body pull taut.

'You do not.' His voice rasped over them. 'I remember it vividly. I've been remembering it vividly ever since it happened.'

He didn't know what it was that made him reach out to take a strand of her long, damp hair—tumbling from the towel and around her face as it was—in his fingers. He wasn't sure what made him twist it around his finger as he gazed deeply into her eyes—this woman who he now called his wife. He tugged the stray strand behind her ear as the jagged sound of her breathing seemed to echo that thing which moved within him. And he certainly couldn't explain what made him step closer to her again and lower his mouth to hers.

She melted against him instantly. The sigh she emitted

was like the hottest, longest lick against the hardest part of him. Driving him crazy and making him ache all the more.

Kissing her more deeply, and angling his head for a better fit, he allowed his free hand to snake around to pull the towel from her head, dropping it to the ground before he slid his fingers into her hair.

He explored her mouth, using his lips, his tongue, his teeth. And then he explored that line over her jaw and down her neck, right round to her sensitive earlobe, and the pressure point behind.

He pressed closer and she arched against him, pressing her breasts into his chest, tight nipples grazing him even through the thin top that she wore. Enough for him to realise she wasn't wearing anything underneath it, and he lost whatever sliver of self-control he had left.

It was everything he hadn't been able to stop thinking about ever since that night. Or maybe his whole life.

With a low groan of need, Lukas brought his other hand off the wall to slide down her back, taking his time tracing her spine and over her peachy backside, before reaching for the hem of her dress and pulling it upwards. Exposing one nipple, which he proceeded to take into his mouth, drawing it against the length of his tongue.

'We shouldn't…' she rasped, though he noticed her choice of word was *shouldn't*, not *mustn't*.

'Everyone else is already at the party, unless they're working,' he murmured against the satin-soft feel of her skin, not wanting to lose contact for a second. 'They won't come in here.'

'I know,' she managed. 'We're the last…'

'So stop talking,' he growled, shifting his attention to the other side, and lavishing it with the same attention.

Her gasp of pleasure was so raw as she moaned out his name, and Lukas was lost. So lost in her heat, and her taste, and her scent. With her still arching against him, he let his hand glide down her body, taking his time to reacquaint himself with her. As though it had been years since he'd last held her, rather than a few weeks.

He let his fingers walk over every dip and every curve. Playing with her belly button and the faint swell of her belly, toying with that mouth-wateringly neat triangle before tugging aside the flimsy lace barrier and inching painfully slowly to her core.

'So wet,' he muttered, his mouth still full of her. He slipped his finger though her slick folds and revelled in the way she bumped against him already. 'So perfect.'

She moaned his name again, and it was all he could do not to wrap her legs around his hips and bury deep himself inside her. She was going to be the death of him.

He thought she probably already had been.

And then Lukas began to stroke her. Taking his time. Long, slow sweeps designed to build the tension slowly, no matter how much his hungry bride bucked against his hand.

She was breathing harder now. Choppy, ragged little sounds that made his own sex ache all the more. He couldn't remember anything ever being hotter than this. *Never.*

Carefully, he built the pace. Alternating between his mouth on her breasts, where he paid attention to one hardened nipple and then the other, to his hand between her legs. Setting the rhythm for her to follow, every breathtaking inch of her responding perfectly to his touch, he built her up, and up, until he could feel her racing towards that peak.

With a final twist of his hand that felt as though he'd been perfecting it just for this moment with *her*, Lukas sent his new bride soaring. Her head tipped back as she came apart against his hand. Shattering in his arms.

'My beautiful wife…' The words slipped out before he could bite them back, and yet he couldn't bring himself to care the way he should.

Oti was all he'd never realised he wanted, and he felt

wonderfully lost in her. So lost that he almost missed the voices approaching the shower block.

'Hold still,' he commanded quietly, not letting Oti go, even as he reached behind him and pulled the shower curtain closed.

He'd been so lost in her that he hadn't even thought to do it sooner. He couldn't imagine any other woman making him this out of control. This fervent. Only her.

Only ever her.

A few moments and the newcomers would be in their respective cubicles, leaving it free for him and Oti to make their escape. It was surprising how silly and youthful he felt. It had been so long since he'd been that way. Had he ever been that way? Now he thought about it, perhaps not.

He'd begun taking care of his mother from such an early age that the usual schoolkid pranks and fun had bypassed him completely. And then he'd been so busy building up his business that there hadn't been time for frivolity.

Yet Oti made him feel fun. And youthful. It occurred to Lukas that maybe he needed a little more of this in his life.

A little more *Oti.*

A few moments later and he heard first one shower start up and then another. Carefully peering out to ensure the coast was clear, he sent his wide-eyed bride on her way back to their *tukul,* waiting a minute or so longer for the sake of appearance before following.

Oti stood hesitantly by the side of the bed, waiting for Lukas to follow her. Was their intimacy over, or was she supposed to wait for him? Her whole body still seared from his touch, and a part of her was terrified that he might have changed his mind in the moments between the shower block and their hut.

She had never, *ever* done anything that crazy before, and she'd never wanted to—though she'd never judged any of the other volunteers who might have bed—or shower—hopped over the years. It wasn't a daily occurrence, though it was common enough. They might be out here to try to do good work, but they were still red-blooded young men and women at the end of the day.

And all she wanted now was to be back in their bed. Truth be told, she'd never really wanted to leave it after their first night together. But she'd been frightened. Scared off by the intensity of her feelings for him. Now it occurred to Oti that if she wanted him she could always stop waiting for him to come to her. She could take more charge over her own destiny.

With a deep, steadying sigh, Oti pushed open the mosquito net and climbed onto the bed, her pulse racing. Moments later, Lukas crashed through the door and as he looked at her on the middle of the king-size bed she held her breath.

'Stay there,' he commanded, his voice low and rough because she affected him too much.

'I wasn't going anywhere,' she told him solemnly.

She wasn't entirely sure where that had come from; she only knew that she liked the effect it had on her husband. More than liked it.

His eyes were almost black with desire as he stripped off his shorts with ruthless efficiency, then sprang up as proud and magnificent as she remembered. Oti heard her own reverent sigh, and her mouth was suddenly parched.

She paused, a kind of wildness scrambling in her chest, and then he was climbing onto the bed next to her, scooping his arms around and flipping her flat onto her back before she realised what was happening.

This was what she'd been waiting for.

This was…

Abruptly, he stopped, and her eyes flew open.

Was something wrong?

'Condom?' he managed gruffly.

'Condom?' she echoed weakly.

'Do you have any?' he demanded, leaving her blinking for a few seconds.

It took her an inordinate amount of time to process what he was saying.

'We need one.' He sounded pained. As though he could barely stop.

Oti paused, willing herself to think straight.

'I have one.' Eventually, her lips drew into a thin line. 'In the drawer of the dressing table.'

His jaw tightened.

'You keep condoms in your *tukul*? Since me, or before me?'

'It isn't *my tukul*. It's *our tukul*,' Oti pointed out, if a little breathlessly, though she couldn't say that glint of possessiveness in his tone didn't make her heart leap in triumph. 'I've never stayed in this one before you because, strangely enough, I've never been married before.'

He grunted a half acknowledgement, so she pressed on.

'But, in answer to your question, they were given to me by my boss the minute she saw you.'

'I take it that's supposed to be a compliment.' He pulled a face.

'Trust me, it is. We're medical staff. You have no idea quite how weird our sense of humour is sometimes.'

'I'm beginning to learn,' Lukas remarked drily, pulling apart the mosquito net and sliding off the bed to head to the dressing table.

'I do feel bad, though,' Oti continued as she watched him. 'The people here have so little. I feel awful about accepting from their supplies, even though I know it's for the staff too, to keep everyone safe.'

'I'll send out a hundred to replace them,' he declared, crossing back to the bed. 'A thousand. Hell, I'll even send a million, just for you to shut up and either slide that on me or give it to me to do.'

A ridiculous giggle escaped her, like some kind of schoolgirl, but Oti couldn't lament it. It felt like a side of her—the sillier side—that had been missing for so long had returned.

'I'd rather have a million tetanus shots,' she joked, as he finished pulling the net back into place, so they didn't get bitten alive.

'Done,' he ground out, flicking the condom onto the bed with his thumb and forefinger. 'It's worth it just for this.'

'Do you have any idea how much a million tetanus shots would cost?' She laughed, tearing the wrapper and sliding out the sleeve of rubber,

Hopefully, he wouldn't see how much her hands were shaking. He was so hot, so ready, and it sent a glorious, heavy heat permeating through her entire body.

'If it means you stop worrying about using a couple of condoms from the supplies,' he managed thickly, his eyes still gratifyingly riveted on the sight of her sliding the protection over his impressive length, 'then I think I can spare the money. Didn't you know that I'm a billionaire?'

'No, I think that detail might have escaped me,' she tried for levity, but there was no escaping the need that laced her voice.

She was grateful when he took control again.

'Now stop talking and come here.'

Scooping her up, he brought her back beneath him before she'd even realised it.

'Much better,' he approved, letting his gaze roam over her, leaving a trail of fire in its wake.

And then he took his time, as if committing every dip and every curve to memory. As if he couldn't get enough of her.

Oti watched him, unable to drag her gaze away. There

was an almost fierceness in his expression as he took her in. A reverence that made her feel more beautiful than she thought she'd ever felt. And then he settled between her legs again, every inch of his sex pressed into her heat, and that primitive need surged through him all over again.

'Lukas…'

'Hush, *my lady*,' he teased, his teeth grazing her neck halfway between pleasure and pain. 'Now is not the time for more words.'

As if to prove his point, he sat back on his heels, nestled between her legs. Then he reached out and simply tore her lace panties off, the raunchy sound seeming to echo in their private hut.

And finally, *finally*, he was there—where she ached for him the most. He took care lining himself up, but still he held back. She could sense it. Almost feverishly, she lifted her legs to wrap right around his body, thrilling as his blunt tip inched deeper.

'Careful,' he warned hoarsely. 'I'm not sure how long I can resist you.'

She moved her hands down his back, her fingernails skimming over his skin and making him shudder with pleasure.

'What if I don't want you to resist me?' she murmured, tilting her pelvis up.

'Oti,' he groaned. 'You deserve more…'

'Now, Lukas,' she hardly recognised the need in her own voice. 'Please…'

He slid home in an instant, a long, low sound escaping his lips. And hers. He drew out and repeated it. Over and over. Faster and faster. And each time she met him stroke for stroke, her legs pulling him tighter in, whilst she ran her hands down his muscular back and obliques, her palms searing everywhere she touched him.

All she could do was wrap her arms around him and

cling on. Letting him drive them nearer to that exalted edge, watching it get closer and closer as her breath grew more ragged in the silent night air.

Primitive and perfect, and never-ending, until he reached down between their bodies and into her molten heat, where he performed another incredible sleight of hand trick on her core, and tumbled her into that great white void.

And as he followed her, calling out her name into her neck, Oti realised that she never wanted it to end. There was no denying the truth that was in her heart any longer.

Their wedding might have been fake, but the fact that she was falling for him was very much for real.

CHAPTER TWELVE

'DID I TELL you that I managed to call Edward on the satellite phone?'

She knew he was awake. It was hours later. After they'd slept a little, only for her to wake up in his arms and make love a second time.

The bed moved as he reached up to the frame inside the safety of the insect net and turned on the torch, the diffused light falling softly around them as he sat up and drew her in closer to him.

'He's had his surgery?'

'No, but he'll be going in for it later this week.'

'That's great news.'

'It is,' she agreed. 'He had the assessment the day after you gave us the funds. There had been a slot and I'd taken it. It's why I needed the money so urgently. He was classified as a suitable candidate, and he'll undergo the operation this week.'

'And when will you know if it worked?'

'Three months will give some indication, but nine months should give a clearer picture.'

'If he needs anything else, you come to me, right?' Without warning, he lifted his hand and slid his fingers under her chin.

It was so unexpected, and so intimate, that Oti wanted to cry. But she refused to.

'Of course. Thank you. I just…never thought he would go through with it.'

'Why not?' Lukas cast her a curious look. 'Do you think he was afraid it wouldn't work?'

'Maybe.' She lifted her shoulders. 'Or maybe he was afraid that it *would* work.'

She wasn't surprised he eyed her strangely. Scrunching her face, she tried to find a way to explain it.

'The night my mother died she'd asked Edward to drive her to her meeting. She hated driving at night—she always said the lights dazzled her. But that night he had a work meeting, and he didn't want to drive back home to collect her, then back to the office for the meeting, only to return to pick her up. So she drove herself.'

'He blames himself,' Lukas realised. 'So why do you blame yourself for *his* accident?'

Oti didn't move. She hadn't known Lukas had been able to read that in her.

'Your father used your brother as leverage against you for years. That's more than just being a good sister. That's guilt.'

She tried to swallow, a thick ball of emotion wedged in her throat.

And then Lukas whispered to her, 'I'm on your side, no matter what, Oti.'

She choked back a sob. 'You're right,' she managed. 'Edward blamed himself for our mother's accident. And I blamed myself for Edward's. The night of his crash, that Christmas Eve, he was coming to pick me up. I'd gone to a party with some old friends—more acquaintances—but Rockman's son was there and I panicked.'

'The one who attacked you?'

'It was the first time I'd seen him since that holiday, and

I was scared. I called Edward and he said he was an hour away but to hold on and he'd come and get me. The next time I saw him, he was in a coma. I believe the report that stated the accident wasn't his fault, but there's a part of me that wonders if he was maybe speeding. Just to get to me.'

'I wish you hadn't had to go through any of that, Oti,' Lukas said fiercely, after what felt like an age. 'You deserve better.'

'So did Edward. Look at him. If the operation is successful, he'll regain some use of his arms. But that's it. He'll never be back to how he was. And it will always have been my fault.'

'No, not your fault,' Lukas growled. 'It's Rockman's fault. If he hadn't assaulted you…'

There was such fury in his tone that it almost made Oti feel safe and comforted.

'So why did you marry me, Lukas? I mean, I realise that paying some obscene sum of money was to secure my brother's company—but whose idea was it for you to marry me?'

It took a moment longer to answer, as if he wished he could give her another answer. Or maybe that was just her imagination.

'It was part of your father's price. He wanted the money, and you married off to me.'

It wasn't a surprise; she'd always known it. But still, she couldn't help but wish it was different.

Oti struggled to keep her voice even. 'Why agree? It seems like a high price.'

'It did,' he agreed, making her heart kick at his choice of the past tense. 'At the time.'

'Oh?'

'It has been a lot more…enlightening than I'd anticipated.'

She didn't need to lift her head to hear that he was smiling.

'So what do you get out of it, Lukas?'

'I get the truth.'

That did surprise her. Pulling out of his arms, she sat up so that she could look directly at him.

'What truth?'

Another pause, though he held her gaze, clearly weighing up whether or not he was finally going to share his secret. Oti didn't realise she had been holding her breath until he finally began to speak.

'I told you about my mother. I'm not going into that story again.' His voice was a study in control, and she hated it. 'But I didn't tell you about my father.'

'You told me that you didn't know who he was,' Oti said carefully.

'I lied.'

'Why?'

'It wasn't your business,' he ground out and then, looking at her again he seemed to soften, just for a moment. 'And I've never spoken about him to anyone.'

She didn't respond. What could she answer to that?

'I told you that my mother was a hotel chambermaid. Well, the man she slept with—my biological father—' he practically spat the word out '—was the son of the family who owned the hotel.'

Slowly, things began making a little more sense in Oti's head. The marriage arrangement. The man who'd so vehemently opposed it. Lukas's hostile takeover of Rockman's hotel chain.

'Your biological father is Andrew,' she breathed. 'Rockman. The Earl of Highmount.'

'He is.' Lukas could barely say the words. 'And it wasn't a one-night stand. He and my mother had a secret affair for over two years. She was deeply in love with him and, for his part, he pretended that he loved her too. But he claimed that he had to prove himself competent to run the family businesses and gain respect before he could present her to his father. My mother was stupid enough to believe him.'

She had to be careful. She could feel his pain and his rage.

'This is what your mother told you?'

Those granite-grey eyes bored into her.

'You think she lied.' There was no rancour in his tone. 'So did I, at first. But I know it to be true because I visited him when I was about twelve, when she was dying.'

'Lukas...' His name came out as a shocked whisper, but he carried on as though he hadn't heard.

'Obviously he'd married someone far more respectable by then, but my mother begged me to tell him that she was ill. She believed that he loved her deep down, but hadn't had any choice but to do what he did. So I went, and he laughed in my face.'

'That's horrible.'

'It's characteristic Rockman.' Lukas waved it aside. 'He then called my mother a multitude of names that I won't repeat, and said that her gullibility was only one of the pathetic things about her, but that he'd *kept her on his leash* because she'd known how to satisfy him in bed.'

'How cruel,' she gasped, but again he cut her off as though, now that he'd started, he needed to get his story out.

'He also had a few choice words for me, of course. The headlines were *illegitimate*, *worthless*, *never amount to anything* and, of course, the ubiquitous *bastard*. Then he had me thrown out of his house. In fact, I think the only reason he let me in was to hear me beg for my mother, and then he could see my reaction and feed off it.'

'So he wasn't shocked by what you had to tell him? He'd known she'd fallen pregnant, and yet he'd abandoned her,' Oti said quietly. 'Both of you.'

Lukas's face twisted into something bitter and dark.

'You're not even close. He hadn't just turned his back

on my mother. He'd decided the best way to keep his own image intact was to sully hers. After that first meeting with him, I decided to dig around a bit.'

'You were twelve?'

'And I was determined. My mother had never told me who he was before that day, but once I knew I went all out. It didn't take much for me to discover that her pregnancy hadn't been the secret she'd told me it had been but that his entire family had known about it. About me.'

'Yet they'd never reached out to you? Either of you?'

'No. Though I've no doubt they knew the truth, publicly they claimed he'd never touched her, and that the first time he'd ever had cause to meet her had been because he'd had to fire her from her job when he'd discovered that she had a reputation at the hotel of sleeping with the guests.'

'She didn't, though?' Oti gasped, knowing the answer but needing to ask the question all the same.

'Of course she didn't. She was besotted with him. Only him. She never even looked at another man, certainly not when I was a kid. But he also claimed that her assertion that he was the father of her unborn baby had simply been her way of getting revenge and attention, simply to wheedle a hush money payment out of his hotel chain.'

'Oh, Lukas.'

'My mother was hounded from her home, and from the village. She had no job, no husband and a baby on the way. It's an age-old story, but it's all the more devastating when the man concerned is from a powerful family, and can destroy a life—two lives—with a whisper in his friends' ears.'

'I'm so sorry. And yet she loved him all her life?'

'To the exclusion of anyone else,' he confirmed bitterly. 'Even me. Especially me. It's why she wouldn't prove that he was the father or demand a DNA test. She always claimed that if I had never been born then they would still have their *relationship*. She said he'd only done what he did because he'd had to, and that she didn't want to ruin his reputation.'

'So this is why you've never spoken about it. Because you were ashamed.' She shook her head. 'But you have nothing to be ashamed over, Lukas. This is his wrong-doing, not yours.'

'You misunderstand,' Lukas said harshly, his eyes so hard that she felt almost crushed. 'I'm not ashamed. I never was. I'm telling you this because it was the moment I vowed to myself that I would get my revenge. The moment I vowed that I would do what my mother couldn't, and *I* would ruin his reputation.'

'Is he worth it?'

'He was determined to punish me—a twelve-year-old kid who went to see him because it was what my *dying* mother had begged me to do.'

'When he threw you out of his house.' She nodded, able to see how hurtful that must have been to an already trau-matised kid.

Lukas was such a strong man that it was sometimes easy to forget he had once been a young boy. And probably a terrified one at that.

'No. Because after I left him, before I had even got back home, there were lawyers and police there threatening to send her to jail if she ever repeated her so-called lie that she had slept with him. And that I was his son. Oti, she wasn't able to get up off the couch, she was so ill, so they had broken down the door and entered, anyway. That was how much power he had then.'

'My God, Lukas...'

Oti hesitated, trying to understand. Trying to work it out.

'I can see that's how you felt as a twelve-year-old, Lukas. But why now? Why this? You're globally success-ful. Haven't you already won? Why not just walk away?'

'Because you can't walk away from people like the

Rockmans. They're relentless. If you walk away, they take it as a sign of weakness and come after you all the harder. And when my company first started out, he used every trick he could to wipe me out.'

'He tried to wipe *you* out?'

'People said the way I took over Roc Holdings was uncharacteristically hostile.' He shrugged. 'Now you know why. But he struck the first blow. Roc Holdings was all about hotels and exclusive boutiques. They weren't interested in the tech game, or the fourth industrial revolution. But he knew who I was, and he pulled in every contact he could to try to destroy me and my business.'

'It didn't work, though,' she pointed out. 'Which surely shows how successful you are. LVW Industries is world-renowned.'

'It wasn't LVW Industries that he tried to destroy. It was my first company, one I set up as a teenager. He bankrupted me. More than that, he trampled my reputation with lies. It nearly destroyed me. And the only reason was because it was me. My company. Just because he could. He wanted me to see that he had that much power.'

'I never knew.' She shook her head, shocked. 'I still don't see how marrying me could help you,' she said dubiously.

'The reason Rockman got away with saying the things he did about my mother was because he had friends—well-connected, respected friends—who could back up what he'd said,' Lukas continued. 'Friends who could provide alibis for all the nights my mother had claimed to be with him. I vowed to make them pay too.'

'But…' she began. And then, suddenly, it all fell into place. She stared at him in horror. 'My father?'

His silence was all the confirmation she needed.

'My father was one of his friends.' She felt suddenly sick.

'Your father is the one person who could have given my mother some degree of peace before she died,' Lukas gritted out. 'If he'd only told the truth and admitted that he knew they'd been in a relationship—even if he'd simply admitted that they'd slept together.'

'Because he definitely knew?' How could she doubt it? She was under no illusions that her father had ever been honourable.

'Your father knew,' Lukas confirmed, his voice painfully raw. 'He provided Rockman with alibis for the occasions he'd been with my mother. And then your father backed up his lies that my mother was delusional, claiming they'd never met, let alone slept together.'

'My God, you must hate him, almost as much as you hate your own father,' she breathed. 'And he knew, but he pushed me to marry you, anyway.'

'Did you really expect any better from a man who sided with his friend over his daughter, when that man's son assaulted you?'

She felt herself blanch. It was one thing knowing the truth, but it was worse hearing someone else say the words out loud.

'Maybe it wasn't...quite the way it sounds,' she managed, even as she could hear how brittle and fragile her voice was.

But the look of disgust that twisted Lukas's face terrified her.

'Are you making excuses for him?'

'No, of course not,' she denied, wondering if that was exactly what she'd been doing.

And, if so, *why?*

Already, Lukas was moving off the bed and she knew what he was about to say even before he said it; even as she scrabbled for the words to silence him, she knew she wouldn't be able to get them out.

'I should never have slept with you, especially after I assured you that I wouldn't.'

'It takes two, as they say,' she managed, though her tongue felt altogether too thick for her mouth.

How could she reverse all this? How could they get back to where they'd been a few hours before? Even just an hour ago?

'I warned you that I wasn't a good man.' Lukas was shaking his head. 'I hurt people.'

'What? No...that isn't who you are.'

'You don't know me at all,' he snarled suddenly, taking her aback. 'You don't know how bad the Rockmans are. It seems you don't even fully appreciate how duplicitous your own father is.'

'Then why don't you tell me?'

He glared at her, and Oti couldn't look away, even as she didn't dare speak.

'That man who spilled his seed into my mother claimed that I would never amount to anything, and he called me a bastard. The two things that man believes in are money and station in life. He tried to deny me both.'

'You have more money than he could ever dream of,' she told him abruptly. 'As well as respect from your peers that he has never enjoyed. And my father?'

'Your father is his last so-called friend. He is the one who allowed my mother to suffer as she did. And now he claims to have some proof of the affair my mother and Andrew Rockman were having for years. It would prove my mother truly believed he loved her, and that she wasn't sleeping with anyone else. It would clear her reputation and finally set her free, Oti.'

And himself besides, by the sound of it, though she knew better than to voice it aloud. Instead, she took a moment to absorb that.

'And you believe my father?'

'I believe that he has something. If it hadn't been for the things he said over thirty years ago, then Rockman would never have got away with painting my mother as some kind of unhinged, desperate woman. And your father may not be honourable, but he *is* self-serving. He would certainly have made sure he had something in his back pocket all these years. Otherwise Rockman would have stuck the knife in years ago.'

She paused as disbelief began to wind through her. But the more she considered it, the more she realised Lukas had a point. She'd always wondered what bonds had kept her father and the Earl of Highmount so closely tied all these years. She'd never believed they were friends in the truest sense of the word—but it made sense that her father would have kept something up his sleeve to ensure he always had the support of a family as powerful as the Rockmans.

'You can't really believe he'll tell you, though. And betray Andrew? He values the Rockman name too much.'

Lukas's expression was impassive and as hard as she tried to get a read on him, it was proving impossible.

'It was a chance I had to take,' Lukas answered evenly, and she hated that his tone was so neutral, so controlled. That he was shutting her out from whatever was really going on. 'Your father is like a rat with a nose for the safest bet. He'll go where the power is and, these days, I hold far more of that than the Rockman family. What better way to secure his support than to marry his daughter?'

'So that's his issue.' Her voice trembled, though, and she couldn't control it. 'Not yours.'

'I should have drawn the line at the man pimping his daughter out to me. At the very least, I should never have touched you.'

'Because, of course, I had absolutely no say in the matter.' She sat up on the pallet bed, her voice as bold as she could make it.

'It's hardly the point.' Lukas didn't look impressed. 'I

never should have put you in this position in the first place. I never should have come out here. This is your sanctuary.'

'I like having you here,' she murmured, but she knew he wasn't listening.

'It's done, Oti. It's over. I never should have slept with you. I told you it was a mistake.'

And then, tipping out his shoes, he pulled them on.

'I promised Clay I would check all the wells in the surrounding villages. I should be out of camp for the rest of the mission. The marriage is over, Oti. Don't try to contact me again.'

Before she could speak, he walked away. And although she tried to follow, by the time she was dressed and outside, he was gone.

CHAPTER THIRTEEN

'YOU SHOULDN'T HAVE come here, Octavia,' Lukas ground out, not even waiting until the door to his office was closed. 'I believe I made it clear back in Sudan that whatever foolish thing we'd indulged in was over. It should never have happened.'

If he'd hoped that the month apart would make it easier to remember the terms of his agreement with her odious father, then he was beginning to realise how mistaken he'd been.

The separation had only made it even harder now to resist crossing that room and hauling her back into his arms.

Back where she belonged.

'You made that abundantly clear, yes, but I needed to see you.'

She stood across the room from him, her eyes somewhat over-bright, her face slightly pale, and evidently fighting against clenching her hands.

It made something pull tightly within his chest, but he knew better than to allow it any airtime in his brain.

'My assistant is at your disposal. As is my driver, and the housekeeper. I can't imagine there's any requirement that they can't handle between them.'

'I'm pregnant.'

Pregnant?

Lukas froze as the word echoed around his head. It was as though the bottom had fallen out of his world and he was tumbling, hurtling through space, and there was nothing he could do to stop himself.

'You can't be,' he bit out roughly, his brain still not engaging. 'A baby was never part of the plan.'

How could it be when he'd always sworn that he would never father a child? Any baby deserved better than him.

'Then you'll have to adjust your plans.' She flashed another dazzling smile. This one didn't reach her eyes either.

'We used protection.' He was still blurting out sentences at random, as though the words were bypassing his brain.

'Not that first time.' She narrowed her eyes at him, though he at least noticed the dart of concern that flashed through them.

For a moment Lukas didn't breathe. He couldn't think straight. Come to that, he couldn't think at all. His brain felt thick, and foggy. All he could think about was old Rockman's face, right before his heart attack, when he'd imagined the day when Lukas's own son would stand in front of Lukas with the same hatred in his eyes that Lukas had shown when he was talking to Rockman.

It was why Lukas had sworn to himself that he would never have kids of his own. He'd vowed to himself that this tainted bloodline would not continue.

And now Oti was pregnant.

'You'll have to leave.'

'Leave?' She frowned at him, and he found that he hated that expression in her eyes.

As if he was somehow letting her down.

'I mean that you're free. Of me.' He bit each word out, as though that somehow made them easier to say. 'You're released from the agreement. I'll grant you a divorce now.'

'No…' she gasped, but he cut her off.

'You'll want for nothing, I'll take care of that,' he continued. 'I'll see to it that you and the baby always…'

'Our baby.'

'Pardon?' He stared at her, uncomprehending.

'*Our* baby, not *the* baby.'

His chest pulled even tighter, but Lukas was determined to ignore it.

'I'll see to it that you and the baby always have everything you need.'

'*You're* all we need.' There was a desperation to her tone now, and it threatened to unravel things within him that had been tied up—for good reason—for so many years.

'No, I'm not what anyone needs.'

'You're wrong,' Oti exclaimed. 'You're the only thing we need.'

And it worried him how much he wanted to believe her.

'This thing between us should never have happened,' he forced himself to say flatly, as though frightened to show any emotion, lest he betray himself. 'But, now that it has, the best thing you can do is put some distance between us. That baby deserves better than me for a father.'

'Why would you even think that?' she cried.

'Because I'm not a good man.' It was a fact that had never bothered him before. 'I've spent decades trying to run away from it, but I can't. Like it or not, I'm my father's own son.'

She'd crossed the room before he'd even registered that she'd moved. And her hand on his chest was threatening to make his head spin.

'You're nothing like Rockman,' she told him fiercely. 'You're a good man, Lukas. A generous man.'

'You don't know me at all,' he thundered, needing to get her hand off him, but unable to even move. Paralysed.

His brain couldn't analyse what was happening.

'Then what am I missing?' she demanded. And it seemed

that the more out of control he was feeling, the more in control she was becoming. 'Because I obviously don't see the same thing that you do.'

'You see what you want to see.' He finally managed to find it in him to lift his hand and remove hers from his chest.

But, instead of resolving the issue, he found his skin was cold without her touch. And he lamented the loss.

'No, Lukas, I've finally found out the truth about you.' She offered a lopsided smile that he couldn't even begin to draw his gaze away from. 'You know, Edward has been doing a little research since his operation, reaching out to all his old friends and allies. It seems you're one of the most generous philanthropists globally, right now. You've given millions to so many charities anonymously over the years.'

'Hearsay.'

'Do you think I don't know it was you who got all those tetanus vaccines to our camp in South Sudan within a matter of weeks? No company has ever managed that before. Not to mention the other drugs, new equipment, even new vehicles you had sent through.'

'That wasn't for public consumption,' he heard himself growl out.

'I'm not *public*, Lukas. I'm your wife. And I know you're a good man.'

'I married you because I could use you, Oti. And your father.' He made himself say it, even though he knew he would hate himself for it. 'Those weren't the actions of a good man.'

'If it hadn't been you, then my father would have married me off to someone. We both know it. And I would have had no choice but to agree because I needed to try everything I could to get the surgery for Edward. You saved me.'

She spoke so softly yet with such conviction, and the

words tore into him more than any harsh words she might have thrown his way.

'By chance, not by design.'

'I don't think so.' Another killer smile. 'You could have walked away, but you didn't. I think, deep down, you knew I needed you. And, somewhere along the line, I think you've fallen in love with me.'

'You're wholly mistaken,' he ground out, barely recognising his own voice. 'I have never loved you.'

'Yes, you do.'

'No, I've never loved anyone. Not even my own mother. I'm simply not capable of it.'

And this, at least, was the truth.

'You loved your foster parents. You *are* capable of it, Lukas. And you have fallen in love with me. Just as I have with you.'

And he felt as though his entire world was imploding because he'd never before known a woman like Oti, who could level him with just one of those looks of hers.

Suddenly, he wished he was a different man. A better man. The kind of man who could say the words that this incredible, huge-hearted woman wanted to hear, and mean it.

But he couldn't.

He was too damaged. Too set in his ways.

He made himself take a step away from her. Then another. He wasn't the man she thought she loved. He certainly wasn't the man he'd pretended to be in South Sudan. Or the month before that, since their wedding. Or even the five months before that, since the first moment he'd talked to her at Sedeshire Hall.

He was a man people feared, and obeyed, and envied, but he wasn't a man who people loved. That was why no one ever had.

He was as ruthless and unlovable as his own father, but

then, that wasn't a surprise; they were cut from the same damaged cloth.

And no child deserved a father like him.

For a while back there, she'd thought she'd been getting through to him. She'd felt as though the wall he kept around him had begun to crumble. But then something had changed, and he'd stopped hearing her, and started to push her away again.

She couldn't put her finger on why, but now he stood apart from her, so intransigent, so distant that he might as well have been a world away, not a few feet. And something cleaved in two inside her chest. She was terribly afraid that it was her heart.

'You think you understand me, Octavia, but you don't know me at all.' It was that crisp, businesslike tone that she found she suddenly abhorred.

'I spent those weeks with you, night and day, through some pretty stressful situations, saving lives in the middle of South Sudan. I think I know you pretty well.'

'You see what you want to see,' he bit out. 'But you ignore the fact that my whole business—my entire life—has been built on revenge. On taking down the man who threw my mother and me into the gutter like used garbage the moment he found out about me.'

'You could look at it that way.' She dipped her head slowly. 'And perhaps there has been a bit of revenge in the mix, but I don't believe that is what really spurs you.'

'And how do you figure that?' he grated out. But the very fact that he was asking was enough for Oti to feel encouraged.

'I believe that what really drives you is love, Lukas. Love for your mother. And yes, that means you hated the way your father treated her, but you've just been nursing it for so long—ever since you were twelve—that you've let it get turned upside down in your head.'

'You're wrong.'

'I don't think I am,' she pressed on earnestly, desperate to make him see it from where she stood. 'You're trapped in this suit of armour because you made it for yourself when you were a twelve-year-old, and you'd long since outgrown it and moved on, but Rockman shoved you back into it when he went after your company. Just because he could. Because that's the kind of ignoble man that he is. Believe me, Lukas, I understand. Your father is no better than mine. But that isn't who you are. I know that for a fact.'

She needed him to see the man she—and everyone back in that medical camp—saw. Probably the same man that most of his business partners and employees saw, given the way she'd seen him treat them. He knew them all by name. How many times had she heard him ask after their families, always taking the time to really stop and listen to them?

She took a chance and crossed the room again, lifting her arms to press her hands on either side of his face, forcing him to look at her.

'Lukas, you're a good man. You show this ruthless side to the world, but you sacrifice yourself for those you care about. That's how I know you love me, because you sacrificed what you wanted to go out to Sudan with me, just because you wanted to understand why I love my work so much.'

'I was curious.'

'You cared,' she corrected. 'You always care. And that's what will make you a good father. Because you'll put your child first in a way that neither of our fathers ever put us—or their other kids—first. You are your own man, Lukas. You're not Rockman. You never were.'

All she could hear was their breathing—shallow and slightly fast. He was silent for so long after that, but he didn't remove her hands. Slowly, so slowly, he dropped his forehead so that it was almost touching hers.

And then, abruptly, he straightened up again.

'You're describing the man you want me to be, Oti. An idealistic version of me. But that isn't who I am.' The agony in his voice made her heart ache. 'I'm damaged and damaging. He once said that I would ruin you, just as he ruined my mother. And he's right. How could I be anything other when I have Rockman blood running through my veins?'

'You're nothing like him.' She thumped her fist against his chest, but Lukas just grabbed it and held it still, his large hand tight around hers, and she wished he would hold on to her for ever.

'I am like him. And nowhere was it clearer than the day I married you. I didn't just choose you because I could buy off your father. I targeted you because I could manipulate you, Oti. I used you.'

'And, once again, you conveniently forget the fact that you gave me a choice. No one forced me. You dismissed my father that night and asked if I really understood what I was doing. And what of me, Lukas? Am I a bad person? I could have refused but, instead, I asked you for even more money.'

'For a noble reason,' he snorted. 'For your brother.'

'Yet I still used you.' She slid her hand from his cheek to the back of his head. 'Yet what you're saying is that I'm more than just that one action? That I deserve to be judged on more than that one less than honourable decision.'

'You're twisting things to suit your argument. Are you so blind to the truth, when I've shown you the man I really am?'

'No,' she whispered. 'You've *told* me who you *think* you are, but almost the entire time I've known you, you've shown me a completely different person. He's the man I fell in love with. And he's the man my baby needs for a father.'

'It was a lie, Oti. Everyone lies. I'm not cut out to be a husband, and I'm sure as hell not cut out to be a father. I won't do to my child the things…*he* did to me.'

'Like abandoning them, you mean?'

Lukas's head snapped back as his eyes met hers. Black and furious again.

'I'm nothing like him. And it isn't the same thing.'

'A moment ago, you were telling me that you were just like him,' she pointed out. 'Now you're saying that you're nothing like him. Which is it to be, Lukas?'

'Does it matter?' he roared. 'You seem determined to twist my words, no matter what.'

'Only because I don't think you know the truth for yourself. You've been in the middle of this fight for so long now that you aren't sure whether you're honouring your vow as a twelve-year-old or seeing it as the good, rounded man you've become. Despite all the odds.'

'I'm trying to save you here, Oti.'

'By turning your back on your child, just as he turned his back on you? So what's the difference between you and him?'

He looked at her as though she'd just driven a knife through his ribs. In a way, given her experience with the Earl, she felt as though she might have done just that.

But she was battling for her baby. For *their* baby. And if she had to shock him into realising the truth, then she was prepared to do it.

'The difference—' his fury practically simmered '—is that I'm sending you away to protect you.'

'How does that protect me?' she demanded.

'Because when I take Rockman down for good, when I prove how he lied all these years, he's going to want revenge, Oti. But I'm relatively protected. There's very little the world doesn't already know about me. So who do you think he'll go after?'

'So you think sending me away will keep me safe?'

'Because it will. But I'll still provide for you financially—whatever you both need, it'll be yours. And I will never, *never* deny my child.'

'Don't be an Icarus,' she begged, 'flying too close to the sun.'

'This isn't about ambition, Oti. This is about revenge. I want to take the man down. He *deserves* to be destroyed.'

'I understand,' she said quietly, her heart and soul aching for him. For the man he was now, but especially for the little boy he'd been back then. 'Believe me, I know. But you know if you do that you'll end up destroying yourself too.'

'I know. And that's why I'm divorcing you.' He moved to the door, turning back only once as he stood, holding it open for her. And the look he shot her was nothing short of bleak. 'I need you to leave.'

'But I love you,' she pleaded. As if that could somehow solve everything.

She thought he hesitated for a brief moment, as though a part of him desperately wanted to believe her but he couldn't quite let himself. And then he went cold again, his expression almost forbidding.

'Then, believe me, Oti, you're the only one who ever has. Now, leave.'

CHAPTER FOURTEEN

OTI STARED OUTSIDE. The rain lashed against the windows, the wind screaming around the building. A perfect storm to match the one howling inside her, just as it had been for the last two days, since Lukas had thrown her out of his office.

But she was going to let it roar and rage for as long as it took, because it couldn't go on for ever. And when it eventually blew itself out, she would pick up the pieces of her shattered heart and she would move on, just as she'd told Lukas he needed to do where his father was concerned, and she would make a life for herself, and this precious baby she carried inside her.

Lukas's baby.

And no matter how much he'd hurt her—because she had sobbed for hours and hours when he'd sent her away—or how much she'd tried to tell herself that she was better off without him, she couldn't bring herself to hate him.

He had given her this inestimable gift, which meant she could never regret a moment of their time together. No matter that she was humbled by it, whilst he was immune to it.

The knock at the door caught her off guard.

Unfolding herself from the sofa, she moved across the room. She knew it was him even as her hand reached for the handle.

Hesitating for a fraction of a second, she closed her fin-

gers around the cold metal and carefully opened the door to
see him braced against her door frame. A bleak expression
that she didn't think she'd ever seen before clouded his face.

It was a small comfort that he looked as drawn and
drained as she felt. Perhaps worse.

He didn't move at first, and she didn't speak. And then,
without waiting for an invitation, he moved past her into
her apartment. Belatedly, she realised that she had stepped
aside enough to allow it, her guard down.

A mistake she wouldn't make again.

Those granite-grey eyes seemed to root her to the spot,
made her skin pull tight.

Jerking herself back to the moment, she would never
know how she managed to galvanise her legs into action,
carrying her away from him as though mere physical distance could somehow protect her heart.

'Did you mean it when you said you love me?' he demanded.

She drew in a deep breath. 'I love the man I saw in
Sudan. The one who was full of life and fun. Not this version of you, mired in the past and weighed down by revenge
that is, frankly, beneath you.'

It wasn't a complete answer, yet Lukas nodded, as
though this was enough for him.

'I contacted your brother the other day, Oti.'

The heavy door slipped from her fingers as she turned
to look at Lukas. Neither of them heard the loud bang as it
slammed closed in the breeze.

'You spoke to Edward?'

'I did. I asked him how he was doing after his operation,
and then I told him that he was getting his company back.'

'You're returning Sedeshire International to him?'

She wanted to ask more. She needed to understand. But
her entire body felt numb. Paralysed. Her tongue was glued

to the roof of her mouth, as if she'd just eaten one of her brother's infamous peanut butter sandwiches.

'It was his company, his baby. Edward's hard work built it into what it was. And he only lost it all because the board lost faith in him after the accident. And because your father is too weak and incompetent to make a business decision if it killed him.'

'Sedeshire International *was* Edward's baby. Just like LVW Industries is yours,' she managed.

'Not any more.' Lukas shocked her by shaking his head. 'Not now I know what it's like to be expecting a different kind of baby. *Our* baby.'

Her heart stuttered and leapt. He'd said *'our* baby.'

'What about taking down the Rockman family?'

'I think Edward can do that all by himself. Turns out your brother may hate them even more than I do.'

He didn't add that it was because of Louis Rockman attacking her. He didn't need to.

'He does,' she agreed quietly. 'You know, in many ways we are the same, you and I.'

'You are the daughter of an earl. And I am the son of a single, unwed mother. I hardly think that makes us the same.'

'We both had mothers who loved bad men, oblivious to their faults. Mothers who couldn't see the truth even though it was staring them in the face. The only difference was that you had to see your mother worship your father from afar, whilst I had to watch mine do it right before my eyes.'

There was sheer torment in Lukas's eyes just then. But he simply pulled his jaw taut, took a breath and then released it.

'In any case, I should go.'

'So…that is what you came here to say?' Oti asked in disbelief.

'It is.'

'That is *all* you came here to say? Nothing more?'

'Nothing more. I just wanted to tell you that you were right,' Lukas acknowledged with a rueful upturn of his mouth. 'And to thank you.'

'To thank me?'

'For showing me a different way to be. For seeing past the demons in me, to the good, I guess. If someone as gentle and good as you can love even a little bit of me, it gives me hope.'

'Hope?' she echoed again.

'Yes.' He cast her an odd look. 'Anyway, I've had an account set up in your name. Tell me how much you need for you, and for our baby. It will be in there.'

'I don't want your money, Lukas,' she choked out. 'I don't want anything from you.'

She couldn't have said what that expression was that twisted his features. Or perhaps it was more that she didn't want to identify it. It made his words echo too loudly around her head.

That if she loved him, then she was the only one who ever had.

It tore her up, and yet simultaneously made her more determined.

His situation was heartbreaking, and it made his rejection of her all the more understandable, even if it didn't make it hurt any less. But she refused to allow him to throw it all away, just because he didn't understand it.

She'd helped him see a better way once. Surely she could do it again.

'Is that all you really came here to say?' she challenged. 'You're going to throw away the fact that I love you? The fact that you love me?'

'I don't even know what love is, Oti. I wish I did. I wish I was that kind of man. But you wouldn't want whatever half-baked idea of love that I could offer.'

'You know how to love, as determined as you might be to pretend otherwise.'

'And you're determined to ignore what's right in front of your face,' he growled, misery etched into his ridiculously handsome face, which looked all the more beautiful to her right at that moment.

'You do,' she urged him softly. 'You've already shown me you do, several times. You just can't bring yourself to see it. But I can help you...if you'll let me.'

She watched him hesitate, those grey eyes shot through with uncertainty, but also with a kind of longing that pulled at her heart.

She had him. For better or worse, she had him. Relief and triumph punched through her.

'I want you, Oti, with every fibre of my being,' he told her fiercely. 'And I don't believe that feeling will ever diminish. More than that, I don't want it to. But I also want what's best for you and for our baby, and I don't believe that's me.'

Subconsciously, his eyes dropped to her belly, and she took the opportunity to close the gap between them. Then, taking his large hands in her own, she placed them over her stomach.

'It is what's best for us,' she confirmed softly. 'And what you've just described is the very definition of love.'

It felt as though her heart was lodged somewhere in the vicinity of her throat.

'You love me, Lukas, and I love you. It really is as simple as that.'

'I still don't know what that is,' he told her, but this time his voice was softer. Awed. 'I don't know if I can be what you need.'

'You can,' she assured him. 'I know you can make me happy, Lukas.'

'If you truly believe that, then I'll willingly spend my whole life trying to make it so.'

She patted his hand where it still lay over her belly.

'What's more, you will make our baby happy.'

He watched her for a moment, speechless. And then, at long last, he kissed her.

It poured through her, wild, and hot, and perfect. As if she—and their baby—were the only things that mattered to him.

It said all the things that he couldn't yet say, and it spoke of for ever. And as Oti wrapped her arms around his neck and kissed him back, she decided happily that was more than enough to be getting on with.

EPILOGUE

MAXIMILIAN CHARLES WOODS roared into the world seven months later. A gloriously bawling eight-pound bundle who sounded as fiercely determined as his father had always been.

He wrapped his fingers around his father's large thumb and squeezed mightily, and Lukas was besotted.

So was Edward, who had wheeled himself to the hospital as soon as Lukas had called him. He had taken his young nephew in his arms and held him in the way he would never have believed possible nine months earlier.

And later that night, when Lukas and Oti were alone again, their cherished baby in their arms, Lukas lifted his eyes to his wife, those granite-grey depths spilling over with emotion.

'I never knew my heart could feel so full,' he told her huskily.

'You love us.' She nodded solemnly.

'I love you,' he confirmed, as he had so many times before. It had come hesitantly at first, but then, as if that first time was all he'd needed, she'd heard it again and again.

More than that, he had shown her he loved her, wholly and thoroughly, each and every day. He'd applied himself to it with the same drive and focus that he applied to everything that he did.

He had turned out to be an even better husband than Octavia had dreamed, and already he had proved that he would never be the kind of father that his, or hers, had been.

Max would never want for love, and he was going to have the role model that Lukas had never had. She had known that Lukas would make her happy, but she hadn't appreciated just how much he would make her heart swell.

'I never dreamed that I could have a wife. A family,' he marvelled. 'People who want me for *me*. Not for the billionaire, or the knighthood. Yet you looked past all that. You looked past the broken man inside, empty and unfulfilled, and you saw who I could be.'

'Only after I'd dragged you halfway around the world to live in a *tukul*. I saw the version of you that no one else got to see.'

'And about a million mosquitoes.' He laughed, leaning down to press his lips to her forehead. 'But I want to be that version of myself. For you. With you. And with our son. I couldn't want for anything more.'

'Don't be too sure,' she told him, her voice thick with love. 'I have plans for a whole team of little Woods children running around.'

And Oti was true to her word.

Two years later, they added a daughter to their family, who came out less fiercely than her brother, but with a grip on life—and her father's thumb—that was equally strong. And, two years after that, twins, a girl and a boy.

They were sitting in the snug at Sedeshire Hall, having settled the last of their brood to sleep, and having bid farewell to both Edward, who lived independently in the gatehouse, and her father, who had mellowed considerably at the arrival of his grandchildren and now lived in his own apartment in the north wing.

'He wants to be a part of Max's life.' Oti had bitten her lip as she'd told Lukas, a few months after their eldest son's birth. 'He asked for a second chance, but I don't know if it's a good idea.'

'What would have happened if you hadn't given me a second chance?' Lukas had replied softly. 'I would have stayed bitter and lost, seeking revenge and destroying myself in the process.'

'But now…?' she had prompted gently.

'Now I'm happy, contented. I'm fulfilled. Driven by the love of a family who I love, rather than driven by revenge for a man who I don't even waste a thought on any more. Just as you told me would happen.'

'So I should give him a second chance?'

'That's your decision.' He'd laughed, dropping a kiss onto her lips. First one side, then the other, as she'd sighed and silently prayed their baby son would give them an hour of quiet to themselves. 'But I will support any decision you make.'

As he had done. And in all the years since. They had supported each other, and together they'd set up the Woods Foundation, offering not just a financial boost to any number of charities, but advice, experience and services. From setting up cold storage facilities to store vaccines for medical camps or desalination plants providing fresh water to desert communities, to local community projects like planting trees in parks, and setting up centres for children who acted as carers for their parents.

But as they snuggled together, their four children miraculously all asleep at the same time, Oti turned her face up to her husband's.

'You really have made me happy,' she whispered.

'I told you that I would,' he deadpanned, lowering his head to claim her mouth with his before she could object. A deep, stirring kiss that made promises for the rest of the night. Five years after their first kiss at the altar, he still had the same power to set her heart thumping and leave her feverish for more.

Even so, she managed to punch his chest lightly.

'I think you'll find it was me who said that you would,' she managed when they finally surfaced.

'Are you quite sure? I seem to remember it differently.'

'You really are the most aggravating man.' She laughed.

'Yes, I think that was what you were lamenting this morning into the pillow, when your legs were draped over my shoulders.'

'You're impossible.' Oti batted him as he offered a wicked smile that shot straight through her body.

'I am,' he agreed. 'And I love you, Lady Octavia Woods, just as I love our family. My only goal is to make you the happiest family alive. It always will be.'

And then he lowered his mouth to hers and set about proving it. Right until the stars began to twinkle in the inky blue sky. Then again, just before the sunrise began to turn the sky a welcoming yellow, and the first of the Woods brood began to roar at the top of his lungs.

* * * * *

COMING SOON!

We really hope you enjoyed reading this book.
If you're looking for more romance, be sure to
head to the shops when new books are
available on

Thursday 16th September

To see which titles are coming soon, please visit
millsandboon.co.uk/nextmonth

MILLS & BOON

Coming next month

REAWAKENED AT THE SOUTH POLE
Juliette Hyland

Helena Mathews put Kelly Jenkins's shoulder X-rays on
the light box. Carter still couldn't believe his eyes. If it
hadn't felt ridiculous, he'd have pinched himself. Not
that it would do any good. This wasn't a dream.

She was truly here. At the Amundsen-Scott South
Pole Station. The odds were astronomical. This was a
situation that one saw in cheesy movies. Not actual
life.

Time had been exceedingly kind to Helena. Her
features were more refined now, but the beautiful young
girl had transformed into a stunning woman. The long
blond hair she'd worn in braids was shorn close to her
head in an adorable pixie cut. It was a cut that her
parents—particularly her mother—probably would have
hated, just like she probably disliked the small diamond
stud in Helena's nose. But both seemed to suit the woman
standing next to him.

And some things hadn't changed. Like her jade eyes
or the full lips that barely stuck out in a pout. Kissable
lips.

Carter shook himself as he stared at the light box.
He needed to pull his shaken core together. Seeing
Helena was a shock, but it changed nothing. He wanted
to believe the lie, but his heart hammered against his

chest, denying that anything about this winter assignment would be the same.

For the first time since he'd ended his engagement, he felt like he was at a crossroads. In those broken moments he'd sworn he'd never step off the isolated path he'd chosen, and nothing was going to change that. Yes, Helena was here, but that didn't have to mean anything significant for him. She was just another medical professional wintering at the research station.

Except…

His brain cut that thought off before he allowed it to wander.

Crossing his arms, he studied the X-ray. It was Kelly's shoulder that mattered right now. Not the soft woman standing inches from him.

"I don't see any breaks, Carter."

His name on her lips sent a wave of unwelcome emotions through the darkened corners of his soul. Light poured into places that had been dormant for years. Home…it felt like home. Warm, welcoming, supportive. All the things he'd taken for granted. All the things he did not need.

Home.

Continue reading
REAWAKENED AT THE SOUTH POLE
Juliette Hyland

Available next month
www.millsandboon.co.uk